STAR WARS

THRAWN

STAR WARS BOOKS BY TIMOTHY ZAHN

THRAWN

TIMOTHY ZAHN

DEL REY • NEW YORK

Thrawn is a work of fiction. Names, places, and incidents either are products of the author's imagination or are used fictitiously. Any resemblance to actual events, locales, or persons, living or dead, is entirely coincidental.

2018 Del Rey Mass Market Edition

Published in the United States by Del Rey, an imprint of Random House, a division of Penguin Random House LLC, New York.

DEL REY and the HOUSE colophon are registered trademarks of Penguin Random House LLC.

Originally published in hardcover in the United States by Del Rey, an imprint of Random House, a division of Penguin Random House LLC, in 2017.

ISBN 978-1-101-96702-7
Ebook ISBN 978-0-345-54284-7

Printed in the United States of America

randomhousebooks.com

19 18 17 16 15 14 13

Del Rey mass market edition: February 2018

For all those who have wished for more stories of
Grand Admiral Thrawn
And to all those at Lucasfilm and Del Rey
who made it happen
Thank you

THE DEL REY

STAR WARS™

TIMELINE

A long time ago in a galaxy far, far away. . . .

STAR WARS

THRAWN

CHAPTER 1

*All beings begin their lives with hopes and aspirations.
Among these aspirations is the desire that there will
be a straight path to those goals.*

It is seldom so. Perhaps never.

*Sometimes the turns are of one's own volition, as one's
thoughts and goals change over time. But more often the
turns are mandated by outside forces.*

*It was so with me. The memory is vivid, unsullied by
ago: the five admirals rising from their chairs as I am
escorted into the chamber. The decision of the Ascendancy has been made, and they are here to deliver it.*

*None of them is happy with the decision. I can read
that in their faces. But they are officers and servants of
the Chiss, and they will carry out their orders. Protocol
alone demands that.*

The word is as I expected.

Exile.

*The planet has already been chosen. The Aristocra
will assemble the equipment necessary to ensure that
solitude does not quickly become death from predators
or the elements.*

*I am led away. Once again, my path has turned.
Where it will lead, I cannot say.*

. . .

The hut was small, apparently made from local materials, situated in the center of the forest clearing. Surrounding it were eight tall, rectangular boxes with two distinct sets of markings. "So *this*," Captain Voss Parck said, "is what you brought me all the way down from the *Strikefast* to see?"

"Yes, Captain, I did," Colonel Mosh Barris said sourly. "Turns out we may have a problem. You see those markings?"

"Of course," Parck said. "Bogolan script, isn't it?"

"It's Bogolan script, but not Bogolanese," Barris said. "The translator droids can't make top or bottom of it. *And* the two power generators behind the hut don't match any Imperial designs."

Standing to the side, watching his captain and the *Strikefast*'s senior troop commander discuss the mysterious settlement they'd found on this unnamed world, Cadet First Class Eli Vanto tried to make himself as inconspicuous as possible.

And wondered what he was doing here.

None of the other ten Myomar Academy cadets had been ordered down with Parck's shuttle. Eli didn't have any particular expertise in unknown artifacts or tech. It wasn't like he needed planetside experience, anyway— he was on track to become a supply officer. There was no reason he could think of why he'd been singled out this way.

"Cadet Vanto?" Barris said.

Eli wrenched his mind back from his musings. "Yes, Colonel?"

"The droids said there are half a dozen trade languages out here that use Bogolan script. You're our expert on obscure local languages." He gestured to the crates. "So?"

Eli moved closer, wincing a little. So *that* was why he was here. He'd grown up on the planet Lysatra in this part of Wild Space, pressed up against the so-called Unknown Regions. His family's shipping company worked mostly in and around their homeworld, but they did enough business in the Unknown Regions that Eli had picked up proficiency in several of the local trade languages.

But that hardly made him an expert.

"It could be a variant of Sy Bisti, sir," he said. "Some of the words are familiar, and the syntax is right. But it's not standard."

Barris snorted. "Hard to imagine a *standard* for a language so obscure that even the droids don't bother with it."

Eli held his tongue. Sy Bisti was actually a perfectly well-defined and eminently useful language. It was the people who still used it, and the worlds they lived on, that were obscure.

"You said you can read some of it?" Parck prompted.

"Yes, sir," Eli said. "It seems to be mostly tracking information and the name of the company that supplied the contents. Also a short bit proclaiming the grandeur and honor of that company."

"What, they engrave promotionals right on their shipping crates?" Barris asked.

"Yes, sir. A lot of small business out here do that."

"You don't recognize the business name, I assume?" Parck asked.

"No, sir. I believe it's Red Bype or Redder Bype. Possibly the owner's name."

Parck nodded. "We can see if there's anything in our records. What about the second script?"

"Sorry, sir," Eli said. "I've never seen it before."

"Terrific," Barris muttered. "So whether it's a smuggler base or the survival camp from a shipwreck, it still comes under UA protocols."

Eli winced. The Unknown Alien protocols were a relic from the glory days of the Republic, when a new species was being discovered every other week and the Senate wanted every one of them contacted and studied. The modern Imperial Navy had no business handling such chores, and even less interest in doing so, and the High Command had repeatedly said so.

Rumor at the Academy was that Emperor Palpatine was working to revoke the protocols. But for the moment they were still standard orders, and far too many of the senators supported them.

Which was going to put a crimp in the *Strikefast*'s schedule. The ship's officers and crew weren't exactly thrilled at having a bunch of cadets underfoot anyway, and Eli could tell they were looking forward to dumping them back on Myomar. This was going to delay that happy send-off for at least a couple of extra days.

"Agreed," Parck said. "Very well. Have your troops make themselves comfortable while I have a tech analysis team sent down. Keep an eye out in case your smuggler or castaway comes back."

"Yes, sir." Barris's comlink signaled, and the colonel pulled it out. "Barris."

"This is Major Wyan at the crash site, Colonel," a taut voice came. "Sorry to interrupt, but I think you'd better come see this."

Eli frowned. He hadn't heard anything about a crash. "There was a *crash*, sir?" he asked.

"One of the V-wing starfighters went down," Parck said, nodding across the clearing where distant lights could be seen flickering through the tendrils of evening mist wafting through the trees.

Eli nodded silently. He'd noticed the lights earlier, but had assumed they were just more of Barris's survey team.

"I'll be right there," Barris said. "With your permission, Captain?"

"Go ahead," Parck said. "I'll stay here with Cadet Vanto and see what else he can tell us about the writing on these crates."

Eli had gone through nearly all of it when Barris and a black-uniformed, black-helmeted navy trooper returned carrying a V-wing pilot's flight suit.

A flight suit stuffed with grass, leaves, and strange-smelling red berries.

"What is *this*?" Parck demanded.

"This is what we found near the crash site," Barris said grimly as they set the suit on the ground in front of the captain. "The body's gone. Nothing left but this—this—" He waved a hand.

"Scarecrow," Eli murmured.

Parck sent him a sharp look. "Is this something you people do out here?"

"Some farmers still use scarecrows to keep birds out of their crops," Eli said, his face warming. *You people.* Parck was letting his Core World prejudices peek out. "They're also used in festivals and parades."

Parck looked back at Barris. "Have you looked for the pilot?"

"Not yet, sir," Barris said. "I've ordered a troop perimeter set up around the settlement, and I'm having another platoon of troopers sent down."

"Good," Parck said. "Once they're here, expand your search and find the body."

"Yes, sir," Barris said. "We might want to wait until morning, though."

"Your soldiers afraid of the dark?"

"No, sir," Barris said stiffly. "It's just that we also found the V-wing's survival pack. The blaster, spare power packs, and concussion grenades are missing."

Parck's lip twitched. "Primitives with weapons. Wonderful. Very well. Search until dark, then resume in the morning."

"We can keep the search going all night if you'd like."

Parck shook his head. "Hard enough to navigate unfamiliar terrain in the dark. I've seen too many night patrols get disoriented and start jumping or shooting at one another, and the mist you've got rolling in will just make it worse. We'll keep aerial surveillance going, but your troopers would do better to stay in camp until daybreak."

"Yes, sir," Barris said. "Maybe whoever took the grenades will be considerate enough to blow themselves to pieces before they get to us."

"Perhaps." Parck looked up at the darkening sky. "I'll head back to the ship and arrange for a wider starfighter cover pattern." He lowered his gaze to Eli. "Cadet, you'll stay here with Colonel Barris's team. Study the settlement, and see if there are any more inscriptions. The sooner we learn everything we can, the sooner we can leave."

It was nearly full dark by the time Barris's men finished creating their perimeter. The tech team had set up an examination table protected by a transparent weather canopy where they could study the grass and leaves they'd taken from the flight suit. They'd started their work when Major Wyan and his search party returned empty-handed from the forest.

So they hadn't found the V-wing pilot's body. Still, there were no indications of wounded or dead among his team, either. With grenades and a blaster in the hands of primitives or a castaway of unknown species, Eli was privately willing to call it a draw.

"So that's what was in the flight suit?" Wyan asked, walking over to where Barris was watching as the two techs spread out the scarecrow's stuffing.

"Yes," Barris said. The breeze momentarily shifted direction, and Eli caught a whiff of an odd aroma he'd smelled earlier. Probably from some of the berries the techs had crushed for analysis. "So far it seems to be just local flora. Maybe the whole thing was some kind of religious ritual—"

And without warning there came the flash and thunder crack of an explosion from behind them.

"Cover!" Barris shouted, spinning around and dropping to one knee as he hauled out his blaster. Eli hit the ground behind one of the big crates, then peeked cautiously around its side. Halfway to the edge of the clearing, a patch of grass was smoldering with the afterburn of the explosion; beyond it, navy troopers were running toward the closest part of the sentry line, blasters drawn and ready. Someone flicked on a searchlight, the brilliant glow sweeping across the forest and lighting up the mist flowing between the trees. Eli followed the spot of light with his eyes, searching for a glimpse of the enemy who was attacking them—

And instead watched as Barris was slammed flat on his face by a second explosion.

"Colonel!" Wyan shouted.

"I'm all right," Barris shouted back. Behind him, the collection of grasses and leaves on the examination table was burning brilliantly, the table itself canted half over by the blast. On the table's far side, the two techs were shakily getting back up onto hands and knees. Swearing under his breath, Eli stayed flat on the ground, bracing himself for the inevitable third explosion.

The inevitable failed to happen. One by one, he heard the perimeter troops check in with Barris, confirming the defenses were secure. Wyan conducted a search of the first twenty meters of forest outside the clearing and reported that the unknown attackers had fled.

Though considering that no one had apparently seen anything in the first place, the fact they didn't now didn't strike Eli as being very comforting.

The explosions themselves were equally mysterious.

"They definitely weren't concussion grenades," Wyan said. "Not nearly powerful enough. Our best guess is that they were blaster power packs with the sturm dowels pulled out."

"That doesn't sound like something 'savages' would be able to figure out," Eli said, frowning.

"Very well deduced, Cadet," Wyan said sarcastically. "Colonel Barris thinks our castaway has come back." He gestured to the hut. "I didn't call you over here to get your opinion on our tactical situation. I called you to see if you'd found anything in the hut or storage crates that would give us a hint as to his appearance or tech level."

"Not really, sir," Eli said. "From the shape of the bed and design of the eating utensils, he's probably humanoid. But there's really nothing more."

"What about the power generators? He has to have some tech skill to work those, doesn't he?"

"Not necessarily," Eli said. "They're mostly automated."

Wyan scowled into the night. "So why the attack?" he muttered under his breath. "And why such a puny one? If he's smart enough to figure out sturm dowels, he's smart enough to pop a grenade."

"Maybe he's trying to scare us away without wrecking his home," Eli offered.

Wyan gave him a sharp look, perhaps preparing to repeat his warning not to offer military advice. But he didn't. Perhaps he was remembering that Eli had experience in this unimportant part of the galaxy. "And how did he get into the camp?"

There was a small scratching sound near Eli's feet. He started; but it was only some small ground creature scurrying through the grass. "Maybe he lobbed the blaster packs in with a catapult or something."

Wyan raised his eyebrows. "Through the weather canopy?"

Eli winced as he looked over at the still-smoldering mass of burned grass. No, of course not—a lobbed-in explosive would have bounced off the canopy and never made it to the table. Stupid of him. "I guess not, sir."

"You guess not, sir," Wyan echoed sarcastically. "Thank you, Cadet. Get back to your work, and this time find us something useful."

"Yes, sir."

"Major?" Barris called, striding across the clearing.

"Sir?" Wyan said, turning to face him.

"Captain's sending some V-wings for a grid search," the colonel told him. "In the meantime, take a squad and set up some floodlights at the perimeter—I want the forest rim lit up like the inside of a spark module. Then fine-mesh the hemisphere sensor screen. I don't want any more explosives getting through without us at least knowing they're coming."

Wyan's reply was lost in the sudden roar as a pair of V-wings shot past at treetop level. "What?" Barris asked.

"I was reminding the colonel that there are a lot of birds flying around," Wyan repeated. "Small ground animals, too—I nearly twisted my ankle stepping on one a minute ago. If we fine-mesh the screen too far, we'll have alarms triggering all night."

"Fine—forget the fine-meshing," Barris said. "Just get those lights—"

And suddenly, directly ahead, the nearest trees were silhouetted by a fireball erupting somewhere in the distance. "What the—?" Wyan barked.

"V-wing crash!" Barris snapped, keying his comlink. "Rescue team to the transport. Now!"

At least this time the pilot's body hadn't been taken. Unfortunately, his blaster, power packs, and concussion grenades had.

And the rumors and speculations were flying.

Eli was out of most of the quiet discussions, working as he was in the castaway's hut. But every now and then, one of the techs would come in to collect something else to analyze. They were usually eager to talk, to lay out their own thoughts and pretend they didn't have any fears.

But they did.

So did Eli. The floodlights blazing away at the edge of the forest had succeeded in warding off further attacks, but the masses of insects and night birds the glow attracted were almost as unnerving. The V-wings flying overhead gave an illusion of safety and protection, but

Eli tensed every time one went past, wondering if this would be the next one to be knocked out of the sky.

And on top of it all was the *why*.

Why was this happening? Was someone trying to scare the Imperials away? Or was the attacker trying to pin them down, or run them in circles? Or, worst of all, was this some kind of macabre game?

And was the grass-filled flight suit a feint, a distraction, or just some native ritual?

That one, at least, received an answer. About midnight, after a comm consultation with Captain Parck, Barris ordered the stuffed flight suit to be thoroughly examined.

Only then did they discover that the helmet's comlink was missing.

"Clever little snakes," Barris growled as Eli edged closer to the conversation. "What about that one?"

"The comlink's still here," Wyan confirmed, peering into the second downed pilot's helmet. "They must not have had time to remove it."

"Or just didn't bother," Barris said.

"Because they could already eavesdrop on our communications?"

"Exactly," Barris said. "Well, that ends now. Call the *Strikefast* and have them shut down that circuit."

"Yes, sir."

Barris shifted his glare to Eli. "You have something to add, Cadet? Or were you just doing a little eavesdropping of your own?"

"Yes, sir," Eli said. "I mean, no, sir. I wanted to report that I found a couple of coins between the inner and outer shells of one of the crates that date to the beginning of the Clone Wars. So it looks like our castaway's been here at least that long—"

"Hold on," Barris said. *"Coins?"*

"A lot of shippers out here put freshly minted low-value coins in with their crates," Eli explained. "It's a good-luck thing, as well as a way to make sure the dates on the manifests don't get altered. They take them out and put in new ones whenever that crate comes back to them."

"So assuming the castaway got the crates new, it means he's been here for several years," Wyan said thoughtfully. "Might explain some of his behavior."

"Not to me it doesn't," Barris said. "If all he wants is a ride back to civilization, why doesn't he just walk out of the forest and ask?"

"Maybe he was on the run when he crashed," Wyan suggested. "Or maybe he came here voluntarily and just wants us to go away."

"In which case he's going to be sadly disappointed," Barris said. "All right, Cadet, keep looking. Do you want me to assign a tech to help?"

"There's not much room, sir. We'd probably just get in each other's way."

"Then get back to it," Barris said. "Sooner or later, our friend's going to push his luck too far. When he does, we'll be ready."

They had five casualties among the sentry perimeter navy troopers that night. Three of them were incapacitated at the hand of the unseen enemy, their chests or helmets slammed by concussion grenades. No one saw anything, either before the attacks or afterward. The other two casualties were accidentally shot by their own nervous comrades, who mistook them for intruders in the misty darkness.

By the time dawn began to lighten the sky, Barris was back on the comlink to the *Strikefast*. By the time the sun finished burning off the nighttime mist, two squads of stormtroopers had arrived. They consulted with Barris, then headed briskly into the forest, blaster rifles held ready across their chests.

Personally, Eli doubted they would have any better luck finding the mysterious attacker than Barris's own troopers had. But he had to admit that the presence of the white-armored warriors brought a welcome boost to morale.

He was taking apart the last crate to look for more marker coins when he heard a soft but pervasive screech erupt from somewhere outside the hut, followed instantly by shouts and curses.

A general alert? Snatching out his comlink, he keyed it on.

And just as quickly keyed it off, holding it as far away from himself as he could, as the screech from outside exploded in his ears.

Someone was jamming their comlinks.

"Full alert!" he heard Barris bellow from across the clearing. "All troopers, full alert. Major Wyan, where are you?"

Eli hurried around the side of the hut, nearly getting bowled over by a navy trooper heading toward the perimeter. The woman's face was ashy under her heavy black helmet, her expression grim, her uniform spattered with dust. Eli came within sight of Barris just as Wyan reached him. "All comlink channels are out, sir," Wyan reported.

"I know," Barris snarled. "Enough is enough. There are eighteen stormtroopers beating the bushes out there—send some navy troopers to recall them. We're pulling out."

"We're *leaving,* sir?"

"You have an objection?"

"No, sir. But what about that?" Wyan jerked a thumb at the hut. "The protocols require us to study it."

Barris glared at the hut for a couple of seconds. Then his face cleared. "But they don't require us to study it *here,*" he said. "We'll take it with us."

Wyan's jaw dropped. "To the *Strikefast?*"

"Why not?" Barris said, as if still thinking it through. "There's plenty of room in the transport for all of it. Tell the techs to break out the heavy repulsorlifts and get busy."

Wyan threw a considerably less-than-enthusiastic look at the settlement. "Yes, sir."

"And tell them to move it," Barris called after Wyan as the major hurried away. "The only reason to jam our comlinks is if he's getting ready to launch a major attack."

Eli pressed himself close to the hut as he looked around the edge of the forest. He couldn't see any lurking enemies out there. But then, none of them ever had.

Three minutes later a squad of grim-faced troopers and techs arrived at the encampment and began attaching repulsorlift hoists to the generators and storage crates. One of the techs stayed with Eli as the others began transferring their prizes to the transport, the two of them studying the hut's exterior and figuring out where to attach the hoists in order to keep the building intact.

They were still discussing the procedure when the first of the stormtroopers began to reemerge from the forest in response to Barris's orders. The jamming continued as the rest of the troops filtered into the encampment, turning to face the forest in defensive formation for the attack they all knew was coming.

Only it didn't. Barris's stipulated half hour ended with the encampment packed aboard the transport, leaving the entire group ready to leave.

Except for one small hitch. One of the eighteen stormtroopers was missing.

"What do you mean, missing?" Barris demanded in a voice that carried across nearly the entire clearing as three of the stormtroopers headed purposefully into the forest again. "How does a stormtrooper go *missing*?"

"I don't know, sir," Wyan said, looking around. "But you're right. The sooner we get out of here, the better."

"Damn right I'm right," Barris said. "That's it, Major.

Get the techs aboard the transport, with your troopers following in standard rearguard formation."

"What about the stormtroopers?" Wyan asked.

"They've got their own troop carrier," Barris said. "They can stay behind and beat the bushes to their hearts' content. We'll leave as soon as everyone else is aboard."

Eli didn't wait to hear more. Barris's order hadn't specifically mentioned him, but he was more tech than trooper. Close enough. He turned toward the transport.

And paused. One of the stormtroopers was standing rigid guard just outside the hatchway, his weapon held ready across his chest. If he took exception to Barris's order abandoning him and his companions . . .

Without twitch or warning, the stormtrooper abruptly dissolved in a violent explosion.

Eli was flat on the ground in an instant. "Alert!" he heard someone shout, the voice distorted by the ringing in his ears. A handful of troopers were charging toward the forest, but Eli couldn't tell if they were on an actual trail or just hoping to randomly catch their attacker. He looked back at the transport—

His breath caught in his throat. The smoke of the explosion was clearing away, revealing that the ship itself had sustained only minor damage. Mostly cosmetic, nothing that should interfere with flight operation or hull integrity. The stormtrooper's armor, no longer pristine white, was scattered in bits and pieces in a small radius around the spot where the man had been standing.

The armor was all there was. The body itself was gone.

"No," Eli heard himself mutter under his breath. It was impossible. A blast that caused so little damage to the ship behind it couldn't possibly have disintegrated a body so completely. Especially not without doing the same to the armor that had encased it.

A movement to his left caught his eye. Emerging into

the clearing were the three stormtroopers who'd gone to look for their missing comrade. They had indeed found him.

Or at least, what was left of him.

Eli had half expected the transport and troop carrier would be attacked as they lifted into the sky. But no missiles, laser pulses, or catapulted grenades followed them up. Soon, to his relief, they were safe in the *Strikefast*'s hangar bay.

Captain Parck was waiting beside the transport's hatch as the men filed out. "Colonel," he said, nodding gravely as Barris emerged behind Eli. "I don't recall giving you permission to leave your position."

"No, sir, you didn't," Barris said, and Eli had no trouble hearing the weariness in his voice. "But I was the commander on the scene. I did what I deemed best."

"Yes," Parck murmured. Eli looked back over his shoulder, to see the captain shift his gaze from Barris to the transport itself. "I'm told you brought the alien settlement up with you."

"Yes, sir," Barris said. "Everything that was there, right down to the dirt. I can put the techs back to work on it whenever you want."

"There's no hurry," Parck said. "You'll accompany me back to my office. Everyone else is to report for debriefing." He turned to face the line of techs and navy troopers.

And his eyes fell on Eli.

Quickly, Eli twisted his head back around. Eavesdropping on officers was very bad form. Hopefully, Parck hadn't noticed.

Unfortunately, he had. "Cadet Vanto?"

Bracing himself, Eli stopped and turned around. "Yes, sir?"

"You'll accompany us, as well," Parck said. "Come." With Parck in the lead, they left the hangar bay.

But to Eli's surprise they didn't go to the captain's office. Instead, Parck led the way up to the hangar bay control tower, the lights of which had been inexplicably darkened. "Sir?" Barris asked as Parck stepped to the observation window.

"An experiment, Colonel." Parck gestured to the man at the control board. "Everyone out? Good. Dim the lights in the bay."

Barris stepped to Parck's side as the lights outside the observation window faded to nighttime levels. Cautiously, trying to stay as inconspicuous as possible while still getting a good look, Eli eased to a spot just behind Parck on his other side. The transport and troop carrier were prominently visible directly below; beyond them at the other end of the bay were three *Zeta*-class shuttles and a Harbinger courier ship. "What sort of experiment?" Barris asked.

"The testing of a theory," Parck said. "Make yourselves comfortable, Colonel; Cadet. We may be here awhile."

They'd been there nearly two hours when a shadowy, human-shaped figure emerged stealthily from the transport. Silently, it slipped across the darkened hangar bay toward the other ships, taking advantage of the sparse cover along the way.

"Who is *that*?" Barris asked, leaning a little closer to the transparisteel divider.

"Unless I'm mistaken, that's the source of your troubles down on the surface," Parck said with obvious satisfaction. "I believe that's the castaway whose home you invaded."

Eli blinked, frowned. One man? *One* man?

Barris apparently didn't believe it, either. "That's impossible, sir," he protested. "Those attacks couldn't have been the work of a single person. He must have had *some* help."

"We'll wait a moment and see if anyone joins him," Parck said.

No one did. The shadowy figure moved across the floor to the other ships, where it paused for a moment as if considering. Then, deliberately, it stepped to the door of the middle Zeta shuttle and slipped inside. "It appears he was indeed alone," Parck said, pulling out his comlink. "He's in the middle Zeta. All weapons on stun: I want him alive and unharmed."

After all the trouble the castaway had created on the planet surface, Eli had expected him to put up a terrific fight against his captors. To his surprise, he apparently surrendered to the stormtroopers without any resistance at all.

Perhaps he was taken by surprise. More likely, he knew when resistance was futile.

At least Eli understood now why Parck wanted him along. The prisoner's cargo crates were labeled with a Sy Bisti variant. If he spoke the language itself—and if it was the *only* language he spoke—the Imperials would need a translator.

The group was halfway to the hatchway where Parck, Barris, Eli, and their stormtrooper escort waited when the hangar bay lights came back up.

The prisoner, as Eli had already noted, was of human shape and dimensions. But there the resemblance to normal humans ended. His skin was blue, his eyes a glowing red, and his hair a shimmering blue-black.

Eli stiffened. Back home on Lysatra, there were myths about beings like that. Proud, deadly warriors that the stories named Chiss.

With an effort, he tore his eyes away from the face and his mind away from the old myths. The prisoner was dressed in what appeared to be skins and furs, apparently sewn together from the indigenous animals of the forest where he'd been living. Even marching in the center of a rectangle of armed stormtroopers, he had an air of almost regal confidence about him.

Confidence. That was definitely part of the stories.

The stormtroopers brought him to within a few meters of Parck and nudged him to a halt. "Welcome aboard the Venator Star Destroyer *Strikefast*," the captain said. "Do you speak Basic?"

For a moment the alien seemed to be studying him. "Or would Sy Bisti be better?" Eli added in that language.

Barris threw a glare at him, and Eli winced. Again, stupid. He should have waited for orders. The prisoner, too, was gazing at him, though his expression seemed more thoughtful than angry.

Captain Parck, for his part, only had eyes for the prisoner. "You asked him whether he spoke Sy Bisti, I assume?"

"Yes, sir," Eli said. "My apologies, Captain. I just thought—the stories all say that the Chiss used Sy Bisti in their—"

"The *what*?" Parck asked.

"The Chiss," Eli said, feeling his face warming. "They're a . . . well, they've always been thought of as a Wild Space myth."

"Have they, now," Parck said, eying the prisoner. "It would appear they're a bit more substantial than that. But I interrupted. You were saying?"

"Just that in the stories the Chiss used Sy Bisti in their dealings with us."

"As you also used that language with us," the prisoner said calmly in Sy Bisti.

Eli twitched. The prisoner had answered in Sy Bisti . . . but he'd responded to a comment that Eli had made in Basic. "Do you understand Basic?" he asked in Sy Bisti.

"I understand some," the Chiss answered in the same language. "But I'm more comfortable with this one."

Eli nodded. "He says he understands some Basic, but is more comfortable with Sy Bisti."

"I see," Parck said. "Very well. I'm Captain Parck, commander of this ship. What's your name?"

Eli opened his mouth to translate—"No," Parck stopped him with an upraised hand. "You can translate his answers, but I want to see how much Basic he understands. Your name, please?"

For a moment the Chiss was silent, his gaze drifting around the hangar bay. Not like a primitive overwhelmed by the size and magnificence of the place, Eli thought, but like another military man sizing up his enemy's strengths and weaknesses. "Mitth'raw'nuruodo," he said, bringing his glowing eyes back to Parck.

"But I believe it would be easier for you to call me *Thrawn.*"

CHAPTER 2

━━━━━━━━━━━━━━●━━━━━━━━━━━━━━

A life path may change because of important decisions or events. Those were what drove my current path.

But sometimes the smallest event can also drive a turn. In the case of Eli Vanto, that force was a single, overheard word.

Chiss. Where had Cadet Vanto heard that name? What did it mean to him? He had already spoken one reason, but there might well be others. Indeed, the full truth might have several layers. But what were they?

On a ship as large as this, there was only one practical way to find out.

Thus did my path take yet another turn. As, certainly, did his.

"Thrawn," Parck repeated, as if trying out the name. "Very well. As I said, welcome. I want you to know that we didn't intend to intrude on your privacy. We were looking for smugglers, and happened upon your home. One of our standing orders is to study all unknown species we come across."

"Yes," Thrawn said in Sy Bisti. "So also said the traders who first contacted my people."

"He understands, sir," Eli translated. "He knows about that order from traders who've contacted his people."

"Then why didn't you come out?" Barris demanded. "Why did you harass and kill my men?"

"It was necessary—" Thrawn began in Sy Bisti.

"Enough," Barris cut in. "He understands Basic. That means he can speak it. So speak. Why did you harass and kill my men?"

For a moment Thrawn gazed thoughtfully at him. Eli looked at Parck, but the captain also remained silent.

"Very well," Thrawn said in Basic. The words were heavily accented, but understandable. "It was necessary."

"Why?" Parck asked. "What did you hope to accomplish here?"

"I hoped to return home."

"You were shipwrecked?"

"I was—" He looked at Eli. *"Xishu azwane."*

Eli blinked. He was—? "He says he was exiled," he told the others.

The word seemed to hang in the fume-scented air of the hangar bay. Eli stared at Thrawn, thinking back to the campfire stories of his childhood. The tales had spoken of Chiss unity and military prowess.

Never once had the stories talked about them exiling one another.

"Why?" Parck asked.

Thrawn looked at Eli. "In Basic, if you can," Eli said.

The Chiss looked back at Parck. "The leaders and I disagreed."

"Disagreed to the point of exile?"

"Yes."

"Interesting," Parck murmured. "All right. So that's *why* you ran Colonel Barris's men in circles. Now tell us *how*."

"It was undifficult," Thrawn said. "Your spacecraft crashed near my place of exile. I had opportunity to examine before following soldiers arrived. The pilot was dead. I took his body and hid it away."

"And filled his flight suit with grass," Barris put in. "Hoping we wouldn't notice you'd stolen his equipment."

"Nor did you," the Chiss said. "Important most was that you would take the flight suit and rotted *pyussh* berries with you."

"The berries?" Barris echoed.

"Yes. Rotted crushed *pyussh* berries are lure for small animals of night."

Eli nodded to himself. *Rotted—fermented; animals of night—nocturnal.* It was as if Thrawn had had a fairly good Basic dictionary to work with but was missing some of the more technical words and had to improvise. His grammar was a bit shaky, too, again suggesting that he'd learned it out of books instead of from practical conversational experience.

Did that imply the Chiss had had only limited recent contact with anyone outside Unknown Space?

"So you strapped the gimmicked blaster power packs to the animals," Barris said. "That's how you got them past our sentry perimeter."

"Yes," the Chiss said. "Also how I later attacked soldiers. With a sling I threw more berries to their armor."

"You then crashed a starfighter," Parck said. "How?"

"I knew spacecraft would come to search. In preparation I had strung some . . ." He paused. *"Ohuludwu."*

"Monofilament line," Eli supplied.

". . . monofilament line between treetops. The spacecraft struck."

"And at that altitude, the pilot wouldn't have time to recover," Parck said, nodding. "It wouldn't have done you any good to capture the fighter intact, by the way. They don't have hyperdrives."

"I did not want the spacecraft," Thrawn said. "I wanted the pilot's . . ." Again a pause. *"Ezenti ophu ocengi."*

"Equipment and comlink," Eli said.

"But you didn't take his comlink," Barris objected. "We checked the suit at the encampment. It was still there."

"No," Thrawn said. "What was there was the comlink from the first pilot."

Eli nodded to himself. Cleverness, tactics, and maintaining control of the situation. Those were indeed the hallmarks of the Chiss, at least according to the stories.

But still: *Exile?*

"Ingenious," Parck said. "And we thought we knew what had happened, so we never bothered to check the serial number. So when we discovered the first comlink was missing and locked it out of the circuit, you still had one that functioned."

"So you killed a man just to get his comlink," Barris said harshly. Clearly, he wasn't as impressed by the alien's resourcefulness as the captain. "Why did you keep attacking my men? For the fun of it?"

"I regret the loss of life," Thrawn said gravely. "But I needed soldiers with fuller armor to come."

"With fuller—?" Barris broke off. "The stormtroopers? You wanted *stormtroopers* to come?"

"Your soldiers wear helmets," the Chiss said, tracing an imaginary brim around his forehead. "No good for me." He touched a hand to his face. "I needed cover of face."

"The only way you could enter the encampment undetected," Parck said, nodding.

"Yes," Thrawn agreed. "I used explosive on one, to obtain armor I could study—"

"How did you do that without anyone hearing the explosion?" Barris interrupted.

"It was as I began feedback noise from comlink," the Chiss said. "The noise enclosed the noise of explosive. From the armor I learned how to kill the soldier without noise or observable damage. I took a second soldier and his armor and walked to the ship."

"While we were moving your equipment inside?" Barris asked.

"I selected a moment when no one was inside," Thrawn said. "With small branches I stood the armor upright and set it outside the doorway. An explosive inside destroyed it."

"A distraction so that we wouldn't realize there were actually *two* missing stormtroopers," Parck said. "Where did you hide during the trip up?"

"Inside the second power generator casing," Thrawn told him. "It is nearly empty, as I have used its parts to maintain the first."

"I gather you've been here for quite a while," Parck said. "I can see why you wanted so desperately to leave."

Thrawn drew himself up. "I was not desperate. But my people need me."

"Why?"

"They are in danger. There are many dangers in the galaxy. Dangers to my people. Dangers to yours." He made an odd gesture. "You would do well to learn of them."

"Yet your people exiled you here," Parck pointed out. "Do they disagree with you as to the magnitude of these threats?"

Thrawn looked at Eli. "Repeat?" he asked in Sy Bisti.

Eli translated the captain's question. "We do not disagree on threat," Thrawn answered in his accented Basic. "We disagree on process. They do not accept belief in . . . *ezeboli hlusalu.*"

Eli swallowed hard. "They don't believe in preemptive strikes."

"So your people need protection," Parck said, his voice subtly changed. "How would you do this, alone and without ships or allies?"

Eli frowned. An odd question, in an odd tone of voice. Was the captain fishing for information on possible Chiss allies?

Thrawn didn't seem to notice. "I do not know," he said calmly. "I will find a way."

"I'm sure you will," Parck said. "In the meantime, you've had a busy day, and I'm sure you could use some rest. Commander?"

"Sir?" One of the stormtroopers stepped forward.

"You and your squad will escort our guest to the deck officer's office while suitable accommodations and refreshments are prepared," Parck ordered. "Thrawn, I take my leave now. We shall speak again later."

"Thank you, Captain Parck," the Chiss said. "I will look ahead to it."

Eli was in his quarters, working on the after-action report he'd been ordered to complete, when they came for him.

Eli had never been in the captain's private office. He'd never even been in this part of the *Strikefast*.

And he'd *never* been in the company of this many high-ranking officers. It was like a board certification session.

Or a court-martial.

"Cadet Vanto," Captain Parck greeted him. He gestured to a chair that had been set in front of the line of officers. "Be seated."

"Yes, sir." Eli sat down, fervently hoping that his shaking wasn't visible.

"First, I want to commend you for your conduct during the recent action," Parck said. "You behaved admirably under fire."

"Thank you, sir," Eli said. Though as he remembered it, he'd done very little except stay as clear of the fighting and confusion as he possibly could.

"Tell me, what do you think of our prisoner?"

"He seems very confident, sir," Eli said. Why were they asking *him*? "Very much in control." He considered. "Except maybe when he was captured in the hangar bay. You may have caught him by surprise there."

"I don't think so," Parck said. "He surrendered quite readily, with no attempt at resistance or escape." He cocked his head slightly. "You seem to know something about his people."

"Not really, sir," Eli said. "We have stories about the Chiss—more like myths, really—that have been passed down through the generations. As far as I know, none of them has been seen on Lysatra or anywhere in the area for hundreds of years."

"But you *do* at least have myths, which is more than we have in the *Strikefast*'s records," Parck said. "What do these stories say about them?"

"They're supposed to be great warriors," Eli said. "Clever, resourceful, proud. Intensely loyal to one another, too. This exile . . . they must *really* hate the idea of preemptive strikes to do that to him."

"So it would appear," Parck agreed. "I see you're on track at Myomar to become a supply officer."

"Yes, sir," Eli said, the change in subject momentarily throwing him off balance. "My family is in the shipping business, and they thought Imperial service would be a step up—"

"Have you had any training in teaching or tutoring?"

"Nothing formal, sir," Eli said. Was Parck going to recommend he switch to a teaching track?

He hoped not. He'd spent his youth flying cargoes for his family, and he didn't want to be stuck in an office or classroom somewhere.

For a moment the captain gazed at him. Then he leaned back in his seat and looked at the other officers flanking him. A wordless signal passed among them . . .

"Very well, Cadet," Parck said, turning back to Eli. "As of this moment, you're assigned as liaison, translator, and aide to our prisoner. You will also—"

"Sir?" Eli blurted out, feeling his eyes go wide. "But I'm just a cadet—"

"I wasn't finished," Parck said. "Along with translation, you'll also be coaching him in Basic. He has the fundamentals, as you saw, but he needs a more extensive vocabulary and some correction with pronunciation and grammar. Any questions?"

"No, sir," Eli managed. The surprises were coming way too fast. "Actually, yes, sir, I do. Why does he need to know Basic? Aren't we putting him back on the planet?"

There was a quiet stir among the officers, and Eli had the sudden sense that he'd just crossed an invisible line. He tensed—

"No," Parck said. His voice was calm, but there was an edge to it, as if this was a question he and the others had already hashed over. And hadn't necessarily agreed on. "We're taking him to Coruscant."

"To—?" Eli clamped his mouth shut, visions of ancient kings parading defeated enemies through the streets flashing through his mind.

But surely that wasn't what Parck had in mind. Was it?

"I believe the Emperor will be interested in meeting him and learning about these Chiss," Parck said. There was something in his tone that suggested the explanation was as much for his officers' benefit as for Eli's. "I also believe that they could prove an important asset to the Empire. Do your myths include any suggestion of where their home planet might be located?"

"Just that they come from the Unknown Regions, sir. Nothing more specific."

"Pity," Parck said. "No matter. That will be another of your duties over the next few days: to learn as much as you can about him, his homeworld, and his people."

"Yes, sir," Eli said, feeling his heart doing bounce-ups. From lowly cadet to translator and tutor to a being straight out of Lysatra's stories.

And the only downside was what it might cost his future.

Because he'd already seen that the Empire was a massive construct of giant, unforgiving machinery. If he strayed even a few degrees off his chosen career path, he might suddenly find himself relegated to some other track, something obscure that might send him to the core deck of a forgotten starbase and abandon him there.

Still, this little detour in his path should only fill a week or so while the *Strikefast* transported Thrawn to Coruscant. After that, Eli would return to Myomar with the other cadets, and with a story he'd be able to tell people for the rest of his life.

And really, what could go wrong?

"You seem amused," Cadet Vanto said. *He leans back in his seat.*

"Amused?" Thrawn asked.

"Entertained with a feeling of humor," Vanto said. *He switches back to Sy Bisti for the explanation.* "Was there anything in particular about this story that you found humorous?"

"I found the story quite interesting."

"Some of my stories you find interesting," Vanto said. *Wrinkles form across his forehead.* "Others you seem to find unbelievable. A few of them you find amusing. This was one of those."

"I do not mean to offend," Thrawn said. "But I myself am Chiss, and never have I heard of any of my people wielding such a power."

"I'll concede that one," Vanto said. *The wrinkles partially smooth out.* "I told you right from the beginning that these stories are barely above the level of myths. But you asked to hear them."

"I appreciate your willingness to share," Thrawn said. "One may learn a great deal about a people by the stories they tell of others."

"And?" Vanto asked. *The wrinkles return. His head turns slightly to his right.*

"I do not understand."

"I ask what you have learned about humans," Vanto said. *His eyes narrow slightly.*

"I misspoke. Apologies. I meant to say I could learn about one person, you, from the stories you choose to tell."

"And what have you learned about me?" Vanto asked. *His eyes return to normal size. His vocal tone lowers in pitch.*

"That you do not wish to be here," Thrawn said. "You do not wish to act as translator and assistant. You certainly do not wish to act as interrogator."

"Who said I was an interrogator?" Vanto asked. *His tone rises slightly in pitch and volume. The musculature beneath his sleeves tightens.*

"You wish to return to your numbers and inventory lists," Thrawn said. "That is where your talents lie, and where you desire your path to lead."

"Fascinating," Vanto said. *His tone takes on a new, rumbling texture. The corners of his lips tighten briefly.* "I suppose that as a big important military commander you find logistics and supply beneath your dignity?"

"Do *you*?"

"Of course not," Vanto said. *His torso stretches slightly upward in his chair. His voice takes on a fuller tone.* "Because I know better. My family has done that kind of work for three generations. I'm just doing it for the Imperial Navy now instead of for my own family, that's all."

"I presume you are good at it."

"I'm *very* good at it," Vanto said. "Lieutenant Osteregi told me I'm one of the best cadets he's ever had aboard. As soon as I finish my last term at the Academy, I'll be guaranteed an assignment aboard a ship of the line."

"Is what you wish?" Thrawn asked.

"Absolutely," Vanto said. *The fuller tone partially*

fades from his voice. "What I don't know is why you care."

"Why I care about what?"

"Why you care about *me*," Vanto said. *His eyes narrow again. His tone returns to the lower pitch.* "You've been studying me—don't think I haven't noticed. You ask me to tell you one of the legends I learned as a child, then you ask about my home or background or childhood. Always small questions, always delivered very casually. What I want to know is why." *He folds his arms in a crisscross pattern across his chest.*

"I am sorry," Thrawn said. "I meant no harm. I was merely interested in you, as I am interested in everything about your Empire."

"But why *me*?" Vanto asked. "You never ask about Captain Parck or Colonel Barris or any of the other senior officers. Or even about Emperor Palpatine or the Imperial Senate."

"They are not connected to my immediate survival," Thrawn said. "You are."

"With all due respect, you couldn't be more wrong," Vanto said. *He shakes his head, back and forth, sideways.* "Captain Parck could order you shoved out an air lock at any time. Colonel Barris could trump up charges or implicate you in something and have you shot. As for the Emperor—" *The musculature of his throat tightens briefly. There is an enhanced infrared glow from his face.* "He has absolute power over everyone and everything in the Empire. If he isn't amused or pleased with you, you'll end up dead."

"Captain Parck seeks honor and promotion," Thrawn said. "He believes me to be the path to that end. Colonel Barris dislikes me but will not risk angering his captain. As for the Emperor . . . we shall see."

"Fine," Vanto said. *The musculature of his throat relaxes partially, but not fully.* "Personally, I'd be a *lot* more concerned about him, but that's up to you. But I'm still the bottom man on the roster. Why do you even care about me?"

"You are my translator. You hold my words in your hand, and their meanings. A misjudged translation will confuse or anger. A deliberate error could lead to death."

"Krayt spit," Vanto said. *He makes a snorting sound through his nose.*

"Forgive me?"

"I call krayt spit," Vanto said. "You've picked up a *lot* of Basic in the past couple of days. You speak it as well as I do. Probably better—you don't have a Wild Space accent people can make fun of. The last thing you need is a translator."

"You make my case for me," Thrawn said. "What is meant by *krayt spit*?"

"It's a slang term for nonsense," Vanto said. *The left corner of his lip twists upward.* "Especially nonsense that the speaker *knows* is nonsense."

"I see. *Krayt spit.* I will remember that."

"Don't," Vanto said. *His tone is deep, the word sharply clipped.* "It's not polite. It also reeks of backwater places like Lysatra. *Backwater* means any planet that's not part of the Core Worlds and the elite and powerful people who live there."

"I presume there exists a hierarchy of worlds and the people who inhabit them?"

"Finally—a question about the actual Empire," Vanto said. "Yes, absolutely there's a hierarchy. A big, impressive, mostly unwritten, but absolutely rigid hierarchy. If you were counting on me to introduce you to the high and mighty, you're going to be seriously disappointed."

"You give yourself too little credit, Cadet Vanto," Thrawn said. "Or perhaps you give the social hierarchy too much. I am content to have you as my translator."

"I'm glad you're pleased," Vanto said. *His tone rises*

slightly in pitch. His throat musculature still shows tightness. "Not that you had any choice in the matter."

"Perhaps," Thrawn said. "Tell me, when do we arrive at your capital world?"

"My orders are to have you in the forward hangar bay—that's the one you tried to escape from—at oh-seven-hundred tomorrow morning," Vanto said.

"And I will meet with the Emperor soon after that?"

"I have no idea what happens after that," Vanto said. *The muscles under his tunic stiffen slightly, and wrinkles return to his forehead.* "But odds are it won't be anyone even close to the Emperor. Probably some senior administrator. Maybe even a junior one."

"Will you come with me?"

"That's up to the captain," Vanto said. "I *do* still have other duties aboard the *Strikefast*. I also need to prepare for my return to the Myomar Academy."

"Your duties and studies are of course important," Thrawn said. "We shall see what decision Captain Parck comes to. Until morning, Cadet, I bid you farewell and good evening."

"Yes," Vanto said. *The tension in his musculature decreases. But it is not entirely gone.* "Until morning."

Captain Parck's personal Lambda shuttle left the hangar at precisely oh-seven-oh-five the next morning. Apart from Parck, Thrawn, and Eli, the passenger list included Colonel Barris, three of the navy troopers who'd been on the planet when Thrawn was running everyone in circles, and two stormtroopers, presumably also part of the group who'd seen the alien in action.

There were also ten heavily armed navy troopers. If Parck was worried about hard-eyed High Command administrators, he also wasn't taking any chances on his prisoner making a break for it once they reached the planet.

Like everyone else in the Empire, Eli had seen hundreds of holos of Coruscant. He'd also spent a couple of hours studying planetary maps the day after Parck announced they were heading there.

None of it prepared him for the breathtaking grandeur of the real thing.

He gazed at the passenger cabin's repeater display, watching in utter fascination. The entire planet was surrounded by half a dozen rings of orbiting transports, passenger ships, and military vessels, each awaiting its turn to head to the surface. Elsewhere, steady streams of outgoing ships created subtle fountains of light as they joined the various exit corridors for passage through the atmosphere, then scattered in all directions once they reached space.

As the Lambda continued inward, Eli watched the array of glittering starlike points that covered the planet slowly resolve into buildings and towers. Still closer, and the gridlines of repulsorlift vehicles wove their packed way between the towering buildings, doing their intricate dance as they headed for a thousand destinations. A sobering thought occurred to him: Right now he could probably see more vehicles than were on his entire home planet.

The pilot eased them into one of the higher lanes, one that seemed reserved for military vehicles. They were close enough now that Eli could pick out specific landmarks. There was the Royal Imperial Academy, where the Empire's elite trained for the army and navy. Beyond it and to the east was one of the industrial areas, with tall towers spewing superheated wastewater vapor high into the atmosphere. In the distance beyond that he could see an open area that was far below the tops of the surrounding towers, yet still many levels above the actual planetary surface. A landing area, most likely, probably for elite politicians or larger military vessels. He spotted the top of the Imperial Senate Building in the other direction.

He caught his breath. If the Senate was *there* and the Royal Academy back *there* . . .

They weren't heading to either the Admiralty or the Imperial Security Bureau headquarters, which he'd concluded were the two most likely destinations.

They were heading straight for the Imperial Palace.

The Imperial *Palace*?

No—that couldn't be. Not for a single, random, blue-skinned near-human captured on an unnamed world out in Wild Space. There was no possible way the Emperor would even notice such an event, let alone take a personal interest in it.

And yet that seemed to be exactly what had happened.

Surreptitiously, Eli looked across the aisle, where Thrawn and Parck sat together surrounded by guards. The captain looked unnaturally stiff, as if he couldn't believe their destination any more than Eli could. The guards looked the same way, except that some of them looked quietly but genuinely terrified.

As well they should be. These were the men and women whose mistakes had allowed Thrawn to get aboard the *Strikefast* in the first place. There were dark stories about what the Emperor did with people who'd failed him.

But Thrawn himself didn't look frightened, or even concerned. All Eli could see in his face was that maddening confidence of his.

Maybe Parck hadn't told him where they were going. Maybe he hadn't told him about the Emperor's history, or his reputation.

Or maybe he'd told Thrawn everything and the Chiss simply assumed that whatever their destination, he would have things under control.

Eli turned back to the display, the old stories of Chiss military power echoing through his mind. As far as he had been able to ascertain, that whole culture and society had been lost from Republic knowledge for centuries, maybe even millennia. Now, suddenly, they'd reentered history.

Was Thrawn's level of confidence unique to him? Or were all the Chiss like this?

As someone who might someday be called upon to fight them, he hoped fervently it wasn't the latter.

Eli had almost managed to convince himself that the group would merely be meeting with some Palace official when they were ushered past a pair of red-robed and red-helmeted Imperial Guards into the Emperor's throne room.

Even more than Coruscant itself, the holos and vids Eli had seen of Emperor Palpatine paled in comparison with the real thing.

At first glance, the Emperor didn't seem like much. He was dressed in a plain brown hooded robe, with no ornamentation or glitz of any sort. His throne, while massive, was solid black and very simple, again with no ostentation about it, raised a mere four steps above the floor. In fact, the darkness of his robe made him almost disappear from sight into the black of the throne.

It was as the group drew closer that the eeriness began.

First was the Emperor's face. The holos and vids always showed him as a dignified, older man, aged somewhat with the experience of life and the cares of leadership. But the holos were wrong. The face beneath the hood was *old;* old, and creased with a hundred deep wrinkles.

Not ordinary wrinkles, either, the kind Eli's grandparents had earned from years under the open sky. These creases were less like age, and more like scars or burn tissue.

The histories stated that the Jedi traitors' last attempt to seize power had been an attack on then-Chancellor Palpatine. The histories hadn't mentioned that his victory over the assassins had come at such a terrible cost.

Perhaps that was also what had happened to his eyes.

A shiver ran up Eli's back. The eyes were bright and intelligent, all-knowing and utterly powerful. But they were . . . strange. Unique. Disturbing. Damaged, perhaps, by the same treachery that had ravaged his face?

Intelligence, knowledge, power. And even more than with Thrawn, a sense of complete mastery over everything around him.

The Emperor watched in silence as the party walked toward him. Parck led the way, Barris and Eli behind him, followed by Thrawn and the navy trooper and stormtrooper witnesses. The guard contingent Parck had brought remained outside the door, six of the Imperial Guards having taken over their escort duty.

It seemed to take forever to reach the throne. Eli wondered how close they would be permitted to approach, and how Captain Parck would know when he had reached that point. The question was answered as Parck came to within five meters and the two Imperial Guards at the foot of the steps glided to positions directly in front of him. Parck stopped, the rest of them following suit, and waited.

And waited.

It was probably only five seconds. But to Eli it felt like a medium-sized eternity. The entire throne room was utterly still, utterly silent. The only sound was the thudding of his pulse in his ears, the only movement the shaking of his arms in his sleeves.

"Captain Parck," the Emperor said at last, his gravelly voice neutral. "I'm told you bring me a gift."

Eli winced. A *gift*? For the Chiss of the stories, that would have been a deadly insult. Thrawn was behind him, and Eli didn't dare turn around, but he could imagine the expression on that proud face.

"I do, Your Majesty," Parck said, bowing low. "A warrior reportedly of a species known as the Chiss."

"Indeed," the Emperor said, his voice going even

drier. "And what, pray tell, would you have me do with him?"

"If I may, Your Majesty," Thrawn put in before Parck could answer. "I am not merely a gift. I am also a resource. One you have never seen the like of before, and may never see again. You would do well to utilize me."

"Would I?" the Emperor said, sounding amused. "Certainly you're a resource of unlimited confidence. What exactly do you offer, Chiss?"

"As a start, I offer information," Thrawn said. If he was offended, Eli couldn't hear it in his voice. "There are threats lurking in the Unknown Regions, threats that will someday find your Empire. I am familiar with many of them."

"I will learn of them soon enough on my own," the Emperor countered placidly. "Can you offer anything more?"

"Perhaps you will learn of them in time to defeat them," Thrawn said. "Perhaps you will not. What more do I offer? I offer my military skill. You could utilize that skill in making plans to seek out and eliminate these dangers."

"These threats you speak of," the Emperor said. "I presume they're not simply threats to my Empire?"

"No, Your Majesty," Thrawn said. "They are also threats to my people."

"And you seek to eliminate all such threats to your people?"

"I do."

The Emperor's yellowish eyes seemed to glitter. "And you wish the help of my Empire?"

"Your assistance would be welcome."

"You wish me to assist the people who exiled you?" the Emperor said. "Or was Captain Parck incorrect?"

"He spoke correctly," Thrawn said. "I was indeed exiled."

"Yet you still seek to protect them. Why?"

"Because they are my people."

"And if they withhold their gratitude and refuse to accept you back? What then?"

There was a slight pause, and Eli had the eerie sense that Thrawn was giving the Emperor one of those small smiles he was so good at. "I do not need their permission to protect them, Your Majesty. Nor do I expect their thanks."

"I've seen others with your sense of nobility," the Emperor said. "Most fell by the wayside when their naïve selflessness collided with the real world."

"I *have* faced the real world, as you call it."

"You have indeed," the Emperor said. "What exactly do you wish from my Empire?"

"A state of mutual gain," Thrawn said. "I offer my knowledge and skill to you now in exchange for your consideration to my people in the future."

"And when that future comes, what if I refuse to grant that consideration?"

"Then I will have gambled and lost," Thrawn said calmly. "But I have until that time to convince you that my goals and yours do indeed coincide."

"Interesting," the Emperor murmured. "Tell me. If you served the Empire, yet a threat arose against your people, where would your loyalties lie? Which of us would command your allegiance?"

"I see no conflict in the sharing of information."

"I'm not speaking of information," the Emperor said. "I'm speaking of service."

There was a short pause. "If I were to serve the Empire, you would command my allegiance."

"What guarantee do you offer?"

"My word is my guarantee," Thrawn said. "Perhaps your servant can speak to the strength of that vow."

"My servant?" the Emperor asked, his eyes flicking to Parck.

"I do not refer to Captain Parck," Thrawn said. "I speak of another. Perhaps I assumed incorrectly that he was your servant. Yet he always spoke highly of Chancellor Palpatine."

The Emperor leaned forward a little, his yellowish eyes glittering. "And his name?"

"Skywalker," Thrawn said. "Anakin Skywalker."

CHAPTER 3

War is primarily a game of skill. It is a contest of mind matched against mind, tactics matched against tactics.

But there is also an element of chance that is more suited to games of cards or dice. A wise tactician studies those games, as well, and learns from them.

The first lesson of card games is that the cards cannot be played in random order. Only when laid down properly can victory be achieved.

In this case, there were but three cards.

The first was played at the encampment. The result was entrance to the Strikefast. The second was played aboard ship. The result was the promise of passage to Coruscant, and the assignment of Cadet Vanto as my translator.

The third was a name: Anakin Skywalker.

"Interesting," the Emperor said. *His eyes are steady and do not blink. The skin of his face is unmoving.* "And *your* name?"

"You already know it."

"I wish you to speak it."

"Mitth'raw'nuruodo."

"So it *was* you," the Emperor said. *He leans back in his throne. The corners of his lips curve upward. His eyes remain unchanged in size.* "When Captain Parck's message arrived, I'd hoped it was."

"Jedi Skywalker survived the war, then?"

"Sadly, he did not," the Emperor said.

"I mourn his passing," Thrawn said. "He was a most cunning and . . . may I consult my translator?"

"You may," the Emperor said. *His eyes narrow slightly. The yellow tinge now appears stronger.*

"*Eqhuwa.*"

"Courageous," Vanto translated. *His face radiates extra heat. The muscles beneath his tunic show stiffness. His lips compress tightly before and after he speaks the word.*

"He was a most cunning and courageous warrior," Thrawn continued. "I had hoped to meet him again."

"Most courageous indeed," the Emperor said. *His head turns slightly to his left. His eyes rest briefly on Vanto, then return. His fingers press gently against the arms of his throne.* "But before his end he detailed for me the circumstances of your meeting, and spoke highly of your abilities. So you wish to become my adviser on matters of the Unknown Regions?"

"I have said that already."

"And if I offered more?" the Emperor asked.

"What larger offer would you make?"

"You can see the power that I have created," the Emperor said. *His eyes are strongly focused, his lips showing a small curve.* "Or you can be part of it."

"My home is lost to me," Thrawn said. "Jedi Skywalker's services are lost to you. If you wish my direct service as a replacement to his, I am honored to offer it."

"Interesting," the Emperor said. *His eyes linger a moment, then shift their direction and focus on Captain Parck.* "You were correct to bring your prisoner to me, Captain. You and your men will return to your ship and your duties. The High Command will provide a suitable reward for your service and initiative."

"Yes, Your Majesty," Parck said, bowing again. "Thank you."

"A favor, Your Majesty?" Thrawn said.

"Speak, Mitth'raw'nuruodo," the Emperor said. *His eyes narrow.*

"I am still inexpert at your language. I would request that my translator be transferred to duty at my side."

The Emperor sits motionlessly without speaking. He then presses his hands onto the throne's armrests and rises to his feet. "Walk with me, Mitth'raw'nuruodo."

The two guards at the foot of the throne stepped a meter to either side. The Emperor descended to the floor and turned to his left, toward a garden area at the side of the chamber.

The garden is small, but contains a variety of plants. Most are set in large pots or in long floor trenches lining the curved flagstone walkways. A few brightly colored flowers grow directly from the decorative stone. Small trees with shimmering bark stand at the periphery like sentinels of privacy. The distance from garden to throne ensures privacy from those still waiting there.

There is an artistic foundation to the garden's arrangement. There is a pattern in the interaction of curve and line, in the melding and contrast of shape and color, in the subtle play of light and shadow. It bespeaks power and subtlety and great depth of thought.

"An interesting space," Thrawn said. "Did you create it?"

"I designed it," the Emperor said. He stopped within the first curve of bushes. "Tell me, what do you think?"

Subtlety, and depth of thought. "You did not bring me here to speak of translators," Thrawn told him. "But you wish Captain Parck and the others to so believe."

"Good," the Emperor said. *His tone is deeper. The corners of his lips lift. His mouth opens slightly, revealing his teeth.* "Good. Anakin spoke of your insight. I'm pleased to learn he was correct. The Unknown Regions intrigue me, Mitth'raw'nuruodo. There is great potential there."

"There is also great danger."

"There is great danger here as well," the Emperor countered. *The corners of his lips turn downward, and his eyes narrow.*

"Certainly there is *power* here," Thrawn said. "But there is only danger to your enemies."

"You do not consider your people to be among those enemies?"

"You spoke of an interest in the Unknown Regions. How may I assist in satisfying your curiosity?"

"You seek to avoid my question," the Emperor said. *His lips compress together.* "Tell me: Do your people regard the Empire as their enemy?"

"I am not accountable for the future actions or goals of my people," Thrawn said. "I can speak only for myself. And I have said already I will serve you."

"Until you find it convenient to escape from my reach?"

"I am a warrior, Your Majesty," Thrawn said. "A warrior may retreat. He does not flee. He may lie in ambush. He does not hide. He may experience victory or defeat. He does not cease to serve."

"I will hold you to that," the Emperor said. "Why do you wish to have your translator?"

"He knows something of my people," Thrawn said. "I wish to explore the depth of that knowledge."

"If he has knowledge of the Unknown Regions, then perhaps I should instead keep him here with me."

"His knowledge is little more than stories and tales," Thrawn said. "He will not know worlds or peoples. Nor will he know hyperspace lanes and potential safe havens."

"That knowledge lies solely with you?" the Emperor asked. *His tone lowers in pitch.*

"For the moment," Thrawn said. "Later, it will lie also with you."

"Once again, your eloquence belies your need for a

translator," the Emperor said. *His lips again turn upward.* "But I will give him to you. Come, let us rejoin the others."

The group was still waiting between the lines of guards. "This is he?" the Emperor asked, pointing at Vanto.

"It is, Your Majesty," Thrawn said. "Cadet Eli Vanto."

"Captain Parck, how much longer does Cadet Vanto have before graduation?"

"Three standard months, Your Majesty," Parck said. "We were scheduled to return him and his fellow cadets to Myomar when we were sidetracked by the smuggler pursuit that ultimately brought us to Thrawn's place of exile."

"You will return the other cadets as planned," the Emperor said. "Cadet Vanto will remain on Coruscant and finish his training at the Royal Imperial Academy."

"Yes, Your Majesty," Parck said, looking briefly at Vanto, then at Thrawn. "I'll inform Admiral Foss of this change."

Vanto's face radiates more strongly than before, and the muscles in his throat have stiffened. He begins to open his mouth, as if to speak, but closes it with no words spoken.

He does not understand. Nor will he. Not for a long while.

The Myomar Academy, situated in the Expansion Region, was staffed and attended mostly by residents of backwater worlds. There, Eli had been among his own kind, about as relaxed and comfortable as it was possible to be given the excruciating pressure of the Empire's most intense training regimen.

The Royal Imperial Academy, in contrast, was staffed exclusively by the elite of the Empire, with a student body to match. From the moment Eli and Thrawn set foot off the shuttle from the Palace, he could feel everyone's eyes fixed firmly on the newcomers.

And he had no doubt that most of those eyes were hostile.

The alien, and the backwater yokel. This, Eli thought glumly, was a classic joke in the making.

Commandant Deenlark clearly thought likewise.

"So," he ground out, his eyes flicking back and forth between the two of them as they stood at attention in front of his desk. "Is this Admiral Foss's idea of a joke?"

Thrawn didn't answer, apparently leaving this one to Eli. Great. "The Emperor himself sent us here, sir," Eli said, not knowing what else to say.

"That was a rhetorical question, Cadet," Deenlark growled, glaring at him from under bushy eyebrows. "You *do* have complicated words like *rhetorical* in Wild Space, don't you?"

Eli clenched his teeth. "Yes, sir."

"Good," Deenlark said. "Because we use a lot of big words here. We wouldn't want you to get lost." He shifted his glare to Thrawn. "What's *your* excuse, alien?"

"My excuse for what, sir?" Thrawn asked calmly.

"Your excuse for living," Deenlark bit out. "Well?"

Thrawn remained silent, and for a few seconds the two of them locked gazes. Then Deenlark's lip twitched. "Yeah, like I thought," the commandant said sourly. "You're damn lucky the Emperor's taken a fancy to you. Though *why,* I can't guess."

He paused, as if expecting Thrawn to explain it to him. Again, the Chiss didn't respond.

"Fine," Deenlark said at last. "Foss's message said you were some kind of fancy-face soldier already, that all you needed was a little orientation in Imperial procedure, equipment, and terminology. That scans out to a six-month course for the typical raw recruit. Probably two years for cadets from the back end of nowhere," he added, looking at Eli.

There were times, Eli had learned, when it didn't pay

to say anything. This was one of them. He kept his head up, his eyes focused straight ahead, and his mouth closed.

"So here's the deal," Deenlark said, turning back to Thrawn. "Cadet Vanto has three months left before commissioning. That's how long you have to come up to speed. You fail, and you're out."

"The Emperor might disagree," Thrawn said mildly.

Deenlark's lip twitched. "The Emperor would understand," he said. But some of the air had gone out of his bluster. "His own mandate to the Academies is to turn out officers worthy of Imperial service. Anything less, and the whole navy suffers, officers and enlisted alike. Of course, if the Emperor wants to put you in by fiat, he can do that." He raised his eyebrows. "I hope you'll prove good enough that he won't have to do that."

"We shall see," Thrawn said.

"I guess we shall." Deenlark pursed his lips. "One other thing. Foss said you were to leave here as a lieutenant instead of the standard rank of ensign. Something about getting you into command position as quickly as possible. I figure, why waste time?" Pulling open a drawer, he extracted a lieutenant's rank insignia plaque and gave it a spinning flip that landed it on the edge of the desk in front of Thrawn. "There you go. Congratulations, Lieutenant. Cadet Vanto can show you which way is up."

"Thank you, sir," Thrawn said politely, picking up the plaque. "I assume the proper uniforms will be delivered to our quarters?"

"Yes," Deenlark said, frowning. "You sure you even *need* a translator? Your Basic seems pretty good."

Eli felt a flicker of hope. Deenlark had already made it clear he wasn't happy with this arrangement. He couldn't touch Thrawn directly, but maybe he could express some of his displeasure by refusing to accept Eli as Thrawn's translator. If he did, maybe there was still time for Eli to get back to Myomar and finish his schooling in more comfortable surroundings.

"There are yet many idioms and technical terms I am unfamiliar with," Thrawn said. "His service will be most valuable."

"I'm sure it will," Deenlark conceded reluctantly. "Fine. Now get the hell out of here. I mean, *Dismissed, Cadets.* You've been assigned a split double—the yeoman outside will have a mouse droid take you there. Schedules and directions are on your computer. Assuming you've figured out how to turn it on."

"I'm familiar with your computer systems," Thrawn said.

"I was talking to Vanto," Deenlark said sarcastically. "Dismissed."

The yeoman was as stiff as the commandant. But he was efficient enough. Two minutes later, Eli and Thrawn were following a mouse droid as it skittered its way along the walkway leading to Barracks Two.

And just like that, Eli's life had been completely upended.

His career trajectory with the navy, so carefully calculated and implemented, was gone. Worse, just because he'd been solidly on track to graduate from Myomar didn't mean he would make it in the much tougher environment of Royal Imperial. Even with only three months to go, he could still wash out.

Especially since his time would now be split between his studies and playing word games with Thrawn. An alien who was even more of a fish ashore than Eli himself.

An alien who could not possibly succeed.

Eli knew what Imperial Academies were like. He'd heard all the running jokes about Falleen, Umbarans, Neimoidians, and other aliens. And Royal Imperial, smack at the center of the Empire, would almost certainly be the worst of the lot. Thrawn had as much chance of surviving here as a wounded bird in a nest of blood spites.

When he went down, would Eli go down with him?

He had no idea. But he guessed he probably would.

"You seem thoughtful," Thrawn said.

Eli made a face. The Chiss had no idea what he'd let himself in for. "Just wondering how we're going to do here."

"Yes." Thrawn was silent a moment "You spoke once of a planetary and social hierarchy. Tell me how that hierarchy . . ." He paused. *"Binesu."*

Eli sighed. "Manifests."

"Thank you. How that hierarchy manifests here."

"Probably the same as in any military academy," Eli said. "The commandant is on top, the instructors are below him, and the cadets are below them. Pretty simple, really."

"Are there good relations between each level of authority?"

"I don't know," Eli said. "They all have to work together, so I suppose they all get along."

"But there is rivalry between cadets?"

"Of course."

"And the cadets have no official military rank or hierarchy until graduation?"

"There's an unspoken social order," Eli said, frowning. "Nothing official. Why all the questions?"

"This." Thrawn opened his hand and gazed down at the lieutenant's rank plaque lying across his palm. "I wish to understand why he gave it to me."

"Well, it wasn't from the goodness of his heart," Eli growled. "It wasn't to save time, either."

"Explain."

Eli huffed out a breath. "Look. There are three reactions you're going to get as soon as you start flashing that plaque around. One: Some students and instructors will see you as Deenlark's pet and resent you for it."

"What is a *pet*?"

"In this case, slang for a favored student," Eli told

him. "That group will resent you for all the privileges you're supposedly getting."

"I do not expect to get privileges."

"Doesn't matter—they'll still figure you're getting some. Reaction number two: Some will see you as a failed officer who's been sent back for a refresher. That group will treat you with complete contempt."

"So this is not so much a gift as a weapon?"

"A weapon against *you*, yeah," Eli said. "And then there's group three. They'll think you're a joke. No, on second thought, they'll probably think you're a test."

"What sort of test?"

"The really hard kind," Eli said. Yes, this had to be what Deenlark was going for. "Okay. Here you're not supposed to show disrespect to superior officers. I assume it's also like that in the Chiss military, right?"

"Normally," Thrawn said, his voice going a little dry.

Eli winced. For a moment he'd forgotten how Thrawn had arrived in the Empire in the first place. "Well, officially we're not allowed to disrespect aliens, either," he went on hurriedly. "I say *officially*, because that's what the General Orders say we're supposed to do. But that's not always what we *really* do."

"You dislike nonhumans?"

Eli hesitated. How was he supposed to answer that? "There were a lot of different nonhuman groups in the Separatist movement," he said, choosing his words carefully. "The Clone Wars killed a lot of people and devastated whole worlds. There's still a lot of resentment about that, especially among humans."

"But were not other nonhuman groups allied with the Republic?"

"Sure," Eli said. "And most of them did all right. But humans still carried most of the weight." He considered. "Well, that's the perception, anyway. I don't know if it's actually true."

Thrawn nodded, either agreement or simple acknowledgment. "Either way, would it not be more reasonable to resent only those nonhuman groups that opposed you?"

"Probably," Eli said. "Well, okay—definitely. And it probably started that way. But sometimes that sort of thing seeps down to other groups." He hesitated. "On top of that, there's a lot of contempt in the Core Worlds toward the people anywhere past the Mid Rim, humans and nonhumans alike. And with me from Wild Space and you from the Unknown Regions, we're about as far into the Sneer Zone as you can get."

"I see," Thrawn said. "If I understand, I am untouchable for three reasons: I am an officer, I am not human, and I am from the disrespected edge of the Empire. So the test for the cadets would be to see how creative they can be in their disrespect toward me?"

"Basically," Eli said. "And how close to the line they can get without stepping over it."

"Which line?"

"The line where they've done something that can't be ignored," Eli said, trying to think. "Okay, try this. Someone could shove you off a walkway and claim *you* were the one who bumped into *him*. But he couldn't break into your quarters and wreck your computer. See the difference? In the second case, there's no way he could claim you were the one at fault."

"Unless he claimed I had stored stolen data on the computer and he was attempting to retrieve it."

Eli winced. "I hadn't thought of that," he said. "But yeah, that's exactly how it would work. Though in that case he'd have to prove you *had* stolen data in order to get away with it."

"It could be planted after my quarters were entered."

"I suppose," Eli said. This just got better and better. "Looks like we're going to be walking on eggshells for the next three months."

Thrawn was silent another few steps. "I assume that is another idiom," he said. "Perhaps it would be better if you did not walk on these eggshells alongside me."

"Yeah, well, you should have thought about that before you asked the Emperor to stick me as your translator," Eli said sourly. "You want to call the Palace and tell them you've changed your mind?"

"I still require your services," Thrawn said. "But you could join the others in expressing your contempt for me."

Eli frowned. "Come again?"

"Excuse me?"

Eli rolled his eyes. Sometimes Thrawn caught these idioms right away. Other times, he didn't have a clue. "That means I want you to repeat that, or otherwise explain what you mean."

"Were the words not clear? Very well. You may make it clear to the others that I am no more than an assignment. One, moreover, that you resisted and thoroughly dislike."

"I don't dislike my assignment," Eli protested, the polite lie automatically coming to his lips. "And I don't dislike you."

"Do you not?" Thrawn countered. "Because of me you were taken from your ship and brought to this Academy, which you fear."

Eli felt something stir inside him. "Who said I was afraid?" he demanded. "I'm not afraid. I'm just not looking forward to spending my last term with a bunch of Core World snobs, that's all."

"I am glad to hear that," Thrawn said gravely. "We shall endure it together."

"Yeah," Eli said, frowning hard at him. Had he just been maneuvered into supporting the Chiss against whatever the Royal Imperial could throw at them? Apparently, he had.

Which didn't mean he couldn't backpedal on that anytime he wanted to. And that time might very well come. "I can hardly wait," he said. "Change of subject. Did you really meet General Skywalker?"

"I did," Thrawn said, his voice going distant. "It was an interesting time."

"That's it? That's all you're going to tell me? That it was *interesting*?"

"For now," Thrawn said. "Perhaps we will speak more of it later." He opened his hand and looked at his new rank plaque. "I cannot help being nonhuman or coming from a region of low respect," he said. "But perhaps it would be best if we kept this a secret between us." He slipped the plaque out of sight into his tunic.

Eli nodded. "Works for me."

Ahead, the mouse droid rolled to the front of a three-story building and stopped, waiting for someone to open the door for it. "I guess we're here," Eli added. "Let's see what the Admiralty has sent ahead for us."

"And then we will learn our schedule and duties," Thrawn said. "And prepare as best we can for the onslaught."

Eli sighed. "Yeah. And that."

CHAPTER 4

To some extent, the direction of one's chosen path automatically selects for the paths that may cross it. A warrior's path will intersect the paths of other warriors, allies and enemies alike. A worker's path will intersect the paths of other workers.

But as with games of cards or dice, sometimes unexpected crossings occur. Some are driven by chance, others by design, others by a change in one's goals.

Some are driven by malice.

Such manipulations can prove effective in the short term. But the longer-term consequences can be perilously difficult to predict.

The path of Arihnda Pryce is one such example. A deep and perceptive study of it can serve as a valuable lesson.

And as an even more valuable warning.

"Ms. Pryce?"

Arihnda Pryce paused and turned around. Hurrying toward her down the long corridor was Arik Uvis, a datapad in his hand, an intense expression on his face.

Arihnda glowered to herself. Uvis with one of his rock-brained questions or comments wasn't something she really wanted to deal with right now.

But he wasn't going away, and the Pryce Mining's corporate building was far too small for her to successfully avoid him all day. Might as well get it over with.

He caught up to her and stopped. "Ms. Pryce," he repeated, breathing a little heavily. The man was in his mid-thirties, about Arihnda's own age, but in far worse shape. "Glad I caught you."

"What can I do for you, Mr. Uvis?" Arihnda asked, keeping her face and voice neutral.

"I heard a rumor that your father's just uncovered a heretofore unknown vein of doonium," Uvis said. "Is that true?"

"It is," Arihnda said, wondering darkly who had let the news slip. Doonium was one of the hardest metals known, making it a key component in the manufacture of warship hulls, and under the Imperial Navy's recently accelerated shipbuilding program the price of the metal had skyrocketed. Even a hint that a fresh line had been found would be enough to initiate a feeding frenzy among refiners and ore buyers alike. "May I ask how you heard of it?"

"That's not important," Uvis said. "What's important is that we guard the find so that we can take full advantage of it."

"I'm sure my mother's already on it," Arihnda assured him. "We have several contacts among brokers capable of handling something like this."

Uvis snorted. "I'm sure you do," he said in a vaguely condescending tone. "Small, local people, no doubt, who work on a promise and a handshake?"

"Not all of them are small," Arihnda said, trying hard not to let her irritation show. Uvis was an outsider from the Core who'd been more or less forced on them by Governor Azadi's office six standard months ago. She could probably count his trips outside the Capital City area during that time on one hand. Not only did he know virtually nothing about Lothal, but he clearly didn't care to learn. "But so what if they are? If any one of them can't handle the full contract, we'll just make deals with two or three or four. Everything's interconnected here."

"And I have no doubt that system works fine for the average backwoods Outer Rim world," Uvis said with strained patience. "But some of us have higher ambitions for Lothal."

Arihnda snorted under her breath. Ambitions for a backwater dirtball like Lothal. Right. "Good luck with that one."

"I'm serious," Uvis insisted. "Now that we have a doonium vein—"

"*We* have a doonium vein," Arihnda cut him off. "Pryce Mining. Not you, and not Lothal. *We* have it."

"Fine," Uvis said. "Just remember the governor's office and I are included in that *we*. We're your partners, remember?"

"Not for long," Arihnda said. "As soon as the profits from the doonium start rolling in, we're buying out of your loan. We can do that—the contract says so."

"The contract didn't anticipate something like this." Uvis took a deep breath. "Look, Arihnda. Here's the reality. Yes, you've got wealth now, more than you ever dreamed of. That means it's your big chance. Not just Pryce Mining's, but yours—personally—as well."

"Really," Arihnda said, trying to make the word sarcastic. But she couldn't quite pull it off.

Because he was right. This kind of sudden wealth might finally make it possible for her to get out of here. Not just out of the family business, but off Lothal completely.

"But it's also going to attract attention, and not necessarily the good kind," Uvis continued. "You need—"

He broke off as a hammerheaded Ithorian appeared around the corner and hurried past them, a stack of data cards in her hand. Someone's niece, Arihnda vaguely remembered, working a two-week internship. The Ithorian grunted a *Good morning,* then disappeared around a different corner. "You need support," Uvis said. "More than that, you need protection. Governor Azadi can give you that."

The nebulous thought of finally getting off Lothal vanished in a sudden cloud of suspicion. "Protection?" she countered. "Or do you mean *takeover*?"

"No, of course not," Uvis protested.

"Really," Arihnda said. "Because we've heard this before. Other people have come to Lothal, lots of them, looking for ways to lift us up out of the dust and coincidentally make themselves rich. Sooner or later, they all find out that the people here are stubborn, set in their ways, and not interested in having fancy-hats from the Core tell them what to do."

"I'm glad Lothal has come to terms with mediocrity," Uvis ground out. "But that pattern is over. The fancy-hats will be coming back, this time to stay. And they'll eat small fish like Pryce Mining for breakfast."

"Don't threaten me, Uvis," she warned.

"I'm not threatening you," he said. "I'm trying to tell you that everything's about to change. There are a dozen ways a big mining corporation can move in on a small operation like yours and either take it over or bleed it dry. I don't want that, you don't want that, and Governor Azadi most definitely doesn't want that."

With an effort, Arihnda got a fresh grip on her temper. So Uvis had already told Azadi about the doonium?

Damn. In a tight-knit community like Capital City, that meant half the citizens knew by now. And if half the citizens knew, a good quarter of the outsiders in the area probably knew, too. "I assume you have a solution to offer?"

"We do," Uvis assured her. "We start with you selling the governor another twenty-one percent of Pryce Mining. That would—"

"*What?*" Arihnda demanded, feeling her jaw drop. "Absolutely not. You're not getting a controlling interest."

"It's the only way to keep some predatory mega-corporation off your back," Uvis said. "With the power and office of the governor protecting you, we can make deals with *real* refineries, the kind with money and influence—"

"No," Arihnda said flatly.

Uvis took a deep breath. "I know this is a big step," he said, his tone soothing now. "But it's the only way—"

"I said *no*," Arihnda repeated.

"You need to at least tell your parents about the governor's offer," Uvis persisted. "At least your mother. As the general manager, she needs to know—"

"Which part of *no* is confusing you?"

Uvis's face darkened. "If you don't, I will."

"No, what you'll do is get out of my sight," Arihnda told him. "Actually, what you can do is get off our property."

He snorted. "Please. I own thirty percent of Pryce Mining. You can't just throw me out."

"The Pryce family owns seventy percent," Arihnda countered, "and the guard droids answer to us."

For a long moment they stared at each other. Then Uvis inclined his head. "Very well, Ms. Pryce," he said. "But hear this. You can sit on your dirty little world, a big frog in a small dust puddle, and think you can stand alone against the galaxy. But you can't. The sooner you realize that, the less it'll cost you." He raised his eyebrows. "*And* your parents."

"Goodbye, Mr. Uvis," Arihnda said.

"Goodbye, Ms. Pryce," he said. "Call me when you're ready to see reason."

Uvis himself was gone. But the cloud he'd left over Arihnda persisted.

A dozen times that day she thought about going to her mother and letting her know about Uvis's warning and offer. But each time she decided not to. The mine had been in her family almost all the way back to the first planetary settlements, and she knew that both her parents would go down fighting rather than give it up.

They had full legal rights to the mine, the land, and the business. Moreover, the Lothal legal system, where any challenges would be heard, was loaded with acquaintances, suppliers, clients, friends, and friends of friends. The one advantage of living on a sleepy frontier world. Whatever corporations or slicksters or sleazy grubbers from the governor's office tried to throw at them, they would weather the storm.

She worked late, finishing up the day's data sorting and drafting a data release for whenever her parents decided to announce the news. Just because half of Lothal probably knew by now didn't mean they wouldn't eventually have to say something official.

It was nearly sundown when she finally left the office. She headed for home, driving slower than usual, watching the colors in the western sky and the fading light as it bounced sparkles off the shrubs and intricate rock formations lining the roadway. On the horizon, the lights of Capital City's buildings were coming on, a softer and whiter glow than the reds and pinks of the setting sun. From somewhere in the distance came the happy shrieking of children at play. Off on the horizon she could see a pair of airspeeders, probably with teenagers at the controls, showboating over the rolling, grass-covered hills as they chased the setting sun. It was the kind of primitive beauty that travel advisers raved about.

Arihnda hated it.

That hadn't always been the case. For a while, back when she was a child, she'd loved the quiet life, the wide-open spaces, and the companionship of children of so many different species and backgrounds. But during her teen years she'd begun to see the quietness as dullness, the open spaces as lack of culture or excitement, the familiar acquaintances as stifling and boring. Often, lying awake in bed, she'd gazed out the window at the stars and wished with all her heart that she could escape to a *real* world somewhere, a place with excitement and bright lights and sophisticated people.

But she never had. And with the passing of her teen years, and her transition to the responsibilities of adulthood, she knew she never would.

The pain and frustration had subsided somewhat over the last decade. But they had never entirely disappeared. She still hated her life here, but it was a familiar, constant hatred, like a dull ache that had never quite healed.

She slowed the landspeeder a little more, watching the interplay of city light and sunset glow. In worlds with excitement and bright lights, she suspected, many of the inhabitants never even saw the horizon, let alone a sunset.

Of course, they probably didn't care about such things. If she were there, she doubted she would care, either.

Could Uvis have been right about the doonium deposits being her chance to finally escape?

She snorted. Of course not. That whole pitch had been a mind game, designed to distract her from his attempt to talk his way into controlling the company.

Let him try. She didn't especially like her life here; but it was *her* life, and Pryce Mining was *her* company, and she would see Uvis in hell before she would let anyone steal it.

The last wisps of color had faded away, and she was pulling her landspeeder into her garage, when her comm chimed. She glanced at the ID—it was her father—and keyed it on. "Hello, Father," she greeted him. "What's up?"

"Arihnda, you need to get to the police station right away," Talmoor Pryce said, his voice nearly unrecognizable. "Your mother's been arrested."

Arihnda stared. "*What?* What in the world for? And who ordered it?"

"The complaint came from the governor's office,"

Talmoor said, his breath coming in short spurts. "The charge is embezzlement."

Talmoor Pryce had worked in the family mine all his life, and Arihnda had seen him act calmly and decisively in dozens of crisis situations. But this crisis wasn't mine-based, and for once he clearly had no idea what to do.

The police didn't seem to know what to do, either. Talmoor and Arihnda were on a first-name basis with several of them, but this time those personal contacts weren't enough to smooth things out or even cut through the bureaucratic clutter. All the police could say was that Elainye was in custody, her bail request had been denied, and they'd been ordered not to allow her visitors. The person behind the order hadn't been named, but everything had come directly from the governor's office.

Not that Arihnda didn't already know who was behind it.

"Arik Uvis works with Azadi's office," Talmoor pointed out as he and Arihnda left the station. "Maybe he can help."

"Maybe," Arihnda said, a twinge of guilt briefly warming the ice that had formed in her soul. In retrospect, she *should* have told her parents about her last conversation with Uvis. At least they wouldn't have been so utterly blindsided by this cowardly attack. "I'll go see him after I drop you off."

"Thanks, but I'm okay," Talmoor said. "We can go see him together."

"I really think you should go home," Arihnda persisted. A plan was slowly forming in the back of her mind, the kind that worked best without witnesses present. "Barkin was going to keep trying for bail. If he gets it, you don't want to be all the way across Capital City when Mother's ready for you to come get her."

"I suppose," Talmoor conceded. "You'll let me know what Uvis says, won't you?"

"Absolutely," Arihnda promised. "But I'm not expecting anything right away. Try to get some sleep, okay?"

"I'll try." He eyed her, his eyes narrowing slightly. "Be careful, Arihnda."

"Don't worry," Arihnda assured him grimly. "I will."

It was pure good luck that Senator Domus Renking happened to be on Lothal, instead of on the distant world of Coruscant where he spent most of his time. According to the press releases, he'd come back to his homeworld for a short vacation and some meetings with Governor Azadi and other political and industrial leaders, and was slated to leave in two days.

Arihnda arrived precisely at nine in the morning, when Renking's office opened, and gave her name and reason for her visit to the smiling woman at the reception desk. Two hours later, she was finally ushered inside.

"Ms. Pryce," Renking greeted her, standing courteously as she came in. "Please sit down."

"Thank you, Senator," Arihnda said, passing between the pair of silent guards flanking the doorway and continuing on to the chair in front of Renking's desk. "Thank you for seeing me."

"It was probably inevitable," Renking said with a smile, waiting until she had seated herself before resuming his own seat. "I understand your mother, Elainye, has been arrested for embezzlement."

"Yes, she has," Arihnda said. "And she's innocent."

Renking leaned back in his chair. "Tell me more."

"Yes, Senator." Arihnda keyed her datapad and tapped for the first file. "First of all, my mother's finances," she said, setting the datapad on the desk and turning it around to face him. "You'll see that there isn't a boost in any of her accounts. If she embezzled, the money had to go somewhere."

"She could have set up a secret account," Renking pointed out. "Possibly even offworld."

"Agreed," Arihnda said. "But if she embezzled, the funds by definition had to come from Pryce Mining. I ran everything from the company's side, digging through all the vectors she had access to. There are no indications of missing money, credit, or resources. No virtual transactions, either."

"That you could find."

"I know more about Pryce Mining's computer operations than my mother does," Arihnda said. "There's no way she could pull off something that I couldn't track."

"Mm," Renking said. "I presume you realize how that makes *you* look."

"Yes, and I didn't embezzle, either," Arihnda said, reaching across the desk and keying for the next file. "This is the company's profit data for the past two years. You can see there are regular dips and surges over that time period."

"Galactic market fluctuations," Renking said, nodding. "Happens in every industry. Your point?"

"You can see a pattern," Arihnda said. "Dips here, here, and here. If there was embezzlement, it would probably have been timed to hit just the right spot to—maybe—not get noticed."

"You say *if* there was embezzlement," Renking said. "I was under the impression that Governor Azadi's office had confirmed there were funds missing."

"So I've heard," Arihnda said, bracing herself as she again tapped the datapad. Now came the tricky part. "But it may not be as simple as missing funds. Here's a security video from a party at the company two weeks ago, right in the middle of the latest financial dip." She pointed to a broad-faced being with fuzzy jowls and wide-set eyes dressed in a dark-brown tunic. "You see the Lutrillian here at the side?"

"Yes."

"That's Pomi Harchmak," Arihnda said. "She handles the heavy-equipment inventory operations. Her account is separate from the main operating fund account. Now . . . there. See how she slips out of the room right at the height of the party?"

"Yes," Renking said. "Where does that hallway lead?"

"To the central office cluster," Arihnda said. "Her desk is in there, from which she can access the entire inventory system. Oh, and a fresh order of digging heads had just come in, with the funds slated to go out the next morning. A perfect time for her to act."

"Also a perfect time for a drinking partygoer to go to the restroom," Renking pointed out. "What makes you think that's not what she's doing?"

"Because she leaves three more times in the next two hours and is gone at least ten minutes each time," Arihnda said.

"What does that have to do with anything?"

"Because that's how financial transactions work here," Arihnda said. "I don't know how it is on Coruscant, but on Lothal secure fund-shifting usually requires two or three touchpoints, and the authorization codes sometimes bounce back and forth over an hour or more."

Renking grunted. "Pretty inefficient."

"Extremely inefficient," Arihnda agreed sourly. It was yet another part of Lothal's quaint approach to life that she found infuriating. "But we're stuck with it. The banks and supply houses all have their own ways of doing things, and none of them like turning everything over to computers or droids. Everyone wants to have a personal touch in big transactions."

"Yes, that *does* sound like Lothal," Renking conceded. He poised a finger over the datapad. "May I?"

"Certainly."

He tapped the datapad to fast-forward the recording. As far as Arihnda could tell, he had no suspicions that what she'd told him was anything but the truth.

And it was, really . . . except that Arihnda remembered her mother mentioning earlier that day how Pomi Harchmak had been having digestive problems. Which meant all those disappearances almost certainly *were* to the restroom.

Maybe Harchmak was innocent. Maybe there were no missing funds, and Uvis was simply making a bald-faced play for control. Or maybe the stomach thing had been a deception and excuse and Harchmak was genuinely guilty.

Arihnda didn't know. She also didn't care. All she cared about was drawing enough suspicion off her mother to persuade Renking to intervene. Once he did, Harchmak's guilt or innocence was her own problem.

"May I make a copy of all this?" Renking asked.

"Actually, I already made you one," Arihnda said, pulling a datacard from her pocket and placing it on the desk.

He smiled wryly as he picked it up. "Rather sure of ourselves, are we?"

"Just the opposite," Arihnda said. "If I couldn't get you to see me in person, I thought you might at least look at the evidence I'd compiled."

"I'm glad I decided to take the time," Renking said. "Give me a moment."

He finished watching the security recording, then silently pushed the datapad back across the desk to Arihnda and turned to his computer. For the next few minutes he worked the keys, gazing at the display. Arihnda remained where she was, trying without success to read his expression.

Finally, he hit one last key and turned back to face her. "Here's the situation," he said, his voice grave. "First: As matters stand, I can't lift the embezzlement charge."

Arihnda stared at him. That wasn't the answer she'd been expecting. "What about Harchmak? I just showed you there's another suspect who's at least as viable as my mother."

"Oh, she's viable, all right," Renking agreed. "And I

have no doubt she'll be detained as soon as I pass this on to the police. But without proof of your mother's innocence, Governor Azadi isn't going to release her."

"Can we at least get her out on bail?"

"You really don't understand what this is about?" Renking asked, giving her an odd look. "This is Azadi's attempt to take over Pryce Mining."

"Azadi's, or Uvis's?"

"Does it matter?"

"Probably not," Arihnda conceded. "That's why I came to you instead of pleading my case to him. I hoped that if I gave you enough ammunition you could stop him. Now you're telling me you can't?"

Renking raised his eyebrows. "What makes you think I *want* to stop him?" he asked. "What makes you think I'm not part of his plan?"

Arihnda pursed her lips. What *did* make her think that? "Because if you were part of the plot, you wouldn't have told me about it. You'd have kept quiet, or encouraged me to make a deal to sell out."

"Very good," Renking said, favoring her with a small smile. "You're right, there is a certain . . . rivalry between the governor and me. And there *is* a way I can help your mother. But I don't think you'll like it."

"I'm listening."

"I can get the charges dropped," Renking said.

"Sounds good so far," Arihnda said. "What about the company?"

"That's the part you won't like," Renking said. "You'll have to sign the mine over to the Empire."

Arihnda had suspected something like that was coming. Even so, the words were like a punch in the gut. "The Empire."

Renking held out his hands, palms upward. "You're going to lose the mine, Arihnda," he said. "Either to Azadi, or to the Empire."

"Because of the doonium."

"Basically," Renking said. "Bear in mind that Coruscant can take it by fiat, with no compensation at all. Right now they'd prefer to play nice in this part of the Outer Rim, but that restraint won't last forever. This way, at least, you'll get your mother out and new jobs for your family."

Arihnda shook her head. "I don't think they'd want to work the mine for someone else."

"Oh, I wasn't talking about keeping them here," Renking assured her. "Not at Pryce Mining or anywhere else on Lothal. Governor Azadi is a vindictive man, and as long as they're in his jurisdiction he might be tempted to mess with them out of pure spite. Fortunately, there's a mine I know on Batonn that needs an assistant manager and an experienced foreman. I already have an offer."

Arihnda smiled tightly. "The two hours you kept me waiting outside."

Renking shrugged. "That, and other things. Unfortunately, there's no datawork position for you at the moment, but the owner says he can put you on inventory until something better opens up."

"I see," Arihnda said, watching him closely. Lothal was awash with petty politics, and over the years she'd learned how to navigate them. If the same rules applied to the Imperial version . . . "I suppose I could just stay here on Lothal until then."

"I wouldn't advise that," Renking said quickly. "Not with Azadi unhappy with you."

"Unhappy with *me*?"

Renking's lip twitched in a small smile. "Unhappy with *me*, then," he conceded.

"He probably wouldn't hesitate to try squeezing me, either," Arihnda said slowly, as if she were just now working it out. "That wouldn't be good for either of us."

"Hardly," Renking said, a mixture of amusement and resignation on his face. "Let's skip to the last page. What exactly do you want?"

"I want to go to Coruscant," Arihnda said. "You must have a hundred good assistant positions you can offer. I want one of them."

"In exchange for what?" Renking asked. "Favors have to work both ways."

"In exchange for not making trouble when the Empire takes over Pryce Mining," Arihnda said. "Maybe you've forgotten what people are like here, but they won't be happy about a bald-faced takeover."

"Oh, I remember just fine," Renking assured her. "Why do you think I'm taking this approach instead of just letting the Empire move in directly and cut Azadi off at the knees? Lothal's like every other frontier planet in the Outer Rim: unruly and a potential pain in the rear."

"But a new doonium vein is worth the trouble?"

"It's worth a *lot* of trouble." Renking took a deep breath, eyeing Arihnda closely. "All right. As it happens, I do have a job on Coruscant I can offer you. There's an opening in one of my citizen assistance offices."

"What are those?"

"My job is to represent Lothal's interests on Coruscant," Renking said. "That includes citizens visiting or temporarily working there. It turns out that there's a decent-sized contingent of such displaced citizens working in the Coruscant mines."

Arihnda's surprise must have shown, because he smiled. "Not *real* mines, of course, not like yours," he said. "These are more like reclamation operations, where centuries' worth of dumped slag, metal shards, and other debris is dug up from around the foundations of old industrial plants. The Lothal contingent is always in flux, so I have an assistance office in the area to help them with housing and general orientation, as well as guiding them through the Coruscant bureaucratic maze."

"How many people are we talking about?"

"About five hundred at the moment," Renking said. "But there are miners and support personnel from a dozen other Outer Rim worlds working the reclamation projects, as well, and that number probably comes to ten thousand or more. I have people who understand bureaucracy, but no one who understands mines and the specific needs and language of miners. I think you'd be a great asset to me."

"I'm sure I would," Arihnda said. "What would my housing and salary be? And when would you want me to leave Lothal?"

"Housing would be modest, but salary would be far higher than here," Renking said, studying her face. "Enough to maintain your current lifestyle, even at Coruscant prices. As to leaving, I could take you there as soon as the agreement with the Empire for Pryce Mining is finalized. Unless you'd like to help settle your parents on Batonn first, of course."

"That would probably be best," Arihnda said. "Assuming I can persuade them to go along with this plan in the first place."

"I hope for their sake that you can," Renking warned, his voice going darker. "It's either this, or your mother's next mining job could be on Kessel."

"Then I'd better go talk to them." Arihnda stood up and slipped her datapad back into its pouch. "I assume you can get the visitor ban on my mother lifted?"

"I'll give the order as soon as you're out the door."

"Thank you," Arihnda said. "I'll be in touch."

Five minutes later she was driving down the roadway, her mind spinning with conflicting thoughts and emotions. So this was it. After years of waiting—after years of knowing it would never happen—she was finally getting off Lothal. Not just off Lothal, but to Coruscant.

And all it would cost was her parents' jobs and dignity, and several generations of the Pryce family legacy.

It wasn't as if Renking was being completely altruistic, either. Part of his goal in accepting Arihnda's thinly veiled demand was clearly to split up the family, which would help stifle any legal challenge or local stirring they might decide to mount.

But machinations and plots aside, one point stood out clearly.

Coruscant.

As a child, she'd wanted to see the lights and colors and big buildings of that distant world. In the turmoil of her teenage hopelessness and desperation, the glittering capital had seemed the epitome of the life she so desperately wanted.

Now, when all hope was past, she was finally going to get there.

Renking had his own reasons and agenda. But then, so did Arihnda.

Because along with the lights and colors and big buildings, Coruscant was first and foremost the center of Imperial political power. The power that Azadi had used to put her mother in prison. The power Renking was using to take their mine for the Empire.

The power that Arihnda would someday use to take it back.

So her parents would accept Renking's terms. Arihnda would see to that. And then she would go to Coruscant, and work in Renking's little assistance office, and be a good girl and a model employee.

Right up until the moment when she found a way to take him down.

CHAPTER 5

All opponents are not necessarily enemies. But both enemies and opponents carry certain characteristics in common. Both perceive their opposite as an obstacle, or an opportunity, or a threat. Sometimes the threat is personal; other times it is a perceived violation of standards or accepted norms of society.

In mildest form, the opponent's attacks are verbal. The warrior must choose which of those to stand against, and which to ignore.

Often that decision is taken from his hands by others. In those cases, lack of discipline may dissuade the opponent from further attacks. More often, though, the opponent finds himself encouraged to continue or intensify the attacks.

It is when the attacks become physical that the warrior must make the most dangerous of choices.

"Don't you see?" Vanto demanded. *His voice is harsh and strident. His hand gestures are wide and expansive. He is angry and frustrated.* "If you keep ignoring these episodes, they're just going to get worse."

"How would you have me respond?" Thrawn asked.

"You need to tell Commandant Deenlark," Vanto said. *His voice is still harsh, but his gestures are calm-*

ing. The anger abates, but the frustration remains. "A month in, and you've already had run-ins with four separate cadets."

"Three," Thrawn corrected. "The second incident was unintended."

"You only think that because you're not up on Core World slang," Vanto said. *He makes a gesture mimicking that of the supposed insult.* "*That* isn't in any way a mark of respect."

"But I have seen similar gestures without such intent."

"Not in the Core Worlds you haven't." *Vanto sweeps his hand crosswise in front of him, indicating dismissal.* "Look, three or four—it doesn't matter. What matters is that you're not being respected, and Deenlark needs to know that."

"To what end?" Thrawn asked.

"Look." *Vanto pauses, the muscles in his jaw tensing and relaxing as he prepares his statement.* "The Emperor himself put you here. Even if no one else knows that, Deenlark does. For his sake, you need to let him know. Because if the Emperor finds out that this has been happening and Deenlark hasn't done anything, there *will* be trouble."

"Commandant Deenlark is in a poor tactical position," Thrawn said. "If he is told and does nothing, he risks attack by the Emperor. If he hears and acts, he risks attack by the families of the cadets."

"So what would a good tactician do?"

"Ideally, he would withdraw to a better position or a different time," Thrawn said. "In this case, he can do neither."

Vanto looks toward the window. His facial heat is fading. He grows more deeply in understanding of the situation. "So what you're saying is that we're stuck."

"Only for two more months," Thrawn said. "We then graduate and leave this place."

"And you finally get to put on that lieutenant's rank

plaque," Vanto said. *He returns his gaze and points to the pocket where the plaque is customarily concealed. His facial and throat muscles again tighten briefly. His frustration increases.*

"Are you disturbed by that?"

"Disturbed by what?" Vanto asked. *His voice deepens and grows more harsh. Frustration, but also resentment.* "That you're getting through four years of academy training in three months? And then jumping a rank on everyone else on top of it?"

"Have you forgotten I have already passed through many years of military experience?"

Vanto again turns his face away. "I know that. I just sometimes forget that you . . . I'm sorry I even brought it up." *His face smooths out as the resentment fades. His hands open and close briefly with embarrassment.*

"I understand," Thrawn said. "Do not be concerned. The incidents will stop when the offenders are emboldened enough to push their actions too far."

Vanto's eyes narrow. He is surprised now, with growing disbelief and suspicion. "Are you saying you *want* them to cross the line?"

"I believe the lack of response to verbal attacks makes it inevitable," Thrawn said. "Such actions would put them in position for official discipline, would it not?"

"Probably." *Vanto holds his hands in front of him in a gesture of confusion.* "But didn't you just—hold it; I've got a call." He pulled out his comlink. "Cadet Vanto."

For a minute he listened in silence. *The voice is human, the words indistinguishable. Vanto's facial muscles tighten and his facial heat increases. He is first surprised by what he hears, then wary, then suspicious.* "Sure, sounds like fun," Vanto said. *His voice is guarded, but holds none of the wariness revealed in his expression.* "We'll be there."

He closed down the comlink. "Well, you may just have gotten your wish," he said. "We've been invited to the metallurgy lab tonight to play cards with Spenc Orbar and Rosita Turuy while they run some corrosion tests on one of their alloy boards."

"Are we permitted in the metallurgy lab?" Thrawn asked.

"Not unless we have a project we're working on," Vanto said. *His lips compress briefly. His suspicions change to certainty.* "Which we don't."

"What if we are invited guests of those with such projects?"

"No such thing," Vanto said. "Not in the big labs. If some wandering instructor or officer catches us, they will *not* be happy. *And* if the card game includes betting, it'll go even worse. Gambling for credits is strictly forbidden."

"That assures they will not attempt such a trap."

"No? Why not?"

"Because if we are charged with gambling, they will be also," Thrawn said.

Vanto shook his head. "You still don't get how it works, do you?" *His facial heat increases; his muscle tension also increases. Once again he shows frustration.* "Orbar's family is from here on Coruscant. Worse, they're connected to the planet's senator. He can probably pull anything short of straight-up murder without getting kicked out."

"Then we will simply refuse any offers to gamble."

Vanto exhales noisily. "You're going to go, aren't you?" *His voice is calmer, indicating unwilling acceptance.*

"We were invited," Thrawn reminded him. "You may stay here if you wish."

"Oh, I wish, all right," Vanto said. "But I don't think letting you wander around alone is what the Emperor had in mind when he put me here. Might as well find out what Orbar has planned." *His head turns a few degrees to the side. He is curious, or perhaps perplexed.* "Is this what Chiss do? See a trap, and just walk into it? Because that's not how the stories say you operate."

"You would be wise to tread carefully around such stories," Thrawn said. "Some have been distorted to the point where no truth remains. Some speak only of victories, and are silent about defeats. Some have been deliberately crafted to leave false impressions in the hearer."

"And which one is this?"

"Sometimes walking into a trap is the best strategy," Thrawn said. "There are few traps that cannot be turned against their designers. What card game did he suggest?"

"It's called Highland Challenge," Vanto said. *Resigned acceptance?* "Come on—I think there's a deck in the lounge. I'll teach you how to play."

"I suppose you're wondering," Orbar said as he dealt out the first hand, "why we asked you two here tonight."

"You said it was to play cards," Eli said, watching him closely. Both Orbar and Turuy were playing it cool: greeting Eli and Thrawn at the door, making a big fuss of setting up their corrosion test, then pulling four chairs up to one of the lab tables and bringing out the cards.

But the courtesy and friendliness weren't real.

Maybe Thrawn still couldn't pick up the subtleties of human expressions. But Eli could. He'd been on the receiving end of his own set of sly smiles and whispered comments since the day they'd arrived, and he'd developed a fine-tuned sense of when he was about to be hit with a joke, trick, or insult.

And Orbar and Turuy were definitely winding up for one of the three. Or something worse.

At least it wasn't the gambling thing Eli had worried about. Turuy had put up a small fuss when Eli told her that neither he nor Thrawn could afford the extra credits to bet on their game, and she and Orbar had accepted the condition with rolled eyes and thinly veiled scorn.

But the fuss hadn't been big enough, and they'd given in too easily. Something else was in the works.

He grimaced. Walking into an unknown trap. Was this *really* how Chiss did things?

"Oh, sure, the game was part of it," Orbar said, finishing the deal and picking up his cards. "Corrosion tests are boring, and you get tired of two-handed games." He shifted his gaze to Thrawn. "But mostly I wanted to pick your friend's brain."

"On what subject?" Thrawn asked, his glowing red eyes narrowing slightly as he carefully fanned his cards the way Eli had shown him.

"Tactics and strategy," Orbar said. "I'm having some trouble in a couple of my battle simulation classes, and I figured with all your military experience—"

"At least, that's what we've been told," Turuy put in with a smile. She was smiling way too much tonight.

"Right," Orbar said. "We figured you might be able to help."

"I am happy to share my experience," Thrawn said. "Have you a specific question?"

"I'm interested in the idea of traps," Orbar said, his voice way too casual. "Take these cards. If I'm holding a King's Lane, there's no way any of you can beat me. But you won't know that until it's too late. How would you prepare for that kind of situation?"

"One would first study the probabilities," Thrawn said. "A King's Lane is indeed unbeatable; but recall that there are three equivalent runs in the deck. Any of them would stagger yours and lead to mutual deadlock."

Turuy snorted. "You have any idea what the odds are against getting two King's Lanes in the same deal?" she asked.

"The odds for having two are similar to the odds for having one," Thrawn pointed out. "But as you say, such runs are rare. More likely you hold a Prince's Lane at best, or a Cube or Triad. In that event, what you described as a trap would more likely be termed simply a battle." His eyes glittered. "Or a bluff."

"Okay, but you're avoiding the question," Orbar said. "I asked what you'd do if I *had* a King's Lane. I didn't ask for a dissertation on game theory."

"Let us assume you have the cards you suggest," Thrawn said. "As I said earlier, even in that case your chance of success also depends upon which cards I hold." He lifted his fanned cards slightly. "Knowledge that you do not have."

"The premise is that my hand is unbeatable."

"There is no such hand," Thrawn said flatly. "As I suggested earlier, I might have a King's Lane of my own. In that case, a challenge would mean mutual destruction. Your better option would be to avoid my hand and deliver your challenge to a different player."

Orbar flicked a glance at Eli. "That assumes there's another target worth going after."

"True," Thrawn said. "But mutual destruction is never the preferred option." He gestured around the table. "You have not yet made your challenge. It is not too late to choose another."

"But none would be more satisfying," Orbar said, smiling tightly.

"As you wish," Thrawn said, shrugging. "A moment, if you will." He set his cards facedown on the table and slipped his hand into his tunic.

And drew it out holding his lieutenant's insignia plaque. He fastened it into position on his upper left tunic and picked up his cards again. "I believe you were about to make a challenge?"

Eli looked at Orbar and Turuy. Both cadets were staring at the insignia plaque, their eyes widened, their mouths drooping open. Orbar threw a quick look at Turuy, got a completely unsmiling glance back from her—

"What's going on here?" a hard voice called from behind Thrawn.

Eli jerked his head around. One of the instructors stood in the lab doorway, his fists on his hips, his expression thunderous as he glared at the cadets around the table. "I assume you all have authorization to be in here?" he growled, striding toward the table.

"Cadets Orbar and Turuy are running a test, sir," Thrawn said, standing up and turning to face the instructor.

The other man came to an abrupt halt, his own eyes widening. Enough reaction, Eli thought darkly, to show he'd been in on Orbar's scheme. "Lieutenant," he breathed. "I . . . what about him?" he asked, nodding toward Eli.

"Cadet Vanto is my translator," Thrawn said calmly. "Where I go, he must necessarily accompany me."

The instructor's lip twitched. "I see. I . . . very well, Lieutenant. Carry on." He spun on his heel and beat a hasty retreat.

Thrawn watched him go. Then, very deliberately, he turned back to the table and gazed down upon the others. "There *is* no guaranteed winning hand, Cadet Orbar," he said quietly. "I suggest you not forget that. Cadet Vanto, I believe we are finished here. Good evening, Cadets."

A minute later, he and Eli were back out in the reflected light of the planetwide city surrounding them, walking along the path leading toward Barracks Two. "Well, that was fun," Eli commented, wincing at the slight shaking in his voice. Would he *never* get used to confrontations? "So you knew he was going to pull that?"

"You yourself suggested his tactic this afternoon," Thrawn reminded him. "The timing was the only challenge."

"The timing?"

"If I had brought out my insignia plaque too soon, he

might have been able to warn off his confederate," Thrawn said. "If I had waited until after the instructor's appearance, he could have disciplined me for being improperly uniformed."

"Or could have challenged your right to wear it," Eli pointed out. "You've never worn it before."

"Because I am both officer and cadet," Thrawn said. "It is a unique situation, which leads to unique opportunities." He smiled slightly. "As well as confusion and uncertainties among our opponents. What did you learn tonight?"

Eli wrinkled his nose. That Orbar and Turuy were jerks to be avoided in the future? True enough, but probably not what Thrawn was going for. "Anticipate your enemy," he said. "Figure out what he's doing, then try to stay a step ahead of him."

"A step ahead, or to the side," Thrawn said, nodding. "When an attack comes, it is usually best to be out of the target zone if possible, thus permitting the energy of the assault to be dissipated elsewhere."

"Yes, I can see how that could be handy," Eli said drily. "Though I guess you can't always choose—"

And without warning Thrawn put his hand on Eli's shoulder and gave him a violent shove to the side.

Eli's comment ended in a startled squeak as his legs hit the knee-high hedge bordering the walkway, the impact and his momentum sending him sprawling over the barrier onto the decorative crushed-stone strip on the other side. The squeak turned into a grunt as his arms and shoulder took the brunt of the impact. He shoved himself back up to a sitting position, wincing as the gravel dug into his palms. What the *hell*—

He stiffened. Three hooded men had suddenly appeared, surrounding Thrawn.

And as Eli stared in disbelief, they moved in for the kill.

. . .

For that first stretched-out second, Eli's mind refused to believe it. Things like this didn't happen on the Royal Imperial Academy grounds. They just *didn't*.

But it was happening. Right in front of him.

The first mad charge seemed to have hit a little off center, probably because Thrawn's action in shoving Eli over the hedge had similarly pushed the Chiss a meter in the opposite direction. But the assailants were quick. They were back on track now, and were converging on the Chiss.

And as Eli watched in disbelief and horror, they attacked.

The standard Academy curriculum included a unit on unarmed combat. Unfortunately, with Thrawn's studies focused exclusively on technology and navy protocol, he hadn't been given any time in the combat dojo.

And it showed. He was doing his best to fend off his attackers, but his defense consisted mainly of trying to push them away, ducking away from their attacks, dodging so that they couldn't all come at him at once, and trying to protect his face and torso.

But it wasn't enough. Defense alone was never enough. He needed to start adding in a few counterattacks, to make an effort to reduce the odds against him. Right now he was in a battle of attrition, and no matter how much stamina he had he would almost certainly run out of strength before his attackers did.

And then, unbidden, a thought slipped in at the edge of Eli's mind.

This could be the end of all his problems.

It was a horrible thought. A gruesome thought. And yet, it was startlingly compelling. If Thrawn was so badly injured that he couldn't complete his training, he would have no choice but to drop out. The Emperor's grand experiment—whatever he'd hoped to accomplish by bringing the Chiss into the navy—would have failed. There would be nothing left to do but take Thrawn back to his exile planet and leave him there.

And Eli would be free.

The *Strikefast* was long gone, of course. But he could grab a transport to Myomar, paying for it out of his own pocket if he had to, and be back on track at the Academy there within a week. Surely Commandant Deenlark wouldn't want him to stay at Royal Imperial once Thrawn was gone, any more than Eli himself wanted it. Back on Myomar; back in his proper career path; back to his life.

One of the attackers got in a solid punch to Thrawn's lower torso, sending the Chiss down to one knee.

And a flood of shame abruptly flowed over Eli's soul. What the hell was he *thinking*?

"Hey!" he shouted, pushing himself up into a crouch. As he did so, he dug his fingers into the crushed stone beneath him, ignoring the flickers of pain as the sharp edges dug into his skin. "Hey, you! Bright eyes!"

Two of the three turned to face him—

And with all his strength Eli hurled two handfuls of gravel straight at their faces.

He hadn't really expected it to work. But it did. Both attackers howled in pain, belatedly throwing up their hands against the hail of stone. Eli leaned down and dug his hands into the ground again, wondering if he could get another volley into the air before they could recover and respond.

Because if he couldn't—if they jumped the hedge and got to him first—he was in serious trouble. Thrawn was still down on one knee, unable to help, and two-to-one odds would be more than enough to take Eli down.

Too late, it occurred to him that the assailants had learned their tactics lessons all too well. Splitting the enemy force in two parts and demolishing them one at a time was a classic approach to warfare. They'd successfully focused their efforts on Thrawn, and now they were going to do the same to Eli.

Only they'd miscalculated. Even as the two attackers started toward Eli, the helpless, all-but-demolished Thrawn leaned toward the man standing over him and slammed his forearm with muscle-paralyzing force into the man's thigh.

The man gasped a startled curse, nearly falling as he clutched at his injured leg. His two friends spun back to him, their drive toward Eli wavering as their focus was suddenly split between their two targets. Eli cocked his arms for his next salvo of gravel—

"Hey!" someone shouted from nearby.

Eli turned to look. Five cadets had emerged from one of the buildings and were racing toward the fight.

That was enough for the attackers. They turned and hurried away into the night, the man Thrawn had hit in the leg supported on either side by his two companions.

"Are you all right?"

Eli blinked away the sudden sweat trickling into his eyes, his body shaking with aftershock. Was it over? "I'm fine," he told Thrawn, climbing unsteadily over the hedge. Strangely enough, his voice wasn't trembling at all. "You?"

"My injuries are minor," Thrawn said, easing carefully to a standing position.

"Yeah," Eli said, frowning at him. Thrawn's tunic was badly rumpled, and there were spots of oozing blood on both cheeks. "You sure?"

"It appears worse than it is," Thrawn assured him, gingerly touching one of his cheeks. "Your assistance was most timely. Thank you."

Eli felt his face warm with private shame. If the Chiss knew why he hadn't moved faster . . . "Sorry I couldn't do more," he said. "I was on the wrong side of the hedge, you know. I gather you heard them coming?"

"There is a particular tread all predators tend to use," Thrawn said, walking over to him. "A balance between silence and speed. Humans use a version of this tread."

"Ah." Eli had already known that Chiss eyes were a bit better than those of humans, their visible spectrum edging a bit into the infrared. Apparently, their ears were better, too. "Thanks for getting me out of the way. I've had just enough training to know I'm not very good at this."

"You are welcome." Thrawn looked at the approaching cadets, who had slowed to a jog now that the attackers were gone. "And now, I believe," he added, "it is finally time for us to see Commandant Deenlark."

CHAPTER 6

A leader is responsible for those under his authority. That is the first rule of command. He is responsible for their safety, their provisions, their knowledge, and, ultimately, their lives.

Those whom he commands are in turn responsible for their behavior and their dedication to duty. Any who violates his trust must be disciplined for the good of the others.

But such discipline is not always easy or straightforward. There are many factors, some of them beyond the commander's control. Sometimes those complications involve personal relationships. Other times it is the circumstances themselves that are difficult. There can also be politics and outside intervention.

Failure to act always brings consequences. But sometimes, those consequences can be turned to one's advantage.

"All right," Commandant Deenlark said as he made a final notation on his datapad. *The skin around his eyes is puffy. Perhaps he is newly awakened. His facial heat is bright and the muscles in his throat are tight. There is a thin coating of perspiration on his face. Perhaps he is nervous.* "Cadets Orbar and Turuy set up the assault, you say. Did you actually hear them calling in the men who attacked you?"

"No, sir, we didn't," Vanto said. "But their comlink records—or the lab's own comm system—should give you the necessary indicators."

"Yes, they should," Deenlark agreed. *His voice goes deeper in tone. Reluctance?* "Unless the assailants were an entirely separate bunch."

"They were not," Thrawn said.

"How do you know?" Deenlark asked. *His eyes narrow.*

"They came across the southwest corner of the parade ground," Thrawn said. "At that time, they were already moving with speed and stealth. But the only way for them to have independently identified us was with electrobinoculars."

"Which none of them had," Vanto said. *He nods, a gesture of understanding.* "That also rules out an attack driven by jealousy or xenophobia, since they couldn't have known it was Cadet Thrawn. So it was Orbar or Turuy. Or the instructor?" he added. *His tone rises slightly with thoughtfulness.*

"No," Deenlark said. "It wasn't him."

"It could have been," Thrawn said.

"I said it wasn't," Deenlark repeated. *His tone has gone deeper, his face stiff, his eyes gazing with heightened intent. Perhaps he does not wish it to be possible.* "Bad enough that cadets were mixed up in something like this. We're not going to drag an instructor in, too." *He looks back at his datapad. His facial heat increases as he makes a final note.*

"Sir, with all due respect, I don't think politics should enter into this," Vanto said. *His tone is respectful but firm.*

"Oh, you don't, do you?" Deenlark said. *His voice becomes harsh.* "Are you ready to have your name put on a witness list?"

"I could handle it, sir."

"I doubt that, Cadet," Deenlark said. "Orbar's family has a lot of say about what happens on Coruscant. Even if they let you graduate, you'd probably find yourself assigned to some Wild Space listening post."

"Is not such manipulation of the justice system in itself illegal?" Thrawn asked.

"Of course it is," Deenlark said. *His lips compress, his facial glow fading slowly.* "All right. Assuming your assailants haven't figured out a way to bypass the comlink records, we should have their names by morning."

"It will not be a long search," Thrawn said. "They would not risk going outside their closest circle of friends. There are eight other cadets who typically socialize with them, two of whom may be eliminated by considerations of aura."

"Aura?"

"Esethimba."

"Presence or aura," Vanto translated. "The Sy Bisti term can refer to a person's height, weight, build, vocal quality, mannerisms, profession and expertise, or some combination."

"They're cadets," Deenlark said. "They don't *have* a profession."

"All ten are in the weapons engineering track of study," Thrawn said.

"Yes, I suppose they are," Deenlark said. "Which leaves us six suspects."

"All of them also from the same social level as Cadets Orbar and Turuy, I assume?"

"If you're suggesting I'm going to look the other way on this, Cadet, I strongly suggest you revise your thinking," Deenlark said. *His voice is harsh, his facial heat increased. Perhaps he is angry, or feels guilt.* "Yes, I'm concerned about the potential political fallout here. I've put up with Orbar's antics for almost four years because of it. Two more months, and he'll be someone else's problem. So yes, I'd like to see this go away. But I can't let this one slide. And I won't."

"I am gratified to hear that, Commandant," Thrawn said. "Let me then suggest an alternative means of action. You will find our attackers. But you will not bring charges against them."

Deenlark's eyes narrow. His mouth opens slightly in surprise. "You don't want them charged?" he asked. "Then what the hell are we all doing here?"

"As I said, I want them found," Thrawn said. "I then recommend they be transferred."

Deenlark gave a snort of derision. "To where? Mustafar?"

"To starfighter pilot training."

Deenlark stares. His expression of surprise deepens. "Hardly what I'd consider a punishment."

"It is not intended to be," Thrawn said. "All three show the aptitude and aura necessary for fighter-craft pilots."

"Really." *Deenlark leans back in his chair. He folds his arms across his chest.* "I can't wait to hear this one."

"It was obvious from their method of attack," Thrawn said. "From the way they moved both together and singly. I do not have the words to properly explain it. But it was the mark of instinctive combat pilots."

"Cadet Vanto?" *Deenlark gestures toward Vanto in an inviting manner.* "Can you corroborate that?"

"Sorry, sir," Vanto said. *His expression is thoughtful.* "But I wasn't concentrating on their tactics. And I doubt I would have seen what Cadet Thrawn's talking about even if I had."

"Such an action would also carry an additional bonus," Thrawn said. "The Royal Imperial's starfighter program is excellent, but I believe the program at the Skystrike Academy is equally capable?"

"Nothing equal about it—Skystrike's far better with pilots than we are," Deenlark said. *He sits up straighter in his chair. His frown fades away. He understands.* "And there's no reason to tell Orbar and Turuy where their fellow conspirators have disappeared to, is there?"

"Not at all, sir," Thrawn agreed. "In fact, I would suggest that the three begin their new training—" He paused. "*Ngikotholu*. Is there a word in Basic for that?"

"Yes: incommunicado," Vanto said. "*Can* they be held incommunicado, Commandant?"

"On *Skystrike*?" *Deenlark makes a snorting sound.* "It's hard *not* to be incommunicado there. And you're right—I imagine even Orbar might learn to behave himself after three of his co-conspirators disappear without a trace."

"Uncertainties are often useful in paralyzing an opponent's plans and actions," Thrawn said. "For a human like Cadet Orbar, who believes himself capable of handling all situations, this will also prove a useful lesson for his future. One can hope he will take it to his core, and become a better person and officer."

"Not sure I'd go *that* far," Deenlark said. "Not with Orbar. But it's worth a shot. If you're *sure* you want to do it this way."

"Allow me to state it more strongly," Thrawn said. "If you bring the attackers to court-martial, I will not testify against them."

"Mm." *Deenlark angles his head a few degrees to the side.* "Is this how you do things in the Unknown Regions, Cadet? Bypass the law and regulations and get what you want through blackmail or extortion?"

"We attempt to solve problems. This is the solution that is best for the Empire as a whole."

"You have anything to add, Cadet?" Deenlark asked. *He raises his eyebrows toward Vanto in question.*

"No, sir," Vanto said.

Deenlark shrugs his shoulders. Perhaps reluctant acceptance. "I'll get the process started," he said. "Maybe give Skystrike's commandant a call. We'll have the guilty parties' names by morning, and their hindquarters off Coruscant by dinner." *He smiles. Perhaps sly amusement.* "That should leave them just enough time to tell Orbar and Turuy they have no idea where they're going before they disappear. As you said, Cadet: uncertainties."

"Exactly," Thrawn said. "Thank you, Commandant."

"Don't thank *me*." *Deenlark's tone deepens*. "Just be advised that if this thing blows up, your name will be right under mine on the *hell-to-pay* list." *He inhales deeply*. "You're cleared for duty, both of you. Get back to the barracks and get some sleep. Dismissed."

"Yes, sir," Vanto said as he stood up. "Thank you, sir."

Thrawn and Vanto were again on the walkway before Vanto spoke again. "Interesting solution," he commented. *His voice is thoughtful*. "I'm a little surprised Deenlark went for it."

"I am not," Thrawn said. "Did you observe the flat-sculp on the left side wall?"

"Yes, I think so," Vanto said. *He frowns and his voice becomes more hesitant. He is focusing his memory*. "The one with the ocean waves and the sailing ship?"

"The sailing warship, yes," Thrawn said. "It is a highly valuable work of art, worth far more than a man of Commandant Deenlark's position could afford."

"I doubt it's his," Vanto said. "It's probably part of the office décor."

"And yet still too valuable for even the Academy to purchase," Thrawn said. "I conclude therefore it was a gift from one or more of Coruscant's powerful families."

"Meaning?" Vanto said. *His posture straightens abruptly as he understands*. "Meaning that Deenlark knows Royal Imperial is beholden to the families. Meaning in turn that he would jump at any chance to avoid a public confrontation."

"Beholden?"

"*Ubuphaka.*"

"Ah," Thrawn said. "Yes, that is indeed Commandant Deenlark's position. That was why he so readily accepted my plan. Odd that these comlinks do not have a preset emergency signal."

"What?" *Vanto frowns in surprise or confusion.*

"Chiss comms have an emergency button," Thrawn said. "It allows for aid to be summoned quickly."

"Yeah, that could be useful," Vanto agreed. "You've got them on civilian comms, but not military comlinks. Probably needed the space for all the extra encryption chips to make sure no one's eavesdropping on official chatter."

"It would also be useful to arrange the comlinks so that one would not need to draw them from belt or pocket."

"That would definitely be handy." *Vanto gestures to the lieutenant's rank plaque.* "Maybe you could put it inside the rank plaque. At least you wouldn't have to worry about dropping it."

"Could that be done?"

"What, put a comlink in the rank plaque? Sure. You'd just have to hollow out the tiles from behind. Plenty of room in there for a comlink's worth of electronics." *His eyes narrow in further thought.* "Though on second thought you might not have enough room for all the encryption chips. Probably couldn't squeeze in enough battery power for long-range use, either."

"It would only function aboard ship, then?"

"Right," Vanto said. "Which means you'd still have to carry a long-range version for off-ship use." *He sighs in resignation.* "I guess there's a reason why people do things the way they do."

"Sometimes," Thrawn said. "Not always."

"I suppose," Vanto said. *His tone is thoughtful.* "Could you *really* tell they would be good starfighter pilots? Or was that just a way to get them kicked out of Royal Imperial?"

"I could really tell," Thrawn said. "You could not?"

"Not even close." *He is silent for three more steps. His forehead is creased in a frown.* "Still doesn't address the fact that they attacked you, you know. You're just going to let them get away with that?"

"Your question assumes they will suffer no punishment," Thrawn said. "On the contrary. They will spend tomorrow knowing their deeds are laid bare and wondering what fate Commandant Deenlark has planned for them. They will journey to Skystrike bearing the same fear and uncertainty."

"Ah," Vanto said. "I see where you're going. Even once they're there, they'll never be sure they won't be hauled out of bed in the middle of the night and brought back to Coruscant for trial."

"That fear will eventually fade," Thrawn said. "But not for a considerable time."

"I suppose not," Vanto said. "So they get to walk on eggshells for a few months, Orbar gets to do the same, and Deenlark doesn't have to face Orbar's family."

"You also will not need to face that same pressure."

"I wondered if you'd been thinking about that," Vanto said. "So justice is served—sort of—and everyone else comes out ahead. What we call a win–win." *He points at Thrawn's face.* "Except you."

"My injuries are minor, and will heal. I have endured worse."

"I'll bet you have." *Vanto is silent for another few steps.* "So is this what the Chiss leaders have to look forward to?"

"I do not understand."

"This kind of justice," Vanto said. "Retribution for exiling you. The stories say the Chiss never forget injuries that have been done to them."

"Your stories assume that memory necessarily leads to vengeance," Thrawn said. "That is not always the case. Situations change. Reasons and motivations change. No, I seek no retribution."

"Really? Because it looks to me like they deserve it."

"They had reasons for my exile."

"The preemptive strike thing?" Vanto asked. *His tone is curious but cautious. He sees information within his grasp, but fears to chase it away.* "What happened, anyway? Did you let someone's strike get through the Chiss lines?"

"No," Thrawn said. "I launched a strike of my own."

"Who was it against?"

"Evil," Thrawn said. "Nomadic pirates who preyed on defenseless worlds. I deemed it dishonorable for the Chiss Ascendancy to stand unmoving and not assist the helpless."

"Did you beat them?"

"Yes," Thrawn said. "But my leaders were unhappy."

"Sounds pretty ungrateful," Vanto said. *His voice is firm, without uncertainty.* "Also pretty stupid. Pirates like that would have turned on your people sooner or later. What then?"

"Then we would have fought," Thrawn said. "But then we would have been the victims."

"And you can't fight until that happens?"

"That is the Ascendancy's current military doctrine." *Vanto shakes his head.* "It's still unfair."

"Sometimes a commander's decisions must be made without regard for how they will be perceived," Thrawn said. "What matters is that the commander does what is necessary for victory."

"Yeah," Vanto said. "Lucky for me, I'm on track for a supply officer position. I'll never have to worry about that."

"Yes," Thrawn said. "Perhaps."

"Now watch," Arihnda said, pointing to the discolored spot where the conduit entered the apartment wall. "Okay, Daisie. Turn it on."

From the other room came the sound of the restroom water being turned on. A moment later, a small spray of water spurted from the spot.

"A water leak?" Chesna Braker growled. "You dragged me all the way down here for a *water leak*?"

"It's your building," Arihnda reminded her calmly. "Your maintenance people kept stalling her off, and I couldn't get anyone in your office to take this seriously."

"So like a little girl who's skinned her knee, you go crying to some bureaucrat in the housing department and get him to issue an order for *me* to drop everything and come down here?"

"Your government lease says your company is responsible for repairs," Arihnda said. "You own the company that owns this apartment block. That makes you ultimately responsible. If your people won't obey the law, I guess it'll have to be you. Personally."

"Hmm," Braker said, eyeing her venomously. "Come over here a minute." She turned and crossed to the window that looked out across the massive planetwide city that was Coruscant.

Frowning, Arihnda followed.

"You see that?" Braker asked when the two women were once again standing together. "Out there are the little people you're representing so proudly. You know what they're going to do if you ever get in trouble or need help?"

"No. What?"

"Absolutely nothing," Braker said. "You'll be as forgotten as yesterday's breakfast." She tapped her chest. "*I'm* the one you want to impress, Ms. Pryce. Men and women like me. Not Daisie what's-her-name out there. We're the ones with the power to make or break you. You'd be well advised to remember that."

"I appreciate your concern for my well-being," Arihnda said. "But I already have a friend in high places."

"Who, Senator Renking?" Braker snorted. "You go ahead and believe that if you want. You're just the latest in a long line of people he's dropped in a dead-end job and left to rot."

"I'll keep that in mind," Arihnda said. "In the meantime, you have some repairs to make, and I have fifty-seven more apartment doors to knock on. As long as I'm here, I might as well see what else is wrong with this place."

"Don't bother," Braker growled. "I'll have one of my people—one of my *little* people—check into tenants' complaints. We'll have it all finished by the end of next week."

"I'll hold you to that, Ms. Braker. Good day."

Ten minutes later Arihnda was in her aircar, buzzing her way across the Coruscant sky along with millions of other vehicles. A month ago, she mused, she would have been terrified by the traffic flow. Now she barely noticed it.

Just as a month ago she might have agreed with Braker's suggestion that Renking had stuck her here in order to get rid of her. For the first two months the senator had talked to her maybe twice, for no more than three minutes at a time. It had very much looked like he'd forgotten about her.

That was about to change. Very, very soon.

Her comm chimed, and she pulled it out. The ID said Senator Renking.

She smiled tightly. Very soon; or possibly right now. "Arihnda Pryce," she said.

"Senator Renking, Ms. Pryce," Renking said over the comm. "How are things going?"

"Very well, Senator, thank you," Arihnda said. "I've just taken another landlord to task for failing her responsibilities to her tenants."

"So I hear," Renking said, his voice going a little brittle. "I just heard from Councilor Jonne, who just heard from Ms. Braker. You're causing a real stir down there."

"Just doing my job, Senator," Arihnda said, smiling to

herself. So her little one-woman crusade against corruption and indifference was finally drawing the right kind of attention. "I hope you and Councilor Jonne aren't suggesting I ignore Coruscant laws and regulations."

"No, of course not," Renking assured her.

"Because the Lothal citizens I'm serving certainly seem happy with our progress," Arihnda continued. "And that *is* the reason I'm here."

"Of course," Renking said. "You're doing a very effective job. Which is actually why I called. As you may know, with so many people living on Coruscant, the usual array of government services has been badly strained for many years. A new program has been initiated that encourages senators to set up—and fund, of course—supplementary citizen assistance offices across the planet."

"Offices open to all Coruscant citizens, not just that senator's own transient citizens?"

"Exactly," Renking said. "I have four such offices, and I'm about to open a fifth in the Bartanish Four Sector. It's occurred to me that you're the perfect person to run it."

"Really?" Arihnda breathed, putting some schoolgirl excitement into her voice even as she sent a cynical smile toward the traffic flow outside. "That would be wonderful. When would I start?"

"As soon as you close your office for the day—I'll have someone else reopen it next week—clear out your apartment, and move everything to Bartanish Four. The office there is ready, and I've got an apartment reserved for you two and six away."

"That sounds great," Arihnda said. Two blocks and six levels would put her within perfect walking distance. "I'll head back to the office and get things started right away."

"Good. I'll send you both the office and apartment addresses. Let me know when you'll be arriving, and

I'll have someone meet you with the various keys. All right?"

"Sounds perfect," Arihnda said. "Thank you again."

"No thanks needed," Renking said. "You've earned it. Take care." The connection clicked off.

Arihnda put the comm away, smiling again. Renking didn't mind her annoying the relatively rich and powerful; he just didn't want her activities so closely identified with him. In an anonymous assistance office, with no obvious connection to Renking, she could make all the waves she wanted without nearly so much political blowback.

From Renking's point of view, it had a couple of nice advantages. Arihnda would continue to stir Coruscant's sludge, possibly digging up leverage points against local movers and shakers that Renking could use in the future. At the same time, her new position would hopefully keep her too occupied to worry about the mine she'd lost to the Empire.

What Renking probably didn't realize was that it was just as much a win–win for Arihnda, which was why she'd worked so hard to land this exact job ever since hearing about the project a few weeks earlier. Dealing with actual Coruscant citizens instead of Lothal expatriates would move her a modest step up the social ladder; and in Bartanish Four she would also move several steps physically closer to the all-powerful Federal District.

Small steps, to be sure. But if there was one thing her parents had impressed upon her, it was that the best path didn't have to be quick as long as it was correct.

And Arihnda was in no hurry. No hurry at all.

Suddenly, almost before Eli knew it, it was over.

"Congratulations, son," his father said, gripping his hand tightly.

"Thanks, Dad," Eli said.

But despite the smiles and cheerful words, he could sense an unexpected reserve lurking behind his father's eyes. His mother's concerns were even more visible.

It wasn't hard to figure out the reason. Every glance at the Coruscant skyline, every lingering look at one of the other freshly minted ensigns, every lowering of their voices whenever someone nearby might hear—all of it pointed to the fact that a Wild Space cadet like Eli should never have been at Royal Imperial in the first place.

And then, there was Thrawn.

"You're sure he's okay?" his mother asked as they walked along one of the garden patches leading back to the barracks. "Because if the stories about Chiss are right . . ." She trailed off.

"They aren't, Mom," Eli assured her. "At least, not the ones you're thinking about."

"How do you know which ones I'm thinking about?"

"The ones about cunning and cruel vindictiveness," Eli said. "If they were, a lot of the cadets you're looking at would never have survived long enough to graduate."

He winced as the last words left his mouth. Probably not the best way he could have put that. "He's okay," he assured them. "Really. Very smart."

"So *that* part of the stories is true?" his father put in.

"Yes," Eli said. "Let's not talk about him, okay?"

"Fine," his father said. "Let's talk about you. What happens now that you're off your career track?"

"Who says I'm off it?" Eli countered. "Up until I came here, that was the bulk of my training. As far as I know, that's still where I am."

"Well, I hope so," his father said. "I just . . . you never know about Core World nonsense."

Eli suppressed a sigh. After all he'd put up with at Royal Imperial . . . but then, that was the way of things.

"And hanging around that Chiss might have affected things, too," his mother added.

"I didn't have any choice, Mom," he once again explained as patiently as he could. No matter how far down the social scale a person was, he added sourly to himself, there was always someone lower. "I was assigned to him as his translator."

"Well, hopefully that's over now," his father said. "When do you get your ship assignment?"

"Later today," Eli said. "And it might be a ground assignment, not a ship."

"It'll be a ship, dear," his mother said, patting his arm. "You come from a family of voyagers, and you're good with numbers. They'd be silly to put you on a base."

"Sure," Eli said. Though now that he had a better understanding of navy logistics, he knew that being good with numbers might be the perfect reason for them to put him at a base or supply depot.

"And we have to get going," his father said suddenly.

Eli frowned, looking at him. Out of the corner of his eye he saw Thrawn approaching at a brisk walk. As his father had apparently also noted.

Always someone lower. "You really don't have to," he said. "If you can stay another day, or even another few hours, we can find out my assignment together."

"We have to go," his father said, fumbling in his tunic. "We have to . . . damn."

And then it was too late. "Good afternoon," Thrawn said as he joined their little group. "You are Ensign Vanto's parents, of course. Welcome to Coruscant."

"Thank you," Eli's father said, his voice a little strained. "You are . . . uh . . ."

"I am Lieutenant Thrawn," Thrawn said. "Your son has done quite well. You should be very proud of him."

"We are," Eli's mother said. Her voice was less strained than her husband's, but the blatant curiosity in her face more than made up for it. "You're a—you're really a Chiss?"

"I am," Thrawn confirmed. "Your son has spoken

of your legends concerning us. Be aware that not all of them are accurate."

"But some of them are?" Eli's father asked carefully. "May I ask which ones?"

"Dad!" Eli admonished him, feeling his face warming.

"The most flattering ones, of course," Thrawn said, a small smile touching his lips. "Still, even when false, legends can be most informative."

"I thought you said they weren't all true," Eli's mother said.

"I did not refer to the legends themselves," Thrawn said, turning his glowing eyes on her. "But what is remembered says a great deal about those doing the remembering."

For a moment an awkward silence surrounded the group. "I see," Eli's father said at last. "Very interesting. But as I was saying, we have to go."

"What was the problem?" Eli asked.

"The problem?"

"You said *damn*. That usually implies a problem."

"Oh," his father said. "No, not really. I'd just forgotten we can't use our beckon call here, that's all. We'll have to get an airbus to our landing platform."

"Which they charge an arm and a leg for," his mother added. "But we'll be fine. We need to get back home anyway." She stepped close to Eli and wrapped him in a big hug. "Thank you for inviting us here, Eli. Let us know where they put you, and take care."

"I will, Mom," Eli promised as his father wrapped his arms around them both. "Have a safe trip back."

"We will," his father said. "Goodbye, and take care." He released his hug. "Lieutenant," he said, nodding gingerly at Thrawn.

"Mr. Vanto," Thrawn said, returning the nod. "Ms. Vanto. Safe journeys."

"Thank you." Eli's father took his mother's arm and led her away.

For a moment Eli and Thrawn stood in silence, watching as his parents walked down the path toward the Academy's landing platform. "They are concerned about you," Thrawn said at last.

"Parents' prerogative," Eli said, wondering uncomfortably how much Thrawn had been able to read from his brief encounters with them. Had he figured out that a major part of their concern was that Thrawn's presence in Eli's life might somehow have poisoned his future? "They're also not all that comfortable here. Big city, Core people. You know."

"Yes," Thrawn said. "Your father spoke of a beckon call. What is that?"

"It's a device that can remotely bring your ship to you," Eli said. "All my family's business ships are slave-rigged for beckon calls. With some of our clients, it's a good idea to keep your ship and the rest of your cargo out of sight and reach until you've finished your deal."

"Because of the potential for theft?"

"Basically."

"Why does the Empire not suppress such criminal activity?"

"Because they can't be everywhere," Eli said. "And Wild Space isn't exactly high on Coruscant's list." He nodded at the lieutenant's rank plaque, now attached prominently to Thrawn's tunic. "So is that a new plaque Deenlark gave you at the ceremony? Or did you give him back the old one beforehand?"

"This one is new," Thrawn said, rubbing his fingertips gently across the tiles. "Evidently he forgot he had already given me one."

"Ah," Eli said, nodding. "I guess you can keep the other one as a souvenir."

"Or find another use for it," Thrawn said. "When will we learn our assignments?"

Eli checked his chrono. "Could be any time now." He looked back at his departing parents, now nearly lost among the rest of the family members who'd gathered for the graduation ceremonies. "Might as well head over to the commandant's office and see."

"Very well," Thrawn said. "Why do they not simply send us the assignments on our computers?"

"I don't know," Eli said. Turning his back on the other cadets and their well-wishers, he headed toward the commandant's office. "Probably want to get us used to handling properly encrypted data and orders. Or it's the way they've always done things. Take your pick. Come on—good chance we'll be the first ones in line."

They weren't the first. But they were the second and third.

Eli gazed at his data card as he and Thrawn walked past the line of graduates now starting to form, his eyes lingering on the Royal Imperial Academy logo, a new trickle of satisfaction running through his disappointment at his parents' abrupt departure. They might not think much of his transfer to Coruscant, but everyone else in the navy would.

He'd done it. He'd really and truly done it. Against all odds, the Wild Space yokel had been thrown into the elite of Coruscant and had succeeded.

"Well?" Thrawn prompted.

"You first," Eli said. And as his time at Royal Imperial was coming to an end, so was his time with Thrawn. It had been interesting, but he was ready to move on.

"Very well." Thrawn slipped his card into his datapad and peered at the display. "Interesting. I am to be second weapons officer aboard the *Gozanti*-class cruiser *Blood Crow*."

"Nice," Eli said. Gozantis were Corellian design, about sixty-four meters long, with dorsal and ventral laser turrets. They were a bit old—most were of pre–Clone Wars manufacture—but they could still hold their own alongside newer ships. Most were being used as freighters or evac ships, but some were being retrofitted with external clamps to carry starfighters or walkers, which would bring them into the front lines against pirates, smugglers, and slavers. In any role, though, a Gozanti was a good, solid ship from which to launch a career.

"And you?" Thrawn asked. "I presume you asked for a supply officer position?"

"I did," Eli confirmed as he inserted his own data card. "Good chance I got it, too—the bigger ships are always hurting for supply personnel . . ."

He trailed off. What the *hell*?

"What is it?" Thrawn asked.

It took Eli two tries to find his voice. "The *Blood Crow,*" he choked out. "Aide to . . . Lieutenant Thrawn."

He looked up at Thrawn, a red haze of anger dropping over his vision. "Did you do this?" he demanded.

Thrawn shook his head. "No."

"Don't lie!" Eli snarled. "Lieutenants don't get aides. *Ever.* You set this up with the Emperor, didn't you?"

"The Emperor does not speak to me," Thrawn said. "Nor have I spoken with him since my first day on this world."

"This didn't happen by accident," Eli ground out. "You must have said *something.* What was it? *What was it?*"

Thrawn hesitated, then lowered his head. "The *Blood Crow* is scheduled for duty in border sectors where Sy Bisti and related trade languages may be spoken," he said reluctantly. "I merely pointed out that it might be beneficial to have two officers aboard who understood those languages."

"Since they aren't programmed into translator droids?" Eli bit out, an acid taste in his mouth.

"But I assure you I said nothing about an aide," Thrawn insisted. "If you wish, I will refuse to accept you in that position."

Eli looked down at his datapad, feeling the anger drain

out of him. The anger, and the excitement of graduation. Thrawn could refuse, ask, or demand all he wanted. It wouldn't do any good. Once orders were logged into the navy data system, they might as well be laser-etched into granite.

So that was that. In a single stroke, Eli's life had been completely upended. Again.

Only now it wasn't just his schooling. This time it was his career, so carefully calculated and implemented, that had been snatched away from him. He would enter the navy not as an up-and-coming supply officer, but as an officer's aide. The career path most solidly guaranteed to go nowhere.

And *that* assumed that Thrawn was even up-and-coming himself. What if he wasn't? What if he failed?

Because he might. In fact, the odds were high that he would. Disrespect for nonhumans might not be official policy, but it nonetheless quietly pervaded the navy. Thrawn would have to try twice as hard as anyone else, and succeed twice as often, just to stay even with them.

And when Thrawn went down, it was almost guaranteed that anyone associated with him would go down, too.

"Ensign Vanto?" Thrawn prompted. "Shall I speak with the commandant?"

"No point," Eli said, shutting down the datapad and putting it away. "The navy doesn't change orders just because junior officers don't like them. When you're an admiral, we'll see what you can do."

"I understand," Thrawn said quietly. "Very well. I shall strive to achieve that rank as quickly as possible."

Eli looked sharply at him. Was the damn Chiss mocking him?

But there was no hint of amusement in his face. Thrawn was deadly serious.

A shiver ran up Eli's back, the ghosts of the old stories whispering through his mind. Chiss didn't make idle boasts or promises. And once they set their minds to something, they succeeded or died in the attempt. Maybe he really thought he could make admiral someday.

Maybe he was right.

"I'll look forward to it," Eli said. "Come on. The orders said to be on the Corellia transport at eighteen-hundred hours. We don't want to start our careers by missing our ride."

CHAPTER 7

There is satisfaction in defeating an enemy. But one must never allow oneself to become complacent. There are always more enemies to be identified, faced, and vanquished.

All warriors understand the need to face and defeat the enemy. Both aspects of the task can be challenging. Both can require thought, insight, and planning. Failures in any of those areas can cost unnecessary time and irreplaceable lives.

But a warrior may forget that even the task of identifying the enemy can be difficult. And the cost of that failure can lead to catastrophe.

Eli had occasionally warned Thrawn of the presence of politics within the navy. They'd certainly seen evidence of that influence during the Orbar incident.

Now, once again, politics had arisen that could directly affect them.

"I wasn't able to get anything on why Captain Virgilio was replaced," Eli murmured as they followed the procession of officers escorting the new commander, Captain Filia Rossi, on her tour of the *Blood Crow.* "But everyone agrees that Rossi's very well connected. Nowadays, that's all you need to get a command."

"I see," Thrawn said.

Eli grimaced. *I see.* That was Thrawn's go-to answer when he didn't want to say anything else.

There was certainly plenty that he *could* say.

Starting with the kind of captain Rik Virgilio had been. He'd been excellent at his job, walking the necessary balance between standing orders and flexibility. In the eighteen months Eli and Thrawn had served under him, the captain had built up a fine reputation for trapping smugglers, rendering aid to distressed vessels, and defusing potentially damaging political situations on Mid Rim and Outer Rim worlds. He'd earned the respect of his officers and crew, and highly satisfactory reviews from the governors and other political leaders with whom he'd interacted.

Equally important, certainly from Eli's and Thrawn's point of view, Virgilio had taken in stride the presence of an alien officer on his ship. There had been a degree of tension during the first few weeks as Virgilio tested the limits of Thrawn's intelligence, knowledge, and ability, but once the captain learned his new officer's parameters Eli could detect no difference in the captain's treatment or acceptance of his second weapons officer. When the position of first weapons officer opened up, he'd raised no objections to Thrawn being promoted to that position. In fact, ship's gossip had suggested that Virgilio might have actually recommended the Chiss for the job.

Now, without warning or explanation, Virgilio had been removed from the *Blood Crow* and a younger, less experienced captain brought in.

There was little that Eli had been able to learn about the new captain. Filia Rossi had graduated from the Raithal Academy twelve years earlier and had spent most of her time since then on Socorro, first on the ground, then aboard an orbiting defense platform out in the system's asteroid belts. For the past year she'd been first officer aboard an ore freighter escort.

Now, suddenly, she'd been promoted to command of a cruiser.

It seemed obvious that the decision had been based on politics and influence rather than merit or even seniority. Still, Eli was willing to give Rossi the benefit of the doubt. It was possible that the driving force was less political status than the simple result of personnel transfers. If Captain Virgilio had been promoted to a better, more prestigious command, then someone else had to be brought to the *Blood Crow* to take his place.

But if that was the case, news of Virgilio's promotion had not been passed to the *Blood Crow*'s other officers. Such silence from the High Command lent additional weight to Eli's suspicions that the former captain had been retired or even quietly dismissed.

"Still, there must necessarily be a first command in every officer's career," Thrawn said into Eli's thoughts.

"I suppose," Eli conceded. "I just don't see why her first command has to be on *our* ship."

Ahead, the captain and the short line of officers trailing behind her had reached the Number Two storage bay. The captain hit the hatch release and stepped inside, First Officer Nels Deyland close behind her.

Eli winced. "Uh-oh," he murmured.

The rest of the officers knew what it meant, too. They began drifting to both sides of the passageway, making room for Thrawn to pass when the expected call came.

The wait was barely ten seconds. "Thrawn!" the captain's voice boomed from inside the storage bay. "Get in here. *Now.*"

Captain Rossi and Senior Lieutenant Deyland stood at one side of the storage bay. *Rossi's facial glow is increasing, her eyes narrowed in a frown. Deyland stands motionless, his face showing a partially masked expression of discomfort.* "Senior Lieutenant Deyland tells me this is yours," Rossi said, pointing at the equipment stacked along the bulkhead.

"It is, Captain."

"You mind telling me what the hell it's doing taking up space on my ship?"

"He found it in a scrap market we were investigating for smuggler activity," Deyland put in. "As I mentioned earlier—"

"Your name Lieutenant Thrawn?" Rossi cut him off. *Her facial glow increases. Her stance is stiff, her fingers moving slightly.*

"No, ma'am."

"Then shut it. I asked you a question, Lieutenant."

"As Senior Lieutenant Deyland said, the parts were in a scrap market," Thrawn said. "They are antiques, remnants of the Clone War."

"I know what they are," Rossi growled, looking at the piles again. "Droideka, buzz droid—*two* buzz droids— half a STAP—" Her eyes narrowed. "Is that part of a *hyperdrive ring?*"

"Yes, ma'am."

"These aren't antiques, Lieutenant." *Rossi snorts, her lips curling down briefly.* "These are junk."

"Perhaps, ma'am," Thrawn said. "However, as I am not fully familiar with the technology of that era, I hoped to gain insight by studying them."

"And maybe get them working again?" Rossi asked. "Don't deny it—I can see fill-ins on both buzz droids. Brand-new components." *She raises her eyebrows. Her finger movements intensify briefly.* "They'd better not be components from the *Blood Crow*'s stores."

"No, ma'am," Thrawn said. "They were purchased elsewhere."

"At his own expense," Deyland murmured.

"Senior Lieutenant Deyland is correct," Thrawn said. "The buzz droids in particular struck me as potentially useful. They are compact, with specialized drilling and cutting tools that allow them—"

"Spare me the lecture," Rossi cut him off. *Her hand makes an abbreviated slash through the air. The pitch of her voice lowers.* "You may have read about the Clone Wars, but some of us lived it. And Virgilio just let you bring this stuff aboard?"

"Captain Virgilio permitted me to purchase them, yes, ma'am," Thrawn said. "He also gave me permission to store them here when I was not working on them."

"Very generous of him," Rossi said. "It may have caught your attention that Virgilio isn't captain anymore. *I* am, and I run a clean ship. I want this garbage dumped before your next watch. Clear?"

Beside her, Deyland stirred. *His stance indicates disagreement.* "Ma'am, if I might suggest—"

"I asked if that was clear, Lieutenant."

"Yes, Captain," Thrawn said. "May I offer an alternative?"

"If I didn't want to hear from my first officer, what makes you think I want to hear from you?" Rossi countered. "Senior Lieutenant Deyland, you'll see that he dumps it as ordered. We're done here."

"Yes, ma'am." *Deyland remains standing where he is, making no indication of preparing to leave the bay.* "With your permission, ma'am, I'd like to hear Lieutenant Thrawn's suggestion."

Captain Rossi's eyes narrow further as she stares at Deyland. Her arms are stiff beneath the uniform sleeves, her fingers now motionless, her stance leaning slightly forward. Senior Lieutenant Deyland's expression is tense but his stance indicates firmness. Captain Rossi straightens slightly. "Apparently, no one aboard understands proper respect for their captain," she said, her voice stiff. "We'll have to deal with that." She turned back to Thrawn. "Fine. Let's hear this alternative."

"It is my understanding, ma'am, that matériel aboard an Imperial war vessel is the property of that vessel, and thus under control of the commander," Thrawn said. "When I bought these items for five hundred credits—"

"Five *hundred* credits?" Rossi interrupted. "Are you *serious*? Those things aren't worth a tenth that."

"That would be correct, Captain, were these standard buzz droids," Thrawn said. "But they are of the Mark One version. Quite rare, and apparently quite valuable."

"Really." *Rossi looks at the buzz droids, her lips pursing.* "*How* valuable?"

"When I bought them, they were nonfunctional," Thrawn said. "As you have noted, I have made some progress in repairing them. I would expect that once they are fully restored they will be quite valuable to collectors."

"Collectors." *Rossi's tone is flat.* "People with more money than brains."

"Some also merely have an interest in Clone War antiquities," Thrawn said. "I am told there are members of the High Command with such interests."

Rossi's lips part slightly, her stance straightening. She gazes again at the buzz droids, the muscles in her cheeks tensing then relaxing then tensing again. Her fingers are in motion, the thumb and forefinger of her right hand rubbing gently together. "Mark Ones, you said?"

"I did."

"Mark Ones," she murmured. *Her voice carries the mix of tension and interest that indicates sudden understanding. Her hand makes a small movement toward her datapad, then stops.* "All right, I'll meet you halfway. We're due back at Ansion in three months. You can have until then to play with your toys. Once we reach Ansion, I'm taking them, working or not. Clear?"

"Clear, ma'am," Thrawn said. "Thank you."

Rossi looks at Deyland, then at the droids. The tension lines in her face smooth out. She brushes past Deyland to the bay's exit. "At your convenience, Senior Lieutenant Deyland," she called back over her shoulder.

"Yes, ma'am." *Deyland gives a small smile of satisfaction, then follows the captain back into the corridor. They continue aft, the rest of the officers again forming up behind them.*

"Well?" Vanto asked quietly as he reached the bay. *His expression holds both anticipation and dread.* "Is she making you throw it all out?"

"Why do you assume that?"

"Because Virgilio let you have it, and Rossi's going to try to wipe every trace of him off the *Blood Crow*," Vanto said. *His voice holds a low level of bitterness.* "Trust me—I've seen her type a lot."

"Interesting," Thrawn said. "As it happens, she has agreed to allow me until the end of our current patrol to bring the items to full function."

"Generous of her. I presume there's a catch?"

"I reminded her that they would become her property."

"Ah," Vanto said. *He nods in understanding.* "And you remembered what I said back when you first got them about collectors and non-intrinsic value?"

"I did. I thank you for that insight."

"You're welcome," Vanto said. "I don't suppose you happened to mention that the buzz droids were already fully operational?"

"She did not ask. But I believe she also came to a belated realization that they have a value beyond even the non-intrinsic lure to collectors. Do you remember a metal called *doonium* from our technical classes?"

"Oh, I knew doonium long before I got to Royal Imperial," Vanto said. "Dad always put on extra security whenever we were lucky enough to carry a crate or two of the stuff. But there's no doonium in buzz droids."

"There was in the Mark One models," Thrawn said. "It was a shell protecting the brain core. It was removed in later models because the cost outweighed the defensive benefits."

"So, rare *and* intrinsically valuable," Vanto said. *He*

nods understanding. "You say the captain figured out that last part herself?"

"I believe so. She reached for her datapad, presumably intending to confirm her memory of the Mark One construction, but then changed her mind."

"Didn't want to make a big deal of it in front of everyone," Vanto said. "She'll wait until she's alone." *He smiles with cynical amusement.* "And then will no doubt congratulate herself on her memory and insight and on putting one over on her poor naïve weapons officer."

"Perhaps," Thrawn said. "And we should probably rejoin the others."

"Right." *Vanto starts down the corridor at a quick walk.* "Hopefully, Deyland also won't mention the droids are functional. If he does, Rossi will probably take them right now, and you won't get to fiddle with them anymore."

"He said nothing at the time."

"Good for him," Vanto said. "Of course, he *does* owe you. Getting blindsided when those Delphidians made a run for it could have been embarrassing."

"Possibly lethal, as well."

"Very possibly," Vanto agreed.

"Thrawn!" A distant bellow echoed down the passageway.

"I believe they have reached the electronics repair shop," Thrawn said.

"And found the other part of your hyperdrive ring," Vanto said. "Yeah. We might want to hurry."

It took a week for Captain Rossi to come fully up to speed on her new command, and to acquaint herself with her ship, her officers, and her crew.

She was, Eli had to admit, pretty good at it. By the end of the second week she was being spoken of with cautious acceptance by most of the crew, and was well on her way to good working relationships with most of her officers.

With two glaring exceptions.

Eli, of course, was the second one.

The most frustrating part was that he'd predicted the problem right from the start. The captain had an aide; nonhuman Lieutenant Thrawn had one; and no one else aboard ship did.

It wasn't proper protocol. It certainly wasn't proper tradition. And in the Imperial Navy, those two things were the bedrock on which everything else was built.

It had taken Captain Virgilio some time to get used to the idea. It had taken Senior Lieutenant Deyland even longer. Neither man, Eli suspected, had ever been really happy with it.

Eli wasn't expecting Rossi to ever get used to it, or accept it. Unfortunately, there were an infinite number of ways a commander could show her displeasure with something. Or with someone.

Sure enough, over the next month Eli saw a clear pattern developing. Every nasty, dirty, or undesirable job somehow ended up on Thrawn's list. If it was a job that an officer couldn't legitimately be ordered to do, Thrawn would still be tasked with overseeing the procedure.

And as Thrawn's aide, Eli was usually assigned the job right along with him.

Thrawn took it with stoic good grace. Eli made sure his own annoyance was equally invisible. The slightest hint of insubordination, he knew, and Rossi would be on him like a tusk-cat on a shaak.

So when the *Blood Crow* picked up a distress call from a freighter carrying a cargo of static-locked tibanna gas, Eli knew exactly who would be leading the boarding party.

"If I understand correctly," Thrawn said as Ensign Merri Barlin maneuvered their shuttle between the *Blood Crow* and the derelict freighter *Dromedar,* "the most disagreeable part of this duty is the dust?"

"Yes, sir," Eli said, looking at the man and woman sitting silently in the jump seats along the shuttle's walls. Neither of them looked particularly happy with their assignment, either. "Electronics Tech Layneo has had experience with static-locking," Eli continued, gesturing to the woman. "Care to elaborate on the problem?"

"As Ensign Vanto says, sir, there's dust," Layneo said, her face wrinkling briefly with disgust. "A lot of it. Something about static-locking brings the stuff out of every nook and cranny on a ship and deposits it neatly on your uniform and skin. You come out looking like a dirt miner."

"It sticks to fabrics especially well," Engineering Tech Jakeeb added. "You usually have to run your uniform through the cleaner twice to get everything out."

"And we all know how Captain Rossi likes her crew to look sharp," Barlin called back from the cockpit.

"How does it affect electronic equipment?" Thrawn asked.

"Luckily, the dust is usually coarse enough not to get into properly sealed gear," Layneo said. "Emphasis on *properly*. I've never seen a civilian transport yet where everything was up to proper code."

"In fact, I'd bet fifty credits we don't find anyone aboard," Jakeeb said. "Automated beacon, dead in space—odds are they got dust in their hyperdrive, couldn't fix it, and took off."

"I'll take that bet," Layneo said.

"Easy," Eli warned. "No gambling aboard ship, re-member?"

"But we're not aboard ship, sir," Jakeeb said inno-cently.

"This vessel is considered part of the *Blood Crow*," Thrawn said. "If static-locking has such serious disad-vantages, why is it still used?"

"It's really only used with tibanna gas, sir," Layneo said. "The stuff's highly explosive and highly valuable.

Big draw for hijackers. Static-locking the tanks makes stealing them a risky business."

"Which means it'll be equally tricky for us if Captain Rossi wants them brought aboard," Jakeeb warned. "Hopefully, it'll just be a matter of fixing whatever's wrong and flying the whole freighter to Ansion."

There was a gentle bump. "We're here, sir," Barlin reported. "Engaging locking collar . . . okay, we're set. Atmosphere inside reading normal. Lights on low, temperature mid-range, gravity functional and standard. Scrub is still running."

"Life-form readings?" Thrawn asked.

"Nothing useful, sir," she replied. "The static-locking's still screwing all that up. Okay, scrub's finished . . . negative on dangerous chemicals or microorganisms. We're good to go, Lieutenant."

"Thank you," Thrawn said. "Ensign Vanto, take Techs Layneo and Jakeeb aft to the engine section. Ensign Barlin and I will go forward to the bridge."

Two minutes later, Eli and the two techs were moving down the freighter's central passageway, their footsteps echoing in the gloom. "*Really* hate derelicts, sir," Layneo muttered as they walked. Her hand, Eli noted, was resting on the grip of her holstered blaster. "Too many ghost-ship stories when I was growing up."

"I heard my share, too," Eli said. "Most are just stories. The rest are real incidents embellished out of all recognition."

"I'm sure this place will look a lot cheerier once Barlin gets to the lighting controls," Jakeeb said helpfully.

"Yeah, I don't think so," Layneo growled. "All the light in the world—"

Without warning, the corridor erupted in a blinding blaze of light.

"Freeze!" a taut voice said from somewhere behind them. "You hear me? Freeze! Or I *swear* I'll shoot you where you stand."

. . .

Vanto's expression is wary as he comes into view, but the tension that was in his voice when he gave the alarm has subsided. He holds an unfamiliar blaster loosely in his hand. "Ensign Vanto: Report," Thrawn ordered.

"Lieutenant," Vanto said. *He gives a brief, formal nod of greeting and acknowledgment. His fingers are half curled in the silent signal that confirms all is indeed well.* "May I present Nevil Cygni. He apparently mistook us for someone else."

"Did he," Thrawn said. *Cygni is a human with dark hair and the textured skin of one who has worked long years in bright sunlight. He sits on the deck at Vanto's feet. His torso is hunched forward, his face buried in his hands. His expression is largely hidden, but the tensed muscles in his neck and arms hold fear and weariness. His clothes are stained with the same dust that clings to the Imperials' own uniforms. His hands show the scarring and calluses of mild physical labor.* "Whom did he mistake us for?"

"Cygni?" Vanto prompted.

"Yes, sir," Cygni said. *Still seated, he straightens up and lowers his hands. His face is well fleshed, with no signs of malnutrition. The skin around his eyes is taut with stress, as are the muscles in his throat. His eyes are dark and wary.* "Please believe that I thought you were—" *He breaks off and his eyes widen.* "I—uh—"

"Lieutenant Thrawn asked you a question, Cygni," Vanto said.

"Yes," Cygni said. *He blinks twice and turns his eyes to Vanto.* "Sorry. My name—no; you already know my name. Sorry. The thing is, we were attacked. By pirates."

"Who were they?" Vanto asked. "Did they mention any names? Were they wearing any kind of insignia?"

"No," Cygni said. "No names." *His lips twitch.* "At least, nothing I heard. I sort of . . . ran."

There is a brief silence. "Where did you run?" Vanto asked.

"There's a storage locker back there where Captain Fitz stores her private food stocks." *Cygni angles his head behind him.* "Specialized stuff she picks up along our route that she sells wherever she can make a profit. We used to pilfer it, taking from the back and keeping the front intact so she wouldn't notice as quickly."

"Which left enough room behind the packages where you could hide?"

"I know what you're thinking," Cygni said. *His voice becomes harsh.* "I should have stood with the others. Maybe fought, maybe—" He broke off, his throat working. "And then they took them." *His voice drops in volume.* "All of them. I heard someone say they were going to go back to their base and find a slicer to get the ship running. But they took everyone else with them."

"What happened to the hyperdrive?" Thrawn asked.

"I've got Layneo checking it out," Vanto said. "Best guess is that someone locked it down before the pirates could get to it."

"Yes—that was it," Cygni said. "Captain Fitz locked the hyperdrive. I heard them threatening her. Or maybe it was Toom, our engineer, who locked it." *He squeezes his eyes tightly shut.* "I heard . . . screams."

"You thought we were the returning pirates?" Thrawn asked.

"Yes." *Cygni opens his eyes and waves one hand at Vanto.* "I was scared, and I didn't focus on the uniforms. I never thought anyone would hear the beacon or come looking anyway. When I saw who you were . . ." *He trails off.* "I guess I'm lucky you didn't just shoot me for pulling a blaster on you."

"We have better self-control than that," Vanto said. *He looks at Thrawn.* "Orders, sir?"

"Contact the *Blood Crow*," Thrawn said. *Cygni buries his face in his hands again. The muscles in his hands are tight with tension.* "Report the situation to the captain, and inform her I will be making a thorough examination of the ship."

"Except for the power compartment, sir," Layneo said as she joined them from around a corner. "There's a bad leak in the main reactor."

"Oh, yes—don't go in there," Cygni said quickly. *He drops his hands from his face. His back stiffens as he looks up.* "Sorry—I should have warned you about that."

"It's okay," Layneo said, her voice dry. "The indicators and hatch interlocks were a pretty solid hint."

"Oh. Right." *Cygni sighs. His torso folds over again in a slump.*

"And then tell her," Thrawn continued to Vanto, "that I recommend bringing a full operational crew aboard while we attempt to restart the hyperdrive. If we are unable to do so, I recommend attempting to disengage the static-locks so that the tibanna cylinders can be removed and transferred to the *Blood Crow*."

Layneo's mouth drops open a few millimeters. "Ah . . . yes," Vanto said cautiously. "Sir, I suspect the captain will find your suggestions . . . a bit excessive."

"She may," Thrawn said. *Cygni's face is still hidden in his hands.* "Nevertheless, those are my recommendations."

"Yes, sir," Vanto said. "I'll submit them immediately."

"Thank you, Ensign," Thrawn said. "While you do that, Tech Layneo will show me to the tibanna cylinders."

Layneo clenches her jaw firmly. "Yes, sir," she said. "This way."

CHAPTER 8

Leadership and obedience are the two legs on which a warrior's life is balanced. Without both, victory cannot be achieved.

Leadership depends on information and comprehension. Not so obedience. Sometimes a commander may choose to share details of his plan. Often he may not. In either case, obedience must be instant and complete.

Such automatic response relies on trust between commander and those commanded. And that trust can only be obtained through leadership.

Eli had expected Captain Rossi to take Thrawn's recommendations badly. He wasn't disappointed.

"A *full* op crew?" Rossi echoed incredulously. "Is he out of his mind?"

"Ma'am, the cargo is extremely valuable," Eli pointed out, fighting back a growing annoyance. Rossi had no business simply rejecting Thrawn's suggestions out of hand. But Thrawn likewise shouldn't have put Eli in the middle of this in the first place. If he wanted to pitch this crazy plan he should have done it himself. "If we can move either the ship or the tibanna—"

"And if he thinks he's going to play around with

twenty tibanna cylinders while my ship is in even the same solar system, he's *very* much mistaken," Rossi cut him off.

"Yes, ma'am," Eli said, glowering at his comlink. Now the captain was just being overdramatic. A cascading tibanna explosion was seriously nasty, but it wasn't *that* bad. "But if Lieutenant Thrawn thinks it can be done, it may be worth letting him try."

"It would hardly be a major loss for the navy if he blew himself to atoms," Rossi countered sarcastically. "But I'm not risking that much of my crew on those odds. Anyway, it's a moot point. A Ho'Din settlement on Moltok is getting shot at by the local Makurth boss, and they need some Imperial muscle to knock their little heads together before it becomes a full-fledged war. We need to go."

"Yes, ma'am," Eli said, wishing he could just let it go and let Rossi's decision play out, for better or worse, upon her own head.

But Cygni needed protection and justice, too. So did the Imperial base or local planetary defense force that had ordered that tibanna shipment.

Besides, Thrawn was counting on him.

"What if just Lieutenant Thrawn and I stayed behind?" he suggested to Rossi. "Possibly with one of the techs along to assist? We could try to get the ship started, and maybe work on the tibanna a little. You could come back and get us after you've settled the Moltok situation."

There was a short pause, and Eli could visualize Rossi tapping her fingers on her armrest as she weighed her options.

If Eli were a betting man—and if gambling were allowed aboard the *Blood Crow*—he would bet on the captain going with whatever option had the best chance of Thrawn blowing himself up. If the tibanna didn't do the trick, a shipload of returning pirates might.

"Very well, Ensign," Rossi said. "Inform Lieutenant

Thrawn that he can have whatever equipment he needs, and up to three crew, assuming he can find that many willing to volunteer. You'll stay with him regardless, of course. An important officer like that can't be without his aide."

Eli scowled. He'd called it, all right. "Yes, ma'am," he said. "I'll deliver your message immediately."

Given the circumstances, Rossi no doubt assumed the repair party would consist only of Thrawn and Eli. It was probably a surprise to her, and not a pleasant one, when Barlin, Layneo, and Jakeeb all instantly volunteered to stay, as well.

"I'm gratified you were all willing to help," Cygni said as he and the others watched from the *Dromedar*'s bridge as the *Blood Crow* jumped to lightspeed. "I just hope it doesn't end badly for you."

"It will not," Thrawn assured him. "Ensign Barlin, Tech Layneo: You may begin when ready."

"Yes, sir," Barlin said, seating herself at the helm station. "Layneo?"

"On it, ma'am," Layneo said, pulling a chair over to the main computer station. "Here we go."

"What are they doing?" Cygni asked, lowering his voice to a whisper as if afraid he would disturb their work.

"They are attempting what is known as an asymmetric backdoor," Thrawn told him. "It is a hidden code programmed into many ship computers for precisely this purpose."

Cygni whistled softly. "I've never heard of that. Nice." He threw a sideways look toward Thrawn. "Never heard of a nonhuman as an Imperial officer, either. You're some sort of Pantoran, right?"

Eli took a breath, preparing to point out that Pantorans didn't have red eyes—

"Of a sort, yes," Thrawn said. "What I am is a lieutenant in the Imperial Navy."

"Right," Cygni said again. "Sorry—I didn't mean to pry. I just . . . no offense."

"None taken," Thrawn said. "Ensign Vanto, go to engineering and unpack the crate I had delivered aboard. We shall join you shortly."

"Yes, sir," Eli said, frowning slightly. There was something about the way Thrawn was acting, something he couldn't quite put his finger on. Was he worried about the ship? The tibanna gas? The pirates? Captain Rossi?

Actually, when he put it that way, it wasn't surprising at all that Thrawn might feel preoccupied.

The crate had been left just outside the cargo bay where the line of tibanna cylinders stood against the hull. Eli glanced into the bay—Jakeeb was in there taking the readings Thrawn had ordered—then set to work on the crate. He got the end open.

And felt his eyes widen. He'd had no idea that Thrawn was bringing—

"What in the *world*?" Cygni's stunned voice came from behind him. "Is that a *buzz droid*?"

"It is," Thrawn said calmly. "I am surprised you recognize it."

"They weren't exactly a secret weapon," Cygni said, walking up to Eli and crouching beside him to peer into the crate. "That's a Mark One, isn't it? Rare. Is it functional? Please tell me it isn't functional."

"Of course it is functional," Thrawn said. "It would hardly be of use otherwise."

Cygni looked at Thrawn, then at the buzz droid, then back at Thrawn. "Okay, you've lost me," he said. "These things were designed to eat starfighters, right?"

"They also have other uses," Thrawn said. "Come. I will explain."

He turned and walked through the hatchway into the cargo bay. Cygni watched him go, then turned to Eli. "Is he serious? About using buzz droids in there, I mean?"

"I assume so," Eli said.

"Really." Cygni looked at the hatchway again, then

shrugged and gestured to Eli. "After you," he said. "This I *have* to see."

Thrawn was standing with Jakeeb, the two having a quiet discussion, when Eli and Cygni joined them. "Tech Jakeeb confirms my earlier assumptions," Thrawn said. "The static-lock does indeed seal the tibanna cylinders, but only from this side."

"Excuse me?" Cygni asked, sounding even more confused. "What do you mean, *this* side?"

Thrawn gestured. "Tech Jakeeb?"

"The lock's only on the cargo bay side of the cylinders," Jakeeb explained. "See, they're fastened right against the hull with half-meter struts. That's too short a distance for the lock to go all the way around—it would short out or power-drain itself out of existence. So the lock is just on the surfaces inside the bay."

"Though also around the ends of the cylinder row, I assume," Eli said. He saw where Thrawn was going with this now.

"Correct," Jakeeb confirmed. "Just not on the backside. So if you want to get to them, your best bet is to go through the hull."

"Hence, the buzz droid," Cygni said, sounding awed. "I'll be damned. Why hasn't anyone thought of that before?"

"Oh, they have," Jakeeb said. "Thing is, it's not quite as simple as it sounds."

"Because?"

"One, you have to get a buzz droid and probably rebuild it," Jakeeb said, ticking off fingers. "Two, once you've done that, big-ship hulls are thicker and tougher than the old starfighters. Fair chance you'll wreck your droid before you're halfway through. Third—" He looked at Thrawn, raised his eyebrows.

"Third is that you will necessarily drain one of the cylinders into space when you cut through," Thrawn said. "That represents a loss that many are unwilling to accept."

"Though losing one out of twenty isn't bad, percentage-wise," Cygni mused. "Especially if the alternative is to lose all of them. So I gather once you have that cylinder drained, you can cut it into little pieces and dump it out your gap in the hull, which then gives you access to the others from the back. Then you just work your way down the line, cutting all the struts and freeing them one by one?"

"Exactly," Jakeeb said. "Takes a while, but once you've got the first one out it's a purely mechanical operation." He looked at Thrawn again. "There is one other *slight* problem, of course. Venting the tibanna outside the ship theoretically works just fine. But if you spark the vapor in just the right way . . . well, there could be trouble."

"As in blowing up the ship?" Cygni asked.

"Not *that* much trouble," Jakeeb said. "But it would be a mess."

"Fortunately, that will not be necessary after all," Thrawn said. His head was cocked a little to the side, Eli saw, as if he was listening to something.

"Why not?" Cygni asked.

In answer, Thrawn pulled out his comlink. "Ensign Barlin? Do I hear the hyperdrive going active?"

"Yes, sir, you do," Barlin's voice came faintly from the comlink. "Got through the lock, and we're just about ready to go. Does Cygni have the destination coordinates? Or are we just going to take the ship to Ansion?"

"Neither, I'm afraid," Cygni said softly.

Frowning, Eli turned to him.

And froze. The wretched, nervous, ill-fated crewman had vanished. In his place was someone else: quiet, calm, and supremely confident.

A small blaster held steady in his hand.

"What the *hell*?" Jakeeb breathed.

Cygni ignored the comment. Pulling out a comlink with his free hand, he flicked it on. "We're good," he said. "Three with the tibanna; two on the bridge." He raised his eyebrows toward Thrawn. "I'd appreciate it if you'd order Barlin and Layneo to surrender quietly."

"Why should I deprive them of their right and duty to defend their lives?" Thrawn countered.

"Because if they surrender, they won't be harmed," Cygni said. "I give you my word."

"And these?" Thrawn asked, inclining his head toward Eli and Jakeeb.

"None of you will be harmed," Cygni said. "All we want is the tibanna." He wrinkled his nose. "Well, and the ship, too. I guess that goes without saying."

Before Thrawn could answer, a dozen large, rough-looking men appeared, swarming through the hatchway into the cargo bay. One of them, a thin man with a braided beard, raised his blaster—

"Blasters down," Cygni snapped. "They've surrendered. No shooting. Angel, I said *down.*"

The man with the braided beard ignored him. "What the hell is *that*?" he demanded, jabbing the blaster at Thrawn.

"*That,*" Cygni said, "is a lieutenant of the Imperial Navy. Now lower your weapon." He looked at Thrawn. "Lieutenant?"

For a moment Thrawn studied him. Then he raised his comlink again. "Ensign Barlin, a group of pirates are on their way. They've been ordered not to harm you if you surrender without resistance. You will do so."

"Sir?"

"Surrender, Ensign. That is an order." Thrawn put the comlink away. "Would you care to accept my surrender personally, Mr. Cygni?"

"That's all right, Lieutenant," Cygni said, not moving. "I get no particular enjoyment out of defeating my opponents. Angel? Disarm them, please."

"Yeah." Angel grinned evilly. "'Cause I *do* enjoy it. So don't get clever." He gestured three of his soldiers forward.

Out of the corner of his eye, Eli saw Jakeeb brace

himself as he prepared for action. "As you were, Jakeeb," he murmured. "You've been given an order."

Jakeeb hissed out a sigh. "Yes, sir."

A moment later, the Imperials were disarmed.

"Good," Cygni said. To Eli's eye he looked more relaxed now that the risk of combat was past. "Better call your ship, Angel."

"Already called," Angel said. "I suppose you want me to toss this crowd in with the others?"

"That was the deal," Cygni said. "No deaths; no injuries. Oh, and in case I didn't mention it, I already have people on the ground at the drop point to make sure you deliver everyone safely."

"Well, you know, now, things don't always go the way you want 'em to," Angel warned. His eyes, Eli noted, hadn't left Thrawn for a minute. "Sometimes there are accidents. Sometimes there's trouble. There can be—"

"Sometimes there are consequences you really don't want to face," Cygni said. He hadn't raised his voice, but something in his tone nevertheless sent a chill up Eli's back. "Enough posturing. You have the other two Imperials? Good. Bring them down here. As soon as your ship arrives, we'll transfer them over. I trust you've decided which of your men will help me bring the *Dromedar* to port?"

"Oh, yeah, I got your team," Angel said, still eyeing Thrawn. "Starting with me."

Cygni frowned. "There's no need for you to come personally," he said. "Getting the cylinders will take some time, whether we break the static-lock or use Lieutenant Thrawn's idea of cutting them out through the hull. Plenty of time for you to drop the prisoners and rejoin us."

"I know," Angel said. "I just like your company, that's all." He nodded toward Thrawn. "I was just saying that accidents *do* happen. Not saying they would or wouldn't, just saying they could."

Cygni gazed at him, an unreadable expression on his

face. He looked at Thrawn, back at Angel. Eli held his breath . . .

"Let me sweeten the pot," Cygni said. "Did you notice that box in the passageway on your way in?"

"Yeah," Angel said. "Is that a buzz droid?"

"It is indeed," Cygni said. "Take it as a bonus. It's probably worth, what—?" He held up a hand toward Thrawn.

"Two hundred credits as it is," Thrawn said.

Cygni snorted. "You have no idea, Lieutenant. That's a Mark One, Angel. At current prices, it's probably a thousand credits just for the core's doonium shell."

Angel threw a startled look at the droid. "It's got a *doonium* shell?"

"Refined, case-hardened, and ready for the right buyer to pull it off and drop it on the black market," Cygni confirmed. "A thousand credits. Two hundred each for five otherwise worthless Imperials. Just to keep them alive."

Angel scrunched up his nose. "Fine," he said reluctantly. "Sure. I guess so."

"If that's not good enough, consider this," Cygni said. "If I hadn't persuaded them to surrender, they would have fought, and some of your men would be dead right now. Maybe even you."

"I said *fine*," Angel said scornfully. "They keep their noses clean, I'll dump 'em with the rest. Happy?"

Cygni inclined his head. "You may not realize this, Angel, but it pays to build a reputation for keeping your word."

"Not to the folks I work with it doesn't," Angel said sourly. "Fine. Let's get this over with."

"So just because I don't have your plate-crystal reputation, you think I can't be trusted to do what I said?" *Angel looks back over his shoulder at his prisoners and the other pirates. His eyes are narrowed, his lips twisted*

*with the corners downward. The muscles in his throat
and back are tight.*

"Not at all," Cygni said. *His tone is calm, his words
conciliatory. His movements are careful and precise.
His face shows little expression, but there is a tight
muscle behind his cheek.* "As long as I was here, I
thought I'd check up on the other prisoners. Your men
were a little rough on a couple of them."

"Hey, you throw a punch at a Culoss, it comes back
with interest," Angel growled. "They're lucky I didn't
shoot them dead."

"Yes," Cygni murmured. "I suppose they are."

"What is a Culoss?" Thrawn asked.

"What?" Angel demands. *His eyes narrow, his facial
heat intensifying. His tone is cautious and suddenly
angry, perhaps indicating regret for speaking the word.*

"It is a word I have not heard before," Thrawn said.
"Ensign Vanto?"

"I don't know it, either," Vanto said. *His tone is cautious, but interested.* "Some slang thing, I'd guess. Probably means 'idiot.'"

*Angel takes a step toward Vanto. His expression is
suddenly furious. His hands form into fists.* "Listen,
pretty boy—"

"Enough," Cygni said. "Move on, Angel. We're on a
schedule."

The *Dromedar*'s crew were locked inside a large metal-
barred cage that had been built into the back third of the
pirate ship's aft-starboard cargo bay. There were ten of
them: seven humans of varying ages, sizes, and skin tones;
two Gran, each with the three eyes and goatlike snouts of
their species; and one Togruta, her cone-horn montrals
and striped head-tails making her prominent among the
prisoners. *The Togruta watches as the new prisoners approach, her hands rubbing slowly vertically along one of
the bars of their prison. She looks briefly at each of the
Imperials, then turns her attention to Angel.*

They reached the cage. Angel took a chained key

from around his neck and unfastened the deadlock securing the cage door. The lock was a mechanical style, impervious to electronic lock breaking. The key itself was an elaborate, wavy shape with multiple nubs and indentations, likely difficult or impossible to duplicate.

Three of the pirates leveled their blasters at the prisoners in the cage as Angel disengaged the lock. He swung the door open and gestured. "Go," he ordered.

Angel waited until the five Imperials were inside, then closed the door behind them and resealed the lock. "Satisfied?" he asked Cygni. Angel handed the key to one of the other pirates, who hung the chain around his own neck and pushed the key deep under his shirt.

"For now," Cygni said. "Remember: They all get dropped off as agreed. Unharmed." *He raises his eyebrows in silent challenge.* "No accidents. Remind your men."

"Don't worry," Angel growled. "You lubs—back to your stations. I want you at the Trapo in six days." *He looks again at Cygni. His eyes narrow.* "And be sure you don't bruise any of them when you drop 'em off. Come on, let's get out of here."

He left the cargo bay and headed forward, followed by his men. *Cygni gives the prisoners a final look, his lips pressed tightly together, then follows.*

"I gather you're our rescue squad?" one of the other humans in the cage asked. *Her lip is twisted, perhaps with contempt or sarcasm.*

"Something like that," Vanto said. "This is Lieutenant Thrawn; I'm Ensign Vanto. Are you Captain Fitz?"

"Yeah," the woman said. "So he snoggered you, too?"

"Who, Cygni?"

"Yeah," Fitz said. "Got aboard the *Dromedar* with a fake authorization and then managed to get the drop on everyone."

"He didn't get *everyone*," Layneo corrected. "He said you locked down the hyperdrive."

"Yeah," Fitz said again. "For all the good it did us. So he talked you into starting it up for him?"

"More or less," Vanto said.

Fitz swore. "So that's it. The ship's gone, the tibanna's gone, and we're done. They might as well kill us."

"I wouldn't give up hope quite yet," Vanto said. "Lieutenant?"

"Not yet, Ensign," Thrawn said. "Patience."

"Not yet what?" Fitz asked. "Hey, bright-eyes—I'm talking to you."

"Probably figuring out what he's going to say in his report," one of the other prisoners said. "Got to make this mess look good somehow."

"Watch your mouths," Vanto warned. "That's an officer of the Imperial Navy you're talking about."

"Yeah, I'm *real* impressed—"

"I said *watch your mouths.*" *Vanto does not raise his voice. But the effect on the prisoners is immediate. Fitz gives him a covert look and lowers her eyes. Her facial glow grows brighter.* "Sorry," she said in a low voice.

"Thank you," Vanto said. "And if you think Lieutenant Thrawn is wasting time with excuses, you're badly mistaken. Lieutenant?"

"Another moment," Thrawn said.

"Look, Lieutenant—" Fitz began.

"He said wait," Vanto said.

"For what?" *Fitz clenches her teeth, then forces them to relax.* "What are we waiting for?"

"For Cygni and the others to reboard the *Dromedar* and jump to lightspeed," Thrawn said. "I am counting out the estimated time now."

"You *want* him to get away with our ship?"

"Be quiet, Captain," Vanto said.

"But—"

"I said *quiet,*" Vanto repeated. *Again, his voice remains steady and controlled. But the purpose and confidence again quiet Fitz's protest.* "I won't ask again."

The cage fell silent. Thrawn continued to count.

And then, it was time.

"Tech Layneo, are you familiar with the control electronics for a ship of this sort?" he asked.

"Not this type specifically, sir," Layneo said. *She peers through the metal bars at the entrance to the cargo bay.* "But I looked at the engine-control layout on our way through, and it seemed pretty standard. What do you need me to do?"

"If we isolate the bridge, can we fly the ship from here?"

A murmur passes among the prisoners. "Probably," Layneo said. "Ensign Barlin?"

"I think we can do it, Lieutenant," Barlin agreed. "It'll take some quick rewiring, though. If the pirates are fast enough, they may be able to disable some of the circuits before we can override them."

"I think we can keep them occupied," Thrawn said.

"Sounds great," Captain Fitz said. "Except that the circuits are out there, and we're in here."

"I'm guessing not much longer, Captain," Vanto said. "Lieutenant, do you need us to give you room?"

"Not at all, Ensign." Thrawn removed his insignia plaque. "You asked me once what I would do with the spare plaque Commandant Deenlark gave me at the Academy."

Vanto leans closer, frowning. He studies the insignia plaque and the electronic components and micro switches partially visible from the back. His frown clears. "That's a beckon call, isn't it?"

"It is," Thrawn said.

"Wait a second," Fitz said. "Are you saying that your ship is close enough to call—? No, that doesn't make any sense."

"Our ship is long gone," Vanto said. *He smiles.* "But that's not what he's calling."

"Then what?" Fitz demanded.

Five seconds later, she received her answer.

Clone War–era holos showing buzz droid attacks on Republic starfighters were impressive enough. But such combat had taken place in the vacuum of space, with only faint sounds recorded via metal conduction. The droid now cutting and grinding its way through the cargo bay bulkhead toward them was far louder than Thrawn had expected. "Move back!" he called over the noise as the edges of the blades, the points of the drill, and the brilliant blade of the plasma torch appeared through the bulkhead metal. Once the droid made it through, the only thing between it and the beckon call would be the cage itself. The timing would be critical to allow it to cut through the bars but not continue toward the remote and the one who held it.

The droid emerged through the bulkhead, throwing off a few final shards of metal. It continued its interrupted vector across the bay, closing into its sphere shape as it flew. It struck the cage and popped open again, its hook appendages gripping one bar as the circular saw and torch attacked two of the others. A meter-long section of one of the bars, sliced through, clattered to the deck, and the blade moved on to the next bar.

"This is going to take too long," Vanto warned.

Thrawn had already estimated the droid's progress. Vanto was correct. "Agreed," Thrawn said. He took two steps to his right, moving the beckon call to the far side of the cage door. The droid shifted toward him. Thrawn repositioned the beckon call, bringing the droid directly onto the door. One final adjustment, and the droid's saw began eating into the lock mechanism.

Thrawn looked at the entrance to the bay. Within a few more seconds, the pirates in this section of the ship would surely come to investigate.

He looked back at the cage door, again gauging the droid's progress. The timing would be close.

"Look out!" one of the prisoners shouted.

Three pirates appeared abruptly through the hatchway. *Their pace falters, their eyes widening and their mouths dropping open as they see the buzz droid eating through the cage.* A second later they recovered from their surprise and reached for their blasters, their hands fumbling slightly with the last remnants of their shock. *Their expressions change from surprise to anger.*

Thrawn reached through the bars of the cage and flipped the beckon call over their heads to land on the engine room deck behind them. Instantly the buzz droid closed down its cutting instruments, unhooked itself from the cage, and shot across the bay toward the pirates.

The pirates' eyes again widen. Their blasters had been lining up on the prisoners. Now they turned the weapons instead toward the approaching droid and fired.

Even with a doonium inner shell, the buzz droid's inner mechanism was vulnerable to blasterfire. But the outer spherical shell was much stronger. All three of the pirates' shots struck, but none made it through. The pirates fired again, all three shots missing. Two of the men hurled themselves to the deck, attempting to evade the droid's approach. The third was too slow and was struck a glancing blow that sent him spinning.

Beside Thrawn, Jakeeb stepped forward, grabbed the top bars of the cage, and slammed the soles of both feet against the door. The remaining undamaged part of the lock mechanism snapped with the impact. Jakeeb dropped back to the floor and ducked out of the cage. Barlin, Layneo, and the rest of the prisoners were right behind them.

There was a brief melee of combat. When it ended, all three pirates had been reduced to unconsciousness.

"Well done," Thrawn said. "Ensign Vanto, Tech Jakeeb, Captain Fitz: Take their blasters and guard the access to this section. Ensign Barlin and Tech Layneo: the control system."

"Yes, sir," Barlin said. She hurried toward the control boards, Layneo and three of the *Dromedar*'s crew behind her.

"We'll need more weapons if we're going to make a stand," Captain Fitz said.

"That will most likely be unnecessary," Thrawn said. "The pirates still forward of the entrance hatch will not be joining us."

"What's going to stop them?" Fitz asked.

"The internal hatch safety interlocks," Thrawn said. He pointed forward, toward the flashing red lights in the distance. "Even now, the entrance chamber and amidships section of the ship have been opened to vacuum."

"*What?*" Fitz asked. *Her muscles tense with surprise and puzzlement.* "How in the world—?"

"Relax, Captain," Vanto said. *He smiles with satisfaction and grim humor.* "Lieutenant Thrawn is always prepared. And as it happens, he also owns a *second* buzz droid."

Fitz is silent two seconds. Then a slow smile spreads across her face. "How very unfortunate for our pirates," she said. "Lieutenant Thrawn, I believe the ship is yours. What course shall we set?"

CHAPTER 9

A great tactician creates plans. A good tactician recognizes the soundness of a plan presented to him. A fair tactician must see the plan succeed before offering approval.

Those with no tactical ability at all may never understand or accept it.

Nor will such people understand or accept the tactician. To those without that ability, those who possess it are a mystery.

And when a mind is too deficient in understanding, the resulting gap is often filled with resentment.

"Let me get this straight," Captain Rossi growled, peering up at Thrawn and Eli. "You're saying you *let* yourself be captured?"

"Yes, ma'am," Thrawn said. "It seemed the simplest way to find and rescue the *Dromedar*'s crew."

"Damn stupid risk," Rossi said flatly. "Especially when you didn't even know if they were still alive."

"I thought the chances were good that they were, ma'am," Thrawn said. "Cygni is not a malicious or casual killer. If he were, he would have simply shot the three of us once Ensign Barlin unlocked the hyperdrive. Our backs were to him, and he had a clear shot."

"Which makes *two* stupid risks," Rossi said. "And not just of your own life, but also those of my crew."

"It was not a serious risk," Thrawn said. "I was watching his reflection in the tibanna cylinders. If he had prepared to shoot, I would have noted the change in his stance in time to stop him."

Rossi gave a snort. "You have an answer for everything, don't you?"

"Part of my job is to anticipate the actions of our enemies."

Rossi threw a look at Eli, as if daring him to say something. But Eli knew better. He'd seen the captain in this mood, and knew she was itching to find something she could throw back in Thrawn's face.

Only in this case, she was out of luck. Thrawn had outmaneuvered Cygni, he'd outmaneuvered the pirates, and he would outmaneuver Rossi, too.

"Sounds more like dumb luck than sound planning," the captain said, shifting her glare back to Thrawn and turning up the intensity a couple of notches. "There's no way you could have known Cygni wasn't exactly who he claimed until he pulled that blaster."

"On the contrary, ma'am, I knew he was a plant from the very beginning," Thrawn said calmly. "His clothing was covered with dust, indicating he had been in the area of the tibanna cylinders and the engine room. A member of the crew would have warned us about the supposed reactor leak as soon as he realized we weren't pirates. Yet he didn't."

Eli winced. He'd missed that one completely. "Big mistake on his part."

"More of a calculated risk," Thrawn said. "He knew there was a danger that someone would notice the lapse. But he also knew that if he drew our attention to the leak we might wonder why he had mentioned that one specific danger. That might cause us to examine the reactor compartment more closely, which he could not afford."

"Because if we had, we'd have walked in on the rest of the pirates," Eli said, nodding.

"That would still have led to our capture, as they outnumbered us significantly," Thrawn said. "But Cygni would then have lost the chance to restart the hyperdrive and take the tibanna, which was his primary objective."

"Unless he forced Barlin and Layneo to do it at blasterpoint," Eli said, a shiver running up his back. Cygni might have some moral limits, but Eli wouldn't put a bent credit on finding any such ethical standards in Angel or the rest of the pirates.

"He would not have succeeded."

"Maybe, maybe not," Rossi said. "Which brings us to *your* sense of priorities."

"Ma'am?"

"You had a decision to make, Lieutenant," Rossi said. "The *Dromedar* and its cargo, or the pirate frigate and the *Dromedar*'s crew. You chose the latter." She shook her head. "Wrong choice."

Thrawn's eyes flicked to Eli. "We saved the crew, ma'am," he said, sounding as confused as Eli had ever seen him. "And captured several pirates and their ship."

"None of which stacks up against even *one* tank of tibanna gas, let alone twenty," Rossi said bluntly. "I'm waiting for a ruling from Coruscant, but until they send one I have no choice but to suspend you from duty."

Eli caught his breath. "Ma'am, you're—"

He broke off as Rossi shifted her glare to him. "You have something to say, Ensign?"

"He does not," Thrawn said, throwing a warning look at Eli. "I presume I will be left behind on Ansion while you continue your patrol?"

"Yes," Rossi said, looking extra annoyed at the fact she hadn't gotten to deliver that bit of the message herself. "Whether you're confined to quarters will be up to Admiral Wiskovis. Dismissed."

Eli clenched his teeth. This was completely unfair. He opened his mouth to say so—

Rossi got there first. "One word out of you, Ensign," she warned, "and you'll stay here with him."

"That won't be necessary, Captain," Thrawn said. "I am certain Ensign Vanto will be of great value to you on the remainder of the patrol."

"Are you, now," Rossi said. "On second thought, I can hardly deprive my special-duty lieutenant of his aide, now, can I? Congratulations, Vanto: You've just been assigned shore leave. *Extended* shore leave."

Eli felt his stomach knot. What the *hell*?

"Barlin will fly you down to the base," Rossi said. Her eyes were still on Eli, as if she still expected some comment or protest. Again, Eli knew better. "I'll tell Wiskovis to expect you. Dismissed."

They left the office, Thrawn silent, Eli silently seething. What had *that* been all about?

Because it had been deliberate. Rossi might not realize it, but then she hadn't spent as much time with Thrawn as Eli had. To Eli the signs had been clear as day: The Chiss had deliberately maneuvered the captain into kicking Eli off the *Blood Crow* along with him.

But why? Why would he do that? Had he manipulated Rossi just for the fun or challenge of it?

Or was there something else going on behind Thrawn's glowing red eyes? Could it be that he was so afraid of losing his aide that he didn't dare let Rossi—or anyone else aboard the *Blood Crow*—see what Eli could actually do?

To be honest, Eli had only a vague idea himself what that could be. He was good with numbers and supply figures—hell, he was *extremely* good with them. But whether he could show any of that talent during the presumably brief time he would be out from under Thrawn's shadow was questionable at best.

"My apologies, Ensign Vanto," Thrawn said quietly into Eli's tangled thoughts. "I realize you wished to return to the *Blood Crow*. Under normal circumstances, I would have been pleased to allow you to show Captain Rossi and the others the depth and range of your abilities. But conditions here are not normal."

"Are conditions *ever* normal in the Imperial Navy, sir?" Eli growled. Still, he could feel curiosity stirring through his resentment. There was an intensity in Thrawn's tone that was oddly contagious. "What's particularly abnormal about this one?"

"Captain Rossi is correct: The tibanna gas is of great value, and therefore of great interest," Thrawn said. "If we are to find the *Dromedar* before the cylinders are removed, we must move quickly."

"I heard the ISB is sending an interrogator," Eli said, his stomach tightening in distaste. The Imperial Security Bureau was a necessary part of keeping order, but it sometimes seemed to go out of its way to be disliked, mistrusted, and feared. "I doubt the pirates will have many secrets left after he's done with them."

"That is indeed the ISB's reputation," Thrawn said. "But the interrogator may not arrive in time, or may not extract the necessary information quickly enough. Remember, we have only four days before Angel will notice his ship's failure to reappear and become suspicious."

"Or at least get mad." Eli frowned sideways at Thrawn as it suddenly hit him. "*You're* going to interrogate them?"

"Assuming I can persuade Admiral Wiskovis to permit me," Thrawn said. "Tell me, what do we already know?"

Eli waved a hand. "Pretty much nothing."

Thrawn remained silent. Eli clenched his teeth. "Fine," he said with a sigh. Another game that Thrawn was very good at. "We know they were six days away from the rendezvous, including a stop to drop us and the other prisoners somewhere. As you said, that leaves us four days to get wherever they were going. But we don't even know which direction to look."

"We have the captured sensor data from the pirate ship," Thrawn reminded him.

Eli shook his head. "You can't tell from the departure vector where a ship is going."

"True," Thrawn said. "But it would have been inefficient to leave in the entirely opposite direction, especially as they know they have limited time before the *Dromedar*'s disappearance becomes general knowledge. We may therefore make an initial assumption that their destination is within a cone of no more than ninety degrees centered around their departure vector."

Eli pursed his lips. And that cone covered their current location at Ansion, so at least getting to Cygni's destination in four days wasn't completely out of the question.

Wherever *there* was. On that, they still didn't have a clue.

"What else do we know?" Thrawn pressed. "What did Angel call their rendezvous?"

Eli had to search his memory. "He called it the Trapo," he said. "I presume you've already looked for a planet by that name?"

"Yes," Thrawn said. "There is no planet or major city listed in the registry. But note that he called it *the* Trapo, not simply Trapo. That may imply a colloquial or slang term."

"A term for what?"

"I do not yet know," Thrawn said. "But I believe that with the right questions we may learn that. What else do we know?"

Eli shrugged. "We have the faces of our prisoners. But even if they haven't altered or deleted their data files—and a lot of criminals do exactly that—it would take days or weeks to sort through all the planetary records and figure out who they are."

"We may also have the pirates' own name for themselves," Thrawn pointed out. "Do you remember? I asked you about it at the time."

"You mean Culoss?" Eli asked, frowning. "I thought that was just some slang word."

"I believe it is more than that," Thrawn said. "Angel reacted too strongly to my interest in the word for it to have been innocent or harmless."

"I didn't notice any reaction."

"It was somewhat subtle."

"I'll take your word for it," Eli said, starting to feel some cautious excitement. A Mid Rim base like Ansion might not have complete files on the Empire's citizens, but it should have a list of the major criminal organizations within its jurisdiction. "Have you looked them up?"

"I have," Thrawn said. "There is nothing listed under that name."

"Oh," Eli said, feeling his excitement fade.

"But there are several possible connections I may be able to exploit," Thrawn continued. "We shall see once I am able to speak with them."

"So what do you want me to do?" Eli asked. "I assume you maneuvered Rossi into leaving me here for a reason."

"Two reasons," Thrawn said. "I need you to monitor my interrogation. There may be a point where you will be uniquely useful."

"All right," Eli said, wondering what Thrawn could possibly mean by that. *Uniquely useful* wasn't a term anyone had ever applied to him. "And the second reason?"

Thrawn was silent a moment. "For what I am planning, I may need a witness," he said quietly. "You, Ensign Vanto, will be that witness."

The three pirates are expressionless as they walk into their side of the interrogation room in single file. Each looks around the room as he enters, noting the gray metal walls, ceiling, and floor. Each also quickly spots the interrogation desk beyond the transparent barrier that bisects the room.

Thrawn waited until they were seated. Then he touched the intercom control set into his desk. On both sides of the barrier, indicator lights blinked on. "Good evening," he said, speaking toward the microphone. "I am Lieutenant Thrawn."

None of the three speak in response. But their facial heat increases. The muscles in their cheeks and throats and around their eyes shift between sullenness and hostility. The larger body muscles beneath their prison clothing twitch and tighten in distinct patterns.

"You are no doubt wondering why you are here," Thrawn continued. "I wish to offer you a deal."

Their facial glows briefly intensify, then fade to their previous levels. "You don't believe me, of course," Thrawn said. "But it is true. We have a saying: *Grasp the useful, let the useless fly.* You three are the useless."

"And you can go plop yourself straight back to Pantora," the tallest of the three retorted. *There is a distinctive twang to his voice, a twang that had become apparent during the passage to Ansion. It is not identical to Vanto's accent but with strong similarities, likely indicating similar Wild Space roots.* "If you came here to insult us, you're wasting your time."

"I intend no insults," Thrawn said. "On the contrary, I am impressed that successors of the pirate queen Q'anah still operate throughout the galaxy."

The pirates' facial heat increases dramatically. Their eyes widen; their throat muscles stiffen. They immediately try to hide their reactions, but they are only partially successful and it is already too late.

"You surely did not believe that you were unnoticed," Thrawn continued. "Indeed, Grand Moff Tarkin has long noted that remnants of Q'anah's Marauders had escaped their captain's fate. I have been in contact with Tarkin, and he has expressed a desire to come to Ansion and deal personally with this last trace of his old enemy."

"We have no idea what you're talking about," the pirate spokesman said.

"A brave but useless bluff," Thrawn said. "However, as I stated, I would prefer to trade you for your leader. Grand Moff Tarkin might not agree. But I am here, and he is not. The true irony is that your leader Angel holds much the same philosophy as I do."

"What do you mean?"

"You surely noted which of your colleagues were selected to travel with him to Cygni's rendezvous," Thrawn said. "More important, you surely noted which of you were *not* chosen. You and the remainder, who were left to die."

One of the pirates looks at their spokesman, his expression tense. The spokesman ignores him, but his own facial glow intensifies.

"From both short-term and long-term perspectives it was a reasonable decision," Thrawn continued. "In the short term, Angel loses several experienced crew, but your capture and interrogation gain him additional time to remove the tibanna cylinders from the *Dromedar*. In the long term, he pares away those he deems no longer useful to his goals."

"And the *Marauder*?" the spokesman shot back. "Sorry, Blueface, but Angel's not stupid enough to dump a perfectly good frigate for nothing."

"As I said: long-term perspective," Thrawn replied. Now they had the pirate ship's name. "Cygni has demonstrated the efficiency of his more subtle approach to ship capture. He has no doubt persuaded Angel that the *Dromedar* will serve him better than the *Marauder*. Certainly a freighter permits a more stealthy approach to its victim than an armed frigate."

On the desk, his datapad lit up with a message: *Frigate* Marauder *linked to five hijackings under ID code* Elegin's Hope. "Especially one that has come under as much scrutiny as *Elegin's Hope*," he added.

"You're talking parth spit." *The pirate spokesman's voice is low and contemptuous.*

"I applaud your tenacity," Thrawn said. "But surely

you can see it is of no value. I already know too much for you to save yourselves, and once Tarkin arrives we will know everything. Unless you choose to accept my offer, you are lost."

The three pirates look urgently at one another. "Let's hear the deal," the spokesman said.

"I will give you and your fellow prisoners a civilian transport," Thrawn said. "It is partially derelict, but it should safely convey you from this sector before requiring repairs. In return, you will identify the system where Cygni and Angel have taken the *Dromedar* to remove the tibanna."

"What guarantee do we have that you won't take the information and turn us over to Tarkin anyway?"

"I offer my word," Thrawn said. "I also offer simple logic. You three are too young to have been any of Q'anah's original pirates. Tarkin's lingering vengeance will not therefore be directed specifically toward you. More important, I know Tarkin. He will take extra pleasure in the fact that Angel will know you were freed as a reward for betraying him."

"You can't know Tarkin very well if you think he *ever* shows mercy. To *anyone.*"

"Precisely," Thrawn said. "His reputation does not permit such actions. That is why I will release you on my own initiative. He will thus be able to take full pleasure in delivering the news to Angel without the need to make the decision himself."

He paused. The pirates did not speak.

"That is my offer," Thrawn said. "I will wait while you discuss it among yourselves."

He touched the intercom switch again, and the indicator lights went out.

The pirates weren't fooled. They had probably been interrogated in such places before, and knew that the intercom remained live despite the evidence of the indicators.

Thrawn had played all his cards. But the pirates had

a card of their own to play. Leaning close, they began speaking softly together.

In a language they would have learned growing up in Wild Space. A language that was used only there and in the Unknown Regions. A language that had never been programmed into Republic or Imperial translators or protocol droids. A language they could reasonably expect no Imperial had ever even heard of.

Sy Bisti.

"What do you think?" the spokesman asked the others. "You think we can trust him?"

"He's an Imperial," the second scoffed. "Of course not."

"Who cares?" the third retorted. "You heard him. *Tarkin's* coming."

The spokesman snorts. "You listen too much to Angel's ghost stories. Even Tarkin can't be *that* bad."

"No? Then how come Angel keeps telling the stories? I tell you, Tarkin's pure evil."

"Speaking of evil," the second man said, "what do you think Angel's going to do if he finds out we sold him to Blueface?"

"Good point," the spokesman said. "But maybe we can have this both ways. Let's take the offer, spin Blueface some froth, then hightail it to the Trapo and warn Angel. If we're fast enough, we should be able to get there before Tarkin or even Blueface can chase us down."

"Unless they've already cracked the static-lock," the third man warned. "Then we'd get there just in time for our ship to fall apart and leave us stuck until Tarkin catches up with us."

"You think they're going to find an ub-dub squalsh who can do slice-work like that?" the spokesman countered, his voice heavy with contempt. "Not a chance. Angel's going to have to bring in someone from outside."

"Maybe Cygni already did."

"Cygni was *supposed* to get the static-lock off before

we ever came aboard," the spokesman said. "Don't worry, we've got plenty of time to get there."

"Then let's take the offer," the second man said. "Give him—I don't know; give him *something*—and get the hell out of here."

"Before Tarkin gets here?" the spokesman suggested.

"Go ahead and laugh," the third man growled. "I'm not."

"Fine." The spokesman looked up at Thrawn and lifted his hand. "Hey," he called in Basic. "You—Imperial."

Thrawn tapped the intercom switch. "Have you made a decision?"

"We'll take your offer," the spokesman said. "Angel and Cygni went to Cartherston on a planet named Keitum. You need coordinates?"

"Thank you, we can find it," Thrawn assured him. "Anything else?"

"Just that you'd better hurry if you're going to catch them," the spokesman warned. "They won't be there any longer than they have to."

"I agree," Thrawn said. "Thank you for your cooperation. The guards waiting outside will escort you to your new transport."

"And the rest of the crew?" the spokesman asked.

"Your companions are already on their way," Thrawn said. "One more thing. You have been given a second chance. I suggest you use it to remake your lives for the better."

"No need to preach, brother," the spokesman said as they rose from their chairs. "Trust me—you'll never hear from us again."

They filed out. Thrawn watched them leave, and as the door closed behind them he stood and faced the door exiting his side of the room. It slid open to reveal Vanto and Admiral Wiskovis. "Admiral."

"Lieutenant," Wiskovis nodded in return. "That was about as impressive a performance as I've ever seen."

"Thank you, sir," Thrawn said. "Do we have it?"

"We do," Vanto said with satisfaction. "Uba, in Barsa sector. It's a nice quiet place to park a freighter for a while, it's the right distance from where they nabbed the *Dromedar*, and the insulting slang term for it is *ub-dub*. *Squalsh* is also the local slang term for the inhabitants, who are not generally considered technological geniuses." He smiled tightly. "*And* there are a bunch of major merchant centers on the northern continent, which local slang refers to as trading posts. Or, for short, trapos."

"We have it, all right," Wiskovis agreed. "Not that I have the slightest idea *why* we have it. How did you know this group used to work with Q'anah?"

"I did not know for certain," Thrawn said. "It was only a guess, based on their name."

"What name?" Vanto asked. *He frowns in confusion.* "Angel?"

"*Culoss,*" Thrawn said. "The name Angel gave their group. I heard that as *Q-less*, or a group without a Q. After we arrived, while we were waiting for Captain Rossi to return, I did a search of known criminal groups. There were a number that included a *Q* reference, but Q'anah's Marauders seemed the most likely to have the resources, the history, and the contacts to deal with stolen tibanna gas."

"Seems like kind of a long shot."

"It was," Thrawn agreed. "But Q'anah used to sign her thefts with a coded reference to her name. It seemed reasonable that the remnant of her gang would also enjoy leaving such clues."

"Still a long shot." *Wiskovis shakes his head.* "What if you'd been wrong?"

"There would have been no loss," Thrawn said. "The ISB interrogator would have arrived, and the questioning would have proceeded on schedule. All would have been as if I had not made an attempt."

"Except you wouldn't have left yourself wide open to

a court-martial," Wiskovis said. *His voice is grim.* "I should at least release the transport myself."

"I cannot allow you to do that," Thrawn said.

"Excuse me?" *Wiskovis draws himself up stiffly. His expression hardens, his throat muscles tightening. Vanto's expression holds sudden discomfort.* "*You* can't let *me* do that?"

"I think what Lieutenant Thrawn meant, sir, is that he strongly urges you to remain as far outside the situation as possible," Vanto put in quickly. "I believe his goal is to bring any blowback on himself, leaving everyone else out of it."

"Very noble," Wiskovis said. *His expression is still stiff and angry.* "And if I choose to do otherwise? This is *my* base, Lieutenant. What happens here is ultimately my responsibility."

"True," Thrawn acknowledged. "But there is still much that can go wrong, and the balance of success and failure is still undetermined. I would not wish you to bear any blame for my plan and actions."

"Or accept any acclaim for its success?"

Vanto winces. "I don't think that's what Lieutenant Thrawn meant, sir," he said.

"Well, then, maybe I should hear that from the lieutenant himself," Wiskovis said.

"If this succeeds, I would of course freely acknowledge your support," Thrawn said. "But if it fails, be advised that when I am brought before court-martial, Ensign Vanto will testify that I acted alone."

"*Excuse* me?" Wiskovis said again. *His eyes widen as he looks at Vanto. His facial heat increases, and the muscles in his cheeks tighten.* "Did he just say you were prepared to commit perjury, Ensign?"

"Yes, sir, he did," Vanto said. *The tension in his voice increases, his expression showing extreme discomfort.* "As I said, his goal is to protect you and your career from whatever comes of this."

For three seconds, Wiskovis remains silent. There is

no easing of his tension and anger. "This discussion is not over," he said at last. "But right now we have work to do. When do you want me to send a force to Uba?"

"You should wait until the released prisoners have made the jump to lightspeed," Thrawn said. "We do not want them noting the preparations and becoming suspicious. You should also contact the ISB agent and alert him to reroute his ship to Uba."

"And then?"

"Lieutenant Thrawn only promised to let them go," Vanto said. *His tension also has not eased.* "He never said we wouldn't recapture them if they went to Uba."

"Fine," Wiskovis said. "Anything else?"

"I would also suggest you send a force to the other site they mentioned, the city Cartherston on Keitum."

"I thought they just said that to throw us off track."

"That was certainly its primary purpose," Thrawn said. "But the name came too quickly and too easily. We may find that Keitum was where the *Dromedar*'s crew was to be released."

"And Cygni said his people would be watching," Vanto said.

"Yes," Thrawn said. "It may be possible to learn who exactly his people are."

"*If* we can catch them." Wiskovis started to turn back to the doorway, then paused. "You didn't *really* contact Grand Moff Tarkin, did you?"

"No," Thrawn said. "I have never met the man."

"Probably a good thing," Wiskovis said. "And if this is the way you talk to superiors, Lieutenant, you'd better hope you never do. Come on—we have some pirates to capture."

CHAPTER 10

One whose path has taken a new turn is often initially disoriented. But as time passes, and the path continues steadily in its new direction, there is a tendency to believe that it will remain so forever, with no further turns.

Nothing is further from the truth. A path once bent is always susceptible to new changes.

Particularly when the original change came from manipulation by an outside force.

"So," Juahir Madras said, taking a careful sip of the caf Arihnda had poured for her. "Are you going to Core Square for the weekend? Or are you going to be a stickley and just hang out in Bash?"

"Probably be a stickley," Arihnda said regretfully, sniffing at her own mug. Juahir liked her caf much hotter than Arihnda did, so that was how she always prepared it when her friend dropped into the office. Easier to let hers cool than watch Juahir trying not to complain about the tepidness of her own drink. "Core Square is awfully expensive."

"That it is," Juahir agreed soberly. "I thought you used to sleep in your airspeeder when you went there."

"That was before Wapsbur got caught doing spice in

a public parking area," Arihnda reminded her. "After that, Renking banned us from sleeping or living in any of his vehicles."

"I didn't realize it was a complete ban," Juahir said. "I thought he just wanted his people not to get caught doing anything illegal or embarrassing."

Arihnda shrugged. "A complete ban is always easier."

"And more brainless," Juahir said. "And you can't stay in his main office?"

"The office sleeps ten if you push it," Arihnda said. "I'm currently number eighteen on the waiting list. So, no."

"Ah," Juahir said again. "Well, Ascension Week's kind of a big deal."

Arihnda nodded, sniffing again at her caf. A big deal for the average Coruscant resident, but even more of a big deal for the political elite. Grand events like this were the perfect screen for the high and powerful to mingle with one another, and Ascension Week was the ultimate in such things. The weeklong festivities that climaxed in Empire Day drew swarms of people to the center of Imperial society as politicians made quiet contacts and deals without the obviousness of going to one another's offices or the less obvious but theoretically traceable route of comm calls.

A million people, and a million possibilities, and Arihnda had worked very hard to take full advantage of both. She'd started small, making conversation with other senatorial aides and assistants, but over the last couple of festivals she'd also made contact with a low-level journalist and the office manager from one of the Mid Rim moffs. This year, she'd hoped to leverage both of those one step up to their respective bosses.

Now, with Renking's new ban on what his staff had jokingly referred to as portable housing, it looked like that wasn't going to happen.

And she couldn't help but wonder how much of the

ban had been Wapsbur's indiscretion and how much was Renking finally noticing Arihnda's own political machinations and taking steps to block them. Though to be honest, she had to admit that was highly unlikely.

But then, so much on Coruscant tended toward the unlikely.

Her work at Renking's citizen assistance office in Bartanish Four—known universally to its inhabitants as Bash Four—had started off a little rocky. The mostly working-class population was very much in the same mold as the miners of Lothal, but even with such commonplace people her Outer Rim accent and lack of Coruscant breeding had opened her up to both amusement and contempt. But Arihnda had kept at it, and slowly she'd gained their acceptance and trust.

And most unlikely of all, along the way she'd even made a genuine friend.

"So I guess we're going to have to do something about that," Juahir said. She took another sip, then set down her mug. "Okay, I concede. It *is* possible to make this stuff too hot."

"Told you," Arihnda said, smiling. She'd been in Bash Four over a year, and was just starting to win over the populace, when Juahir had come in asking for help finding an apartment. Arihnda had located one in her own building, and later that week had helped carry in her meager collection of belongings. Juahir had thanked her with dinner at an incredible little blink-and-miss-it restaurant Arihnda hadn't even known existed, and from then on they'd been inseparable. "Not worth stressing about. There *will* be celebrations here, too, you know."

Juahir burbled a rude sound through her lips. "Right— Bash Four's Empire Day festivities. Ten minutes' worth of fireworks—two minutes of which are duds from last year—and three minutes of all the airspeeders honking their horns. Listen to Palpatine's pre-recorded speech, two more minutes of honking, and everyone goes home. Big whoop." She shook her head. "It's too bad you don't have a friend who has a friend who has an apartment within view of the Imperial Palace."

Arihnda gave a little snort. "If you mean Senator Renking—"

"Oh, wait," Juahir interrupted, brightening. "That's right—you *do*." She pointed a finger at herself. "*Me.*"

"What in the world are you talking about?" Arihnda asked, frowning.

"I'm talking about Core Square," Juahir said, clearly enjoying herself immensely. "I know a guy who just snagged a place in Sestra Towers."

"Sestra *Towers*?" Arihnda gasped. Sestra was a luxury apartment complex close enough to the center of Federal District that it was visible from Renking's main office. "You're joking."

"Nope," Juahir assured her. "It'll be a little cozy, but we can fit you in."

"You're serious," Arihnda said, almost not daring to believe it. "You sure your friend won't mind?"

"Already cleared it with him," Juahir said. "There's one catch, though." She leveled a finger at Arihnda. "We'll be responsible for transportation and lodging. *You'll* be responsible for getting us into at least one exclusive party or reception. Deal?"

"Deal," Arihnda said, smiling back. "Not a problem—I can get up to two other guests in on my senator's aide pass."

"No, no, no," Juahir chided. "You *never* tell the crowd how the trick is done. So can you sneak out a little early?"

"Sure." Arihnda checked her chrono. "As boss of this office, I'm giving myself the rest of the day off."

"I wish *I* had friends in high places."

"You do. Sestra Towers."

"And don't you forget it," Juahir said. "How long will it take you to pack a bag?"

"Five minutes," Arihnda promised, shutting down her computer and keying for messages to forward to her comm. "Come on—I'll drive us over, you can get your bag while I pack, and we'll meet back at my airspeeder."

"I said I'd provide transportation," Juahir reminded her.

"I know," Arihnda said. "I've also seen your airspeeder. We're taking mine."

The Federal District, known informally as the Core of Coruscant—or, even more informally, Core Square—was the undisputed center of the galaxy, both politically and socially. The Senate was there, as were the Imperial Palace, all the major ministries, and the combined headquarters of the army and the Imperial Navy.

The elite of the Empire lived and worked here. So did those who had ambitions of joining that noble society, as well as those who carried out the elite's will.

"So what's *your* excuse?" Arihnda asked Driller MarDapp as they rode the crowded airbus toward the Alisandre Hotel.

"She means how did you score an apartment here," Juahir translated. "As in, whose pet tooka did you have to feed, walk, and polish?"

"Oh, is *that* what she meant?" Driller asked, grinning. He grinned a lot, Arihnda had noticed in the brief time she'd known him. Fortunately, he had the teeth and dimples for it. "Sorry to disappoint you, but no tooka was involved. I happen to have an uncle who's a senior staff officer at Royal Imperial and who happens to be offplanet for three months. Being as I'm his favorite nephew—"

"Translation: He's the nephew who got in his bid before any of the other relatives did," Juahir interjected.

"—favorite nephew of all those who asked him," Driller amended drily, "I got to move in."

"So what are you doing?" Arihnda asked. "Workwise, I mean?"

"Nothing fancy, I'm afraid. I'm with an advocacy

group that petitions senators and ministers on behalf of ordinary citizens."

"Ah," Arihnda said, mentally crossing him off her checklist. Advocacy groups sometimes had access to the powerful, but they had no power of their own. Nothing there for her to cultivate.

"Sounds a lot like what Arihnda does in Bash Four," Juahir said.

"Pretty similar, yes," Driller said. "Except that you're handling local people and problems, while we speak on behalf of people from other planets. Sometimes on behalf of the whole planet, in fact."

"I thought that was what senators were supposed to do," Arihnda said.

"Emphasis on the *supposed to* part," Driller said. "I'm sorry—that sounded nastier than I meant it to. You know better than anyone how easy it is for someone to fall through the cracks. That's our job: filling in cracks."

"Sounds so exciting when you put it that way," Juahir said. "So any idea which of these parties the Emperor is supposed to be hosting?"

"I'm not sure he's going to host any of them," Arihnda said. "That rumor goes around every year." She squinted toward the hotel they were rapidly approaching. "I don't see any Imperial Guards anywhere, so if it's happening it's not happening here."

"That's okay," Juahir said. "We're going to hit a lot more parties before the week's up, right?"

"As many as you can handle," Arihnda promised. "Or at least until we get thrown out."

"Hey, that can be fun, too."

The Alisandre's grand ballroom was supposed to be one of the biggest in Core Square, with a cluster of smaller rooms surrounding it. The arrangement made it ideal for both large gatherings and the smaller, more intimate get-togethers that inevitably spun off from big crowds. The security men at the door gave Arihnda's ID a good, hard look—and gave Juahir and Driller even harder ones—but passed all three of them without comment.

"Wow," Juahir breathed, looking around as Arihnda led the way through the meandering flow of people. "I feel *very* underdressed."

"You're the guests of a lowly senator's aide," Arihnda reminded her. "You're not expected to have a thousand-credit gown."

"I'm sure there are plenty of us around," Driller added. "You just can't see them for the glare of the gems from everyone else. So who exactly is here, Arihnda?"

"It's a pretty fair mix," Arihnda said, studying the little conversational knots that had formed amid the eddies and flows of partygoers. "Over there are the governors of a couple of the minor Core worlds. There's a Mid Rim moff over there, and I see at least six or seven senators."

"And you know all of them?" Driller asked. "Can you introduce me?"

"I don't really *know* them, but I've met a lot of them," Arihnda said. Though she'd certainly been trying to know most of them better. "Senator Renking sometimes sends me out to deliver confidential data cards when I'm here in Core Square."

"So *that's* where you disappear to all the time," Juahir commented.

"It's hardly *all the time*," Arihnda corrected her severely. "Maybe four days a month if I'm lucky."

"Yeah, but for every one of those days I get twenty calls wondering why you're not in your office fixing someone's problem."

"What are they calling *you* for?" Arihnda asked, frowning. This was the first she'd heard about this. "You don't work there."

"No, but a surprising number of people in our building know we're friends," Juahir said drily. "They figure that I'm responsible for you, or some such."

"Ridiculous," Arihnda said. "You're barely responsible for yourself."

"If you two could stop bickering for just a minute," Driller cut in, "would one of you care to explain *that*?"

Arihnda followed his pointing finger. Across the room was another conversation knot, this one consisting of just four people.

But they were definitely an eye-catching group. One of them was a white-haired man with a matching mustache wearing the white tunic and insignia plaque of an ISB colonel. The second man had his back toward Arihnda, but his formal outfit matched one owned by Senator Renking. The third man was young, and wore the uniform and plaque of a navy ensign. And the fourth man—

Wasn't a man at all. He was human-shaped and had human features, but his skin was blue, his hair was blue-black, and his eyes were glowing red.

And *his* insignia plaque identified him as a senior lieutenant.

"I've never seen anything like that before," Driller continued. "What is he, some kind of Pantoran with an eye condition?"

"Now, that's just rude," Juahir chided him. But she was staring at the strange being just as hard as he was. "Arihnda? Any ideas?"

"Sure," Arihnda said. "Let's go over and ask."

Juahir's gasp was audible even over the hum of conversation filling the ballroom. "You're kidding."

"Not at all," Arihnda said. "Actually, I think that's Senator Renking, so I can just pretend I was checking in to see if he needed anything."

"I thought you were off duty."

"Senator's aides are never off duty," Arihnda said. "Come on."

And if it wasn't Renking, she decided, his outfit tagged him as someone of similar status. Easy enough to flip a humorous case of mistaken identity into a new contact among the elite.

The contingency plan proved unnecessary. The man was, in fact, Senator Renking.

The first thing Arihnda had learned as his aide was to never interrupt a conversation. The second thing she'd learned was how to edge herself into those conversations. In this case, the best approach was to position herself at a discreet distance, outside the group but inside the edge of the senator's peripheral vision. Eventually, she knew, he would notice her.

In this instance, the wait was barely ten seconds. "Ah—Arihnda," Renking said, interrupting himself and holding out an inviting hand. "I was hoping to run into you—your comm said you were here, but I didn't want to interrupt you with a call unless I had to."

"Not a problem, Senator," Arihnda said. "What can I do for you?"

"I need a favor." Renking half turned to the other three people. "But I'm forgetting my manners. Colonel, Lieutenant, Ensign: This is Arihnda Pryce, one of my aides. Ms. Pryce: This is Colonel Wullf Yularen of the Imperial Security Bureau; Senior Lieutenant Thrawn, a rising star in the navy; and Ensign Eli Vanto, the lieutenant's aide and translator."

"Honored, noble sirs," Arihnda said, bowing respectfully.

"Colonel Yularen was just telling me about an intriguing operation the lieutenant and ensign were recently involved with out in the Mid Rim," Renking continued.

"Really," Arihnda said, putting some fascination—most of it genuine—into her voice. The elite loved to hear themselves talk, but most of the time their stories were worth listening to.

"Really," Yularen confirmed, his eyes flicking over her shoulder to Juahir and Driller. Probably making sure they were out of eavesdropping range. "The lieutenant more or less single-handedly captured a pirate ship and most of its crew, and saved a valuable shipment of tibanna gas on top of it."

"It was hardly single-handed, Colonel," the non-human said. His voice was calm and respectful, with a quiet underpinning of confidence and intelligence.

"You had only four crew with you, including Ensign Vanto," Yularen said. "I call that close enough to single-handed. What do *you* say, Ensign? Was I overstating the case?"

"Not at all, sir," Ensign Vanto said politely. He looked and sounded a little pained, as if he had no idea what he was doing here and just wanted to go home.

Which, from his distinctive accent, Arihnda guessed to be somewhere in the Outer Rim or even Wild Space, which likely made his forced presence here among the elite even more awkward and uncomfortable. Arihnda herself had worked very hard to get rid of her own Outer Rim accent, but she still felt self-conscious about her roots.

"Ensign Vanto is perhaps too modest about his and the others' contributions," Thrawn said. "But what matters is the result."

"Well, however it untangles, congratulations to you both," Renking said. "I presume you're here on Coruscant for commendation?" He raised his eyebrows. "Or promotions?"

"Not exactly," Yularen said. "There's some additional . . . datawork, shall we say, that needs to be looked at."

"How serious are we talking?" Renking asked, eyeing Thrawn.

"Serious enough," Yularen said. "But I'm not particularly worried. I was an admiral during the Clone Wars, and I still have friends in high places."

"And are no doubt making a few more tonight," Arihnda murmured.

Yularen looked at her with fresh interest. "Very perceptive, Ms. Pryce," he complimented her. "Yes, that's exactly why I'm putting the lieutenant through the Coruscant social grinder. I think he did a remarkable job, and I want to make sure as much of the Senate knows about it as possible."

"Well, I personally will be sure to look into the details when I get a chance," Renking said. "But right now, as I said, I need Ms. Pryce to run an errand for me. Arihnda, I need to leave, but I also need to get a data card to Moff Ghadi. You know who he is, right?"

"Yes, sir, of course," Arihnda said. Actually, she'd made quite a few private deliveries to Ghadi over the past two years. Ghadi was always too busy to talk to her during those visits, but she'd always made a point of engaging his reception and staff people in friendly conversation. This might finally be her chance to make contact with the moff himself.

"Good," Renking said. "He'll need to load it into a secure datapad, download the files, then return the card to you."

"Understood," Arihnda said. A slightly unusual procedure, but still one she'd occasionally done before. "Do you want me to take it to your office when he's finished?"

"Please," Renking said. "Just put it in the drop slot." He nodded to Yularen and the others. "And now, I really must take my leave. Colonel, good luck. Lieutenant, and Ensign, even better luck." He turned and began weaving his way through the crowd toward the main entrance.

"If you'll excuse us, Ms. Pryce," Yularen said with a courteous bow, "I have a few more people I want to introduce Senior Lieutenant Thrawn to before we head across Core Square to the next reception."

"Of course, Colonel," Arihnda said, bowing in return. "Lieutenant; Ensign."

She turned and headed away, noting that Yularen and the other officers were heading toward a knot of other senators.

"I thought you were going to introduce us," Driller complained as he and Juahir came up beside her.

"Sorry," Arihnda apologized. "Wasn't really an opportunity. Next group."

"So who is he?" Juahir asked. "And *what* is he?"

"Mostly what he is is in trouble with the High Command," Arihnda said. "We didn't get any further than that."

"Interesting," Driller said. "High Command doesn't usually bother with junior officers. Wonder whose tooka he ran over."

"You can ask your uncle when he gets back," Arihnda said. "All I know is that when someone like Colonel Yularen says *additional datawork* with a pause between the words, he's talking about something serious."

"Or more precisely, *not* talking about it," Driller said.

"Exactly," Arihnda said. "But that's Thrawn's problem. *My* problem is that I have to go to work."

"Yeah, we saw the handoff," Juahir said. "Delivery, right?"

"Right."

"And during an Ascension Week party, too." Juahir shook her head. "Renking's a slave driver. You want us to come with you?"

"No, that's okay," Arihnda said, craning her neck. She couldn't see Ghadi, but if he was here it shouldn't take long to track him down. "I'll be back as quick as I can. Have fun, enjoy yourselves, and don't get drunk on the swirlydips."

"Swirlydips have alcohol in them?" Juahir asked, brightening.

"They do here," Arihnda said. "Stay out of trouble, okay?"

With Moff Ghadi's distinctive appearance, Arihnda spotted him within three minutes of starting her search.

"So Renking has you working tonight, does he?"

Ghadi asked, fingering the data card. His eyes were bright and intense, Arihnda noted a little uneasily. Swirlydips, or something stronger. Hopefully, he was functional enough to get this over with quickly so she could get back to working the party.

"Yes, Your Excellency," she said. "But I'm sure he wouldn't have interrupted you if it wasn't important."

"And he even sent *you*," Ghadi said, smiling crookedly. "Well, come on." He turned, sending his patterned red-and-yellow cloak swirling through the air around him as he headed for the lifts. "My secure datapad's in my suite," he added as Arihnda hurried to catch up. "It'll just take a minute, and then you can get back to enjoying yourself."

"Yes, Your Excellency," Arihnda said, glancing around as they worked their way through the crowd. She'd never even seen pictures of what the Alisandre's suites looked like. If the ballroom was anything to go by, Ghadi's suite would be well worth a quick visit.

It was.

"Get yourself a drink if you'd like," Ghadi said as he crossed the plush carpet of the main living area toward one of the side doors. "The droid can fix anything you can name."

"Thank you, Your Excellency," Arihnda said, eyeing the extensive bar off to one side, and the exquisitely restored classic LeisureMech C5 bartender droid standing motionless beside it. She was tempted; but for the moment, at least, she was officially on duty. Instead, she contented herself with looking at the carvings, the artwork, and the decorative panel inlays. This room alone was twice the size of her apartment, and probably cost her entire year's salary per night.

"I'm glad it was you he sent," Ghadi called from the other room. "I've seen you in my office several times over the past few months, usually playing courier. Renking obviously has a high opinion of you."

"Thank you, Your Excellency."

"As, of course, do I," Ghadi added. "A very high opinion indeed. Tell me, have you enjoyed working for him?"

"It's been very interesting," Arihnda said, frowning. That wasn't the kind of question she was usually asked. Was Ghadi just making conversation? Or was something else going on?

"Of course: interesting," Ghadi said. "The most diplomatic word possible, as well as the most insipid." He stepped back into the living area, Renking's data card in hand, and walked back across the carpet to her. "Here you go," he said, handing it to her. "You may take it back to him now."

"Thank you, Your Excellency," she said, frowning down at it. It looked like the one Renking had given her . . . but at the same time, something about it seemed different. The color was right, and the senator's logo on the upper corner seemed correct. Could it be the weight? She hefted it gently, trying to decide.

No, she realized suddenly—it was the logo. Senator Renking's logo was etched into the surface of all the office's data cards. But the logo on this card was embossed rather than etched.

This wasn't the same card she'd just handed Ghadi.

She looked up at the moff, to find him gazing back at her, a hard-edged half smile on his face. "Very good, Ms. Pryce," Ghadi said quietly. "Too bad, really."

"Your Excellency?" she asked carefully.

"You noticed there was something different about the data card," Ghadi said. "A shame. If you'd just taken it back to him . . . as I say, too bad."

Without warning, his hand snapped out toward her. She had just enough time to see a small tube concealed in his palm as a spray of fine powder showered her face and chest. She flinched back, reflexively squeezing her eyes shut—

"So now we have to do it the hard way," Ghadi continued. "That, Ms. Pryce, is polstine spice. Highly prized, highly expensive. And highly illegal.

"And you, my dear, have enough of it on you to guarantee that you spend the rest of your life in prison."

CHAPTER 11

Military leadership is a journey, not a destination. It is continually challenged, and must continually prove itself anew against fresh obstacles. Sometimes those obstacles are external events. Other times they are the doubts of those being led. Still other times they are a result of the leader's own failures and shortcomings.

Political power and influence are different. Once certain levels have been reached, there is no need to prove leadership or competence. A person with such power is accustomed to having every word carefully considered, and every whim treated as an order. And all who recognize that power know to bow to it.

A few have the courage or the foolishness to resist. Some succeed in standing firm against the storm. More often, they find their paths yet again turned from their hoped-for goal.

But such a turn does not always mean that the victim has lost. Or that the victor has won.

Eli had no business being here. He knew it, Yularen surely knew it, and he was pretty sure everyone else in the ballroom knew it, too.

It just made no sense. He was too backwater for these Core people. He was too junior in rank for the scattering of admirals and generals in attendance. And he was far too lower-class to be rubbing shoulders with the elite of the Empire.

The same drawbacks also applied to Thrawn, of course, plus the added one of being a nonhuman in a society that, while tolerant for the most part, wasn't exactly welcoming. But at least there was a reason why Yularen had dragged him here to show off to the men and women of power. If the High Command decided to get serious over their threatened court-martial, an interested civilian base could be useful as a counterweight against offended admirals.

Thrawn needed to be here. Eli's presence was completely unnecessary.

Though even with Thrawn he couldn't avoid the sense that the Chiss was being seen less as an unfairly charged officer and more as an unusual prize fish.

"Interesting," Yularen murmured.

Eli turned back from the shimmering color-changing gown he'd been eyeing to find the colonel gazing at his datapad. "Sir?" he asked.

"A note from HQ," Yularen said. "Lieutenant Thrawn's latest suggestion seems to have paid off."

Eli looked at Thrawn. "Is this the backtrack of Cygni you suggested a couple of days ago?"

"No," Thrawn said, eyeing Yularen closely. "As it turned out, Colonel Yularen was unable to establish enough data points with that inquiry to yield useful results. In this case, I noted that the planet Kril'dor, a known source of tibanna gas, is quite close to the Uba system. It occurred to me that if Cygni intended to simply sell the cylinders, he would have taken the *Dromedar* there, where extra tibanna could easily and invisibly be added into their own distribution channels."

"Which suggested that his intended recipients wanted the tibanna as is," Yularen said. "Which immediately pointed to either arms dealers or people who already have blasters and wanted to be able to shoot them."

Eli winced. "Criminals or insurgents."

"Yes," Thrawn confirmed. "We have been profiling many of them, looking for indicators and markers."

"Really," Eli said, frowning. He hadn't heard anything about criminal profiling work. "When have you been doing all this?"

Thrawn inclined his head. "You sleep more than I do."

Eli felt his face warm. "Sorry."

"Don't apologize," Yularen said with a grunt. "And don't worry—a career with the navy will knock that out of you soon enough. The point is that if you throw Thrawn's latest filter in with all the rest, here's what pops up."

He handed the datapad to Thrawn. Eli leaned close to the Chiss and peered at the display. There was a full report there, but in the center Yularen had highlighted a single word.

Nightswan.

"We've been hearing rumors about someone calling himself Nightswan for the past year or so," Yularen continued. "At first, he seemed to be some sort of consultant, planning jobs like this for various groups."

"And now?" Thrawn asked, handing back the datapad.

"Now we're not sure," Yularen said, his eyes darting back and forth as he skimmed the report. "A couple of the analysts are suggesting he may have settled down with a single organization. I'm not sure I buy that, myself." He pursed his lips. "Well, we'll keep an eye out for him. At least now we know one of his aliases."

Which the man would probably never use again, Eli knew. No one had yet figured out how Cygni had slipped through the cordon that Admiral Wiskovis had thrown around Uba, but somehow he'd gotten away.

Maybe the interrogations of the surviving pirates would give them some clues. Eli rather doubted it.

"Anyway, this came through while you were talking

with that last group of senators, and I thought you'd like to know," Yularen said.

"I appreciate that, Colonel," Thrawn said. "Thank you."

"No thanks needed—it was your suggestion that got us there," Yularen reminded him. He started to put the datapad away, paused as something caught his eye. "Wait a moment—something new coming through. The tibanna cylinders . . ."

He trailed off. "Is there trouble, Colonel?" Thrawn asked.

"You could say that, Lieutenant." Yularen took a deep breath. "It seems that twelve of the twenty cylinders we recovered along with the *Dromedar*"—again, he offered Thrawn the datapad—"were empty."

Eli felt his mouth drop open. "*Empty? But that's impossible. They were still static-locked.*"

"Our friend Cygni apparently found a way to get the gas out anyway," Yularen growled. "Looks like he went in through the cylinders' backs."

Eli winced. The very technique that Thrawn had suggested. Terrific. "Through the hull?"

"The hull was untouched," Yularen said, shaking his head. "No, they're going to have to pull everything apart to figure out how he did it."

For a long moment the three of them just looked at one another. "You still saved the ship," Yularen said at last. "Along with almost half the tibanna and the *Dromedar*'s crew. And you caught most of the pirates."

"Considering the value the High Command places on tibanna," Thrawn said, "they may not consider that a sufficient victory." His voice was calm enough.

But the expression on his face sent a shiver up Eli's back.

Some of the myths talked about what happened when Chiss were defeated or outsmarted. None of those stories ended well.

"If they don't, they should," Yularen said flatly.

"Never mind. There's still a long way to go, and I, for one, have always considered half a loaf far superior to no loaf at all. We'll make this work." He gave Thrawn a twisted smile. "And if the navy decides to toss you out, the ISB would be more than happy to take you." He tapped his white tunic. "I daresay you'd look good in white."

"Thank you, Colonel," Thrawn said. "But my skills and aptitudes are best suited for ships and open warfare."

"Then let's make sure you stay there." Yularen looked around. "I believe that's the minister of war over there. No point aiming low when you can aim high. If we're lucky—and if he's been drinking—we might get him to drop the court-martial completely."

"Your Excellency, please," Arihnda said carefully, backing toward the door, her lungs alternately burning and icing with the bits of spice she'd accidentally inhaled. What the *hell* was going on?

Whatever it was, there was precious little she could do about it. The door was presumably locked, the windows were unbreakable, and she was on the five thousandth floor anyway.

"He's very clever, your Senator Renking," Ghadi said. His voice was cool, almost conversational. "Did he really think he could get away with this?"

Arihnda shook her head. "I'm sorry, Your Excellency, but I have no idea what you're talking about."

"I'm talking about planting false data in a senior Imperial official's computer," Ghadi said, his voice going soft and menacing. "Apparently, Renking expected me to be so taken with you that I'd just load the data card without checking it first."

Arihnda felt her eyes widen. "Wait a minute. Planting false *data*? What kind of false data?"

"So here's what you're going to do," Ghadi continued, ignoring her question. "You're going to take that data card"—he pointed languidly toward the card in her hand—"and do whatever Renking told you to do with it. Leave it on his desk, file it, hide it under the carpet; whatever he said. And you will never, *ever* tell him about the switch or about this conversation." Ghadi raised his eyebrows. "Follow my instructions, and that'll be the end of it. Deviate from them, and I'll see that you're arrested for possession. Your choice."

Arihnda's lungs were slowly starting to clear. But at the same time, the room was starting to take on a strange clarity, with colors and textures more and more sharply defined and light and shadow pulsing back and forth. "What is this stuff doing to me?" she asked. Her voice, she noticed, was throbbing in time with the light/shadow dance.

"Nothing much," Ghadi said. "It needs to be cooked to release its full potency. Of course, the fact that it's raw means you'd be identified as a dealer or courier instead of simply a user. Much harsher sentence. I need your decision."

Arihnda squeezed her eyes shut. Even through closed lids she seemed able to see the room's new vibrancy. "How do I know you'll keep your word?" she asked, opening her eyes again.

"Why wouldn't I?" Ghadi countered with a shrug. "You're a very small fish, not worth the time and effort of gutting."

"I see," Arihnda said. "What was on the data card I gave you?"

Ghadi frowned. "You ask a lot of questions, Ms. Pryce," he said thoughtfully. "Are you *trying* to make me think you're worth gutting?"

"You're asking me to do to Renking the same thing he tried to do to you," Arihnda pointed out. "I don't want to escape your bonfire just to get dropped into his."

"Do your job and he'll never know it was you,"

Ghadi said. "Besides, you don't really have a choice, do you?"

Arihnda looked at the powder Ghadi had thrown on her tunic. The bright white was fading as the dust was absorbed into the fabric, but she knew that with the right equipment it would be detectable for days. "I suppose not."

"And don't forget it." Ghadi smiled, a tight, bitter, evil smile. "Welcome to politics, Ms. Pryce.

"Welcome to the *real* Coruscant."

Arihnda managed to slip out of the ballroom without Juahir or Driller spotting her. She caught an air taxi, rode to Renking's office, and put Ghadi's data card in the slot in the desk safe as she'd been instructed. Then, calling another air taxi, she returned to Driller's borrowed apartment. The last thing she wanted to do was stay in Core Square a second longer than she had to, but she knew that running would make her look guilty.

Besides, her lungs and vision were still showing the effects of the spice, and there were probably other visual cues that would tag her to anyone who knew what to look for. It would be the height of irony if Ghadi kept his word not to turn her in only to have some random security guard do it for him.

She lay awake on the daybed for the next three hours, waiting for the symptoms to fade, wondering what was on the card. Wondering what it would do. Wondering what *she* would do.

She had no answers.

It was after two in the morning when Juahir and Driller finally returned. Arihnda brushed off Juahir's questions with a story about not feeling well, then fended off the other woman's efforts to help. Eventually, Juahir gave up, and she and Driller drifted off to their own beds.

It wasn't until dawn was starting to lighten the sky

that Arihnda finally nodded off. Her last thought as she fell asleep was to wonder when the blow would fall.

It fell very quickly.

The general comm call came at oh-nine-hundred, barely three hours after Arihnda fell asleep. She arrived at Renking's office to find most of the local staff already assembled, whispering urgently and apprehensively among themselves. Renking arrived a few minutes later, his eyes cold, his face dark and stiff.

"I have some bad news," he said without preamble. His gaze moved across the crowd as he talked, but Arihnda noted that his eyes never seemed to touch her face. "Some allegations have recently arisen of financial and corporate discrepancies coming from my office. While these allegations are categorically false, I must nonetheless address them as quickly as possible. I will therefore be returning to Lothal for a time, and will probably need to make brief visits to other worlds before I return.

"Unfortunately, until the situation has been straightened out, my funding levels will be severely restricted. I have no choice but to close several of my outlying offices and relieve those assigned there of your duties. Here are the offices affected."

He read off a list of seven offices from his datapad. It wasn't coincidence, Arihnda suspected, that he saved Bash Four for the very end.

"Thank you all for coming," he concluded. "My apologies to those of you whom I'm no longer able to employ, but I'm certain you'll find other positions soon. Enjoy the rest of your Ascension Week festivities. Ms. Pryce, if you'd stay a moment?"

Arihnda remained standing beside the wall as the others filed out. Renking busied himself with his datapad, or at least pretended to do so, until the two of them were alone.

And then, for the first time since entering the office, he looked at her.

Arihnda had expected to see anger in his eyes. She saw only ice. She expected him to shout or curse. His voice, when he finally spoke, was soft and infinitely more frightening. "I hope you're proud of yourself."

"I didn't have any choice," Arihnda said, silently cursing the shaking that had suddenly afflicted her voice. She'd promised herself that she would match him tone for tone, but an Imperial senator in full-blown anger was more intimidating than she'd expected. "He said he would have me arrested."

"And you *believed* him?" Renking demanded. "You honestly believed you were important enough to waste even the time of a single police call on?" He shook his head. "You really *are* a fool, aren't you?"

"What about *you*?" Arihnda countered. How was this *her* fault? "Whatever you were trying to do, you must not have disguised it very well. If I'd known what was going on, I would at least have been ready for him."

"Oh, right," he bit back. "A wet-eared Lothal yokel would have been ready for a moff. Yes, I'd have paid good money to watch *that* match." He held out his hand. "Your airspeeder key."

Arihnda handed it over, clamping her mouth shut against the retort that wanted to come out. "I assume you'll be taking back my apartment, too," she said instead. "I'll go over and start clearing it out."

"It's already being emptied," Renking said. "Your things will be waiting in the outer office tomorrow." His lip twisted. "We could have done great things together, Arihnda. I'm sorry I couldn't rely on you."

"I'm sorry I couldn't trust *you*, either," Arihnda said.

"Trust?" Renking snorted. "Don't be a fool. There's no trust in politics. Never has been. Never will be. Now get out. I'm sure you'll be very happy back on Lothal."

•　•　•

To Arihnda's surprise, Juahir and Driller were waiting outside the office. "Are you all right?" Juahir asked anxiously. "I got a call from the landlady that a group of Ugnaughts were in your apartment packing everything up and figured you were here."

"I just got fired," Arihnda told her. The trembling was starting to creep back into her voice. Ruthlessly, she forced it down. "The apartment disappeared when the job did."

"Ouch." Juahir peered closely at her. "Does this have anything to do with why you bailed on us last night?"

"Yes, and I don't want to talk about it." Arihnda looked around at the cityscape rising all around them, at the majestic buildings and the never-ending flow of airspeeder traffic. When she'd first arrived she'd found the view exotic and exciting. Later, it had become familiar and commonplace.

Now it was ominous. Billions of humans and aliens were crammed together out there, all jockeying for the same jobs and the same living space.

And Arihnda was now one of them.

"Okay," Juahir said briskly. "Well, you can stay with me for the moment. A little cramped, but we'll make do. Work-wise . . . well, you know what Topple's clientele is like, so you might not want to even consider it. But the server droids are always breaking down, so Walt's always hiring."

"Yes," Arihnda murmured. Renking's words, *I'm sorry I couldn't rely on you*, echoed accusingly through her mind.

Maybe that was the trick to surviving on Coruscant: never relying on anyone.

If that was what it took, Arihnda could do it.

"Or you could stay with me for the next two months if you'd rather," Driller offered. "Closer to the center of things and the fancier jobs. Though it's probably hard to get one of those."

"Probably," Arihnda said. She took a deep breath.

She could do this. "Thanks for your offers. What I need, Driller, if you're willing, is to stay with you and Juahir for the rest of Ascension Week. After that, I'll be out of your hair."

Juahir and Driller exchanged glances. "Okay," Juahir said carefully. "You sure you don't want to come back with me?"

"No," Arihnda said. "Thank you."

"Isn't there *anything* else we can do for you?" Driller pressed. "Nothing else you need?"

"Just one more thing," Arihnda said, pulling out her datapad. The datapad, at least, was hers, not Renking's. "I need the address of the nearest citizen assistance office."

"... and it is therefore the decision of this panel that Lieutenant Thrawn be cleared of all charges."

Eli took a deep breath. So that was that. The court-martial panel had taken the full details of the *Dromedar* incident into account, specifically made note of Captain Rossi's pettiness, and rendered the correct decision.

It was a solid vindication. Still, Eli found himself having mixed feelings as he and Thrawn walked together from the room. He himself had been under the edge of the cloud on this one, but as a subordinate officer his career hadn't been at risk nearly as much as Thrawn's. If Thrawn *had* been convicted and discharged from the navy, would Eli have been returned to his old supply officer career path?

And if he had, would he have been pleased or disappointed?

He scowled at the flat gray walls around them. He hadn't asked for the role that had been thrust upon him, and he definitely hadn't wanted it. As he'd long suspected, his position as Thrawn's aide was having a dampening effect on his own advancement, and there were many times over the past couple of years when he would have given anything to be free and clear of the Chiss.

But then there were the other times. The times when Thrawn made some connection or noticed some small fact that nailed a smuggler or racketeer red-handed. The times when the Chiss suggested a tactical maneuver that pulled an unexpected victory out of defeat. The times, as with Cygni and his pirates, when Thrawn was two steps ahead of the enemy at every turn.

Or at least, most of the turns. The lost tibanna still rankled him. It rankled Thrawn even more, he could tell.

So what did Eli *really* want? A calm, safe pathway that utilized his talents and skills to their maximum potential and took him to the top of his chosen field? Or a path where he nearly always felt like a fish flopping on the shore, but where he got to see true genius in action?

He'd been mulling that question ever since Royal Imperial. He still didn't have an answer.

"Your family still engages in private shipping, does it not?" Thrawn asked into his thoughts.

"Yes, sir," Eli confirmed, wincing a little. He still wasn't sure how he felt about being Thrawn's aide, but his parents had made their thoughts about his stagnating career *very* clear. It had gotten so bad that he no longer looked forward to their letters and calls.

"I assume that such work also includes a knowledge of supply and demand?"

"Shipping by itself doesn't," Eli said, "but they also do a lot of purchasing, and that definitely does. Why, is there something you need?"

Thrawn was silent another few steps. "Doonium," he said. "Cygni identified my buzz droid as a Mark One model, and clearly recognized its value. That can only be due to its doonium content."

Eli shrugged. "No surprise there. The price of doonium has gone through the roof since the navy started its latest shipbuilding surge."

"That is the tale," Thrawn agreed. "But I wonder. Do you know how many ships are being constructed, and how much doonium they require?"

"Not offhand, but I could probably find out," Eli said, frowning. "Are you thinking the navy might be stockpiling the stuff?"

"That is one possibility," Thrawn said. "The other possibility is more . . . intriguing."

"That possibility being . . . ?"

"Some other project," Thrawn said thoughtfully. "Something large, and unannounced."

"Militaries sometimes have off-the-list projects going on," Eli pointed out. "But I don't know how large it could be. I suppose the first step would be to check the Senate and finance ministry's public records."

"Unless the project has been made invisible even to them."

"That would argue something even smaller," Eli said. "Secret project or not, the money has to come from *somewhere*. Not just material costs, but engineering, worker payments, and resource transport. The bigger it is, the harder all that is to hide."

"But not impossible?"

"My parents always said that nothing was impossible," Eli said. "If you'd like, I can look into it."

"I would be most appreciative," Thrawn said. "Thank you." He gestured to a door ahead. "I was told our new orders would be waiting for us here."

"Ah," Eli said. That was fast. Apparently the High Command had known in advance what the panel's verdict would be. At least he and Thrawn wouldn't just be sitting around in limbo.

Still, the news was likely to be mixed. From what he'd read, courts-martial were the ultimate in career killers. Even if the officer was acquitted, he was usually given only ground or orbital assignments for the next few years. Given the navy's attitude toward nonhumans— and given the way Thrawn had ruffled both Admiral

Wiskovis's and Captain Rossi's feathers on his way to scoring only half a victory—he doubted it would be one of the nicer or more prestigious ground assignments, either.

And where Thrawn went, would Eli follow?

"Ensign Eli Vanto?" a voice came from behind them.

"Yes, ma'am," Eli confirmed, turning around.

The woman striding toward them was middle-aged, dressed in a quiet but expensive-looking business outfit topped by a short cloak. Her expression was cool, her skin smooth with the look of someone who rarely if ever walked beneath an open sky. "A word, if you please?" she asked.

Eli looked at Thrawn. "You may speak with her," Thrawn said. "I will get our orders and return." He sent the newcomer a brief look, then continued on toward the door he'd indicated. It slid open, and he disappeared inside.

"*You may speak with her?*" the woman echoed. "I didn't know even ensigns needed permission from their superiors to talk with people."

"That's just the way he talks," Eli said, feeling his face warming. Thrawn had long since become fluent in Basic, but his ability to phrase his comments in polite or diplomatic ways was still sometimes woefully lacking. "You are . . . ?"

"My name is Culper," the woman said. "I'm an aide to Moff Ghadi." Her eyebrows lifted slightly. "You *do* know who Moff Ghadi is, I assume?"

"Of course," Eli said. He actually *had* heard of Ghadi—the moff of the important Tangenine sector here in the Core, he vaguely remembered. Beyond that one fact, though, the details of Ghadi's life and position were somewhat fuzzy.

"Good," Culper said briskly. "His Excellency has been following this case with some interest. He concurs with the outcome, but is somewhat displeased that your role in the lieutenant's success was not more fully acknowledged."

"Not hard to explain," Eli said. "Lieutenant Thrawn was the one who identified the impostor Cygni as a plant, laid out a plan to capture him, then executed that plan with skill and efficiency."

"But hardly alone," Culper pointed out. "You and the other members of the *Blood Crow*'s crew were vital to his achieving that result."

"Which has been stated time and again," Eli reminded her. "Mostly by Lieutenant Thrawn himself. Who I believe has also recommended commendations for all of us."

"But not promotions."

"Junior officers don't get to tell senior officers how to do their job," Eli said. "I trust High Command and the Imperial Navy to do what is right and proper."

Culper smiled thinly. "Ah, yes. Right and proper. Two high-sounding but meaningless words. One doesn't get what one deserves in this universe, Ensign Vanto. One certainly shouldn't wait for what someone else considers right or proper. No, one must be alert for opportunities and take firm grasp of them." She lifted a hand, closed it emphatically into a fist.

"Is there an opportunity out there that I'm missing?"

"Indeed," Culper said. "His Excellency Moff Ghadi has many contacts and associates across the Empire. One of them, a governor in a prestigious Inner Rim system, is in need of an assistant military attaché. A single word from His Excellency, and the job is yours." Another thin smile. "And you would certainly be promoted to lieutenant along the way, with promotion to captain soon following."

"Interesting," Eli said. "Unfortunately, I'm committed to three more years of service to the navy before I could even consider such an offer."

"Not a problem," Culper assured him. "In the particular system at issue, the attaché's office is an extension of the Imperial Navy. You'd be serving out your Imperial commitment even while establishing yourself in the local hierarchy."

"Sounds even better," Eli said. "I appreciate the offer, but I'm not yet ready for a desk job."

"This would hardly be a desk job," Culper said, her lips twisting just slightly with amusement or contempt. Apparently, Eli was even less well informed about such things than he'd realized. "You'd liaison with the Imperial Navy, yes; but you'd also be an officer in the system fleet's own defense force. Before you know it, you'd have a command of your own. A patrol craft to start with, then a frigate, up to a light or even heavy cruiser."

"Sounds intriguing," Eli said.

"More than simply *intriguing,* I would hope," Culper said, her smooth forehead wrinkling. "You seem oddly hesitant, Ensign. I trust you realize that there are senior officers throughout the navy who would jump at a chance like this. For His Excellency to offer it to an officer as junior as you is unheard of."

"I don't doubt it," Eli agreed. "Which leads to the obvious question: Why me?"

Culper shrugged. "One might just as well ask why *not* you? You've proved yourself capable in an unusual situation, you've made a name for yourself—" She paused, her eyes flicking to the door through which Thrawn had just exited. "And it's not like the navy has your future in mind."

Eli looked away, a knot forming in his stomach. Culper was right on that one, anyway. Thrawn was on his way to a desk assignment of his own, with his aide likely falling meteorlike alongside him.

Or instead, Eli could take Moff Ghadi up on his offer and command his own ship.

He'd never considered that as a possibility for his future. He'd been in supply at the Academy, and the best that career track had to offer was chief supply officer on a Star Destroyer or possibly command of a major ground-based depot.

But that career track was long gone. Now he was an officer's aide . . . and if there were ever a path that led nowhere, that was it. He might end up a captain, possibly even a lieutenant commander; but he would always be standing in the shadow of a full commander, an admiral, or a grand admiral.

Or instead, he could be captain of his own ship.

It was the opportunity of a lifetime. He would be a fool to turn it down.

But could he really pull this off? *Could* he command an entire ship, even one as small as a system patrol craft? He didn't have the training or the experience. He certainly didn't have the gifts of leadership or charisma.

But still. Captain of his own ship . . .

"I trust the location is not a problem," Culper said into his hesitation. "To be perfectly honest, an Inner Rim assignment is more than generous."

Eli's thoughts froze. "What do you mean, more than generous?"

Culper's lips compressed briefly. "I mean that for a Wild Space person like yourself, the Inner Rim is an incredible move upward."

"I see," Eli said, a trickle of anger tugging at him. He'd seen plenty of superiority and disdain from the Core cadets at the Royal Imperial Academy, but he'd never thought he would hear that same prejudice from a senior government official. "Tell me, Ms. Culper: Why exactly have I been singled out for this honor?"

"Because His Excellency considers you worthy of promotion."

"So you said," Eli agreed. "What's the *real* reason?"

Culper's lips compressed again. "If you don't wish to avail yourself of this opportunity—"

"It's because of Thrawn, isn't it?" Eli cut in as he suddenly understood. "Moff Ghadi doesn't care if I succeed. What he wants is for Thrawn to fail."

"His Excellency has no interest in what happens to a lowly senior lieutenant."

Eli looked at the door ahead with a sudden flash of understanding. "Only he's not a senior lieutenant anymore, is he? He's been promoted to captain."

Culper's lip twitched. Not much, but enough to show that Eli had hit the mark. "Fine," she said, her smooth voice going dark. "Yes, he's being promoted; and yes, there are a few of us who aren't pleased by all the attention the alien is getting. His actions cost the Empire hundreds of thousands of credits' worth of lost tibanna gas."

"He saved half of it."

"Forty percent," Culper said frostily. "And that was Admiral Wiskovis's doing, not his. All your alien friend cared about was showing how clever he was."

"He also rescued the freighter crew."

"Three of whom were aliens."

Eli felt his skin prickle. "What difference does that make?"

"Do you really not understand?" Culper demanded. "The Empire's priority was to retrieve the tibanna. *That* was what was valuable. *That* was what a good Imperial officer should have focused on. Instead, he risked the lives of you and the other *Blood Crow* crew to rescue some aliens. What do you think he'll do the next time such a decision is required?"

"I see," Eli said. So there it was. He wasn't being cited for ability and groomed for a prestigious post. He was nothing more than a tool with which Ghadi and his friends hoped to topple the non-elite, nonhuman threat to their comfortable little universe. "I appreciate your honesty, Ms. Culper. Please thank His Excellency Moff Ghadi for his offer. But I'm happy right where I am."

"Then you're a fool," Culper said acidly. "He *will* go down someday. Even with you there to smooth the political path for him, he'll go down. He was lucky this time. But luck never lasts. And when he goes down, anyone too close will go down with him."

"Moff Ghadi will make sure of that?"

Culper smiled. "Good day, Ensign," she said.

She started to turn away, then paused. "Oh, and if I were you, I'd get comfortable with that title," she added. "You'll be holding it for quite some time."

She turned again, swirling her cape this time, and strode toward the exit. Eli watched her go, the emotional tangle emerging again as the disgust receded.

But while his feelings were still mixed, his course was now clear. One way or another, his career was linked to Thrawn's.

"You are disturbed." Thrawn's voice came from behind him.

"I'm fine," Eli growled. Was it too much to ask that people stop sneaking up on him? "Did you get your orders?"

"Yes," Thrawn said. "What did she want from you?"

"She was offering me a job," Eli said shortly. "What's your new assignment?"

Thrawn looked down at the datapad in his hand. "First officer aboard the *Thunder Wasp*. It is listed as an *Arquitens*-class light cruiser currently on patrol duty in the Mid Rim."

"And you've been promoted to captain?"

Thrawn inclined his head, his glowing eyes narrowing slightly. "How did you know?"

"Lucky guess," Eli said. "I assume you picked up my orders while you were at it?"

"Yes." Thrawn held out a data card. "Also the *Thunder Wasp*, as my aide-de-camp."

"With no promotion."

"No," Thrawn said. "My apologies, Ensign. I *had* recommended you for both promotion and for a combat station."

"Which I'm not really trained for," Eli pointed out. "Where I *should* be is in supply."

Thrawn was silent a moment. "This job you were offered. Was it better than the one the navy has assigned you?"

Eli looked over just in time to see Culper leave the room. Captain of his own ship . . . "No," he said. "Not really."

It took Arihnda four tries to find what she was looking for.

But it was time well spent.

The place she was now in was without a doubt the most poorly staffed citizen assistance office she'd ever seen. Only four of the twelve desks were occupied, two by humans, one each by a Rodian and a Duros. There was a light coming from the supervisor's office door, so apparently there was at least one other person here.

The lack of personnel was likely an artifact of the timing, with the Ascension Week festivities having taken their toll on the office's staff. The obvious corollary was that the ones who *were* here would be the ones who couldn't get time off, which likely meant the newest and least competent.

Of course, since ordinary citizens didn't get weeklong holidays off, either, the line was just as long as usual. Longer, really, since only a third of the staff was there to handle their problems.

Arihnda smiled to herself. Perfect.

She had plenty of time during her wait in line to evaluate the workers. She finally settled on one of the humans, a squat woman whose face and body language silently proclaimed the fact that she didn't want to be there. Arihnda deftly tweaked her position in line just enough to make sure that Grouchy's desk was the one she finally sat down at.

"Welcome to Proam Avenue Citizen Assistance," the woman said in a voice that was more mechanical than that of some droids Arihnda had worked with. "My name is Nariba. How can I help you?"

"I'm Arihnda," Arihnda said. "I recently lost my job, and I need another one. Something interesting and fun would be the best. Oh, and I also need a place to stay."

"Is *that* all?" Nariba said with a grunt, peering down at her computer. "References? Qualifications? Job history? Come on, come on—I don't have all day."

"I used to work for a senator," Arihnda said brightly. "But all I've been offered since then was a waitress job."

"And you didn't take it?" Nariba growled. "Not smart. You're not going to get anything better around here."

"But I used to work for a *senator*."

"Hey, honey, look around you," Nariba said in a voice of strained patience. "Half the people in Core Square used to work for a senator. You're lucky you didn't have to work *under* a senator, if you know what I mean." She peered a little more closely. "Or maybe you did. You're the type a lot of them would like."

"Are you suggesting my senator would act *immorally*?" Arihnda asked, a small part of her appreciating the irony of the question.

"What, you just fall off the Rimma transport?" Nariba puckered her lips in a condescending smile. "Of *course* you did. Worked on your accent, I see. Need to work a little harder."

"I will," Arihnda promised. "But about my job and an apartment . . . ?"

Nariba rolled her eyes. "Sure, why not? There are still people who believe in miracles. Give me your comm number and I'll put you on the list."

Arihnda did so. Thanking Nariba, she stood up and waved over the next person in line.

And then headed straight to the supervisor's office.

There was a buzzer by the door. Arihnda tapped it and waited a moment. She tapped it again, and again. On the fourth buzz, the door slid open.

The office was smaller than Arihnda would have guessed, not much bigger than the medium-sized desk and full-wall data card shelves filling most of the space. Behind the desk sat a harried-looking middle-aged man. "Who are you, and what do you want?" he growled.

"My name is Arihnda Pryce," Arihnda said, stepping inside and glancing at the name plaque on the desk. *Alistar Sinclar.* "You have a problem, Mr. Sinclar, and I have the solution."

Sinclar blinked. "Excuse me?"

"I just spoke with Nariba," Arihnda said. "Your employee at desk three. She's not very good at her job. She's rude and insulting; and worst of all, she isn't helpful. Between you and me, she needs to be fired."

"Does she, now?" Sinclar said. "I hardly think you're in a position to make that kind of judgment."

"No, but *you* are," Arihnda said. "That's where my solution comes in. Hire me to replace her."

Sinclar raised his eyebrows. "Your credentials?"

"I worked for the past two years in Senator Renking's assistance office in Bash Four," Arihnda said. "And I was very good at my job."

Sinclar pursed his lips. "Working for a senator is a *bit* insular—"

"I've dealt with angry landlords, angry tenants, reluctant employers, and panicky job-seekers," Arihnda continued. "Also union bosses, would-be union bosses, striking miners, strike-breaking miners, angry men and women who wanted to tear up my office, low-level criminals, high-level criminals, and politicians from the rawest hack to the most entrenched fossil."

She stopped for air. From the look on Sinclar's face, he probably hadn't heard anyone throw quite this depth of a list at him before. "Really," he said, a bit lamely.

"Really," she assured him. "But don't take my word for it." She nodded toward the main office behind her. "You have eight empty desks out there. Let me work the rest of Ascension Week for free. After that, you can decide for yourself which of us you want to keep."

Sinclar smiled. "You *are* brash, aren't you?"

"I am," Arihnda agreed. "But I've been told that it isn't brashness if you succeed."

"Interesting point." Sinclar stood up and offered his hand across the desk. "You're on, Ms. Pryce. Take desk eight. Let's see if you're as good as you think."

CHAPTER 12

No one can say where his path will take him, even for the duration of a single day. More difficult still is to see where one's path will intersect that of another warrior.

A warrior must always be alert for such meetings. Some are generated by happenstance, and those may be benign. But others are arranged with purpose. Those must never be underestimated.

Fortunately, there are always signs. Before any trap is sprung, it must be prepared and primed and armed. If one reads the signs properly, the pattern of the attack will be clear.

But one must always remember that launching a trap is easier than defeating it.

The smugglers had been escorted aboard, scowling or cursing, and sent one by one into the brig. Commander Alfren Cheno stood by the brig's outer hatch, fingering a large grist mollusk shell. "Shells," he said flatly. "They were smuggling iridium inside *shells.*"

"Yes, sir," Eli said. Cheno was an old-school type, having risen to the peak of his ability as captain of the *Thunder Wasp.* He was probably destined to end his career aboard it, or another ship just like it.

Given the captain's age and upbringing, Eli had feared that he would show either the prejudices of Moff Ghadi's patronizing mouthpiece Culper or the disdain of the *Blood Crow*'s Captain Rossi. Instead, Cheno had taken Thrawn's assignment in stride, though with a certain degree of quiet yet unmistakable misgiving. But over time the Chiss had slowly won him over with his ability to see through the clutter to the heart of whatever matter they were dealing with.

Still, the commander had never lost his ability to be dumbfounded. Which was what made moments like this so entertaining.

"They were taking the stolen iridium from the mines to an old surplus underwater transport, sir," Eli explained. "Possibly Gungan; we still haven't positively identified the vehicle. They then transported it to a group of fishing boats where they formed it into small disks and hid them inside the shells for shipment off-planet."

"The discrepancy in weight didn't give the show away?"

"There wasn't any, sir," Eli said. "The disks were small, and grist mollusk meat is unusually dense. They had the whole thing down to a science."

"Mm." Cheno puckered his lips. "Dare I ask who tumbled the scheme?"

"Do you really need to, sir?"

"I suppose not," Cheno said. "Fine. How did he do it?"

As recently as a year ago, Eli mused, when he and Thrawn had first come aboard the *Thunder Wasp,* it had hurt a little to have to explain how Thrawn had pulled off the most recent of his long string of miracles. Now Eli was so used to it that it was almost fun. Rather like being the assistant of an illusionist who knew the secrets of how the tricks worked.

Which wasn't to say that he would ever be able to pull off the tricks himself. But he was becoming surprisingly okay with that. "It was the makorr, sir," he said. "One of the local water predator species. Captain Thrawn noticed that they were unusually active near these particular boats. Something seemed to be drawing them."

"That mysterious lure being free food," Cheno said, nodding understanding. "The smugglers had to get rid of the mollusk meat to make room for the iridium, and they simply dumped it overboard." He shook his head. "It's really quite simple once you see it."

"Yes, sir," Eli said. Illusionist's assistant . . . "Most things are."

The hatch slid open, and Thrawn appeared. "Captain," Cheno greeted him. "Our guests all packed away for the night?"

"Yes, sir," Thrawn said. "They seem somewhat bewildered, though."

"Good," Cheno said. "I like bewildered prisoners. Gives them something to think about besides escape. Speaking of packing, I understand we have more antiques on their way?"

"Yes, sir," Thrawn said. "My apologies for not informing you sooner."

"No problem," Cheno said. "What is it this time? Another piece of hyperdrive ring?"

"No, sir. A piece of a buzz droid and a section of an attack weapon I believe was called a vulture droid."

Cheno grunted. "Clone Wars matériel again," he said, eyeing Thrawn closely. "Something about that era that interests you?"

"In point of fact, sir, *everything* about that era interests me," Thrawn said. "May I continue to store the items in the aft hangar bay?"

"Absolutely," Cheno said. "Mind you, if we ever get those new TIE fighters they keep promising us, we'll need to come to some other arrangement. But until then, I see no reason why the space can't be yours."

"Thank you, sir," Thrawn said. "With your permission, I will go and see about getting them properly stowed."

"Of course," Cheno said. "Carry on, Captain. Ensign." With a nod to each of them, he turned and headed toward the bridge.

"Would you walk with me, Ensign?" Thrawn invited, gesturing in the direction of the unused hangar bay.

"Certainly, sir," Eli said as they headed out. "Bewildered, you say?"

"They are angry at the manner in which they were captured."

"I'll bet they are," Eli said. "Maybe the next group will be smart enough to save up the mollusk meat and dump it in bits and pieces the whole length of the way back to port. That way they won't draw a crowd."

"Excellent," Thrawn said.

Eli frowned. "What's excellent?"

"Your growing aptitude for the art of tactics." Thrawn handed him his datapad. "What do you make of this?"

"What is it?" Eli asked as he took the device. It was hardly tactics to see the stupid moves a group of over-confident smugglers had made. As Cheno had said, everything was obvious in hindsight.

"A listing of the prices of various Clone War artifacts in various antiques shops, surplus stores, and salvage yards over the past three years."

Eli frowned. "You mean all the way back to when you started collecting them on the *Blood Crow*?"

"Yes," Thrawn said. "The oldest numbers are at the top. Study them, and tell me what you see."

Eli peered at the list. It was an impressive document, long and detailed. It wasn't just the items Thrawn had bought, either, but an entire spectrum of Clone Wars weaponry and equipment. He gazed at the list, his mind slipping automatically into the supply and shipping mode that he hadn't had much opportunity to use since graduating from the Academy. "Well, the Mark One buzz droids are through the roof," he said. "But with the price of doonium still going up, that one was inevitable."

"Indeed," Thrawn said. "Continue scrolling down the list, if you would. Search for a pattern."

Eli nodded absently, already ahead of the suggestion. Items, prices, dates . . .

And there it was. "The vulture droids," he said, tapping the datapad. "The prices have been stable until five months ago."

"When they suddenly began moving upward," Thrawn said, nodding. "What do you conclude from that?"

"Obviously, someone's buying them. Someone's buying a *lot* of them." Eli raised his eyebrows. "More doonium?"

"Not with these droids," Thrawn said. "But you remind me. Have you made any progress in your analysis of the navy's warship program?"

"Some," Eli said cautiously. In truth, they'd been so busy over the past few months that he'd only had occasional moments to devote to that project. "There are a lot of nooks and crannies in that kind of matrix sheet, so I can't say for certain. But right now, I can't find any building project that could be absorbing anywhere near the amount of doonium that's been disappearing from the markets."

"And the finances themselves?"

"Again, nothing obvious. If something's going on, it's being *very* well hidden."

"Interesting," Thrawn murmured. "I trust you will continue your investigation." He gestured toward the datapad. "In the meantime, we have these vulture droids to consider. You say they are being purchased?"

"Yes," Eli said. "And the buy-up's not just local, either. You can't get numbers rising this fast unless all the surrounding sectors are being drained, too."

"That was my assumption, as well," Thrawn agreed. "And with no other obvious value to the droids, the likely conclusion is that the buyer intends to use them."

"Not much a vulture droid can be used for except to shoot at other people," Eli pointed out. "And their tech has to be at least a couple of decades old. I was under the impression that we'd pretty much learned how to deal with them."

"It is possible we have forgotten," Thrawn pointed out. "As weaponry advances, the techniques used against obsolete ordnance may be neglected or lost."

"Possibly," Eli said. "Takes a pretty confident person to think he can beat modern turbolasers with blaster cannons, though."

Thrawn shrugged. "I could."

"Right, but you're on our side," Eli said drily. "Who else could?"

Thrawn raised his eyebrows in silent question. Eli frowned . . . "Let me guess. Nightswan?"

"The Rodian who sold me the vulture droid part had an order for more such parts under the name Nightswan," Thrawn confirmed.

"The merchant let you see his order requests?"

"He was unaware that I did so."

"Ah," Eli said, peering closely at him. Ever since Uba and the lost tibanna, Thrawn had had a subtle but strong focus—Eli refused to call it an obsession, even in the privacy of his own mind—toward Nightswan. Over the past year Thrawn had been summoned back to Coruscant four times to consult with the Emperor, and during each of those visits he'd made time to visit Colonel Yularen for a private and unofficial update on Nightswan's activities. "I don't suppose there could be a second Nightswan out there?"

"That is always possible," Thrawn said. "But consider. We know our Nightswan specializes in clever strategies. We know he has seen firsthand the effectiveness of old technology and weapons that no one expects to face. And along with the name, the request specified that payment would be in iridium."

"So you're also tagging him for the operation we just took down?" Eli shook his head. "I don't know. Nightswan is smart. These guys are idiots."

"Indeed they are," Thrawn agreed. "Which is why I asked one of them about the mollusk meat as they were being locked away. He admitted that the man who set up the scheme specifically told them to disperse the meat over their entire path. They told him that was too much trouble."

"Interesting," Eli said. "Still doesn't qualify as proof."

"True, but it bears further examination," Thrawn said. "I will inform the commander of my thoughts and speculations. Meanwhile, perhaps you could track the smuggled metals and look for a connection to vulture droid purchases."

"I'll do what I can," Eli said. "But lines like that are pretty easy to cover up."

"I trust your abilities," Thrawn said. "We must also watch for reports of trouble on the planet Umbara."

"Why Umbara?"

"The smugglers remembered that the man who instructed them mentioned that world."

"Sounds like misdirection," Eli warned. "Umbara was one of the major Separatist planets. The locals fought pretty hard, and got stomped pretty solidly. Hard to believe they'd want to go through that again."

"Agreed," Thrawn said. "But we will watch for reports from there just the same." His expression hardened. "Nightswan escaped the Empire once. I'm sure the Empire would appreciate it if we remedied that failure."

Art.

For some it was a measure of culture. For others it

was a measure of wealth. For most it was a matter of simple enjoyment.

For Thrawn, it was an invaluable tool.

The *Thunder Wasp*'s computer library had only a limited catalog of art reproductions, and only three pieces of those were from Umbara. Fortunately, Thrawn had spent the past three years building up an extensive collection of data cards that rivaled the best art archives in the Empire.

He sat in his cabin, surrounded by holograms of sculptures, flats, mobiles, kinetics, interactives, and the other art forms the Umbarans had developed and explored over the centuries. Of particular interest were the subtle changes that had taken place between works created before and after the Clone War.

The other Chiss didn't understand. They never had. He'd been asked innumerable times how he was able to build such detailed tactical knowledge from such obscure and insignificant ingredients.

The question carried its own answer. To Thrawn, nothing in a species' art was obscure or insignificant. All the threads tied together; all the brushstrokes spoke to him; all the light curves told the story of their creator.

Artists were individuals. But they were also products of their culture and history and philosophy. The weave of artist and culture was evident to the discerning eye. The fundamental pattern of a species could be sketched, then drawn, then fully fleshed out. Most important of all, the relationships among art, culture, and military doctrine could be deduced.

And what could be deduced could be countered.

Distantly, Thrawn became aware that a new image had entered the pattern of Umbaran art flowing around him. Reluctantly, he withdrew his mind from contemplation and reflection and narrowed his focus.

Ensign Vanto had entered his cabin.

"Ensign," Thrawn said. "You disturb my solitude."

"You worried us," Vanto countered. *His expression is concerned.* "Commander Cheno has been trying to reach you by intercom for the past ten minutes. We've entered the Umbara system, and he wants you on the bridge."

"My apologies," Thrawn said. "I was more focused than I realized."

"Sure," Vanto said. *He looks around at the artwork.* "The commander thought you might have become ill. What's all this?"

"Art of the Umbaran people," Thrawn said. "Has the rest of the task force arrived?"

"Our Star Destroyer has," Vanto said. *He continues to study the artwork with interest.* "The ISD *Foremost*, Admiral Carlou Gendling commanding. He has two of his four corvettes with him, but he sent the other two and his light cruiser off to investigate a problem that just cropped up in another system."

"Is Admiral Gendling planning to wait for the other ships?"

"He seems confident that we can handle the matter without their help," Vanto said. "I'm assuming that once we reach orbit, he'll order the dissidents to proceed to the nearest garrison or police station and surrender themselves and their weapons. Commander Cheno wants you on the bridge just in case they don't."

"Understood," Thrawn said. "Please convey my apologies to the commander, and tell him I shall join him momentarily."

He reached the bridge to find the combat crew assembled and at their proper stations. All indicators showed the *Thunder Wasp* at full battle readiness. "Reporting for duty, Commander," he said. "My apologies for the delay."

"No problem," Cheno said. *He peers closely at Thrawn's face.* "Are you all right? I thought you might have been taken ill."

"I am well," Thrawn assured him. "I understand Admiral Gendling is preparing to deliver an ultimatum?"

"Yes," Cheno said. *His expression indicates apprehension.* "I advised him to wait for the rest of the task force, but Gendling's an impatient sort." *He steps closer to Thrawn and lowers the volume of his voice.* "He also has a somewhat overinflated view of himself and his capabilities," he added. "Though that's just my opinion."

"Not simply your opinion, sir," Thrawn said. "The overall pattern of his career validates your assessment."

"Really?" Cheno said. *He is surprised.* "You've studied his career?"

"I have given it a cursory examination."

"Really. Have you made the same cursory examination of *my* career?"

"You have not been offered the same opportunities as Admiral Gendling," Thrawn said. "Without such, there is little chance for you to prove your abilities."

"Even if I could?" Cheno said. *His expression is wry and understanding.* "No, don't try to spare my feelings. You're a brilliant officer. I'm an adequate one. You'll rise through the ranks. I'll end my career quietly." He turned back to the forward viewport. "But maybe we'll be lucky. Maybe we'll have to fight a battle, and you'll win it for me. At least the *Thunder Wasp* will finally get some recognition." He nodded aft. "The starboard turbolaser targeting system has been giving us some problems. Go see if Ensign Vanto needs assistance checking the diagnostics, if you would."

"Yes, sir."

Vanto was standing by the weapons diagnostic station when Thrawn arrived. "Ensign," Thrawn greeted him. "Report on the starboard targeting system."

"They just ran a diagnostic," Vanto said. "No obvious problem, but the thing's been twitchy so we're running it again. Did I hear Commander Cheno hoping the Umbarans take a shot at us?"

"You did," Thrawn confirmed. "But his hope will likely remain unfulfilled. The Umbarans will not attack."

"Really, sir?" Vanto said, his tone one of surprise. "Because they attacked just fine during the Clone Wars."

"But only when they perceived themselves as having an advantage in numbers or position or command capability," Thrawn said. "Those factors do not exist here. Furthermore, their homeworld stands to absorb severe damage from orbital bombardment if they initiate combat."

"Ah," Vanto said. "Too bad for Commander Cheno, I guess."

On the main comm display, Admiral Gendling's face appeared. "People of Umbara," he said. *His voice is strong and proud, carrying both challenge and contempt.* "Or perhaps I should say, insurgents of Umbara. This is Admiral Carlou Gendling of the Imperial Star Destroyer *Foremost*. You have engaged in sedition and gathered weapons in defiance of Imperial law. In the name of the Emperor, I order you to turn in yourselves and your weapons to the nearest military garrison or police station. Your leaders will be charged according to the severity of their crimes; those who simply followed out of ignorance or family ties will be permitted to return to their homes and lives without punishment. If you do not comply, your world will face the full destructive force that an Imperial Star Destroyer can bring to bear. I give you one hour."

"And that's that," Vanto said. *There is a level of regret in his voice. As Commander Cheno wishes to test himself in full combat, so, too, does Vanto.* "He'll probably end up sending in a few stormtrooper squads to keep order and make sure the troublemakers remember what's sitting over their heads. But for us—"

"Incoming!" Senior Lieutenant Hammerly called from the sensor station. *Her voice holds surprise and ten-*

sion. "Numerous craft, incoming from behind the outer moon. Two hundred—three hundred—*four* hundred. Four hundred craft incoming on our starboard-aft quarter, moving on attack vectors.

"Identification: vulture droids."

CHAPTER 13

No battle plan can anticipate all contingencies. There are always unexpected factors, including those stemming from the opponent's initiative. A battle thus becomes a balance between plan and improvisation, between intellect and reflex, between error and correction.

It is a narrow line. But it is a line one's opponent must also walk. For all the balance of experience and cleverness, it is often the warrior who acts quickest who will prevail.

"All ships disperse," Admiral Gendling's voice boomed across the bridge. "One-eighty-degree turn. Prepare for combat."

Eli snarled under his breath. What did the overblown excuse for an admiral *think* they'd been doing?

But one of the *Thunder Wasp*'s officers, at least, didn't seem to hear any implied slight in the order. Commander Cheno was standing stiff and tall on the command walkway, his head held high, his shoulders back. This was his chance—maybe his last chance—to shine in combat. "Turbolasers, stand ready," he called. "Helm, bring us aft and above the *Foremost*. Gunners, your job is to intercept and destroy enemy fighters targeting the *Foremost*'s dorsal surfaces."

A chorus of acknowledgments came from the crew pits. "Looks like he got his wish after all, sir," Eli murmured to Thrawn.

"No," Thrawn said.

"Excuse me?"

"He wished to meet the Umbarans in combat. But this attack is not theirs."

"It's coming from an Umbaran moon," Eli pointed out, trying to filter the sarcasm out of his voice. Thrawn's unshakable confidence still sometimes got to him. "The whole system is full of Umbarans. The Umbaran leaders aren't screaming to Gendling that it's not them and please don't shoot."

"Because they do not yet see themselves in a position of weakness," Thrawn said. "They are watching the attack to see if we are weakened sufficiently for them to engage us."

Eli shook his head. "How do you *know* all this?"

"All weapons: *Fire*!" Cheno called.

The *Thunder Wasp*'s bridge lit up with flickers of green light as turbolaser bolts shot outward toward the incoming fighters. A few of the vulture droids were hit, shattering instantly into brilliant explosions of smoke and debris. But most of them avoided the cruiser's attack with ease.

"Fire again!" Cheno bit out. "And this time, *hit* them."

"They're too small, sir," Weapons Officer Osgoode called back. "We're going to have to wait until they're closer."

Before Cheno could answer, the vulture droids opened up with their own volley of return fire.

"Deflectors!" Cheno snapped. His voice, Eli noted, was starting to sound strained.

Small wonder. Theoretically, vulture droids should be

no match for Imperial ships-of-the-line. But there were a hell of a lot of them.

The cruiser's gunners tried their best. But they could do little against the incoming swarm. The smaller craft were too fast, too distant, and too nimble. The *Thunder Wasp* kept firing, but only a few of the bolts found their targets.

Meanwhile, the vulture droids' own return fire was tearing into the *Thunder Wasp*'s hull, penetrating gaps in overloaded shields to destroy sensors, weapons emplacements, and a small but rapidly growing number of outer hull plates.

Eli looked at the tactical display. So far the *Foremost* seemed to be holding its own, but the two *Raider*-class corvettes were being pummeled even harder than the *Thunder Wasp*.

And still Commander Cheno stood on the command walkway. Unmoving. Silent.

In over his head.

Helpless.

Eli stole a look at Thrawn. The Chiss was also standing motionless, his face as impassive as Cheno's.

But there was something about him that sent a shiver up Eli's back. Thrawn saw something. Somewhere in all that chaos and destruction, he saw something.

Abruptly, he seemed to come to a decision. "Who here has had combat experience with vulture droids?" he called.

"I have, sir," Hammerly called back, raising her hand.

"Turbolaser station one, Lieutenant," Thrawn ordered.

"Commander?" Hammerly asked, looking at Cheno for confirmation.

"Go," Cheno ordered her, his voice grim. "Secondary Sensor Officer—"

"I will take the chief sensor officer's position," Thrawn interrupted. "Ensign Vanto, with me."

A few seconds later Thrawn was seated at Ham-

merly's console. Eli stood behind him, trying very hard
not to look as nervous as he felt. Bad enough that they
were being taken apart by an attacking force they
couldn't stop. But by throwing orders around without
Cheno's approval, Thrawn had effectively usurped command. Eli's mind flashed back to Captain Rossi and Admiral Wiskovis, and their reactions to Thrawn's casual
disregard for chain-of-command protocol. "Now what?"
he asked in a low voice. "Did you already know Hammerly had been in combat?"

"I needed a reason to take her station," Thrawn replied quietly. "I have studied vulture droids, Ensign.
They do not normally fight this effectively."

Eli looked at the display. The fighters had closed
with the four Imperial ships and were swarming around
them, pouring in continual fire while still largely managing to dodge the defenders' counterattack. "Well, they
weren't designed to be very smart on their own," he
pointed out. "A few simple pre-programmed maneuvers
and combat patterns, throw in huge numbers to overwhelm their targets—"

"There!" Thrawn jabbed a finger. "That group of
four. Did you see it?"

Eli frowned. "No."

"Their drive emissions suddenly increased, allowing
them to speed up," Thrawn said. "But there was no reason for extra speed. They were already evading our attack quite effectively."

"Okay," Eli said, frowning harder. The group Thrawn
had tagged were weaving through the turbolaser blasts
and coming around for another volley—

He stiffened. There it was. "I saw it."

"Good," Thrawn said. "Note how their combat style
also changes. Instead of firing with deliberation at vulnerable spots, they fire indiscriminately whether the target point is worth shooting at or not."

"Got it," Eli said. The shifts in combat style were

subtle, but now that he knew what to look for they were quite visible. "So what does it mean?"

"You said yourself that these droids are not clever," Thrawn said. "Their creators assumed a given fighter would not survive long, and so programmed them to be swarming weapons."

"So burning through their resources as fast as possible, without any long-term considerations?" Eli asked, frowning. "You sure?"

"Look at the curve of the combat pods," Thrawn said. "The shape of the stripes, the positions of the blaster barrels. Weapons such as this not only are functional, but also incorporate the artistry of their creators. The beings who created and built these fighters believe in short, quick answers to questions and problems."

"I'll take your word for it," Eli said. The explanation sounded ridiculous, but he'd seen Thrawn pull equally obscure facts out of equally imperceptible visuals. "Where does that leave us?"

"They are designed to swarm," Thrawn said. "But they only briefly show that tactic. That leads to the conclusion . . . ?" He paused expectantly.

"That the rest of the time they're under direct command from somewhere," Eli said as it suddenly clicked. "Somewhere on the outer moon?"

"They were launched from there," Thrawn agreed. "But they are not being controlled from there. The changes occur when the fighters fly through the transmission shadow of one of our ships."

"So if we can find and analyze all the shadows, we can backtrack to the transmitter," Eli said with a sudden surge of hope. "And you came here because you needed the sensor station to power through that kind of calculation?"

"Precisely," Thrawn said.

Eli felt his lip twitch as the final element fell into place. By masking his insight and revelation this way, Thrawn was hoping to pass on more of the credit to the rest of the *Thunder Wasp*'s crew. And, by logical extension, to Commander Cheno. One last chance for him to shine in combat. "What do you want me to do?"

"I will run the calculations and coordinate the locations and vectors," Thrawn said. "You will watch for other shadows and mark them."

"Right." Eli glanced at the tactical, wincing at all the spots of red that marked major damage to the Imperial ships. "Work fast."

The next two minutes dragged by. Eli looked back and forth across the battle, catching three more of the subtle changes that marked a fighter briefly running on its own programming. He had no idea how many Thrawn spotted in that same time period, but the Chiss turned abruptly to his board no fewer than ten times.

"Corvette down!"

Eli looked at the tactical, his stomach knotting. Where one of the Raider corvettes had been, there was now a roiling cloud of shattered metal and fire-tinged debris. "Sir?" he murmured urgently.

"Done." Thrawn touched a final key.

And abruptly, bright yellow crosshairs appeared on the planetary display. "Commander Cheno?" Thrawn called up toward the command walkway. "I believe we have isolated the ground-based transmitter that is coordinating the attack. I recommend that you pass this information to Admiral Gendling and request he target and destroy it."

"What are you talking about?" Cheno asked, frowning down at him. "What transmitter?"

"The one feeding tactical data to the vulture droids," Thrawn said. "The *Foremost*'s turbolasers are the only ones that can reach effectively to the surface."

"I see," Cheno said. He didn't, Eli suspected, but he knew better than to ignore his first officer's advice. "Comm: Contact the *Foremost*. Inform the admiral that I need to speak with him immediately."

Eli huffed out a long sigh. And with that, it was over. Thrawn had come through again, and it was over.

Only this time, it wasn't.

"Ridiculous," Admiral Gendling scoffed. "Even if these fighters *are* being controlled and haven't simply been reprogrammed, there's no possible way for you to have located the transmitter."

"Sir, as I explained—"

"And I'm not about to go shooting at random into a civilian city on the strength of some mid-level officer's wild guesswork," Gendling interrupted. "Less talk, Commander. More fighting."

Eli winced. In general, not shooting into a civilian population was a perfectly sensible approach to combat. More sensible, in fact, than he would have expected from a lot of Imperial officers.

But in this case, the proposed attack was hardly random, and failing to act was likely to be very costly. "Now what?" he asked Thrawn.

For a moment Thrawn stared at the tactical in silence. Then, reaching to the board again, he keyed in a new order.

And on both the sensor and tactical displays a set of moving gray wedges appeared.

"Signal all ships," he ordered the comm officer. "The gray wedges mark the transmission shadows where the vulture droids rely on their own programming. Within those shadows they will be most vulnerable and therefore most easily destroyed." He raised his voice. "Senior Lieutenant Hammerly?"

"On it, sir," she called back. On the tactical, four droids flying through the *Thunder Wasp*'s shadow disintegrated in four bursts of turbolaser fire. "That what you had in mind, sir?"

"It is indeed," Thrawn confirmed. "Well done."

"All ships acknowledge our transmission," the comm officer added. "Gunners are switching tactics."

And with that, the tide finally began to turn.

But it was bloody. In the end, Gendling's remaining corvette was severely damaged, nearly half its crew dead or wounded. The *Thunder Wasp* and *Foremost* were in better shape, but both ships would need time in a shipyard before they would be combat-ready again.

The vulture droids were all destroyed. The Umbarans had surrendered unconditionally. The *Foremost*'s stormtrooper squads were on the surface and supervising the surrender of the insurgents.

And Admiral Gendling was furious.

"You're lucky I don't bring you up on charges right here and now, Commander," the admiral said. *His expression holds embarrassment and guilt. His tone holds harshness and anger.* "You do not—do *not*—usurp an admiral's authority and command that way. I speak *for* my crew and *to* my crew."

"I'm sorry you feel that way, Admiral," Commander Cheno said. *His tone holds tension, but also resolve.* "I was simply trying to recapture the initiative in the most efficient way possible and save the battle. And with it, a few lives."

"Are you mocking me, Commander?" Admiral Gendling demanded. "Because if you are, as the Emperor is my witness, I'll take you down so hard and so fast they'll have to scrape up what's left of your career with a flatcake turner. Whose bright idea was it, anyway? I know you didn't come up with any of that yourself."

Commander Cheno's expression remains resolved. "I ordered the information passed to the *Foremost* and the remaining corvette," he said. *There is a small emphasis on the word* remaining. "As for the discovery of the enemy's weakness, that was a joint effort of my bridge crew."

With slow deliberation, Admiral Gendling turned his eyes to Thrawn. *His arm and torso muscles are rigid.* "Your first officer has built himself quite a reputation," he said to Cheno. "Maybe I should ask *him* who came up with the transmitter idea."

"Or maybe you should speak directly with me," Cheno said. "As you said, the commander speaks for his crew."

For three seconds, Gendling continues to stare. Then he turns back to Cheno. "I'll have your career, Commander," he said. "I'd take your ship, too, but it's clear that some upstart half your age will do *that.*"

"If the upstart is deserving, more power to him," Cheno said.

Gendling smiles with malice and pride. "This isn't over, Commander. You can be *very* sure of that. I'll see you at your court-martial. Dismissed."

Commander Cheno is silent while returning to the shuttle. Only once aboard, and in flight, does he speak. "Well," he said. *His voice holds weariness.* "It looks as if I may not be ending my career quite as quietly as I expected."

"There is no need to protect me," Thrawn said. "The *Thunder Wasp*'s log will answer all his suspicions."

"Perhaps," Cheno said. "Logs *can* be altered, you know."

"I did not know that."

"Not easily, of course," Cheno said. *He offers a small smile.* "Certainly not legally. Doesn't matter. As he said, you have a reputation. More to the point, he can't really bring up all the details of this supposed breach of protocol without exposing his own ineptitude. No, he'll satisfy himself with destroying my career and leave you and the rest of the *Thunder Wasp*'s crew alone."

"That is not right or proper."

"No, but it *is* reality," Cheno said. "As I said, my career isn't important. What's important is the future of the Imperial Navy." *He gestures with respect and admiration.* "You're that future, Thrawn. It's been a privilege to be your commander."

"Thank you, sir," Thrawn said. "I have learned a great deal serving under you."

"I doubt that," Cheno said. *His tone holds dry humor, with no bitterness or resentment.* "But I thank you. And I, too, have learned a great deal."

Eli had half expected the shuttle to return empty, with both of its passengers consigned to the *Foremost*'s brig. To his relief, both Cheno and Thrawn emerged from the docking bay. Cheno murmured something to Thrawn and then headed toward the bridge. Thrawn watched until the commander's turbolift car departed, then beckoned Eli to join him. "Ensign," he greeted Eli quietly. "I presume you wish to know how our meeting with Admiral Gendling went. In brief, not very well."

"I'm not surprised," Eli said, wincing. The look on Cheno's face as he left the docking bay . . . "I take it the commander took the brunt of it."

"Yes," Thrawn said. "Partly because he was in command during the battle. Partly because he attempted to shield my role in the outcome."

"So because Gendling screwed up, he's taking it out on you," Eli growled. "I thought only politicians were that level of stupid and nasty."

"I have found those characteristics in all fields of endeavor," Thrawn said. "Has your research uncovered anything of use?"

"Maybe." Eli handed Thrawn his datapad. "The building the transmitter was operating from is owned by a group of humans. The locals don't know their names and can't give anything useful in the way of descriptions. But it's clear you were right about no Umbarans being directly involved in the attack."

"I doubt Admiral Gendling will take that into consideration."

"*No* one's taking that into consideration," Eli said sourly. "Since most of the unrest and turmoil was concentrated in the mining districts, Gendling's already called for the Empire to take direct control of Umbara's entire mining and refining sector."

"Interesting," Thrawn said. "Did you find any indication that Nightswan was directly involved?"

"The transmitter was run by humans," Eli said. "That's as close as we've gotten right now."

"Still, we know that Nightswan has been involved in mining and metal smuggling elsewhere," Thrawn said. "Tell me, how valuable are the Umbaran mineral deposits?"

"Very," Vanto said. He took back his datapad and keyed in a few commands. "Several important ones. Key among them: doonium."

Thrawn pondered a moment. "Is there any way to calculate a system's success rate against smugglers?"

"You can get a rough figure, anyway," Eli said. "You take the amount of legitimate shipping on some easily identifiable product—those Paklarn grist mollusks, for example—and compare it with the amount being sold elsewhere. The numbers are a little loose, and they obviously don't apply to every product type. But as I said, it gives you a rough figure."

"Understood," Thrawn said. "Do you have that figure for Umbara? If possible, I would like it for the success rate for smugglers of rare metals or rare metal ores."

Eli called up the relevant numbers, ran a quick mental calculation. "It's very good," he said. "Somewhere in the ninety percent range."

"And the number for a comparable Imperial-controlled world?"

Eli nodded and busied himself with his datapad. "Looks like . . . whoa. Sixty-five to seventy percent. Though from personal family experience, I'd guess it could actually be as low as forty or forty-five."

"It would seem we have found the reason for the attack," Thrawn said. "The purpose for a clearly futile assault upon an Imperial force. Nightswan wished for the Empire to take control of Umbara's mines."

"Because it's easier for him and his smugglers to cheat material past Imperial inspectors than past the Umbarans." Eli huffed out a breath. "I'll grant that it sounds like Nightswan's brand of deviousness. But we don't even know for sure that he was involved."

"He was," Thrawn said. "He is. Who else would invite me here to demonstrate his handiwork?"

Eli blinked. "He *what*?"

"Surely it is clear," Thrawn said. "He set up his mollusk smuggling group in an area he knew the *Thunder Wasp* was patrolling. He made certain that Umbara was mentioned within the smugglers' hearing. He knew of my interest in Clone War weaponry and made certain the name *Nightswan* was on at least one order."

"Interesting," Eli murmured. On the surface, for Thrawn to even suggest such a thing bordered on the egomaniacal.

Still, the Chiss was seldom wrong about tactical matters. And Nightswan wasn't exactly an ordinary mastermind, either. It was entirely possible that he would do such a thing simply for the challenge of it all. "Well, if it *is* him, he lost this one."

"Not at all," Thrawn said, his voice grim. "I defeated his vulture droid attack, but winning that encounter was not his true goal."

"The Imperial takeover."

"Or perhaps the Imperial takeover itself was merely a step," Thrawn said. "It may have been his final goal if he was merely a smuggler. But he is more."

"So if he's not a smuggler, what is he?"

"I do not yet know," Thrawn said. "Possibly his activities are building to a political confrontation or resolution on some planet or system. Possibly he seeks vengeance or humiliation against some person or organization. But whatever his goals and motivations, he is a person of extreme interest."

"I guess we'd better keep an eye out for him, then," Eli said. "Sooner or later, he has to surface."

"Incorrect, Ensign. Sooner or later, he will *choose* to surface."

CHAPTER 14

One is born with a unique set of talents and abilities. One must choose which of those talents to nurture, which to set aside for a time, which to ignore completely.

Sometimes the choice is obvious. Other times, the hints and proddings are more obscure. Then, one may need to undergo several regimens of training and sample several different professions before determining where one's strongest talents lie. This is the driving force behind many life-path alterations.

There are few sets of skills that match only one specific job. More often they are adaptable to many different professions. Sometimes, one can plan such a change. Other times, the change appears without warning.

In both instances, one must be alert and carefully consider all options. Not every change is a step forward.

It had been a hard day, full of desperate and petty people with desperate and petty problems. By all rights, Arihnda should be exhausted.

At the same time, it had been a resoundingly successful day, with solutions for nearly all those problems and gushings of heartfelt gratitude. By all rights she should be ecstatic.

She was trying to decide which feeling would dominate her evening, and anticipating the start of that evening, when there was a warning beep from the outer door.

She glanced at the chrono, suppressing a sigh. Technically, the office still had two minutes to go. Realistically, none of today's problems had been solved in less than twenty. Her evening was evidently going to start later than she'd hoped.

But this was her job, and she was good at it, and there wasn't anything better for ten kilometers in any direction, including up or down. So however long this took—

"Hey, stranger," Juahir said cheerfully as she walked through the inner door. "How are you doing?"

"Juahir!" Arihnda all but gasped, feeling her face light up in a smile. "I'm fine. What are you doing in the pricey end of the planet?"

"Oh, this is the pricey end, is it?" Driller asked, walking in behind her. "Hey, at least you make enough to actually *live* here."

"Just barely," Arihnda said, feeling her smile grow a little brighter. Driller had dropped in on the office a couple of times before his uncle came back to reclaim his apartment, but she hadn't seen him since.

As for Juahir, she'd come by only once, and that had been nearly six months ago. They'd talked a few times on the comm, though, and Juahir had a standing invitation to tour the Federal District if she ever found the time to come to this side of the planet.

Apparently, she just had.

"It's great to see both of you," Arihnda said, coming around her desk and giving each of them a quick hug. "How long are you going to be here? Do you have plans for the evening? I'm off duty in about a minute and a half."

"You sure they can do without you?" Driller asked,

looking pointedly at the line of empty desks. "Or did the supervisor decide you were so good they didn't need anyone else?"

"No, we're still a fully staffed and thoroughly over-worked office," Arihnda said. "Everyone else just happened to have evening plans and I volunteered to do the last half hour alone."

"Well, *that's* not fair," Juahir said with mock outrage. "Serve them right if someone came in here and swept you off your feet."

"It's not so bad," Arihnda said. "Actually, I do my best work when I'm alone."

"You like the extra pressure?" Driller asked.

"I like the lack of witnesses."

He gave her a sideways look. "You're kidding, right?"

Arihnda shrugged. "You'd be amazed how far a little insinuation will get you with an apartment owner."

"What kind of insinuation?" Juahir asked.

"Hints that you know what she did last night," Arihnda said. "Or last month, or last year. Throw out a few vague comments, and most people will fill in the rest. Once they do, they're a lot more open to settling the problem the tenant is having."

"Assuming they have some hidden dirt to fill in," Juahir pointed out.

"Everyone has hidden dirt," Arihnda said. "You never said how long you would be here."

"*You* never answered my comment about someone sweeping you off your feet," Juahir countered.

"I thought you were joking," Arihnda said, aware of the permanent hollow spot in the core of her being. She'd met many men over the past year, some of whom had tried to befriend or romance her. She'd tried with a few of them—really, really tried—but nothing had worked out.

Nor had she met anyone, man *or* woman, whom she could call a friend. In her line of work, everyone she encountered started by thinking of her as a helper, champion, or even mother figure. None of those was a good basis for a balanced emotional connection.

"I never joke about food," Juahir said solemnly. "We're hungry, and we bet you are, too. So shut this place down and let's go."

"I'm with you," Arihnda said, starting her computer's lockdown procedure. "Fair warning: I can't afford to take you anywhere near as fancy as the Alisandre Hotel this time around."

"Don't worry, we've got it covered," Juahir said with an impish smile. "We already have reservations."

"At the *Alisandre*? Seriously?"

"No, no, no." Juahir pointed upward. "At the Pinnacle."

Arihnda felt her eyes widen. "The *Pinnacle*? You're joking."

"Nope," Juahir said, grinning even more broadly. "You game?"

"Sure." Arihnda looked down at her clothing. "In that case, I need to change."

"No problem," Juahir said. "We budgeted time for that."

The Pinnacle wasn't the highest point on Coruscant. But it was the highest point in the Federal District, and it provided magnificent views of the Palace, the Senate Building, and the various ministries and monuments clustered around them.

The clientele matched the view. Every third table, it seemed, sported a face Arihnda remembered from her days working for Senator Renking.

It was exhilarating. But at the same time it was vaguely depressing. She'd come to Coruscant to gain connections and influence and to work her way up the political ladder. Instead, she'd ended up stuck barely a few rungs from the bottom.

And as she gazed across the room, and up the ladder

looming mockingly over her, her onetime goal of regaining Pryce Mining faded ever more into the mists of never.

But the food was good enough to almost drive away the wistful pangs of resentment at how she'd been treated. Once or twice along the way she wondered how Juahir and Driller were paying for all this, but what with the excitement, the memories, and the sheer taste sensations she didn't wonder very much or very hard.

"So how does it feel being back in the skylanes of power?" Juahir asked as the waiter delivered their dessert plates.

"Very nice," Arihnda said. "I thought I'd put all this behind me, but there really is a lure to it all."

"So if you could come back to this life, you would?"

Arihnda gave a little snort. "What, is Senator Renking hiring?"

"Probably not." Juahir nodded sideways to Driller. "But Driller is."

Arihnda frowned at him. "Really? For what?"

"For a position with my advocacy group," he said. "You *do* remember that's what I do, right?"

"Of course," Arihnda said. "I just assumed that people like you were on a hook-string budget. You're really hiring?"

"We really are," he said, nodding.

"And *you* didn't snatch it up?" Arihnda asked, looking at Juahir. "Whatever it is has to be a hundred steps up from waitressing at Topple's."

"I'm not waitressing anymore," Juahir said, frowning. "You know that. I dusted off my old martial arts stuff and got into bodyguard training, remember?"

"Since when?" Arihnda asked, frowning right back. Juahir had sometimes talked about her school-age hand-to-hand combat work, but she'd never even hinted she might want to do that sort of thing professionally.

"Since about four months after you moved here from Bash Four," Juahir said. "I started part-time with a little dojo four hundred levels down from my apartment, and when a full-time position opened up—look, I told you all this."

"You most certainly did not," Arihnda said.

"But—" Juahir looked entreatingly at Driller.

"Hey, don't look at me," he said quickly. "You told *me* you told her."

"I'm so sorry, Arihnda," Juahir said, wincing. "I would have *sworn* . . . anyway, I've moved over here and have a job at the Yinchom Dojo now. We do civilian training, but we're also licensed to train government bodyguards. We've got a handful of guards from the Senate, with some good word-of-mouth bringing in new ones."

"They're a hundred thirty levels down from your office but thinking of looking for someplace higher," Driller added.

"Pluses and minuses," Juahir said. "The lower levels are more discreet for aides and assistants whose senators want them to double as bodyguards, but don't want the whole world to know they've been training. The higher levels are more prestigious and might draw more people who are *supposed* to look like guards."

"And are more expensive," Driller murmured.

"A *lot* more expensive," Juahir agreed, crinkling her nose. "Anyway, to get back to your original question, that's one reason Driller didn't offer me the job."

Arihnda had almost forgotten that was where this conversation had started. "And the other reason?"

"We're looking for an expert in mines, mining, and refining," Driller said. "Juahir doesn't know the first thing about that stuff, while you know the first thing, the last thing, and all the things in between."

"I wouldn't go *that* far," Arihnda said modestly, her mind racing. Working for an advocacy group wasn't a huge step up, status-wise, but it would once again take her into the centers of political power. That alone made it worth pursuing.

Not to mention it would get her away from desperate citizens and their desperate problems.

"The downside of the job is that it doesn't come with an apartment like your assistance office job does," Driller continued. "But Juahir's got a decent-sized place, it's closer to the Senate Building, and she's already told me she'd love a roommate."

"Absolutely," Juahir confirmed. "You have no idea how many times I've collapsed onto the couch, every muscle aching, and wished there was someone there to make dinner without me having to move."

"I'm pretty good with dinner," Arihnda said with a shrug. In politics, she'd learned, it never paid to look too eager. "And I'm definitely ready to move on to something else. Where and when do I apply for the job?"

"You just did," Driller said with a grin. "Seriously. I've already floated your name, and the rest of the group has already vetted you. If you want the job, it's yours."

Arihnda took a deep breath. The hell with not looking too eager. "I want the job."

"Great." Driller picked up his dessert, frowning a little at Juahir. "So. Is it proper etiquette to toast a momentous event with a dessert plate?"

"I don't know," Juahir said, picking up her own plate. "Let's find out."

And just like that, Arihnda was back.

It was like waking up from a bad dream. Suddenly, she was among the elite again, walking the ornate hallways of the Senate and office buildings, speaking to the people who ruled the Empire.

Not just speaking, either, but actually being listened to. Back when she'd been delivering data card packets for Senator Renking, most of the recipients had barely noticed her. But licensed advocacy groups had prestige, if not any actual power, and they *were* noticed. Now, suddenly, it seemed like everyone knew her face and her advocacy group. Some of them even remembered her name.

Arihnda had survived the lower levels of the Federal District. But up here, where the sun shone and the brightest lights glittered, was where she wanted to be.

She was back. And she would never leave it. Ever. Whatever it took to stay in the skylanes of power, she would do it.

"Okay," Driller said, sitting Arihnda down in front of the Higher Skies Advocacy Group's main computer. "Last job of the day, I promise."

"You promised that two jobs ago," she reminded him.

"Who, me?" he said, looking innocent. "I know, I know. What can I say? You're the mining expert. That means you get all the mining expert jobs."

"Right," Arihnda agreed. It wasn't like anyone else could do it, after all.

Mainly because there never seemed to be anyone else around.

At first, she'd puzzled about that. Driller had explained that most of the time the other members were out of the office, talking to senators or aides, visiting the various ministries, or traveling offplanet to talk with governors or moffs or just gather firsthand information. He'd also reminded Arihnda that she herself was often out of the office, and suggested that it was simple bad luck that she'd missed crossing paths with any of the others.

It was a lie, of course. Arihnda had figured that out very early on. Either the rest of the staff was off doing nefarious things, or else there *was* no other staff.

But she didn't care. Driller paid on time, and he had enough spare credits to keep her in outfits suitable for the rarefied company she kept these days.

More important, his license continued to give her access to the Empire's powerful. Ultimately, that was all that mattered.

"So here's what we need," Driller said, reaching over her shoulder and tapping a few keys. "There seems to have been an unusual number of Imperial takeovers lately, mining facilities and sometimes whole planets. I want you to pull up the list and evaluate it for the importance of the mines in question, the circumstances of the Imperial takeover, and anything else that might establish a pattern as to what's going on. What?"

"What do you mean, what?" Arihnda asked.

"Your face went all puckered just then," Driller said. "Is there a problem?"

"No," Arihnda said. She hadn't realized she'd reacted. "Sorry. I was just thinking about the Empire taking over our family's mine three years ago."

"Sorry, I'd forgotten about that," Driller apologized. "If it's too uncomfortable for you to do this . . . ?"

"No, no, I'm fine," Arihnda assured him.

"Okay," he said. "And don't feel like you have to finish tonight. I've got a late appointment—you okay with closing up alone?"

"Sure," Arihnda said. The apartment she shared with Juahir was two hundred levels down and not in the best part of the district, but the rowdies usually didn't come out into the walkways and platforms until the sunlight had faded from the bits of clear sky above. At this time of year, that was a good two hours away. "Enjoy."

"Right," he said drily. "A meeting with a Senate doorkeeper. It's going to be *so* much fun."

He headed out, locking the door behind him, and Arihnda settled in to read.

She had assumed Driller was imagining things, seeing patterns and conspiracies that turned out to be figments of his overblown imagination. He had a tendency to do that.

But in this case, he was right on the mark.

There were twenty-eight mines on the list: twenty-eight Imperial takeovers dating back to a year before Renking had ripped Pryce Mining out of Arihnda's hands. The majority of them, though—twenty-one, to be precise—had occurred during the past year. She dug through the list, scanning the basic elements, occasionally digging into or at least skimming the accompanying subfiles, looking for common threads. She reached the entry on the most recent event, an attack on an Imperial task force off Umbara—

She paused, frowning, as one of the names in the report caught her eye.

Captain Thrawn.

"No," she murmured under her breath. Surely it couldn't be the same blue-skinned nonhuman she'd met at the Alisandre Hotel a year ago. That Thrawn had been a lieutenant, and this one was a captain, and she'd heard somewhere that it typically took ten to fifteen years in the navy to ladder that far up the ranks.

But it was him, all right. There was a subfile attached giving the details of the battle, and the accompanying images left no doubt. The lowly lieutenant that Colonel Yularen had been trying to rescue had leapt to command rank in less than two years.

Mentally, she shook her head. Either he was amazingly competent, or he had impressively powerful friends.

Interesting, but not her concern. Putting him out of her mind, she got back to work.

Focused on her analysis, she didn't notice the time slipping away, and it was a shock when she looked at the chrono and realized the sun had been down for over half an hour. The rowdies would be starting to gather, but the trip back to her apartment should still be safe if she hurried. She closed down the computer system and headed out, locking the door behind her.

The faint daylight from overhead had long since vanished, but the increased intensity from the streetlamps and brassy advertising signs more than made up for it.

Still, the lack of sun somehow created a psychological illusion of darkness.

Up here, where the police were vigilant, things were all right. But in the lower parts of the district, the rowdies would be gathering to drink, spice up, and make noise.

Some of them, eventually, would also start making trouble.

The turbolift car, when it arrived, was packed. The next car might be more comfortable, but Arihnda wasn't in the mood to wait. Fortunately, the passengers began filing out almost immediately as the car stopped at the more elite residence levels just below the government offices. Twenty levels above hers, her last companion got out, leaving her alone.

Not an ideal situation, certainly not at this hour and this deep. But she should be all right.

And as long as she had the car to herself, she might as well take advantage of the unexpected privacy. Pulling out her comm, she keyed for Juahir.

"Hey," Juahir answered cheerfully. "What's up? You got dinner going?"

"Not exactly," Arihnda said. "I got tied up at the office and I'm just heading home now."

"Ooh," Juahir said, her voice going serious. "You okay? Where are you?"

"In the turbolift heading down," Arihnda said, watching the indicator. "I'm almost—"

She broke off, her breath catching in her throat. The car had reached her level; but instead of stopping, it continued moving down.

"Juahir, it didn't stop," Arihnda said, fighting to keep her voice even. Belatedly, she lunged for the control board and punched the next button down.

Too late. The car had already passed that level. She tried again, picking a button ten levels farther down this time. Again, the car reached the landing and continued on without stopping.

"Arihnda? *Arihnda!*"

"It's not stopping," Arihnda ground out. This time she ran her finger down the whole column of buttons. The car ignored all of them.

And it was picking up speed.

"Juahir, I can't stop it," she said. "It's heading down and I can't stop it."

"Okay, don't panic," Juahir said firmly. "There's an emergency stop button. You see it?"

"Yes," Arihnda said. It was at the very bottom of the panel, protected by a faded orange cover. After years of uneventful travel, she'd forgotten it was even there. She flipped up the cover, revealing a less faded orange button underneath, and pressed it.

And grabbed for the handrail as the car screeched to a sudden halt.

For a moment all was silence. "Arihnda?" Juahir called tentatively.

Arihnda found her voice. "I'm okay," she said. "It stopped. Finally."

"Where are you?"

Arihnda peered at the indicator. "Level forty-one twenty."

Juahir whistled softly. "A thousand from the top. Okay. You took your usual turbolift, right?"

"Right." The car doors slid open. Cautiously, Arihnda peered outside.

She'd never been this far down before, but it looked exactly the way the vids and holos portrayed it. Garish display signs blazed everywhere, much brighter and more strident than the ones higher up, promoting shops or advertising products or flickering with the visual static of malfunction or unpaid bills. Contrasting with the bright colors was the stolid faded-white of the street-lamps, about three-quarters of them working, the rest struggling to maintain illumination or gone completely dark. The walkways beneath the lights, like the lights themselves, were mostly fine, but there were enough broken and missing tiles to emphasize that she was no longer in the city's upper levels. The building fronts behind the signs ran the gamut from carefully maintained and almost cheerful, to struggling and faded, to dilapidated and slumlike. And everything, even the bravely painted storefronts, seemed dirty.

And then there were the people.

There weren't many pedestrians on the walkways right now. Most of them were traveling in groups of three or more, as if no one wanted or dared to be alone, and all of them were walking in the odd gait of people who wanted to hurry but didn't want to *look* like they were hurrying.

Like the buildings and the walkways, the people also seemed dirty.

"Okay," Juahir's voice came from the comm. "You're going to have to move—that turbolift's obviously broken, and you don't want to wait there until someone comes to fix it. There's another turbolift about six blocks to the west. Can you see the sign?"

Arihnda squinted down the walkway. But the turbolift indicator sign, if it was even theoretically visible from this angle, was completely swallowed up by the glare of the display signs. "No, but I can get there."

"Okay, go," Juahir ordered. "We're on our way— we'll try to meet you before you get there."

Arihnda frowned. *We?* "Is Driller with you?"

"Just get moving," Juahir said. "Hide your comm— it'll tag you as top-class, and you don't want that. And be careful."

"I will." Keying off, Arihnda tucked her comm back into her pocket. She took a final look around, then headed down the walkway, trying to match the not-hurrying pace of the others.

It wasn't too bad, actually. The people were rough-edged and a little on the skittish side, and she had no doubt they were both willing and able to engage in rough stuff if the mood struck them. But back in Bash

Four she'd learned tricks of expression and body language that made people think twice before engaging with her.

Luckily, the pattern here seemed to be the same as it had back there. The handful of people who got close enough to get a good look at her passed by without comment and without slowing.

She'd made it four blocks, and could finally see the turbolift indicator sign, when it all fell apart.

They came without warning: six of them, gangly youths hopped on spice or something worse, boiling out of a pair of dark doorways between two broken lights. Two of them carried long chains; the other four had short blades held casually in their hands. "Hey, sweets," one of the chain carriers called. "Lookin' for some fun?"

Arihnda threw a quick look over her shoulder. Two more thugs had emerged from concealment behind her.

With a sinking feeling she realized she was trapped. To her left were the windows and doorways of small businesses already shut for the night. To her right was a two-meter-high railing between the walkway and a sheer drop of at least twenty levels before she even hit anything solid.

"Not interested, thanks," she called back, trying to keep her voice steady. She'd tussled with friends when she was growing up, and had had to deal with the occasional drunk or spicehead back on Lothal. But she'd never faced anything like this.

She could call the police. But they were spread all over the district, and the thugs were right here. Trouble would reach her long before any help could. She could turn and run and hope she could somehow get past the two men behind her. But there was nothing back there but unfamiliar walkways and a broken turbolift.

"Aw, don't be like that," the thug said, mock-sweetly. "You want a drink? Sure you do. So do we. You can buy us all one. You got money, right?"

Arihnda felt her stomach tighten into a knot. What the hell was she going to do?

Behind the six thugs, a man and woman had come into view, striding toward the confrontation through the shadows of another pair of broken streetlamps. Arihnda watched them, feeling a surge of hope. This was her chance. If the couple got too close before they realized what was happening, she might be able to point the thugs in that direction and get away while they were occupied with more interesting prey.

Too late. The man came to a stop ten meters behind the thugs as he apparently spotted the trouble. If he and the woman turned and ran right now, they'd probably make it back to the turbolift before the rowdies could catch them.

Except that the woman hadn't stopped when her companion did. She was still walking toward the thugs as if she didn't even see them. Arihnda braced herself . . .

The thug's spokesman must have heard the approaching footsteps. He started to turn as the woman reached him—

Without even pausing, the woman snapped her leg up, jabbing the edge of her foot into the back of his knee.

The leg collapsed beneath him. He got one hand on the pavement, howling in rage and pain as he flailed for balance. His cursing abruptly cut off as the woman slammed the back of her fist into the side of his neck. He collapsed to the walkway and lay still.

For a single second the other thugs froze, gaping in bewilderment. The woman didn't give them time to recover from their shock. Even as her first target fell, she snatched the chain from his nerveless fingers and threw it at the heads of the three youths on her right.

Two of them managed to dodge. The third caught the chain squarely across his throat and dropped with a tortured gurgle as the chain rattled onto the pavement beside him.

The woman spun to face the two standing on her left. But the gang had had enough. The four still on their feet took off at top speed, sprinting past Arihnda on either side without even a glance. Arihnda spun around as they passed, saw that the two who'd been behind her were already tearing into the garish lights of the night.

"You all right?"

Arihnda turned back, feeling her jaw drop. "*Juahir?*"

"Yeah. Hi. You okay?" Juahir gripped Arihnda's shoulder, looking her up and down. "Did they get to you?"

"No," Arihnda managed. The man Juahir had been walking with had finally come unglued from the walk-way and was walking toward them. "I was . . . you surprised me."

"I *said* we were coming," Juahir reminded her, waving her companion forward. "Arihnda Pryce, meet Ottlis Dos. Ottlis is a bodyguard who's been taking some extra hand-to-hand classes at the dojo. We'd just finished our session and were heading home when I got your call. He offered to come along in case I needed him."

"I guess you didn't," Arihnda said, eyeing the man closely. He didn't look much like a bodyguard.

"Nope," Juahir said. "And before you ask, he let me take them on by myself because I told him to. He's a government employee. If he beats someone down, there's a mass of datawork he has to fill out."

"Assuming the victims file a complaint," Arihnda murmured.

"Well, there's that," Juahir conceded. "Regardless, as a private citizen all I have to do is claim self-defense or defense of others and I walk."

"Nice when the law works on the side of the people."

"You mean, for a change?" Ottlis asked. His voice was smooth and resonant, pleasant and almost cheerful. Again, not the kind of voice Arihnda would expect from a man who beat people bloody for a living.

"That's not what I said," Arihnda protested.

"It's okay—Ottlis has no illusions as to how Imperial law is stacked," Juahir said. "He works for—well, actually, he's not supposed to talk about his job or employer. Sorry."

"Not a problem," Arihnda said, taking a second look. That kind of mandated silence usually implied someone very high up the political ladder lurking behind the curtain. This Ottlis character might be worth cultivating. "We should get moving now, don't you think?"

"Absolutely," Juahir said. "Whenever you're ready."

"I'm ready now," Arihnda said. She took a step.

And found herself fighting unexpectedly for balance as one leg tried to collapse beneath her.

"Whoa," Juahir said, catching her arm. "Let me help."

"Thanks," Arihnda said, her face heating with embarrassment. "I'm not scared, you know. Just . . . shaking."

"Don't worry, it happens to everyone," Juahir said, peering closely at her. "Adrenaline and delayed shock. You ever think about taking some self-defense training?"

"I've thought about it a lot," Arihnda assured her as they started walking toward the turbolift. "Mostly in the past three minutes. How much does your dojo charge?"

"Unfortunately, we're totally booked at the moment," Juahir said, wrinkling her nose in thought. "We might be able to refer you to—" She broke off and looked at Ottlis, who'd taken up position on Arihnda's other side. "What about you? Would you be willing to give Arihnda an hour's training before or after your classes? We could work out a discount."

"I couldn't ask you to do that," Arihnda protested. "Juahir, stop it—you're embarrassing him."

"Not at all," Ottlis said, inclining his head to her. "I'd be delighted to give you some instruction. It's been said that a man never truly understands a subject until he teaches it."

"But do you even have the time?" Arihnda pressed. "Juahir said you were someone's bodyguard."

"Yes, but at the moment I'm just helping guard an empty office suite," Ottlis said. "My employer won't be arriving for his next visit for at least six more weeks. More than enough time to instruct you in the basics." He smiled, almost shyly. "And perhaps a bit more."

Arihnda looked back at Juahir. There was an oddly innocent expression on the other woman's face. Was this maybe not *just* about self-defense training?

And suddenly Arihnda realized she didn't care. She could really use another friend in this city. If Juahir wanted to play matchmaker, more power to her.

"Okay, you've got yourself a deal," she said. "Both of you," she added, looking back and forth between them. "On one condition."

"Which is?" Ottlis asked.

"I get to take you out to dinner tonight," Arihnda said. "Both of you."

CHAPTER 15

———————————

Many of those skilled in technological warfare believe that physical training and discipline are unnecessary. With turbolasers, hyperdrives, armor plating, and the mental resources to direct them, muscular strength and agility are thought to be merely conceits.

They are wrong. The mind and body are linked together in a meshwork of oxygen, nutrients, hormones, and neuron health. Physical exercise drives that meshwork, stimulating the brain and freeing one's intellect. Simulated combat has the additional virtue of training the eye to spot small errors and exploit them.

A change in focus can also allow the subconscious mind to focus on unresolved questions. Simulated combat often ends with the warrior discovering that one or more of those questions has been unexpectedly solved.

And occasionally, such exercise can serve other purposes.

"I do not understand," Thrawn said, his usually impassive face troubled as he gazed at the datapad report. If Thrawn were a lesser being, Eli reflected, he would almost say the Chiss was confused.

"What's there to understand?" Eli asked. "It's the result everyone expected."

The glowing red eyes bored into Eli's. *"Everyone?"*

"Mostly," Eli hedged. Yes, that was definitely what he might characterize as confusion. "Really, it's just navy politics as usual."

"But it violates all tactical reason," Thrawn objected. "Commander Cheno acquitted himself well, and the actions of his ship won the battle and saved many lives. How does High Command conclude that he must be relieved of duty?"

"They didn't relieve him, exactly," Eli pointed out. "The communication stated that he'd been permitted to retire."

"Is there a difference in the result?"

"Not really," Eli admitted. "You're right, letting him retire is mostly just a sweet-shell. As I say, politics. Gendling's well connected, and his delicate little pride got bruised, so he's taking it out on Cheno."

Thrawn looked again at the datapad. "It is a foolish waste of resources."

"Agreed," Eli said. "But it could have been worse."

"How so?"

"Really?" Eli asked, frowning. Was it *really* not obvious to him? "You were the one Gendling really wanted to nail to the bulkhead. Cheno might have been able to save himself if he'd told the panel you'd overreached your authority. But he didn't. Since they had nothing on you, they threw him to the wolves instead."

Thrawn was silent another three steps. "A foolish waste," he murmured again.

Eli sighed. "You might as well get used to it."

Again, the glowing red eyes turned on him. "What do you mean?"

Eli hesitated. It really wasn't his place to say this. But if he didn't, who else would? And for all Thrawn's military skill and insight, he seemed incapable of seeing this one on his own. "I mean, sir, there's a good chance that you're going to leave a trail of damaged careers in your wake. In fact, you already have: Commander Cheno,

Admiral Wiskovis, Commandant Deenlark—all of them have had official feathers ruffled in their direction."

"There was no such intent on my part."

"I know that," Eli said. "It's not because of anything you've done. It's just the political reaction to—well, to *you*."

"That was never my intent in accepting the Emperor's service."

"Intent isn't the point," Eli said patiently. "The problem is that you don't fit into the neat little box navy officers are supposed to fill. You're not human; worse, you're not from the Core Worlds."

"Neither are you or many others."

"But the rest of us Wild Space yokels aren't flying rings around all the politically connected elite who think they're such flaming-hot stuff," Eli pointed out. "You're showing them up, and they resent you for it. And if they can't take you down, they'll go after the people they think helped make you who you are."

"People like you?"

Eli let his gaze drift away. *Yes,* people like him. People who still had the lowly rank they'd graduated the Academy with while everyone else was energetically climbing the ladder.

But this conversation wasn't about him. This conversation and warning were about Thrawn. "They'd probably come after me if they thought I was worth the effort," he said, sidestepping the question.

"Do you suggest I try to be less capable?"

"Of course not," Eli said firmly. "You do that and more people will die and more bad guys get away. I'm just pointing out that you need to be aware that you're in the political crosshairs."

"I understand," Thrawn said. "I will endeavor to learn the rules and tactics of this form of warfare. In the meantime, is there anything we can do for Commander Cheno?"

"Just wish him well, I guess," Eli said. "Even if you

could persuade someone to listen to an appeal, he'd never command a ship again. This way, at least he got to go out on a high note."

"Except that we know it was only a partial victory."

"We *suspect*," Eli corrected, lowering his voice. "We don't *know* that's what Nightswan was going for." He pointed to the door ahead, the door with the simple gold IMPERIAL SECURITY BUREAU plaque above the smaller COLONEL WULLF YULAREN nameplate. "Maybe this is where we'll get those answers."

Colonel Yularen was waiting behind his desk when they arrived. "Welcome, Captain Thrawn; Ensign Vanto," he greeted them. "Sit down."

"Thank you, Colonel," Thrawn said. "I trust you have news for us?"

"Yes, but not the news you want," Yularen said sourly. "Speaking of news, I just heard that your Commander Cheno got stabbed in the back by the court-martial panel. I'm sorry."

"Thank you, Colonel," Thrawn said. "He was a good officer."

"So I've heard," Yularen said. "Not great, but he didn't deserve to get bounced out that way." His eyes narrowed. "Any blowback toward you? Either of you?" he added, looking at Eli.

"Not that we've heard, sir," Eli said.

"Good," Yularen said. "They may not especially like you at High Command, Thrawn, but they can't ignore the fact that you get results." He scowled. "Unfortunately, our results aren't quite up to your standards. We've done a complete search of every document ISB can get its hands on. The name *Nightswan* has cropped up on everything from metal smuggling to antiques purchases to the organization of protests and unrest. But we still don't have the slightest idea who he really is."

"Interesting," Thrawn said. "You said he organized protests. Protests against whom?"

"Pretty much everyone," Yularen said. "Mostly

government—local and Imperial both—but also corporations, manufacturing interests, even shipping companies." His eyes flicked back and forth as he read from his computer display. "We haven't found anything in common among his various targets, either. Maybe he just likes making trouble."

"May I have a list of all activities he is associated with?" Thrawn asked.

"Of course." Yularen picked up a data card and handed it across the desk. "What are you hoping to find?"

"A pattern," Thrawn said. "You say his targets appear random, but I believe we will find something connecting the locations, timing, or personnel involved. Many of his schemes involve the theft of doonium or other precious metals. Is there a chance he is driven by what he considers theft or—" He looked at Eli. "*Gubudalu?*"

Eli frowned. *Gubudalu?* What in the world was *that* one? Quickly, he ran the Sy Bisti root and modifiers—

Ah. "Usurpation," he said.

"Thank you," Thrawn said. "Could he be driven by the theft or usurpation of some personal or family mining interests?"

"Interesting thought," Yularen said. "Your typical smugglers, pirates, and thieves don't like to draw attention to themselves. But Nightswan slaps his name all over the place." He pursed his lips. "Could be he's planning some major operation and wants to get everyone looking somewhere else. I remember a group of arms smugglers during the Clone Wars who liked to set fires on one side of a city to draw the police and firefighters there, then hit a weapons depot on the other side."

"Indeed," Thrawn said. "What about Coruscant? Is there unrest here?"

"You must be joking," Yularen said with a snort. "Go down two thousand levels and you'll find all the unrest you could ever want. Go down four thousand and you might as well be in Wild Space."

"So this would be a fertile ground for anti-Imperial protests?"

"It would," Yularen agreed. "Except that all the centers of power are up here, and we've got the best police, military, and private defense forces anywhere in the galaxy. Hell, we've got combat dojos that do nothing but train Senate and ministry bodyguards. Nightswan could agitate from here until Ascension Week without making a single dent in anything that matters."

"One would think Nubia equally immune to such threats." Thrawn indicated an entry on his datapad. "Yet this protest at the Circle Bay mayor's office seems to have been quite effective."

"That was a unique case," Yularen growled. "The perpetrators managed to get the entire kitchen staff fired, then infiltrated the new staff with their own people. Once you've got someone on the inside, you can pull off almost anything."

"Exactly," Thrawn said. "You said there were dojos that specifically work with Senate bodyguards?"

"Yes," Yularen murmured, frowning with sudden interest. "Yes, I see where you're going. But most of the bodyguards who train at those places are already employed. I doubt a senator would go to one of the dojos to hire replacements or extra staff. He or she would probably get those from an accredited agency."

Yularen stood up. "Still, it's been a long time since ISB looked at any of those places. Might be worth taking a tour of the Federal District's combat subculture. Either of you care to join us?"

"Welcome to the Yinchom Dojo." *The boy seated cross-legged on the floor to the right of the door rises to his feet. His voice has the clearness of youth, with cheerfulness beneath the solemnity. He bows at the waist toward Colonel Yularen, then repeats the gesture to each of the other four of the group.* "Abandon the tedium and cares of life, all who enter, and prepare your minds and bodies for the rigors and joys of combat."

"We will," Yularen said. *His voice is calm and official, but there is a hint of humor beneath it, as well as appreciation for the boy's performance.* "I'm Colonel Yularen. I wish to speak to the owner of this place. Can you go and bring her to us?"

"I can," the boy acknowledged. *He bows again to Yularen.* "Please; come inside."

The group filed into the dojo. The boy waited until all five were standing against the wall, then headed off around the edge of the training room.

"Not nearly as impressive as the last one, sir," Vanto murmured.

"No," Thrawn agreed.

"A little small, and a little too far from sunlight to be considered top-line," Yularen agreed. *He looks slowly across the training area, his eyes flicking back and forth, taking in the details. A sparring duo works in each of the central mat's corners: one duo empty hand, the second empty hand against blade, the third and fourth stick against stick. A young human female circles the center of the mat, calling occasional instructions and corrections to each of the pairs.*

"On the other hand, thirty senators have sent one or more of their bodyguards here for updated training or sparring over the past five years," Yularen continued, "so the place must have *something* going for it. Owner's a Togorian named H'sishi."

The boy, continuing around the room, passes a woman seated on a bench against the wall.

"Sir?" Vanto said suddenly. *He nods toward the woman.* "That woman. We've seen her someplace before."

The boy passes the woman, and she stands and makes her way around the edge of the mat. An overly wide round kick comes near. She leans gracefully out of its path. An indication of moderate proficiency and

skill. She reaches the Imperials and inclines her head.
"Welcome to the Yinchom Dojo, Captain Thrawn,"
she said, raising her voice to be heard over the clash of
combat sticks. "I'm Arihnda Pryce. You probably won't
remember, but we met once at an Ascension Week reception in the Alisandre Hotel, back when you were a senior lieutenant."

"Certainly I remember you, Ms. Pryce," Thrawn
said. "You are an aide to Senator Domus Renking."

"You have a remarkable memory, Captain," Pryce
said. "I'm no longer with Senator Renking's office,
though. I work now for an advocacy group."

"I see," Thrawn said. "May I reintroduce my companions, Colonel Yularen and Ensign Vanto."

"I remember you both," Pryce said. *She nods a greeting to each of them. Her eyes shift briefly to the two
ISB agents standing silent watch behind them.* "How
may I assist you?"

"We wish to speak to the owner," Yularen said. "The
boy's gone to get her."

"Who is the woman overseeing the sparring?" Thrawn
asked.

"That's Juahir Madras, one of the instructors," Pryce
said.

"Are you here for a class?" Yularen asked.

"No," Pryce said. "My boss thought I might be able
to establish a few contacts with some of the high-level
bodyguards who train here, so I've been hanging around
for the past few days chatting with people. Ah—here's
H'sishi now."

*A large, feline being appears in one of the doorways
leading from the side of the main room. She is covered
in short brown-white fur and dressed in a combination
kilt and bandolier. Her yellow eyes focus on each of the
visitors in turn. She looks at each of the sparring duos,
then at Instructor Madras.* "Cease!" she called.

Instantly the sparring halted. In the silence, H'sishi
strode across the mat, moving with grace on her back-

jointed legs. She passed Instructor Madras without a glance and came to a halt beside Pryce. "Good day to you, officers of the Empire," she said. *Her voice is sibilant but clear.* "I am H'sishi, master of the Yinchom Dojo. How may I serve you?"

The sparring duos stand facing the visitors, their facial heat intense from heavy exercise. Instructor Madras's expression and stance show uneasiness. Her gaze is on Yularen's chest, not his face.

"I'm Colonel Yularen," Yularen said. "This is Captain Thrawn; Ensign Vanto; Officers Roenton and Brook. We're doing a routine spot-check of the dojos in the Federal District, with particular interest in government contracts and bodyguard training. I presume you have full records of both?"

"Of course," H'sishi said. "I will get them for you."

"Before you do," Thrawn said, "we are also interested in trainers for a possible new urban combat unit. Do you teach advanced stick fighting?"

"We do," H'sishi confirmed. "Have you had training in that art?"

"I have had the basics," Thrawn said. "I would like to observe your best technique firsthand."

"Certainly," H'sishi said. "Instructor Madras and I will offer you a demonstration."

"There is no need to involve any others," Thrawn said. "Instructor Madras, please bring the sticks. Instructor H'sishi and I will spar."

"Sir?" Vanto asked. *His voice is surprised and wary. But there is no understanding in it. He doesn't see the patterns; nor has he woven together the facts and possibilities.*

Madras walks to the center of the mat, the fighting sticks in her hands. Her body stance holds uneasiness.

"Ms. Pryce, please walk alongside me," Thrawn said. "There is a question I wish to ask."

"Of course." Pryce moved to his side.

Thrawn, Pryce, and H'sishi walked to the center of

the mat. "You said you worked for an advocacy group," Thrawn said. "Which one?"

"It's called the Higher Skies Group," Pryce said.

"Thank you," Thrawn said. "Stand clear, now. Instructor H'sishi, let us begin."

Pryce and Madras stepped away. "The timer is for three minutes," H'sishi said. She crossed her sticks in salute. Thrawn mirrored the gesture.

They began.

H'sishi is a good fighter. But her focus is solely on the combat, with no thought for other matters. She does not notice as the relative positions are slowly altered until Pryce and Madras are within view.

Both watch the combat, neither speaking to the other, though a quick conversation could have occurred before they were fully in view.

Their expressions are inconclusive. Both women are fascinated by the combat, with all fears, concerns, and thoughts submerged.

With H'sishi herself there are no longer doubts.

The three minutes end. H'sishi steps back and again crosses her sticks.

"Excellent, Captain," she said. "Your style is unknown to me, but you have clearly been well trained."

"Thank you, Instructor," Thrawn said. He crossed his own sticks and then offered them to Madras. *She walks forward and takes them, her eyes avoiding his gaze.* "Perhaps the next time I have duty on Coruscant you will teach me some of your style. It is of your species?"

"Yes, a Togorian form," she said. "I hope you will find the time. I would welcome you as both student and teacher. And now, Colonel Yularen, I will retrieve the records you requested."

They waited while she went to her office and returned with a data card. Yularen accepted it, then led the group back outside. "Well, *that* was interesting," Yularen commented as they walked toward their aircar. "I assume,

Captain, that you didn't simply feel the need for a little exercise?"

"Indeed," Thrawn said. "I presume you noted that Instructor Madras did not stop the sparring when we first entered?"

"She didn't stop when Pryce came over to talk, either," Yularen said. *His tone conveys thoughtfulness.* "And that despite the fact that the noise made conversation difficult."

"They didn't stop until H'sishi ordered them to," Vanto added.

"I assume you think it wasn't just rudeness?" Yularen asked.

"I think she knows who I am," Thrawn said. "She certainly knows who *you* are, Colonel. And so she stalled our meeting, wishing additional time to prepare herself."

"Interesting," Yularen said. "Unfortunately, it's a reaction ISB agents see all the time. *Everyone* has dirty secrets."

"But not everyone has secrets concerning Higher Skies," Thrawn said.

"The advocacy group?" Yularen asked.

"Yes," Thrawn said. "It is the one with which Ms. Pryce works. I asked about it before the sparring, and watched Instructor Madras as Ms. Pryce supplied me with the name. She reacted with discomfort."

"You're sure?"

"Yes," Thrawn said. "For one reason or another, the group bears investigation."

"So once you had the name and Madras's reaction, why did you go ahead with the fight?" Vanto asked.

"I have developed a certain skill for reading human emotions," Thrawn said. "I do not have such a baseline for Togorians. I wished to know if H'sishi, too, was concerned that I know of Ms. Pryce's connection with Higher Skies."

"So you gave her the chance to take you out," Vanto said slowly. *His tone holds growing understanding.* "You were the only one of us who'd heard the name. So if she'd wanted to, she could knock you down, claim it was an accident, and buy herself and the group some time."

"Correct," Thrawn said. "To be more precise, I offered what *looked* like opportunities to injure me. They were, of course, illusory."

"Of course," Vanto said. *His tone is properly respectful, but also holds irony.* "So when you were attacked at Royal Imperial Academy . . . ?"

"I wished to study the attackers' capabilities," Thrawn said. "I would have protected you from serious harm, as indeed I protected myself."

"You'll have to tell me all about that one sometime, Captain." *Yularen pulls out his comlink.* "I'll get ISB started on Higher Skies and see what we can dig up."

"I would caution that the investigation be careful and low-key," Thrawn said. "They will be alert now to such a probe, and we do not wish to drive them away."

"Yes, we *do* know how to handle investigations, thank you."

"I meant no offense," Thrawn said. "I would also consider it a favor if you would allow me to observe your progress."

"Sorry, but that won't be possible," Yularen said. "New orders came in while you were batting sticks with H'sishi. Ensign Vanto picked them up." *He gestures to Vanto.* "Ensign?"

"Yes, sir," Vanto said. *His voice holds hidden frustration.* "For the next four weeks, while the *Thunder Wasp* undergoes repairs, you'll be at the Palace with Emperor Palpatine. Once the repairs are complete, it'll return to Mid Rim and Outer Rim patrol duties." *He pauses, his frustration growing deeper.* "Under the authority of its newly appointed captain, Commander Thrawn."

"Congratulations, Commander," Yularen murmured.

"Thank you," Thrawn said. He had been promoted. Yet Vanto had not?

That wasn't as it should be. Vanto had held the rank of ensign a full year longer than was customary. Yet there was nothing Vanto had done or failed to do that should have delayed his promotion.

"Impressive achievement," Yularen continued. *His gaze switches between Thrawn and Vanto. He, too, recognizes something is amiss.* "Usually a captain warms that position for at least six years."

"I understand that during the Clone War promotions occurred more quickly."

"Wartime will do that," Yularen said. *His voice holds grim memories.* "Good luck with your new assignment, and your new command. And don't worry about Higher Skies. Whatever's there, we'll find it."

CHAPTER 16

No one is immune from failure. All have tasted the bitterness of defeat and disappointment. A warrior must not dwell on that failure, but must learn from it and continue on.

But not all learn from their errors. That is something those who seek to dominate others know very well, and know how to exploit. If an opponent has failed once at a logic problem, his enemy will first try the same type of problem, hoping the failure will be repeated.

What the manipulator sometimes forgets, and what a warrior must always remember, is that no two sets of circumstances are alike. One challenge is not like another. The would-be victim may have learned from the earlier mistake.

Or there may have been an unanticipated or unknown crossing of life paths.

"Sorry I missed our last two sessions." Ottlis's voice came from Arihnda's comm. "As I told you, my employer has come for a visit, and we've all been pretty busy."

"I understand," Arihnda said.

She did, too. Which wasn't to say she was happy with

the situation. Not just because of the interruption in her combat training, but because she really enjoyed Ottlis's company.

But work was work, and even in the upper echelons of Imperial power only a few had the luxury of picking and choosing their own schedules. "If you ever do get a couple of hours you don't know what to do with, though, let me know," she said.

"Actually, that's why I'm calling," he said. "I'm watching the office alone tonight—everyone else is off to a party—and if we move the table in the conference room over to the wall there should be plenty of room for a sparring session. You game?"

"I think so," Arihnda said, frowning. *This* was out of the blue. Still, it would be a chance to get in some practice. Not to mention a couple of hours of human contact that wasn't just pitching high-minded policies to senators and ministers. "When do you want me? And *where* do you want me—you've never given me the address."

"I haven't? Sorry." He rattled off the address, a place in one of the office spires near the Senate Building. "As to time, the sooner the better. Like I said, everyone's already gone, and we'll have the place to ourselves."

"Aside from the doorwatch droids?"

"Well, of course aside from them," he agreed. "But I'm high enough clearance that I can vouch to them for you. How soon can you be here?"

Arihnda checked the chrono. Technically, she was supposed to keep the office open for another forty minutes, just in case some senator's aide dropped by for more information on one of Higher Skies' policy positions.

But as usual, she was alone here this afternoon. Just this once, she decided, the Empire's movers and shakers could wait until tomorrow. "Ten minutes," she said.

"Ten it is," Ottlis said. "Just buzz the door when you get here, and I'll let you in."

Arihnda backtracked the address on her datapad during the air taxi ride, hoping to find out who exactly Ottlis worked for. But that information was unlisted. Once inside the building—Ottlis had already cleared her with the outer door droids—she looked for a directory or some other index or occupant listing.

Again, nothing. Apparently the residents didn't want even droid-approved visitors to know who was here and where exactly they were located.

She'd already guessed Ottlis's employer was very high up in the official ranks. This merely confirmed it.

The two doorwatch droids in the hallway stared silently at Arihnda as she approached the office door. But they permitted her to touch the buzzer without challenge. Ottlis answered promptly, gave the droids his personal clearance password, and ushered her inside.

"Nice," she commented, looking around as he led the way through the foyer and down a long corridor. The carpeting, wall hangings, and pillar sculpts were elegant but more understated than the décor she'd seen in other senators' offices. Someone who liked luxury, but didn't feel a need to rub people's faces in it. "Your boss must be even more important than I guessed."

"Probably so," Ottlis agreed. "This way."

Arihnda frowned, casually dropping a half step behind him. There was an odd layer of emotional distance in Ottlis's speech and mannerisms tonight. Something wasn't right. "Where's the party?" she asked.

"What party?"

"The party you said everyone else had gone to."

"Oh." He stopped by an open door and gestured her toward it. "In here, please."

"Thank you," she said. Something was definitely wrong, but it was too late to back out now. Brushing past him, she stepped into the room.

And came to an abrupt halt.

This wasn't the conference room Ottlis had promised. It was an office, as luxuriously appointed as the foyer and corridor, with trinkets and trophies from around the galaxy on display and no room whatsoever for sparring.

And seated behind the carved pearl desk—

"Good evening, Ms. Pryce," Moff Ghadi said, rising to his feet. "It's nice to see you again."

For a long moment Arihnda stood where she was, the memory of her last run-in with Ghadi flooding over her. This was the man who'd thrown spice on her and then threatened to have her arrested. The man who'd used that blackmail lever to make her betray Senator Renking. The man who'd sent her entire life into a tailspin.

"Your Excellency," she said, stepping away from the door and walking toward him. "Nice to see you, as well. You really should have taken me into your confidence back in the Alisandre Hotel."

Ghadi's confident smile slipped a bit. "Oh?"

"Absolutely," Arihnda assured him. "If you had, I could have told you that I was just as eager to take down Senator Renking as you were."

"Really," Ghadi said, eyeing her closely. "Your own boss?"

"The man who engineered the Imperial takeover of my family's mining business on Lothal," she corrected. "I just would have preferred to destroy him without messing up my own life in the process." She stopped beside the guest chair in front of his desk. "May I?"

"By all means," Ghadi said, waving her to the chair. His smile, she noted, was back to full confidence. "I would argue from results that the upheaval in your life was the best thing that could have happened to you. Your poise and confidence alone show you've come a long way."

"And I probably would have come still further if I hadn't had to start over at the bottom," Arihnda said. She glanced around as she sat down, noting that Ottlis had taken up position in the center of the doorway behind her as if expecting to thwart an escape attempt. The fact that she hadn't even tried to run seemed to have confused him. "But that's water under the bridge," she added, turning back to Ghadi. "So. To what do I owe the pleasure of this invitation?"

"First poise, and now directness," Ghadi said approvingly. "Excellent. Let's see if we can add honesty to the list. Who do you work for?"

"I'm sure you already know. The Higher Skies Advocacy Group."

"Good," Ghadi said. "Let's continue. Who hired your advocacy group to destroy me?"

Arihnda frowned. "Excuse me?"

"No, no, the useless naïve-child approach won't work anymore," Ghadi said. "Not for you."

"I'm not naïve, and I'm not a child," Arihnda said as calmly as she could. "I'm just confused, because I have no idea what you're talking about."

"Really," Ghadi growled. "You have no idea that very soon after one of your people came to talk to me some of my confidential financial information was recovered from a smuggler gang? Or that one of my mines was hit by raiders barely a week later?"

"What was stolen?" Arihnda asked.

Ghadi frowned. "What?"

"I asked what was stolen," Arihnda repeated. "Maybe whoever took your data is only interested in your mines or other resources."

Ghadi gave a snort. "Don't insult my intelligence," he bit out. "No one robs a moff. Not if they want to continue breathing. These are either the preliminary pinpricks leading to an attack, or else a diversion. Either way I want to know who's behind it." His eyes narrowed. "Is it Renking?"

"Your Excellency—"

"He's the obvious one," Ghadi went on. "But subtlety has never been his strong point. A different senator?

They're forever jockeying for position and advantage. Or maybe a moff?" He barked a cynical laugh. "Of course. It's Tarkin, isn't it? Grand Moff Tarkin, for whom nothing is ever quite enough. He's wanted me gone for years. Tell me it's him."

Arihnda shook her head. "I'm sorry, Your Excellency, but I can't help you."

Ghadi leaned back in his chair, his gaze steady on her face. "Fine. You don't know. Maybe your boss does. Let's call and tell him you've been invited to my office, just as Ottlis set it up. Let's see if he makes any interesting suggestions as to what you should do once you're here."

Arihnda thought about it. Driller seemed way too cheerful and open to be a spy.

But there was the sketchiness about who else was working for him and what they were doing. There was his seemingly never-ending stack of credits.

And maybe the best spies were the ones who didn't look the part.

"All right," she said, pulling out her comm. "I presume you want to listen in?"

"Of course." Ghadi beckoned Ottlis over from the door. "Just in case you're planning to try something," he added.

"All I'm planning is a conversation," Arihnda said. Turning the comm's speaker volume all the way up, she keyed Driller's number.

"Hey, Arihnda," Driller's cheerful voice came on. "What's up?"

"I just got a call from Ottlis," Arihnda said. "He can't come to the dojo tonight, but he has some free time and Moff Ghadi's office to himself, and wants to know if I can come over for a private session."

"Great," Driller said. "What did you say?"

Arihnda felt a cynical smile twitch at her lips. So Driller had known that Ottlis worked for Ghadi, yet hadn't bothered to mention that fact. "I said I needed to check with you and see if I could close up early."

"Sure, go ahead."

"Thanks," Arihnda said. "Any special instructions?"

There was just the briefest hesitation. "What do you mean?" he asked, his voice subtly changed. "Instructions about what?"

"What I should do while I'm there," Arihnda said. "Like—oh, I don't know. Anything I should look at or take notes on?"

"No, no, nothing like that," Driller said, his voice returning to normal. "Just have your session and go home."

Arihnda looked up at Ghadi. His eyes were focused on the comm, his lips puckered in concentration. From the lack of a self-satisfied smirk it didn't look like he'd heard whatever it was he was looking for.

He probably hadn't. Almost certainly hadn't, even. He could hardly know Driller well enough to have noticed the hesitation or the briefly altered tone.

But Arihnda had caught both. Did that mean something *was* going on back at Higher Skies? Or was Driller simply tired or distracted by something else?

Maybe there was a way to find out.

"Thanks," she said. "Listen, there's something else. Ottlis said that there's a position opening up soon for an office assistant with some combat training. He was thinking I might want to apply."

"You mean you'd leave Higher Skies?" Driller asked, his tone suddenly cautious. "You can't do that, Arihnda. There's way too much work to be done, and you're our best rep."

"Thanks, but I don't think you understand," she said. "This isn't just some random office position. It's with Grand Moff Tarkin."

This time, even Ghadi couldn't miss the pause. "Tarkin?" Driller asked carefully.

"That's what Ottlis said," Arihnda said. "And look, it's not like I'd be gone forever. When he's not here on

Coruscant, I'd only be part-time, so I might still be able to do some work for you."

"You'd at least be able to drop by and see us occasionally, right? Maybe have dinner and a chat?"

"Of course," Arihnda said. "I like talking to you. You know that."

"Yeah, and vice versa," Driller said. "Well . . . look, have a good session and . . . if you want to apply for the job, go ahead. Could be interesting."

"Thanks," Arihnda said. "I'll see you in the morning."

"Right. Good night."

Arihnda keyed off the comm. "Well?" she asked, raising her eyebrows at Ghadi.

"Well, what?" he growled. "And what exactly was that nonsense about Tarkin?"

"Proof that you aren't anyone's target," Arihnda said. "If you were, he'd have told me to look around your office while I was here, just like you obviously thought he might. *And* he wouldn't have been willing to let me lose my connection with Ottlis—and therefore with you—to go work for Tarkin."

Slowly, some of the fire went out of Ghadi's eyes. "You spin a good yarn, Ms. Pryce," he said. "You might even be right. But we really need to know for sure, don't we?"

"Meaning?"

"Meaning that from now on, you're my eyes and ears inside Higher Skies," Ghadi said. "You'll copy all their files, report on all their conversations, and make lists of all their contacts."

With an effort Arihnda kept her face expressionless. "I'm sure that's not necessary, Your Excellency."

"Oh, I think it is," Ghadi said. "And you'll do it, or I'll call ISB and tell them you came here tonight to steal confidential files and data cards. Ottlis will confirm that, of course."

Arihnda looked up at Ottlis. He looked back at her, his face expressionless.

"I don't hire fools, Ms. Pryce," Ghadi added quietly. "Ottlis knew from the start that he'd been set up with you. He's kept me fully apprised of the game this whole time."

"I've already told you I'm not playing any games."

"Then you should welcome the chance to prove it," Ghadi said. "Ottlis will give you what you need, and then he'll escort you home."

"I don't need his protection," Arihnda said, looking up again. And to think she'd once thought of this man as a friend. "Or his company."

"I'm sorry you feel that way," Ghadi said. "I also don't care. Good evening, Ms. Pryce. We'll be talking again. Very soon."

The trip to the apartment was very quiet. Ottlis waited until she had unlocked and opened the door, then strode away into the lights and flickering signs of night. Neither had said a word the entire trip.

The apartment was empty. Juahir was probably still at the dojo, or else was meeting with whoever had told her to hook up Ottlis with her dear friend Arihnda.

Just as well. Arihnda wasn't ready to face her right now anyway.

She cooked dinner completely on autopilot, and ate it the same way. Afterward, she sat down at her computer, staring at the display and trying to think.

She'd been dropped into a box. A very small, very uncomfortable box. Even the slightest hint that she was trying to cross Ghadi, and he would hand her over to ISB, and with Ottlis corroborating the charges she would be convicted in record time.

That left her no option but to spy on Higher Skies. But if Driller was in fact spying for someone, that someone wouldn't be happy if he caught Arihnda digging into his secrets. If Driller *wasn't* spying, and if Arihnda proved there was no deliberate threat against Ghadi, the moff might turn her over to ISB anyway as a warning to his hypothetical enemies.

It was the same box Ghadi had trapped her in before. He probably expected it to work the same way again.

Only this time, Arihnda was prepared.

And it was going to cost him.

She worked on the computer for the next hour, pulling up data, digging into rumors and unsubstantiated reports, finding obscure financial records and hints. She spent another hour putting all of it together. Somewhere along the way Juahir called and said she was heading to a party and not to wait up. Arihnda hadn't planned to, anyway.

She waited until she had everything in a neat package. Then, pulling out her comm, she keyed for the Universal Connection system. "My name is Arihnda Pryce," she told the droid who took the call. "I want to send a message to a navy officer whom I believe is on Coruscant."

"Name?"

She braced herself. He was either amazingly competent, she'd told herself once, or else he had powerful friends. Either way, he was worth reaching out to. "Thrawn," she said. "Commander Thrawn."

He was waiting in a corner booth in the Gilroy Plaza Diner when Arihnda arrived, his features half concealed by the hood of his plain robe, his red eyes completely invisible. Her first thought was that it was the wrong person, but as she neared him she saw he was wearing tinted glasses that hid all but the faintest glow.

"Ms. Pryce," he greeted her as she reached the table. "You are late."

"Sorry," she apologized, glancing around as she sat down across from him. The diner was nearly deserted, with the only other patrons in a booth around the corner from the serving bar. That should give them sufficient privacy. "Nice glasses. With your eyes covered, most people would probably assume you're a Pantoran."

"So I have been told," Thrawn said. "Why did you ask me to meet you?"

Arihnda studied him. His face was impassive, giving nothing away. "I'm in something of a situation," she said. "I think you're also dealing with some problems. I'm hoping we can help each other."

He inclined his head slightly beneath the hood. "Continue."

"This evening I was taken to a meeting with a high government official," she said. "He thinks the advocacy group I work with is trying to destroy him. He wants me to spy on them for him, and threatened to turn me over to ISB under false charges of espionage if I refuse."

"Did he seem confident in that threat?"

Arihnda frowned. An odd question. "Very confident."

Thrawn nodded. "Continue."

"That's really about it," Arihnda said. "I was hoping you would help me get out from under him."

"I see," Thrawn said. "And your weapon?"

Arihnda blinked. "What do you mean?"

"Surely you don't expect me to bring turbolaser fire to bear on his office," Thrawn said, a slight dryness to his tone. "I conclude you have some other weapon you believe will be useful against him."

Arihnda smiled tightly. He was good, all right. "I do," she said, pulling out her datapad. "During his rant he mentioned that one of his mines had been recently attacked. I poked around a little and found it." She keyed the datapad and swiveled it around to face him. "Anything interesting jump out at you?"

Thrawn nodded. "Doonium."

"Yes," Arihnda said. "A good-sized vein of it, which

he apparently never registered. He appears to be selling the doonium to the navy through hidden channels, probably at inflated profits, certainly without paying taxes on it."

"Or perhaps is selling it elsewhere," Thrawn said.

"And the current black market in the metal will bring even more ridiculous profits," Arihnda agreed. "Either way, no one knew about it until someone dug up the data and raided the mine. I asked him what was stolen, but he never answered. I'm betting heavily it was some of the doonium."

"And you believe his lack of disclosure is a weapon that can be brought to bear?"

"Exactly," Arihnda said. "I thought that since you're a friend of Colonel Yularen, you could quietly pass this along to him."

"By which I assume you mean anonymously?"

Arihnda felt her throat tighten. "Partly anonymously, yes," she said. "It's a little tricky. I don't want anyone but Yularen knowing I gave it to you. But *he* needs to know, because I want it on his record that I gave him this data so that I don't get arrested or charged if it turns out someone at Higher Skies *was* the thief."

For a moment Thrawn gazed at her from behind his glasses. Then, slowly, he shook his head. "I can give this to Colonel Yularen," he said. "But I cannot do so now."

Arihnda stared at him. "Why not?"

"Because the longer it is in his possession, the more likely it will become known to others within ISB," Thrawn said. "Possibly including the close friend and secret ally of your corrupt official."

"You think he has some specific ally there?"

"I am certain of it," Thrawn said. "You said he threatened to send you to prison for theft. But his word alone would be insufficient to overcome the absence of evidence."

"Not even the word of a senior official?"

"Senior officials are precisely those whom the ISB is

tasked with monitoring," Thrawn said. "Only with a secret ally could he know the charges against you would escape closer scrutiny."

"I don't understand," Arihnda said. "How do you even know he *has* someone like that?"

"You said he was confident," Thrawn reminded her. "A warrior does not threaten an enemy with an unloaded weapon unless he has no other choice." He pulled the card from the datapad and slipped it into a pocket. "I will hold your information for Colonel Yularen. But I will deliver it only when I judge the time to be right."

Arihnda swallowed hard. She could see Thrawn's logic, and it made sense.

But without Yularen and ISB holding something over Ghadi, there was no way she could take him on by herself. "What if I said I was willing to risk it?"

"I am not."

"What if I sweeten the pot?" Arihnda pressed. "You know military tactics, but I know politics. I could help you there."

"I appreciate the offer," Thrawn said. "But I do not need assistance."

"Your aide might disagree," Arihnda said. "Ensign Vanto. In three years you've gone from lieutenant to commander, yet he's still an ensign. Why?"

Even through the glasses she could see his eyes narrow. "That is a military matter."

"Is it?" Arihnda countered. "Remember, I was at the dojo when he got the news of your promotion. He was disappointed. Also resentful, I think, though he tried to hide it."

"How do you know this?"

"He and Colonel Yularen had a short conversation when the report came in," Arihnda said. "You were slapping sticks with H'sishi so you probably couldn't hear them. But I was close enough to catch the gist of what they were saying." Actually, she hadn't heard nearly as much as she was making it sound. But she'd done some digging on Vanto while she was prepping for this meeting, and it hadn't been hard to put the pieces together.

Fortunately, she'd put them together right. Behind the glasses, Thrawn's eyes narrowed. "Promotions should not be affected by politics," he said.

"Maybe they shouldn't, but they are," Arihnda said. "The way I read it, some of the senators and ministers don't like you. You're too good for them to attack directly, so they find other ways. Pressuring the High Command to keep your aide from advancing is one. Putting your ship last in line for repairs is another."

Thrawn seemed to straighten up. "Excuse me?"

"Oh, you hadn't caught that one?" Arihnda asked. "Practically every other ship that needs dockyard space has been put on the list ahead of the *Thunder Wasp*. After all, the best way to make sure you don't outshine all their precious elite Core World officers is to keep you on Coruscant away from any possible battles or engagements."

"Interesting," Thrawn said. "I had of course noted that the *Thunder Wasp* had been placed at the lowest priority. I assumed the repair ranking was based on which ships needed to be returned to patrol duty most quickly."

"You were half right," Arihnda said. "Just substitute which *captains* they want back on duty—and which one they don't—and you'll have the complete picture."

"I see," Thrawn murmured. "Have you an ally who can alter that?"

"I have some contacts," Arihnda said, running quickly through the list of senators and ministers she'd talked to while working with Higher Skies. Without knowing who was behind the vendetta against Thrawn, there was no way to guess which of them might be able to intervene on his behalf. "None of them is really an ally."

He was silent another moment. "Tell me, who does your high government official fear?"

"I don't know that he fears *anyone*."

"Then who does he hate? All who hold positions of power fear or hate someone. Or something."

Arihnda thought back on Ghadi's rantings. Now that Thrawn mentioned it . . . "There *is* someone he hates, yes," she said.

"So you have an enemy, and a threat to that enemy," Thrawn said. "That gives you two possible vectors of attack. One is to turn the threat into an ally, then use him against your enemy. The other—" He paused and cocked his head to the side. "Is to use the threat as a lever against your enemy in order to make *him* into your ally."

"I see," Arihnda said slowly, her mind spinning. When he put it that way . . . "Any recommendation as to which approach would be best?"

"Only you can decide that," Thrawn said. "You must consider which weapons and levers you have available, and which approach offers the best chance of success." He lifted a warning finger. "But remember that in neither case is your new ally likely to be your friend. His association with you will be based solely on fear or need. Fear of what you can do to him, or a need for what you can provide him. If either of those forces loses its value, so does your position."

"Understood," Arihnda said. "Thank you, Commander. I think I know what to do now."

"One other thing." Thrawn's half-hidden eyes seemed to burn into hers. "It may be that your advocacy group will indeed prove to be more than you know. If you are to have Colonel Yularen's ultimate support and protection, you may need to turn your back on your colleagues. Are you prepared to do that?"

Arihnda smiled bitterly. *Her colleagues.* Driller, her boss. Juahir, her roommate. The only two people on

Coruscant she knew well. The only people on this planet she'd ever called friends. "Absolutely," she said.

The Higher Skies office was deserted when Arihnda arrived an hour later. Nor was anyone likely to drop by. Driller knew she'd been off to see Ottlis, and would undoubtedly have relayed that information to Juahir. Arihnda's failure to return to their apartment would probably be seen as evidence that she and Ghadi's bodyguard had progressed from combat sparring to other forms of physical activity.

A year ago, doing something so blatant or obvious would have embarrassed her. Now she barely noticed, let alone cared.

All she cared about was that she now had all night to work without fear of interruption.

It was just past dawn when she finally made the call.

"This had better be important," Ghadi growled. "And I mean *damn* important. I'm *this* close to having Ottlis whipped for waking me up, and you don't even want to know what I want to do to you."

"It's important," Arihnda assured him. "You were right—Higher Skies is keeping watch on many important people. I've found the files."

"Of course I was right," Ghadi said blackly. "Any reason this revelation couldn't have waited until later?"

"It probably could have," Arihnda conceded. "But I thought you'd want to hear as soon as possible about the Tarkin file."

There was a brief silence. "They have a file on *Tarkin*?" he asked, the grumpiness abruptly gone. "What's in it?"

"I don't know," Arihnda said. "This one's under a different encryption than everything else I've found. But if it's like the ones I've been able to read, it probably has a lot of secrets in it. Things Tarkin wouldn't want anyone else knowing about."

"Perfect," Ghadi said. "Yes. I absolutely want those files."

"I thought you would," Arihnda said. "I can collate them with the other files I've been able to find. But I wanted to make sure you wanted this one."

"Don't be stupid," he said. "You have the weapon I need to take down Tarkin, and you want to know if I *want* it? Get it on a data card and bring it to my office. *Now.*"

"Yes, Your Excellency," Arihnda said. "As I said, though, at the moment it's unreadable. If you give me time, I may be able to decrypt it."

"Just bring it to me," Ghadi growled. "*I'll* decrypt it. Let's see how high and mighty Grand Moff Tarkin is when I'm shoving his dirty little secrets down his throat."

"Very well, Your Excellency," Arihnda said. "Do you also want the other information? Or do you want to wait until I've decrypted it?"

"I'll take anything you've found on any of the other moffs," he said. "You can hold off on anything else." He muttered something unintelligible under his breath. *"Tarkin."*

"I'll bring this over at once, then," Arihnda said. "Who in your office shall I give the data card to?"

"Mm—good point," Ghadi said. "Yes, you'd better bring it directly to me here." He gave her a Whitehawk Tower address. "Ottlis will meet you at the door and take the data card. Give it to him, and *only* to him."

"Yes, Your Excellency," Arihnda said. "I'll leave at once." She keyed off the comm.

It was done.

Or at least, half of it was done.

But she had time. She had plenty of time.

CHAPTER 17

There are three ways to take down a wild tusklan.

The average hunter takes a large-bore weapon with which to shoot the animal. When it works, the method is quick and efficient. But if the first shot fails to hit a vital organ, the tusklan may be upon its attacker before a second shot can be aimed and fired.

The wise hunter takes a smaller-bore weapon. The method is less likely to produce a first-shot kill, but the second, third, or fourth shot may succeed. However, if the bore is too small, none of the shots will penetrate to vital points, and the tusklan will again triumph over its attacker.

The subtle hunter takes no visible weapon at all. He instead induces a thousand stingflies to attack the tusklan from all sides. The method is slow, and destructive of the pelt. But in the end, the tusklan is dead.

And it dies never knowing where the attack came from.

Eli sighed as he looked at the navigational repeater display in Thrawn's office. Another day, another crisis.

Another small-time, minor-world, petty-plated crisis. "So what's this one about, sir?" he asked.

"It appears to be a land dispute, Ensign," Thrawn said.

Eli clenched his teeth. *Ensign.* Thrawn had promised that he would try to get him the promotion both agreed was long overdue. So far, it hadn't happened.

And only Eli knew why.

He thought about that brief and long-ago meeting with Moff Ghadi's flunky Culper. He thought about it a lot. At the time, he'd dismissed Culper's threat to keep him at the bottom of the navy's officer corps as empty hyperbole designed to scare him.

But as the old saying said, it wasn't a bluff if you had the cards. Moff Ghadi clearly had the cards.

And for all of Thrawn's military cleverness, he had no idea how to navigate Coruscant politics.

"On one side is the Afe clan of the native Cyphari," Thrawn continued. "On the other side is a group of human colonists in an enclave pressing up against Afe territory. The colonists claim the Afes have been raiding their border settlements, and demand concessions and a safety buffer zone that would together take nearly half the Afes' land and force them to move into territories controlled by their fellow Cyphari. The Afes claim they have lived on that land for centuries, and state their attacks are in retaliation against trespassing and border raids from the humans."

Eli suppressed another sigh. "And we are here why?"

"Because I requested the assignment," Thrawn said. "With the assistance and support of Colonel Yularen."

"I see," Eli murmured. And with the further backing of the Emperor?

Possibly. Thrawn's informal connection to Yularen wasn't something that normally happened between navy officers and ISB, and Eli had long suspected the Emperor's silent hand in the relationship. Certainly it made sense: Yularen could smooth Thrawn's path through the High Command's datawork and sheer inertia, while Thrawn in turn often spotted details that were useful to

Yularen's investigations, particularly with the whole Nightswan puzzle.

But the arrangement, and the perks that went with it, hadn't gone unnoticed by others in the navy. Eli had caught the occasional odd look from other officers in passing, and formal communications with the *Thunder Wasp* sometimes carried undertones of resentment or envy.

Thrawn, naturally, didn't seem to notice anything except the perks.

"Here," Thrawn said, swiveling around his desk display. "Tell me what you see."

Eli leaned closer. It was a summary of the planet's shipping records for the past six months, displayed side by side with a breakdown of cargo types. He ran his eye down them, his brain automatically sorting, merging, and analyzing . . .

He smiled tightly. "Shellfish."

"Precisely," Thrawn said. "The volume of shellfish exports has nearly doubled in the past four months."

"About the time the land dispute began?"

"The dispute has been ramping up for approximately twice that long," Thrawn said. "But the recent escalation in cross-border incidents does date from that point. The petition to Coruscant dates from one month afterward."

"The humans have some precious metals they want to smuggle," Eli said slowly, working out the logic. "Possibly because they discovered a new vein eight months ago." He looked sharply at Thrawn. "Beneath the Afes' territory?"

"That's the most likely reason for the colonists' sudden demand for Afe land."

"So they putter around with their own smuggling efforts for a while," Eli continued. "Then someone calls in Nightswan. He shows them how to do it properly, they start shoving out their backlog inside the shellfish, and decide they want better access to the vein." He shook his head. "Kind of sloppy. You'd think someone as clever as Nightswan could have come up with a new technique instead of repeating himself."

"Come now," Thrawn said, mildly chiding. "Don't you recognize an invitation when you see one?"

Eli looked at the shipping list again. "Pretty daring," he said. "Also pretty stupid. He just barely won the last round. You'd think he'd have learned to quit while he was ahead."

"Ah, but *did* he win the last round?" Thrawn countered. "We agree he won at Umbara, but we really don't know how many other confrontations he and I may have had over the past few months. Only those operations that he signs, as it were, do we know to attribute to him."

"I hadn't thought about that."

"I have," Thrawn said, his voice going dark and thoughtful. "Perhaps you hadn't noticed, but there appears to be a growing number of these incidents around the Empire. There's been an increase in smuggling activity, which robs Coruscant of tariff money. Thefts of metals like doonium have also increased, at the very time the Empire is attempting to gather together as much of those resources as possible. There have been disputes like this one, sometimes between peoples on a single world, sometimes between neighboring systems, all of which distract attention and drain military resources. Even more disturbing, there are a growing number of incidents of unrest or open revolt."

"And you think Nightswan is behind them?"

"*All* of them?" Thrawn shook his head. "No. At the moment the turmoil is unorganized. Nightswan is not a shadowy mirror image of the Emperor, guiding a growing army of disaffection. But I likewise have no doubt that Nightswan has had a hand in some of the incidents. In many of those, I suspect, he achieved his intended goal."

"Whatever that goal happened to be," Eli mused.

"And now, he's invited us to this one. I'm glad we could fit him into our schedule."

"Indeed," Thrawn said. "Let us see what he has arranged for us this time."

"I really don't understand the purpose of this meeting, Commander," Mayor Pord Benchel said. *His expression is tense, the muscles in his throat equally tight. His voice holds resentment and frustration.* "You've asked nothing that wasn't in our reports and sworn statements to Coruscant. Have you even read them?"

"I have," Thrawn said. "The purpose of this meeting is so that I may meet you in person. You, and the rest of the dispute committee."

"It's not a *dispute committee*," Lenora Scath put in. *Her expression holds anger, as does her voice.* "It's a committee for justice. *We're* the ones who've been attacked, Commander, not the Cyphari."

"The reports suggest that is a matter of dispute," Thrawn said. "Hence, the term I have assigned you."

"Not *our* reports," Brigte Polcery retorted. *Her expression and voice also hold anger.* "Not any report that anyone in his right mind could believe."

"Are you suggesting I am *not* in my right mind?" Thrawn asked mildly.

"No, of course not," Polcery said hastily. *Her anger decreases, replaced by caution.* "I'm just saying you can't trust the Cyphari to tell the truth. That clan thing of theirs means everyone always just repeats what the clan leader says."

"I see," Thrawn said. "Do you agree, Mr. Tanoo?"

"Excuse me?" Clay Tanoo asked. *His body stance suggests surprise and nervousness.*

"I asked if you agreed that Cyphari statements cannot be trusted."

"Oh." Tanoo looked at the others. "Yes, of course. The clan thing. You know?"

"I have been told," Thrawn said. "By reliable sources." *Their expressions shift. Benchel and Scath wonder if the statement is an insult. Polcery and Tanoo are certain that it is. Some of the other seventy-three people gathered in the assembly room show similar emotions. Most are merely nervous or frightened. Those in the rear of the room are possibly too far away to hear the testimony. The sides of the room are covered with banners depicting their life on Cyphar. The designs and patterns speak of the hardship and determination of their past, and of their hope for their future. Woven within those patterns are their closeness of family and distrust of outside authority.* "Thank you. You may all return to your other activities."

"Thank you, sir," Benchel said. "May we ask what decision you've come to?"

"I have hardly had time to make a decision, Mayor Benchel. My next task is to view directly the disputed territory."

"I'd advise against that, Commander," Polcery said. "The Cyphari have threatened to attack anyone who comes onto their land without permission."

"So I have heard," Thrawn said. "Fortunately, I have already received Afe Chief Joko's invitation."

The reactions of expression and body stance are brief. But they are sufficient.

"Well, good luck to you," Benchel said. "I'd advise you to take a guard along anyway."

Three minutes later, the shuttle lifted into the air and flew off across the landscape. "Your conclusions, Ensign Vanto?" Thrawn invited.

"Not entirely certain, sir," Vanto said thoughtfully. "Mayor Benchel is an obvious choice—he's loud and passionate and did most of the talking. But I'm thinking he may be a little *too* loud."

"And the others?"

"I'd say Scath and Polcery. Maybe Tanoo, but he

seems a little too slow and simpleminded. I can't see Nightswan trusting him with big secrets."

"You forget that the conspiracy was already in place when Nightswan was brought in," Thrawn said. "He may not have had any choice as to participants. Anyone else?"

"I didn't see anything from the other ten committee members. As far as I could tell, they were just regular colonists who'd been caught up in events, or possibly manipulated into believing what the others told them. Ditto for the onlookers."

"Indeed," Thrawn said. "My congratulations, Ensign. Your skills have improved markedly."

"Thank you, sir," Vanto said drily. "Which ones did I miss?"

"None," Thrawn said. "Scath, Polcery, and Tanoo are indeed involved in the conspiracy. Mayor Benchel, as you have already surmised, is one of the duped. Have you any further thoughts or conclusions?"

"Not yet, sir," Vanto said.

"There is yet time," Thrawn assured him. "Study further. We will speak again after we have met with Chief Joko."

Eli had done a quick study of the Cyphari during the *Thunder Wasp*'s voyage, and the closest image he'd been able to come up with for the natives' appearance was large stick insects with Rodian snouts and neat rows of short red fur.

Which, in real life, turned out to be exactly what they looked like.

"I know not what to tell you, Commander Thrawn," Chief Joko said, his voice simultaneously grating, whiny, and melodious. It was an interesting combination, one Eli hadn't run into before. "The reports of my clansfolk are true and accurate. The humans from the Hollenside Enclave have crossed the border on many occasions, stealing and mistreating our crops and attacking or burning our farm structures." He reached a long arm behind him and tapped the inner surface of the conical meetinghouse he had invited the Imperials into. "Once, a home was also burned."

"Fortunate that it was not the clan meetinghouse," Thrawn said, sending a long gaze around the structure and the dozens of designs decorating it. "This structure is rich with the culture and history of the Afe clan."

"It is," Joko said. "Few of the Empire would notice. Fewer still would appreciate."

"Perhaps. Did you confront the attackers?"

"On three occasions our sentinels arrived at the incursion before the invaders slipped away," Joko said. "On two of those occasions the sentinels were attacked."

"Were any injured or killed?"

"Eight were injured," Joko said. "None was killed."

"There is that, at least," Thrawn said. "Let us hope this can be resolved before it reaches a stage that brings loss of life." He finished his visual survey of the meetinghouse and returned his attention to Joko. "Let us now examine the other side of the blade. I am told members of the Afe clan have also crossed the border into the Hollenside Enclave."

"To sit idly without giving response is to encourage further attacks," Joko said, his snout flattening. "Yes, we have crossed the border. Yes, we have inflicted impairment equal to our suffering. But never have we attacked the humans on their own soil."

"Did you not defend yourself against human guards?"

"We did," Joko said, his snout rounding back again and the tips of his fur going slightly orange. "But we shot only to distract, and to drive away. We did not shoot to injure or kill."

Which wasn't what Mayor Benchel's reports said, Eli remembered. According to him, several of the enclave's hastily organized civilian guard force *had* been shot and wounded. And if Thrawn was right about Benchel not being part of the conspiracy, the mayor would have no reason to lie about that.

Unless he had himself been lied to by one of the others. In that case, his report could be meaningless.

Eli sighed to himself. Thrawn made it look so easy.

"I would like to see where the first of these incursions occurred," Thrawn said. "Will you send a guide with us in our shuttle to that location?"

"There is no need for shuttle or guide," Joko said, unwinding from his cross-legged seated position like hair tresses unbraiding. "We are already here. Will you accompany me?"

"Of course," Thrawn assured him, standing up. Eli, caught by surprise, scrambled to his feet. "It is fortunate that the incursions happened so near the clan meeting-house."

"Fortune follows design," Joko said, his snout widening. "I anticipated your request." He spread his arms to encompass the entire structure. "The clan meeting-house is, of course, mobile. Come; I will show you."

"Here," Joko said. *He pauses at the edge of a field of stiff, desiccated grain stalks*. "Here, when the grain was yet ripe and unharvested, is where humans first came onto Afe land."

Thrawn gazed across the field, wondering what the plants had looked like in full bloom. As it was, there was little left in the stalks for him to see.

He looked back at the clan meetinghouse, a hundred meters behind them. Its shape and structure reinforced the patterns of words and pictures he'd seen on the interior wall.

Patterns and connections. Ultimately, that was what it came down to. Patterns and connections in nature; patterns and connections in created things; patterns and connections in warfare.

Patterns of the humans and human smugglers. Patterns of the Afes and Afe defense. Patterns of Night-swan.

What were the patterns here?

"Do airspeeders regularly cross this area?" he asked.

"Not regularly," Joko said. "Sometimes a craft travels from the human enclave to the Twi'lek settlement."

"Are there pictures of the ground from any of those flights?"

"None that I know of," Joko said. *He touches the skin beside his eyes.* "We have seen the land from the height of the eyes." *He points upward.* "We need not see it from the height of the clouds."

"All information and points of view are useful," Thrawn said. "Ensign Vanto, please calculate the most likely route."

"No need," Joko said. He pulled a small flat box from his waist sash and keyed it on.

A huge holomap of the area, vertical and twenty meters square, appeared ten meters in front of them. Joko adjusted the box, and the view widened out. "There are the two major cities for sky travel," he said, pointing on the holomap. He keyed the box again, and the view zoomed in to where they were standing. "No likely path comes overhead where we now stand."

"Yes, I see," Thrawn said. He studied the holomap, then the cropland, then the holomap again. The overall crop field itself would be in clear view from an airspeeder, though this particular area would be at the edge of observation.

Limited isolation, offering limited anonymity. Perhaps something had been visible before the harvest that was not visible now. "Ensign, I will want a list of all who have traveled this route over the past year. Chief Joko, did any of the Afes note anything unusual about the crops from this field? Was any grain discarded due to disease or malformation?"

"Some plants die in all fields," Joko said. "This field

has a history of such damage. Still, it is mostly fertile, and water is abundant, so it continues to be planted."

"Yes." A group of stalks that were slightly shorter and thinner than the rest was visible, forming a corridor four meters wide that started at the edge of the field and traced a winding path toward the center. "Did the damage occur in this specific part of the field?"

"Yes." *Joko gazes at him, his upper body hunched over as if to bring his eyes closer to the Imperial's level.* "The stunted stalks are a sign of improper development. You have a keen eye, Commander Thrawn."

"Does your map also include the locations of human attacks on Afe territory?"

Joko adjusted the box. The focus of the map widened again. Another touch on the controls, and a dozen pulsing red dots appeared. All were north of the field where the Imperials now stood. "The most recent are colored the darkest red."

"Your counterattacks on the humans?"

Four blue dots appeared, approximately opposite the four northernmost red dots. "We are long-suffering," Joko said. "But we finally had to take a stand."

"Understandable." Patterns; and this pattern was beginning to emerge. "You will be guarding some of your villages tonight. Where will your guards be stationed?"

Joko draws himself up to his full height. "Why do you ask?"

"I believe I can anticipate the human conspirators' plan for tonight," Thrawn said. "I wish to see your deployment so that I may adjust my own plans."

Joko is silent for a few seconds, then touches the control. Three yellow spots appear on the map, one at the northernmost red spot, the other two farther north. "Their boldness takes them ever closer to our main cities," he said. "We will guard these villages in anticipation. We will also hold guards in reserve to pursue them back to their lair and entrap them."

"Yes." The deployment fit the pattern that the meetinghouse artwork had indicated. It was a pattern the conspirators had also likely learned over the many years the two species had lived side by side. "I offer two suggestions. First: Do not hold guards for pursuit. Deploy them solely in protection of your villages."

"You deny us the right of response?"

"I believe your attackers hope to lure you across the border so as to claim you invaded the enclave," Thrawn said. "By remaining on your side, you will deny them that weapon."

"Yet the evidence will demonstrate their attack came first," Joko said. "We have no intent of causing injury. Our pursuit would be solely to identify the invaders."

"Nevertheless, I still caution restraint."

"For how long, Commander Thrawn?" *Joko's fur tips turn briefly orange.* "How long would you have us cower before an enemy?"

"It will end tonight."

Joko's eyes flicked to Vanto, then to each of the five escorting stormtroopers, then back to Thrawn. "Tonight."

"Tonight. In the meantime, I offer you my escort to deploy as you wish in defense of your villages. Be advised that their blasters will be set on stun. I will not kill anyone on either side."

"But some of the humans are criminals."

"When their guilt has been established, they will face Imperial justice," Thrawn said. "Until then, there will be no killing."

"Imperial justice." *Joko's voice and body stance hold contempt.* "Very well, Commander Thrawn. I accept your word. For now. You will return to your ship to ponder?"

"No," Thrawn said. "Ensign Vanto and I will spend the night here."

"Here on our world?"

"Here in this very spot," Thrawn said. "Will you

leave the meeting structure in its current place for our use?"

"Why?"

"I wish to observe the crops in the moonlight," Thrawn said. "Sometimes the altered spectrum offers clues."

"You will find no clues in that fashion," Joko said. "But I will leave the structure. Do as you will."

"Thank you," Thrawn said. "One final request. I know that many of your people live in this district. I request that they leave for tonight."

"*All* of them?"

"All of them," Thrawn confirmed. "They may move up into the hills or across the river. But all must leave this area."

"But it will be disruption," Joko said. "They will need shelter and provisions. Many are the families and young children that must travel."

"The move will be only for this single night," Thrawn said. "Surely the people of the Afe clan can endure a night of hardship in return for the reclamation of their land."

"You can promise so quick a resolution?"

"I promise Imperial justice," Thrawn said. "Move your people. I will contact you when it is safe for them to return."

Five minutes later the stormtroopers and the Afes departed, the first in the *Thunder Wasp*'s shuttle, the second in the clan's ancient landspeeders.

"Ensign?" Thrawn invited.

"You're expecting the conspirators to come here tonight," Vanto said. "Probably in force."

"Why?"

"Because they expect you to rule in favor of the Afes and thereby block their access to the ore," Vanto said. "This may be their last shot, and they'll want to take full advantage of it."

"Very good," Thrawn said. Vanto's pathway was slightly flawed, but his final conclusion was correct. "If they've had experience with Imperial justice, they won't expect an overly quick ruling. But a long investigation will certainly focus attention on this region and prevent them from returning without being observed."

"Ah," Vanto said, his earlier confidence slightly subdued. "I see."

"But your conclusion regarding the raid is still valid," Thrawn said. "What do you conclude from the stunted plants?"

"Heavy-metal poisoning," Vanto said, his confidence returning. "Which further implies that the ore is near the surface. Odd that no one spotted it before."

"The planet's metallurgical needs are satisfied from other, more extensive mines," Thrawn said. "A vein this size may not be worth developing."

"Unless you're a group of ten or twenty that sees easy credits."

"Yes. Did you note the pattern in the humans' raids?"

"They're moving farther and farther northward," Vanto said. "Moving toward the larger population centers. I assume they're trying to provoke a stronger reaction from the Afes."

"Yes," Thrawn said. "They recognize that the usual Cyphari response to such attacks is to defend the last site attacked, plus the next two along the anticipated path. The conspirators' hope is twofold: to draw attention farther away from this spot so their mining operation remains undetected, and to induce an Afe attack that will result in human deaths."

"They want the Afes to *kill* someone? Just so they'll have a better case to present to Coruscant?"

"Partly," Thrawn said. "More significant is the fact that the Afe ethos will cause them to recoil in shame and guilt, which will disadvantage them in future negotiations."

"Which is why you advised Joko to stay on this side of the border," Vanto said, nodding. "Even if they're not trying to kill, they might be manipulated into doing so. You got all that from the artwork in the meetinghouse?"

"I did."

"I wish you could teach me how to do that," Vanto said ruefully. "If we're expecting company, shouldn't we bring down a few more navy troopers or storm-troopers?"

"The two of us will be sufficient," Thrawn said. "They won't expect trouble."

Vanto smiled in grim anticipation. "No," he agreed. "I daresay they won't."

CHAPTER 18

There are many stories and myths about the Chiss. Some are accurate; others have been eroded by the twin forces of distance and time.

But one fact has always remained constant: The Chiss must be approached from a position of strength and respect. One must have strength, for the Chiss will deal only with those capable of keeping their promises. One must have respect, for the Chiss must believe that those promises will be kept.

There will be many cultural differences, and a warrior dealing with the Chiss must be wary of them. But never make the mistake of believing forbearance equates to acceptance, or that all positions are equally valid. There are things in the universe that are simply and purely evil. A warrior does not seek to understand them, or to compromise with them. He seeks only to obliterate them.

There were three open-topped landspeeders' worth, nine men and three women in all. Eli and Thrawn watched through the meetinghouse doorway as the intruders drove carefully into the lane of damaged plants, forcing their way over and through the damaged stalks.

One at a time the vehicles stopped, spacing themselves along the corridor at twenty-meter intervals. The raiders climbed out, scattered along the lane, and got to work.

Eli had hoped that all three of the conspirators Thrawn had identified earlier at the meeting would be present. It would certainly make it easier to file charges if they were caught in the act. But only the nervous one, Tanoo, was present.

Still, the fact that the landspeeders had driven straight into the field, apparently not caring that they were leaving visible damage on the remaining stalks, indicated that Thrawn had been correct in his conclusion that this would be the last raid for a while. The further implication was that everyone who wasn't working the diversionary raids was probably here.

And with Thrawn's stormtroopers backing up the Afes, the raiders weren't going to have the quick and easy smash-and-run they were expecting.

In fact, there was a good chance the whole bunch of them would end up captured. If Eli and Thrawn could take this group as well, the Imperials might indeed roll up the whole conspiracy tonight.

There would certainly be no lack of evidence. Each of the raiders had two long cylindrical bags attached to his or her waist, about fifteen centimeters in diameter, trailing on the ground. They walked steadily along their assigned sections of the ore vein, digging into the soil with small trowels and shoveling their prizes into the bags.

"Interesting," Thrawn murmured. "Tanoo isn't digging."

Eli focused his electrobinoculars. Thrawn was right. Tanoo was going back and forth among the diggers, testing the material they were digging up with a hand-held sensor. "Checking the quality of ore?" he suggested.

"Perhaps," Thrawn said, his voice thoughtful. "Locate his full record. I want a list of his areas of knowledge and expertise."

"Yes, sir." Eli lowered his electrobinoculars and pulled out his datapad. They'd already looked at the summary profiles of the three known conspirators, which had listed Tanoo as a crop geneticist. The record came up, and Eli skimmed it . . .

He frowned as something caught his eye. "His secondary schooling was in organic chemistry."

"Was he ever arrested or charged with a crime?"

"Nothing about that here," Eli said. A thought struck him, and he keyed a new search. "No arrests for Tanoo himself, but his older brother was arrested for . . ." He trailed off, his throat tightening as he read the rest of the entry. "His older brother was arrested for possession of spice," he said. "Specifically, a rare variety called scarn that forms under grain fields."

Thrawn turned his glowing red eyes toward him. "Grain fields such as this one?"

"Yes," Eli said, the taste of bile in the back of his mouth. Spice, in any of its dozens of varieties, was a plague on the galaxy: a horribly addicting drug that its victims would lie, steal, assault, and murder for. "This stuff is more a pre-spice compound, actually. It looks like you have to do some refining and chemical manipulation to make it full-fledged scarn."

"Show me the method."

Eli pulled up the file and handed over his datapad. For a few minutes Thrawn read in silence. Then he handed back the datapad and pulled out his comlink. "This is Commander Thrawn," he said softly. "Are the shuttles and stormtroopers I ordered ready to fly? Good. Send them to this location for prisoner retrieval. Also add Lieutenant Gimm to the TIE escort. Launch when ready." He got an acknowledgment and returned the comlink to his belt.

Eli did a quick run through the numbers. Normally, prep and travel time would mean the shuttles would show up in forty minutes. Thrawn's foresight in having them ready to go should cut that in half. "How many stormtroopers are coming?"

"Twenty," Thrawn said. "I didn't know how large the conspiracy was when I gave the orders."

"Better to err on the side of caution," Eli agreed. And twenty stormtroopers was erring well on the side of caution. "Is Lieutenant Gimm one of the new TIE pilots?"

"Yes," Thrawn said. "He's also the best we currently have."

Eli frowned. Here, on Cyphar's open areas, it didn't exactly take an ace to handle a high-cover mission. Was Thrawn expecting resistance in the form of enemy airspeeders?

He considered asking, decided it would be just as easy to wait and see, and turned his electrobinoculars back on the diggers.

They were making good progress. Already the long bags they were dragging behind them were starting to fill up. By the time the stormtroopers arrived, they might well be ready to scurry back across the border.

"What's that?" A distant voice whipped faintly across the empty field.

Eli winced. Unless, of course, they spooked and took off sooner.

He focused on Tanoo. The man was staring up into the night sky, fumbling a civilian set of electrobinoculars from a pouch at his waist. He lifted them up to his eyes . . .

"Set on stun," Thrawn said quietly as he drew his blaster. "I will move a hundred meters to the right and take up position beside that border-mark stone."

"Understood," Eli said. Peering across the ground, he located the rough obelisk at the edge of the field.

"You'll stay here," Thrawn continued. "I'll deal with the landspeeders, while you target the raiders. Make certain none of them gets past us."

"Understood," Eli said again. Twelve against two . . .

and all twelve of the raiders had holstered blasters. Briefly, he hoped Thrawn had taken those odds into account. "Do we attack together, or does one of us start?"

"I'll start," Thrawn said. "You'll know when to open fire."

Eli frowned. "I'll know? How will I—?"

But Thrawn had already slipped out into the darkness.

Eli mouthed a silent curse. Great. He braced the side of his blaster against the edge of the meetinghouse doorway, hoping those long-ago Academy weapons classes would come back to him.

"It's Lambda shuttles!" Tanoo said anxiously, his voice rising almost to a squeak. "Two of them. Everyone—back in the speeders. Come on, come on, come *on*."

"Oh, bark it down," someone growled contemptuously. "It's probably just that idiot Imp bringing in a late buffet dinner or something."

The words were barely out of his mouth when Thrawn opened fire.

His first shot burned through the rusty plating of the rearmost of the three landspeeders, blasting the starboard-aft repulsorlift. With a metallic screech the front of the vehicle pitched up as that corner slammed onto the ground.

The nearest raiders jerked as if they'd stepped on a static plate. Eli clenched his teeth, wondering if this was when he was supposed to make his appearance. Before he could decide Thrawn fired again, taking out the same repulsorlift on the vehicle in front of it.

That was enough for Tanoo. Shrieking something incomprehensible he dived into the third landspeeder, the one closest to him, and tried to spin it around back toward the border.

But with the disabled vehicles blocking the path behind him, and with the taller and stiffer stalks on either side resisting his attempts to get through them, he was having trouble breaking free. He kept trying anyway, battering at the stalks over and over, gaining a few centimeters with each lunge.

The rest of the raiders weren't so easily rattled. They sprinted instead toward the disabled vehicles, their long bags dragging and bouncing behind them, yanking out their blasters and firing in the general vicinity of Thrawn's concealment as they ran. Eli tensed, but they were in motion and none of them seemed to be particularly good with their weapons, and all the bolts went wild. The raiders tumbled into cover behind the landspeeders and dropped to their knees, ducking lower as Thrawn shifted to a standard rapid-fire pattern designed to keep an enemy pinned down. The raiders responded by popping their heads up at random and squeezing off return fire.

And as both sides settled down for battle, Eli realized that the raiders were now lined up neatly within his field of fire. Even better, pressed against the landspeeders and on their knees, they were not only stationary but also had limited capacity to move or dodge.

Eli smiled tightly. Thrawn had been right: He *did* know when to fire.

Lining up his blaster on the first pair, he squeezed the trigger.

The stun setting had a wider effective range than standard blasterfire, permitting each shot to take down two of the raiders. With their attention on Thrawn and his louder, more dangerous fire, the conspirators lost six of their number to Eli's attack before the rest suddenly woke up to the new threat. Instantly they shifted their fire toward the meetinghouse, forcing Eli to throw himself sideways to avoid getting hit. He slammed onto the ground on his left shoulder, jarring his whole body and momentarily throwing off his aim.

It was, in retrospect, the wrong move. Up to that point his position had been somewhat obscured; now he was out in the open. Shots hammered the meetinghouse and the ground around him as he scuttled as quickly as he could on elbows and knees toward another border stone to the meetinghouse's left.

Five meters into his mad scramble, he belatedly realized he probably should have gone the other way, past the raiders' defense line, and tried instead to reach Thrawn. There, the two of them could have worked in unison to hold off their opponents until the reinforcements arrived from the *Thunder Wasp*.

Too late for that now. Swearing under his breath, Eli kept going, wincing with each shot that burned through the air or sizzled into the ground nearby—

And then, suddenly, all was silence.

Cautiously, Eli wobbled to a halt. Still silence. Even more cautiously, he lifted his head.

The men and women who'd been shooting at him were sprawled on the ground beside the landspeeders. Standing over them, his blaster trained on the still-trapped Tanoo, was Thrawn.

Feeling like a fool, Eli stood up, brushed himself off as best he could, and walked over to his commander.

"Well done, Ensign," Thrawn said, his eyes and blaster still pointed at Tanoo. Tanoo, for his part, had abandoned his attempts to escape and was leaning resignedly over his landspeeder's steering wheel. "Are you injured?"

"No, sir," Eli said, feeling his face warming. *Well done?* Not even close. "Sorry, sir."

Thrawn spared him a quick look. "Why are you sorry? You executed your part perfectly."

"But I didn't get them all," Eli pointed out. "And when they fired at me I went in the wrong direction."

"I did not expect you to defeat them all," Thrawn assured him. "And your decision to draw their fire away from me was what enabled me to move unnoticed to a position where I could bring a final end to their resistance."

"Oh," Eli said lamely, torn between the reflexive desire to tell Thrawn that it hadn't been a decision at all and the equally reflexive reluctance not to argue with his commanding officer when he was being complimented.

Thrawn didn't give him time to resolve either part of the quandary. "Come," he said. "I expect Mr. Tanoo is ready to talk."

Mr. Tanoo was.

"It wasn't my idea," he groaned, still draped across the steering wheel. "It was Polcery—she's the one who came up with it."

"Yet you were the one who refined the pre-spice for smuggling," Thrawn said. "Having learned the technique from your brother."

"They forced me," he moaned. "I didn't want to. But they forced me."

"The technique is quite interesting," Thrawn went on, as if Tanoo hadn't spoken. "A small change in the formulation results in a product that appears to be scarn but with the effects drastically diminished. A man who is being forced to work against his will could easily sabotage their efforts and desires. Yet you did not."

Tanoo raised himself from the steering wheel, and even in the darkness Eli could see the disgust in his face. He didn't like being caught, and he especially didn't like being caught by an alien. "You're a clever little Imp, aren't you? Fine; you caught us. Now what?"

"You will be turned over to a court for trial."

"And what are you going to charge us all with?"

"Possession of an illegal substance," Thrawn said. "Assault on Afe villages and their inhabitants."

"I don't think so," Tanoo said. "See, there aren't any raids going tonight—Polcery didn't trust you not to put some stormtroopers on guard. So that's off the list. And possession of pre-spice isn't illegal."

"Really," Thrawn said. "Ensign?"

Eli already had his datapad out. A quick search . . .

Damn it. "He's right, sir," he said. "Pre-spice isn't an illegal substance. There are too many other products it can be turned into that are perfectly safe and legal."

"But the product you have created *is* illegal," Thrawn pointed out.

"Maybe," Tanoo said. "But you'll never prove it. See, that's what the others are doing tonight instead of poking at the Cyphari. They're hiding all our product where no one will ever find it."

"Perhaps." Thrawn reached into the landspeeder and plucked the sensor from Tanoo's belt. "Perhaps not."

Tanoo barked a laugh. "If you think you're going to search the enclave looking for our supply, you can forget it. That thing's range is only twenty meters, and it only registers pre-spice, anyway. Face it: You've got nothing."

"On the contrary, I have all I need," Thrawn said calmly. "Twenty meters will be quite sufficient. One final question: Which of your group brought in Nightswan to advise you?"

Tanoo's eyes narrowed. "How did you know about him?"

"Answer my question."

Tanoo pursed his lips. "It was Scath," he said. "She knew someone who knew him and thought he could help."

"And so he did," Thrawn said. "But not enough. His end will come. Yours has now arrived."

And with perfect timing, the two shuttles and their three accompanying TIEs swooped past overhead. The shuttles curved around and angled toward the ground near Thrawn, the starfighters rising again into low-cover and high-cover formations.

Ten minutes later, the unconscious conspirators were aboard the first shuttle, binders firmly locked around their wrists and ankles. Eli used that time to check the landspeeders, hoping for contraband or something else that could be used against them in court.

But aside from the material in the collection bags, there was nothing. Unless there was some tweak in local law that made possession of pre-spice illegal, and if the others really had stayed home instead of raiding across the border, then Thrawn might very well have nothing.

"All secured, sir," the stormtrooper commander reported as Tanoo trudged up the shuttle ramp under the blasters of a pair of watchful guards and disappeared inside. "Orders?"

"Take the prisoners back to the enclave by way of the Afe villages I have marked," Thrawn said, handing him a data card. "If you see any fighting there you are to intervene on the side of the Afes. Do your best to take the human attackers alive, but you are free to use deadly force if you deem it necessary."

"Yes, sir," the commander said. "Do you want the other shuttle left here?"

"It will accompany you," Thrawn said. "There will be more prisoners before the night is over, either in the villages or in the enclave. I will keep Lieutenant Gimm; you will take the other two TIEs as escort."

"Yes, sir." Stiffening briefly to attention, he strode toward the shuttles, giving orders as he went.

A few minutes later, the shuttles were back in the sky, the TIEs flying in flanking formation. "And now, we end this," Thrawn said, fingering the sensor he'd taken from Tanoo. "Come."

Lieutenant Gimm was waiting by his TIE, coming to attention as Thrawn and Eli neared him. "I'm told you need some fancy flying, Commander," he said.

"Indeed," Thrawn confirmed. "Running through the ground below our feet is a vein of material that is a precursor to a spice variety called scarn."

The pilot stiffened a little further. "Yes, sir," he said, his voice darkening. "I've heard of it."

"This sensor will show its presence," Thrawn continued. "It does, however, have only a minimal range, twenty meters or less, which will require ground-level flight.

The vein itself almost certainly does not run straight, but twists and turns along its length. Do you think you can follow it?"

"May I see the sensor?"

Thrawn handed it over. The pilot peered at it, waved it back and forth around him, then nodded. "Yes, sir, I can," he said. "May I suggest I also take a little gunnery practice as I fly over it?"

"Your enthusiasm is noted and appreciated, Lieutenant," Thrawn said. "But I am told that the pre-spice runs deep in places, and I understand that a certain degree of heat is part of the refining process. We do not wish to accidentally turn it into the final, deadly product."

"No, sir," the pilot said. "If you just want it mapped, I can do that."

"We will hardly be simply mapping, Lieutenant," Thrawn assured him, pulling out his comlink. "As you said: gunnery practice. Lieutenant Commander Osgoode, this is Commander Thrawn. I have an interesting challenge for you."

It was, Eli would afterward decide, the most insane military operation he'd ever seen or even heard of.

But it worked.

It was spectacular enough from the ground. It was probably even more so from low orbit. Gimm flew his TIE fighter low over the cropland, nearly brushing the tops of the stalks at times, then continued on over grazing lands, marshes, and more cropland. He flew in gentle curves or dizzying zigzags, wherever the trail led him, always following the line of pre-spice lurking beneath the soil.

And following along fifty meters behind him was a blazing wave of ground-shattering flame as the cleansing fire from the *Thunder Wasp*'s turbolasers carved out the same path, their focal point precisely matching the

TIE's maneuvers and burning the pre-spice into oblivion.

By morning, as Thrawn had predicted, it was over.

"What do you do?" Joko demanded. *His voice shakes*. "Do you attack our sovereign land at will?"

"I have destroyed the source of the conspirators' profits," Thrawn said. Did the chief truly not see the pattern nor understand the result? "With the pre-spice gone, they have no further incentive to seek control over Afe land."

"You attacked us," Joko repeated. "You destroyed farmland and damaged homes and water springs."

"If I had not destroyed all the pre-spice, the attacks would have continued."

"The Empire would have given us justice without destruction."

"Without the destruction the justice would have been temporary," Thrawn said. "The value was too great to be ignored. The thieves would have come back. When they did, you would have lost more than just farmland."

"What more?" Joko demanded. "Orchards? Bridges?"

"Lives."

For a few seconds Joko gazed at him in silence. But the silence was stiff, and there was bitterness beneath it. "I see your concern for my people," he said at last. "But their lives and lands could have been protected in a different way. A *better* way."

"You may appeal my actions to Coruscant," Thrawn said. "They may repudiate them."

"Yet the damage will remain," Joko said. "I will appeal your actions. And I will pray we never meet again."

Vanto was waiting when Thrawn emerged from the shuttle. "Ensign Vanto," Thrawn said. "Has Coruscant responded to my report?"

"Yes, sir," Vanto said, his voice dark with contempt. "I'm afraid they're not happy with you."

"No doubt their unhappiness will expand when Chief Joko delivers his own reaction."

"Fine," Vanto said with a resigned sigh. "They're not just not happy. They're furious."

"As expected."

"Which is insane," Vanto said, his anger appearing through his decorum. "You ended the conflict, you exposed a criminal conspiracy, and you kept a deep vein's worth of spice off the market. What more do they want?"

"They want a commander who follows procedures," Thrawn said. "They want a commander who will ask their advice."

"*And* their permission?"

"Perhaps," Thrawn said. "I have found that many admirals aspire to that rank because of a wish to exercise control and authority. Such leaders are threatened if officers of lower rank solve difficult problems without them."

"And of course, there's always politics lurking around the corner." Vanto eyed him thoughtfully. "What about you, Commander? Why do *you* seek high rank?"

It was a question many had asked over the years. Thrawn had asked it of himself. The answer never seemed to satisfy the questioner. "Because there are problems that must be solved. Some cannot be solved by anyone except me."

"I see." Vanto was silent a moment. "Senior Lieutenant Hammerly was able to stall them for a bit by telling them you were consulting with the local chief. But they expect you to call back."

"Of course," Thrawn said. "I will do so immediately."

"What will you tell them?"

"The truth."

Vanto had now asked the question. He was no more satisfied than anyone who had come before him.

Thrawn wondered if anyone would ever be satisfied. Or would ever truly understand.

. . .

The truth.

Eli scowled the words to himself as he strode down the *Thunder Wasp*'s central corridor toward his quarters. *The truth.* When did that ever gain anyone anything?

Thrawn had been telling the truth pretty much since he'd arrived in Imperial space. Yet he was continually getting hauled back to Coruscant to explain himself before increasingly hostile officers' boards. It was only through the intervention and good graces of people like Colonel Yularen that he was still even in the navy, let alone commanding his own ship.

The truth. No, truth never gained anyone anything. All it did was anger those who preferred lies and confusion and backspinning in the hope of making themselves look better.

As far as Eli had been able to tell, that was pretty much everyone.

Ahead, the door to the starfighter hangar slid open and Lieutenant Gimm stepped out. "Lieutenant," Eli greeted him. "Excellent flying down there."

"Thank you," Gimm said, an odd expression on his face. "I'm glad I ran into you."

"You have a question, sir?"

Gimm's lip twisted in an ironic smile. "You don't remember me, do you?"

Eli frowned, studying his face. He couldn't place it. "No, sir," he admitted. "Should I?"

"I would have thought so," Gimm said with a casual shrug. "Of course, it *was* pretty dark at the time. And you probably had other things on your mind."

Eli caught his breath as it suddenly clicked. "You were one of the cadets who attacked Commander Thrawn."

"I categorically deny that, of course." Gimm lowered his eyes pointedly to Eli's insignia plaque. "And you're still an ensign."

"An ensign in service to the best commander in the navy," Eli countered stiffly.

"Maybe," Gimm said. "Though from what I hear, whether he *stays* a commander is somewhat up in the air."

"We'll see," Eli said. "What do you want?"

"Nothing, really," Gimm said. "I just wanted you to know that, despite what I'm sure were Commander Thrawn's best efforts, I wasn't tossed out of the Academy. In fact, things worked out very well for me. Commandant Deenlark was able to pull enough strings to get the three of us transferred to starfighter training at Skystrike Academy."

"Really," Eli said. "Commandant Deenlark did that, did he?"

Gimm's forehead wrinkled, just for a moment. But then it cleared. "Oh, I see. You think my family were the ones who pulled the strings." He shrugged. "Doesn't matter, really, as long as strings were pulled by *someone*. But don't take it too hard, Ensign. Getting to be a commander even this long is pretty impressive for an Unknown Regions alien. If he ends up back as a lieutenant in charge of droid repair, well, he'll still have his memories."

"I'm sure he'll have more than that," Eli said.

Gimm raised his eyebrows. "I'm sure he'll have more than that, *sir*," he corrected.

With a supreme effort, Eli stifled the sudden urge to punch Gimm across the corridor. "I'm sure he'll have more than that, *sir*."

"Better," Gimm said. "I think I'll go have a drink with the *real* officers now. Good night, Ensign."

He turned and strode off down the passageway. Eli watched him, an unpleasant mix of emotions swirling inside him.

Thrawn had been right. The man *had* become an outstanding starfighter pilot.

Only he would probably never know who he had to thank for that. In fact, he'd likely go to his grave thinking that he'd put one over on the poor, dumb alien.

With a sigh, Eli continued on toward his quarters. Wondering if anyone, anywhere, really cared about truth.

CHAPTER 19

————◆————

Alliances are useful in some situations. In others, they are absolutely vital.

But they must always be approached with caution. Unity of that sort is based on mutual advantage. While that advantage exists, the alliance may stand firm. But needs change, and advantages fade, and a day may come when one ally sees new benefits to be gained in betraying another.

The warrior must be alert to such changes if he is to anticipate and survive an unannounced blow. Fortunately, the signs are usually evident in time for defense to be planned and executed.

There is also always the possibility that changes will serve to meld the allies even more closely together. It is rare, but it can happen.

"The four-blend is really the best," Lady Teeyr Hem said, her long, thin Phindian fingers caressing the bottle Arihnda had brought her. "I stand deeply in your debt."

"I'm pleased you are happy," Arihnda said. "I, in turn, am in your debt for your sympathy to the goals of Higher Skies."

"Your goals are much like mine and my husband's," Lady Hem said, still gently stroking the bottle's neck.

"You must have gone long and far to find this particular wine."

"It was my pleasure," Arihnda assured her. It *had*, in fact, been something of a challenge, entailing trips to nearly thirty of the Federal District's finest wine shops and several hours of studying labels until she'd found the exact vintage, blend, and texture she knew Lady Hem wanted.

But it was worth it. The look on the Phindian's face was priceless.

"At any rate, I must leave now," Arihnda added, standing up. "I just wanted to drop off this small token of my appreciation, and to ask if Senator Hem had found time to read the document I sent him."

"He has," Lady Hem said, her fingers now moving to the bottle's textured label. "I believe he agrees with your agenda and your plans. But I will speak to him about that this night." She blinked rapidly, her species' version of a wide smile. "Over a glass of wine, perhaps."

"I'll look forward to hearing from him," Arihnda said, smiling back. "Until we speak again, Lady Hem, farewell."

"Farewell, my good friend Arihnda Pryce."

Driller, not surprisingly, was aghast.

"Two thousand credits for a bottle of *wine*?" he gasped as he stared at Arihnda's receipt. "Are you out of your *mind*?"

"The Phindians are a highly technological species, and are very devoted to family," Arihnda reminded him. "Both of those go double for Senator Hem. A simple bottle of his wife's favorite wine, and he's as good as in our pocket."

"Not exactly a *simple* bottle," Driller growled. "Will this at least buy you access to his office?"

"I'm expecting an invitation by the end of the week," Arihnda assured him. "And yes, I'm sure I'll be able to get some numbers from him about the navy's military budget and the level of Senate support. The *secret* numbers, not the ones the public gets to see."

"Great," Driller said. "It's important to know where the money is going so we can see what's left for schools and hospitals."

"Absolutely," Arihnda said, smiling to cover her sudden surge of contempt. Did he *really* think she was this naïve and stupid? Apparently, he did. "So is there anyone else you want me to pitch Higher Skies to?"

"Let's see," he said, studying his datapad. "A couple of governors are in for a visit. Mid Rim, not too difficult. Or—ooh. How big a fish are you willing to go after?"

"How big a fish have you got?"

"The biggest," he said, eyeing her closely. "The fish you were once going to leave me for until the job offer fell through. Grand Moff Tarkin."

Arihnda felt her stomach tighten. *Tarkin.*

And the timing was absolutely perfect.

"Wow," she said, trying for just the right mix of casualness and interest. "Sure, why not?"

"*Why not* is because he's got a reputation for chewing up advocates and small bureaucrats and spitting them out in neat linear meat strips," Driller warned. "It won't be one of the milk runs you've been doing lately. This'll be more like a dogfight."

"Milk runs are fun," Arihnda said. "But I like dogfights, too. Can you get me in to see him?"

"I think so," Driller said. "You sure?"

Arihnda smiled. "Trust me," she said. "Tarkin's someone I've always wanted to meet."

There were, Arihnda had learned, many tricks politicians and military types used to intimidate, pressure, and otherwise put visitors at a disadvantage.

Tarkin knew them all.

It began with his office: the long walk from the door;

the thick, textured carpet that dragged at a visitor's feet and threatened to trip her up with each step; the sunlight glinting off corners of shelves and display stands and the desk itself, the spots shifting and flickering and distracting. The objects on the shelves and stands were the next layer: mementos of Tarkin's past triumphs, a procession of reminders of his power. Here and there, she spotted some ancient and valuable artifact that he had either bought, stolen, or despoiled. Yet another object lesson: The man got whatever he wanted.

It was an impressive display, especially considering that the grand moff probably only used this office a few weeks each year. His main office, the one from which he controlled a large swath of the Outer Rim, was probably even more intimidating.

At the end of the gauntlet, seated in a tall-backed chair as he watched her approach, was Tarkin.

If the office itself wasn't enough to put guests into defensive mode, Arihnda mused, their first look at the man himself probably did the trick. The gaunt face, gray-white hair, thin lips, and steely eyes were like an image of waiting death; the twelve tiles of his insignia plaque were in deceptively colorful contrast with the dark olive green of his uniform; the stillness of his expression and body as he watched her approach was like that of a jungle predator preparing to strike.

It was an impressive display of power and intimidation, one that no doubt worked well against nearly everyone who dared enter his sanctum.

Arihnda intended to be the exception.

"Governor Tarkin," she greeted him as she reached the desk. "I appreciate you taking the time to see me."

"Ms. Arihnda Pryce," he greeted her in return. His voice was a match for the coolness of his face. "I understand you represent an advocacy group called Higher Skies."

"That's certainly what they think," Arihnda agreed.

"Actually, I'm here to represent myself. And to make you the best offer you'll get today."

His expression didn't change. But his eyes seemed to grow colder. "Really," he said. "I think perhaps you overestimate your charm."

"Oh, I don't run on charm, Governor," Arihnda assured him. "I run on information." She slipped a data card out of her pouch and set it on the desk. "Here's a sample. I'll be happy to wait while you look it over."

For a moment he was silent, his eyes locked on hers. Then, a small smile creased his lips. "Full credit for ingenuity," he said, picking up the data card. "Sit down."

Arihnda stepped to the chair at the corner of his desk and lowered herself into it, trying not to let any of her submerged apprehension make it to the surface. She was 90 percent certain she'd read this man correctly, but that remaining 10 percent could make or break her.

Tarkin watched her another moment, then slipped the data card into his computer. "At least you aren't so obvious as to try a data-thief program," he commented.

"Not at all." Arihnda pulled out another data card and set it on the desk. "*This* is the one with the thief program. It's the Higher Skies brochure and agenda I was supposed to give you."

Tarkin's forehead furrowed briefly. "Really," he said, his tone intrigued. "Who exactly are you, Ms. Pryce?"

"Someone who wants to make a deal that will benefit us both," Arihnda said. "But please—look at the information on that card. It'll give you a taste of what I have to offer."

Again, Tarkin gazed at her a moment before returning his attention to his computer. Arihnda sat silently, watching his eyes track back and forth across the display as he skimmed the file. She'd gotten good at reading faces, human and nonhuman alike, during her time with Higher Skies. But Tarkin's might as well have been a theatrical mask.

He reached the end and turned back to Arihnda. "Interesting," he said.

"You found it informative?" Arihnda asked.

"Hardly," he said. "Most of this I already knew."

Arihnda felt her stomach tighten. "I see."

"Don't look so concerned," Tarkin said with another thin smile. "That's a good thing. It proves you've successfully tapped into Governor Nasling's records, and also lends credence to the one or two items I was unaware of. No, my comment was directed at the skill of your employers. How did they come to create such a clever thief program?"

"I imagine they brought in someone to help," Arihnda said. "You see, I think they're rebels."

For the briefest of moments a flicker of emotion crossed Tarkin's face. Then the mask fell back into place. "Rebels," he repeated.

"Yes, Your Excellency," Arihnda said. "But don't worry. All they have is the merest skeleton of that data file. Just enough to keep them happy with my work so that they'll keep sending me to other officials." She dared a smile. "And keep funding me, of course. Bribery can be expensive."

"Especially on Coruscant," he agreed. "So this is a double-layer thief program?"

"Exactly," Arihnda said. "It was layered on top of the Higher Skies version by an associate. The idea of bringing it to you was inspired by another associate. Both of whom would prefer to remain anonymous," she added, as if it were an afterthought.

The tease worked exactly as she had hoped. Tarkin leaned back in his chair, his eyes boring into hers. "We're far past the point of coyness," he said coldly. "Their names."

"The program was crafted on the orders of ISB Colonel Wullf Yularen," Arihnda said. "The one who advised me to bring the results to you was Commander Thrawn."

"Ah," Tarkin said, his voice dropping a few more degrees. "So you drop the names of two highly respected individuals in the hope that I'll think you have powerful friends and benefactors. Which one of them suggested *that*?"

"Neither," Arihnda said, starting to sweat a little. "I've always considered that you were the only benefactor I needed."

To her relief, he gave her another thin smile. "Thank you for not presuming we would ever be friends." His smile faded, a small frown creasing his forehead. "Interesting about Commander Thrawn. He was on Coruscant just a few weeks ago, explaining himself to yet another court-martial panel."

"What did he do?" Arihnda asked. She'd tried to keep track of Thrawn's activities, but she hadn't heard a whisper of this one.

"Burned off a vein of scarn spice on some alien's territory," Tarkin said. "Direct and efficient. Not as politically astute as some would have liked."

"What was the outcome?"

"He was cleared, of course," Tarkin said. "The High Command doesn't especially like him, but they find it difficult to argue with his results. The Emperor seems to have taken a fancy to him, as well. What exactly did he and our good Colonel Yularen expect from you in return for their help?"

"Colonel Yularen wanted the data, of course," Arihnda said. "He was highly interested in my, shall we say, unofficial survey of the Empire's top politicians."

"I assume you haven't turned it over to him?"

"Not yet," Arihnda said. "I thought you might like a preview. And perhaps to extract a few tidbits you could use for—" She shrugged. "Let's just say for the good of the Empire."

"Very noble of you," Tarkin said. "And Commander Thrawn?"

"Amazingly easy to please," Arihnda said. "All he

asked for were expedited repairs on his ship, and a long-overdue promotion for his aide. The first I've already managed through some of my other contacts. But there's still some political resistance to the second."

"Resistance to a military promotion?" Tarkin asked disbelievingly. "Which of our esteemed politicians has that much time and energy to spare?"

"Moff Ghadi," Arihnda said, watching Tarkin closely.

It was all she had hoped for. More, even. Tarkin's face stiffened, his eyes going bright and narrow.

She'd already known there was a rivalry between the two men. She hadn't realized how deep and bitter that rivalry truly was.

"Moff Ghadi," Tarkin repeated. "I should have guessed."

"I have information on him, of course," Arihnda said, keeping her voice casual. "He was one of the first politicians I targeted."

"You have that information with you?"

"Right here," Arihnda said, touching her hip pouch and then pulling out her datapad. "But first, I thought you might be interested in hearing a recording I made a few months ago." She keyed it on and turned up the volume.

"This had better be important." Ghadi's voice came from the speaker. "And I mean *damn* important. I'm *this* close to having Ottlis whipped for waking me up, and you don't even want to know what I want to do to you."

"It's important," Arihnda's voice came back. "You were right—Higher Skies is keeping watch on many important people. I've found the files."

"Of course I was right. Any reason this revelation couldn't have waited until later?"

"It probably could have. But I thought you'd want to hear as soon as possible about the Tarkin file."

"They have a file on *Tarkin*? What's in it?"

"I don't know. This one's under a different encryption than anything else I've found. But if it's like the ones I've been able to read, it probably has a lot of secrets in it. Things Tarkin wouldn't want anyone else knowing about."

"Perfect. Yes. I absolutely want those files."

"I thought you would. I can collate them with the other files I've been able to find. But I wanted to make sure you wanted this one."

"Don't be stupid. You have the weapon I need to take down Tarkin, and you want to know if I *want* it? Get it on a data card and bring it to my office. *Now.*"

"Yes, Your Excellency. As I said, though, at the moment it's unreadable. If you give me time, I may be able to decrypt it."

"Just bring it to me. *I'll* decrypt it. Let's see how high and mighty Grand Moff Tarkin is when I'm shoving his dirty little secrets down his throat."

"Very well, Your Excellency—"

"That's enough," Tarkin said quietly.

Arihnda shut down the recording. "Imagine that," she said, mock-seriously. "A high official conspiring to use illegally obtained material to topple another high official."

"And being foolish enough to allow that conspiracy to be recorded." Tarkin eyed her. "I notice your own voice wasn't nearly as identifiable as his."

"A malfunction in the recorder."

"Of course," Tarkin said. "Tell me, what exactly did you give him?"

"Absolutely nothing," Arihnda assured him. "It was complete gibberish wrapped in what appeared to be an advanced encryption layer. He's probably still trying to find a coherent sentence in it."

"I see," Tarkin murmured. "So Colonel Yularen will get data on the Empire's politicians. Commander Thrawn will get his aide promoted. I'll have Yularen's data before Yularen gets it, plus the satisfaction of removing Moff Ghadi from the face of the galaxy." He raised his eyebrows. "We haven't yet talked about you. What do *you* get out of this?"

"Your patronage and support," Arihnda said. "The satisfaction of knowing I've helped the true powers that keep the Empire running." She paused. "And if you should find it useful and expedient, I'd like the governorship of Lothal."

"Lothal," Tarkin echoed, leaning forward again and keying his computer. "Not exactly the ground-shaking demand I'd expected. Why there?"

"The rivalry between Governor Azadi and Senator Renking cost my parents their mining company and forced them out of their home," Arihnda said, an unexpected surge of anger rising inside her. She'd thought she'd put the emotion of that betrayal behind her. Apparently not. "Being made governor of Lothal will humiliate the first, and make it easier for me to take down the second."

"A clear vision of one's goals is important in a governor," Tarkin said drily. "But governorships are valuable commodities. I'm afraid this"—he tapped the data cards on his desk—"isn't quite enough."

"I thought it might not be." Taking a deep breath, Arihnda pulled out another data card. "But this is."

"And it is . . . ?"

"Everything about Lothal the Empire would ever want to know," Arihnda said. "Its mines and refineries, including the quiet and secret mines that no one talks about and no one pays taxes or tariffs on. Its infrastructure and factories, including output numbers and efficiency ratings. The banking structure and how assets are hidden or spirited away. Its people, including social frameworks, and which species get along or don't get along together. Summaries of archaeological surveys in the northern areas that suggest the presence of untapped mineral resources, on both protected and unprotected lands."

She straightened up in her chair and set the card on

Tarkin's desk. "The Empire is gathering up the Outer Rim worlds. It might as well be as easy and painless as possible. For everyone."

"Interesting," Tarkin said, making no move to take the card. "Some would consider that a betrayal of their homeworld."

"I prefer to think of it as loyalty to my new homeworld."

"Well said," Tarkin said approvingly. "And if I may say so, your timing is impeccable. As it happens, that particular governorship may soon be vacant."

"Governor Azadi is retiring?" Arihnda asked, frowning. She hadn't heard anything about that.

"Yes," Tarkin said. "Rather against his will, it would seem."

"Interesting," Arihnda said. Not that Azadi didn't deserve it. Whether he'd been actively involved in her mother's arrest and the loss of their company, or whether he'd simply stood aside while others in his office did his dirty work, he still deserved it. "Renking?"

"Perhaps," Tarkin said. "Perhaps other reasons. Still, Senator Renking *is* angling for the governorship." He raised his eyebrows. "I wonder which of you wants it more."

"I've given you the means to take down Moff Ghadi," Arihnda said, forcing calmness through her sudden flash of anger and frustration. She would *not* lose now. Especially not to Renking. "I have inside information on other moffs, governors, and senators. I've given you Lothal. I want that governorship, Your Excellency. What more do you need to make that happen?"

"Oh, much, much more, Ms. Pryce," Tarkin assured her. "There are many people in power whom I would like to know better. Fortunately, I now have you."

Arihnda clenched her teeth. She'd started as a senator's lackey; and now she was being offered the job of a grand moff's lackey? "Your Excellency—"

"Of course, as a governor you'll have much better

access to those people than you will as an advocate," he continued. "Yes, I can see this being advantageous to us both."

Arihnda let out a silent sigh. So he'd just been playing with her. She should have known. "I'm glad you approve, Your Excellency."

"Of course, going from a mere civilian to a planetary governor is quite a step," Tarkin continued. "Still, you've had a great deal of experience and contact with the powerful of the Empire, as well as the advantage of being a local of the world in question. Perhaps we'll begin by designating you as acting governor before granting you the full title."

"For how long?" Arihnda asked.

"Oh, a few months," Tarkin said with a shrug. "A year at the most. Technically, of course, these appointments are supposed to be run through the Palace, but I see no reason we need to bother the bureaucrats. You'll need to spend a fair amount of your first year or two in office here on Coruscant, learning the details of your new position."

"While also gathering the data you want?"

"But a short absence from Lothal shouldn't be a problem," Tarkin continued. "There are several ministers in place there, any of whom can run things while you fulfill your side of our bargain. You'll simply need to pick one before you return to Coruscant."

Arihnda smiled. The governorship of Lothal, a clear shot at taking down Renking, *and* she'd get to live among the elite on Coruscant for a while longer. She couldn't have planned it better if she'd tried. "I think we have an agreement, Your Excellency."

"We do." Tarkin held out a hand. "The rest of your data, please?"

"Here's half of it," Arihnda said, pulling two more data cards from her pouch. "I'll give you the other half once I've been confirmed in the governorship."

"Of course," Tarkin said. "You'll fit in quite well here, Ms. Pryce. Or should I say, Governor Pryce?"

"Thank you, Your Excellency," she said, standing up. "Now, if you'll excuse me, I have one more errand to run. I'm sure you want to look over those data cards anyway." She pointed at them. "Oh, and the recording of Moff Ghadi is on the second card. You'll want to take special care with that one."

Juahir was walking across the Yinchom Dojo's central mat, duffel bag in hand, when Arihnda arrived. "Hey— Arihnda," Juahir greeted her. "You get off early?"

"No, just between jobs," Arihnda said. "You have a good workout?"

"Fair," Juahir said. "Senator Xurfel signed up her two newest bodyguards with us this morning. I had to run them through the grinder to see how good they are."

"And?"

"They've got potential, but they're not up to Coruscant standards," Juahir said. "But we'll get them in shape. So which jobs are you between?"

"Well, I was at Grand Moff Tarkin's office yesterday," Arihnda said. "We had a nice chat."

"Yes, I heard about that," Juahir said, brightening. "Driller said he actually got you in to see him. Congratulations."

"Thank you," Arihnda said. "Not much happening today, so I thought I'd drop by here."

"Great," Juahir said. "So we doing a workout, or lunch?"

"Neither," Arihnda said. "We're making an arrest."

"Who?"

"You." She watched Juahir's mouth drop open as Colonel Yularen and his agents filed silently into the dojo behind her.

"Arihnda, what are you doing?" Juahir asked carefully.

"We're arresting a traitor," Arihnda said. "A woman who's been using her training position to suborn or blackmail high-level bodyguards and send them off to spy on their bosses." She raised her eyebrows. "And, occasionally, to try to murder them."

"*What?*" Juahir breathed, her eyes widening, her skin going ashen.

"Senator Evidorn's bodyguard Kaniki," Yularen said darkly as he walked up to them. "He tried to kill the senator this morning. Apparently, your indoctrination on the evils of the Empire was a little *too* effective."

"We never told them to kill anyone," Juahir protested. "They were just supposed to get information for—" She broke off, throwing a sudden look of understanding at Arihnda.

"That's right," Arihnda confirmed. "I'm the one who pulled the data Driller and Higher Skies have been collecting and handed it over to the ISB. Driller and everyone else connected to the group are being picked up right now, but given the Kaniki incident Colonel Yularen decided he wanted to arrest you personally."

"Arihnda—"

"There's just one thing I want to know," Arihnda said, her throat suddenly aching with suppressed emotion. "Were you ever my friend? Or was I always just a tool to you?"

Juahir stared at her as the ISB agents moved around behind her, binders in hand. "Yes, I was your friend," she said quietly. "I wasn't involved with . . . this . . . until after Senator Renking fired you. That was so horribly unfair. It showed me how corrupt the whole system was. It was only later that Driller approached me and—"

"Driller and Nightswan?" Yularen cut in.

Juahir transferred her stare to him. "Driller mentioned someone with that name. But we only talked about what we could do to fix things. To make the Empire better for everyone."

"And then you thought about me and figured you

could use me," Arihnda said. "Poor Arihnda Pryce, cast adrift in the swirling dregs of Coruscant. The perfect patsy."

"It wasn't like that."

"But close enough," Arihnda said. She looked at Yularen. "I'm finished. Thank you."

"Wait," Juahir pleaded as the ISB agents started her toward the door. "Arihnda, I was your friend. I helped you out when you needed someone. Can't you help me now?"

Arihnda held up her hand. Yularen did likewise, and the agents stopped. "Here's what I'll do, Juahir," she said. "Colonel Yularen is going to interrogate you. If you give him everything—and I mean *everything*—he'll send you to prison instead of having you executed."

Juahir's face had gone even whiter. "Arihnda—"

"I'm on the road to power now," Arihnda interrupted. "If I achieve my goals, I should be able to pull enough strings to get you out in a few years. If not . . ." She shrugged.

"*Arihnda!*"

But Yularen had already gestured, and the men were on the move again. Arihnda remained where she was, not turning, until the door closed again behind her.

"What about her?" Yularen asked.

Arihnda turned, blinking away sudden tears. H'sishi was standing silently in the doorway of her office, watching them.

Had Yularen just asked *her* for advice?

Of course he had. Yularen and Tarkin had been in contact regarding the Higher Skies affair, and while Arihnda's new status hadn't been officially announced the colonel had probably been given the news. "Commander Thrawn said she was in the clear, didn't he?"

"That was his conclusion, yes," Yularen said.

"Did you find anything in the records to contradict that?"

"No."

"Then I suppose we can let her go." Arihnda lifted a warning finger toward the Togorian. "But I'd recommend you leave Coruscant as soon as possible. Your former employee might try to shift some of her guilt onto your back. She does that sort of thing to her friends."

"Thank you," H'sishi said gravely. "Mistress Arihnda; Colonel Yularen." Turning, she disappeared back into her office.

Arihnda smiled. *Mistress Arihnda.* A meaningless title, a veneer of respect overlaying a deeper and more casual disdain. The title of the small and powerless.

But she was done with it now. Done with it forever.

Governor Pryce. Yes, that was better. Much, much better.

Another week, Eli had gotten used to saying to himself, *another mission.*

This time it was smugglers, small gangs working out of obscure systems. The *Thunder Wasp* had proved especially good at rooting out such blights upon Imperial commerce, and Coruscant had apparently taken notice.

Of course, Thrawn owed at least some of that success to Eli's own talent at identifying and tracking shipping and supplies. That had led to successful attacks on no less than four smuggling operations, three of which had included black-market doonium.

Two of which had apparently included Nightswan.

Eli scowled to himself. This whole Nightswan thing was starting to get out of hand. The *Thunder Wasp* had been in time to close down one of the schemes Eli had spotted, but they'd been too late to stop the other before it was abruptly shut down. Worse, Eli had identified at least five other operations that seemed to fit Nightswan's pattern that were out of the *Thunder Wasp*'s patrol area and thus out of Thrawn's ability to defeat.

Thrawn always sent warnings to the commanders in the affected sectors. But the communications were usually too slow, or the ships were too busy with other matters, or the commanders simply didn't believe him. ISB was only marginally better, and even there it was often only Colonel Yularen who took the reports seriously.

Thrawn always spoke of patterns and connections. After nearly four years of serving with him, Eli was only now getting the knack of spotting those patterns. Others in the navy apparently weren't so astute. Possibly they never would be.

The one puzzle neither Eli nor Thrawn had so far been able to figure out was why Nightswan was so obsessed with taking doonium away from the Empire, and what the Empire itself wanted with the stuff.

They weren't building ships with it. Every time Eli ran the numbers, the amount of doonium the Empire was gathering far exceeded any possible need. Were they stockpiling it against some future need for ships? Thrawn's discussions at the Palace—could the Emperor be planning something special? A series of expeditions into the Unknown Regions, perhaps? There were too many questions Eli didn't have answers to.

But those questions paled before the one looming before them today. Namely, the question of why he and Thrawn had been suddenly summoned back to Coruscant.

It couldn't be over the Cyphar incident. Thrawn had already been cleared of misconduct over his actions there. Had Yularen discovered something new about Nightswan that he wanted to share personally? Or had the High Command decided they were tired of Thrawn's continual focus on the man and wanted him to stop harassing the other commanders just because he thought they weren't doing their job?

Or had Eli perhaps crossed some unseen line in his searches and examinations of the subject? The fact that he'd been specifically ordered to appear with Thrawn was more than a little unnerving.

"Do you know what this is about, sir?" Eli murmured

to Thrawn as a group of senior officers filed into the room.

"No," Thrawn said. "But I find it interesting that you were also summoned."

So Thrawn had noticed that, too. Not really surprising.

"Try to read their faces," Thrawn murmured.

Eli suppressed a grimace. He was trying. *Had* been trying since the officers began filing in. Focusing his attention on the admiral in the lead, he studied the man's expression and body language—

And caught his breath, his analysis sputtering to a halt as the last man in line appeared through the doorway.

Grand Moff Tarkin.

And suddenly, all bets were off. Tarkin's title was technically a civilian one, his position giving him authority across a huge swath of the Outer Rim. But he also wore an Imperial Navy uniform, and his duties and authority straddled both civilian and military venues.

Which area, Eli wondered, was he representing today?

The admiral in the center waited until everyone was seated. Then she rose to her feet. "We are met this morning," she said, "to pay special honor to two of our own."

Eli blinked. Honor? So this *wasn't* another inquiry board or court-martial?

"Never has any officer of the Imperial Navy achieved such success in so short a time," the admiral continued.

Eli felt a whisper of relief, mixed with a hint of melancholy. So that was it. Thrawn had been called back to receive yet another promotion.

Not that Eli begrudged him the recognition. On the contrary, he more than deserved it. Aside from the thorn in the side that was Nightswan, his record was an unbroken string of wins against the enemies of the Empire.

"It is therefore with great pleasure that this board

confers upon Commander Thrawn the rank of commodore. Congratulations, Commodore Thrawn."

And there it was. Eli smiled and tried to look happy—
which he was, really—as he joined in the applause.
Coming all the way to Coruscant seemed excessive for
what was, for Thrawn, a fairly commonplace ceremony,
but at least they could get back to space now. Even as
the admiral stepped forward and handed Thrawn his
new insignia plaque, Eli started mentally sorting through
the files that ought to lead them to their next smuggler
nest—

"It is also an honor and privilege," the admiral continued, "for this board to rectify a situation that has too
long been allowed to stand."

Eli frowned, thoughts of lists and supply manifests
vanishing. Was there a situation Thrawn had gotten
himself into that Eli hadn't heard about?

"It is therefore with equal pleasure that this board
confers upon Ensign Eli Vanto—"

Eli caught his breath. It was happening. It was finally
happening. After all this time, they were finally promoting him to lieutenant.

"—the rank—"

Lieutenant Vanto. The sound in his head was like a
drink of cool, clear water after a session in the dojo.
Lieutenant Vanto . . .

"—of lieutenant commander."

Eli felt his whole body stiffen. What had the admiral
said? *Lieutenant commander?*

That was impossible. For an ensign to jump ahead
that many ranks at once was unheard of. He must have
heard it wrong.

"Congratulations, Lieutenant Commander Vanto,"
the admiral finished.

And the insignia plaque in the admiral's extended
hand was indeed that of a lieutenant commander.

"Congratulations," Thrawn repeated from beside him.

"Thank you, sir," Eli managed. "And thank you, ma'am."

There was more: a few short speeches from the others on the board, more congratulations, stirring visions of the glorious future awaiting them all.

Eli didn't really hear any of it.

To his mild surprise, Tarkin lingered after the navy officers had filed out again. "Congratulations, Commodore," the grand moff said, nodding to Thrawn. "And to you, Lieutenant Commander," he added to Eli.

"Thank you, Your Excellency," Thrawn said.

"Thank you, Your Excellency," Eli echoed.

"A fine ceremony," Tarkin continued. "I'm glad I stopped by. Governor Arihnda Pryce sends her regards and her own congratulations."

"I wondered if she might," Thrawn said. There was, Eli noted, a hint of something in his voice. Some kind of private joke between him and Tarkin? "She is well, I trust?"

"Quite well," Tarkin said. "Eagerly preparing to take on her new post."

"I am pleased that things have worked out for her."

"As am I." Tarkin reached forward and touched the new commodore's insignia plaque on Thrawn's chest. "Consider this a bonus."

"Thank you, Your Excellency," Thrawn said. "Please thank the governor when you next see her."

"I will," Tarkin said. "Now I believe you have enemies of the Empire to deal with. Good hunting to you."

With a final nod to Thrawn, he turned and left.

"Once again, congratulations, Lieutenant Commander Vanto," Thrawn said. "I trust the wait has been worth it."

"It has indeed, sir," Eli said. Distantly, he wondered what Lieutenant Gimm would say when he first saw the former ensign's new rank.

Probably nothing. Not much he *could* say to a superior officer.

But his expression would definitely be worth seeing.

"And now, we'd best get to our new ship," Thrawn continued, turning toward the door. "There will be a great deal to learn."

Eli frowned. "Our new ship?"

Thrawn turned, a half-amused, half-knowing smile on his face. "I see you were not paying attention at the end. I thought not. We're being transferred, Commander. I am now the captain of the ISD *Chimaera*."

Eli caught his breath. Thrawn had been given an *Imperial Star Destroyer*? "No, I—congratulations, sir."

"Thank you, Commander," Thrawn said, the amusement growing. "Shall we go?"

"Yes, sir."

They headed for the door. "What did Grand Moff Tarkin mean by your promotion being a bonus?" Eli asked.

"I think it was merely a joke."

"Ah," Eli said. A Star Destroyer was one of the best possible assignments, almost the highest pinnacle of success the Imperial Navy could offer. It would indeed be an honor and a privilege to serve aboard one. And as a lieutenant commander, yet.

Before they left the *Thunder Wasp*, he promised himself, he would *definitely* make a point of looking up Lieutenant Gimm.

CHAPTER 20

Seldom can one attain victory in warfare without allies. Some allies provide direct assistance, the two forces battling side by side. Other allies provide logistical support, whether weapons and combat equipment or simply food and other life needs. Sometimes the most effective use of an ally is as a threat, his very presence creating a distraction or forcing the common enemy to deploy resources away from the main battlefront.

But standing by an ally doesn't necessarily mean one will always agree with that ally. Or with his goals or methods.

The *Chimaera*'s alarm had been muted by the time Eli reached the bridge. *Another day,* he thought tiredly as he stepped out of the turbolift car, *another crisis.* Life under Commodore Thrawn's leadership was exciting enough, but there were times when the pursuit and capture of pirates and smugglers began to feel routine and even a bit boring.

Only today wasn't just another day. Nor was it just another crisis.

His first warning that something serious was going on was the group clustered around Thrawn beside the aft bridge hologram pod. Not only was Senior Comm Officer Lomar there, but also First Officer Karyn Faro and Stormtrooper Commander Ayer.

Thrawn caught Eli's eye and beckoned him over. "Lieutenant Commander Vanto," he said gravely. "Senior Lieutenant Lomar has just received a distress call from the troop transport *Sempre*. The captain reports he is under attack."

Eli shot a look at the tactical display. If the positions and vectors were accurate, they were over two hours away from the scene. "I assume no one else is closer, sir?"

"No one with sufficient firepower." Thrawn gestured to Lomar. "Senior Lieutenant?"

"The *Sempre* has identified its attackers as the frigate *Castilus* and two squadrons of V-19 starfighters," Lomar said. "There may be more—the attackers have jammers going, and the *Sempre*'s transmissions are spotty. I've got my people scrubbing and sifting the recordings now, so if there's anything else in there, we'll find it." He threw a hooded look toward Thrawn. "His last transmission said he'd been breached and was being boarded."

"The attacking ships were reported stolen eight weeks ago," Thrawn added.

Eli frowned. There had been something in the commodore's voice . . . "By Nightswan?"

"Possibly," Thrawn said. "The scheme was quite inventive, which could indicate his hand in the planning. But whether or not he was behind the theft, I do not believe he is involved with this attack. Overly violent attacks are not his usual style."

"Styles can change, Commodore," Faro said, her voice brisk and with a hint of impatience. "And with all due respect, I don't see how the ships' starting point matters right now as much as the fact that they're here and they're shooting at our people."

Eli winced. Commander Faro had come with the

Chimaera, having served as first officer under the previous captain. She was never overtly insubordinate, but she was never far from that line, either. Calling Thrawn's comments into question wasn't something a first officer was supposed to do, especially not in public.

But Thrawn merely inclined his head to her. "We are already moving at the *Chimaera*'s greatest speed to assist, Commander," he said. "And knowing their origin may enable us to anticipate their goals and future actions."

"It's a troop carrier, sir," Faro said, the edge of impatience still there. "I think their goal is probably to kill some Imperial troops."

"Perhaps," Thrawn said. "Perhaps not." He gestured to Ayer. "There seems to be something of a mystery about this particular transport."

"Yes, sir," Ayer said, looking uncomfortably at Eli. "As I told the commodore, Commander Vanto, the *Sempre* isn't carrying troops."

"It's empty?"

"No, sir."

Eli flashed a look at each of the others. "Excuse me?"

"I can't say anything more, sir. To any of you," Ayer added, looking even more uncomfortably at Thrawn.

"Major Ayer has received a direct communication from Coruscant, but is not at liberty to share the contents with us," Thrawn said. "Our orders are to deliver him and his stormtroopers to the *Sempre* while we deal with the attacking ships."

"Understood, sir," Eli said, an unpleasant feeling settling in between his shoulder blades. Secret communications that were outside the normal chain of command always made him nervous. "What if they need help aboard?"

"We won't, sir," Ayer assured him.

"What if you do?" Eli repeated.

"We won't, sir," Ayer repeated. The apology was gone

from his voice, his new tone making it clear that the subject was closed. "I can't say any more."

"I'm sure we will be informed at the appropriate time," Thrawn said. "Until then, our task is to reach the *Sempre* before it is completely overwhelmed. Commander Faro, you will run a complete check on the weapons and weapons crews. We are to be ready for combat the moment we reach the scene of the attack. Lieutenant Commander Vanto, contact engineering. If there is a way to increase the *Chimaera*'s speed, you will implement it."

One hour and forty-nine minutes later, the *Chimaera* arrived.

To find that all their orders were now irrelevant.

The *Sempre* drifted dead in space. Its crew lay scattered across the ship, all dead. The troop compartments were empty.

The attacking ships, of course, were long gone.

"Odd," Vanto said as he and Thrawn picked their way through one of the clusters of bodies. With the need for secrecy gone—whatever that secrecy had been about—Ayer had reluctantly permitted the two of them to join his stormtroopers as they finished sweeping the ship. "Blaster burns on some of the bodies, but not all of them."

"Yes, I noticed that," Thrawn said. "Several of the latter also have injuries to their heads and torsos."

"As if they were physically hit," Vanto said. He pointed at the blood marks on a nearby section of bulkhead. "And then we have those. Looks like most of the beating victims had their heads or bodies slammed against the walls and bulkheads."

"Note, too, that some of the marks are higher than the victims are tall," Thrawn said. "That mark in particular. Do you see a pattern in it?"

Vanto stepped to the wall and looked up at the indicated mark. *His forehead wrinkles with thought. His fingers hover over the mark as if he is mentally tracing it.* "More blood than most of them. Those smears look like they could be finger marks. Somebody writing in the blood?"

"Perhaps," Thrawn said. The mark was blurred and seemed incomplete, as if the writer had been interrupted. Or perhaps it wasn't writing at all. Certainly it didn't look like any letter or combination of letters he was familiar with. Though if the writer had been injured, that might account for the distortion.

But why would an injured person choose to write so high? And if it wasn't a word or the beginning of a word, perhaps it was a symbol or a glyph.

He surveyed the crumpled bodies. As Vanto had noted, two had been killed by blasters, the rest beaten to death. None was tall enough to have easily made the mark.

Vanto had come to the same conclusion. "I'd say this was made by either one of the attackers or one of the passengers."

"Perhaps an examination of the troop quarters will tell us which," Thrawn said. "Come."

A stormtrooper was standing guard at the hatchway leading to the troop quarters. "Sorry, sir," the stormtrooper said. *His filtered voice is stiff and imperious.* "No one is allowed inside."

"I am Commodore Thrawn," Thrawn said. "I wish to enter."

"I'm sorry, sir, but I have my orders."

"I am giving you new orders, stormtrooper," Thrawn said. "The passengers are gone. The secrecy you were ordered to maintain concerning the *Sempre* is no longer an issue. Imperial officers and crew are dead, some of your own colleagues among them. Justice and retribution for the attack depend upon information. Some of that information lies behind you through that hatchway."

"I'm sorry, sir, but I have my orders," the storm-trooper said again. *His voice holds no recognition of the situation's urgency.*

"I am your commander, stormtrooper," Thrawn said. *"You will step aside!"*

Vanto twitches at the sudden volume and vehe-mence. The stormtrooper likewise reacts with surprise. He hastily steps away from the hatchway. "Thank you," Thrawn said.

He and Vanto stepped inside. "You disapprove of my words and tone?"

"I don't disapprove of either, sir," Vanto said. "I was just startled. I don't think I've ever heard you shout in anger before."

"I was not angry," Thrawn said. "Some people will not respond to reason. Others refuse to consider alter-natives to their normal pattern of behavior. In such cases, an unexpected breaking of one's own patterns can be an effective tool. What do you see?"

Vanto stepped to the center of the sleeping area. He turned his head slowly, his eyes lingering on the rows of three-tiered bunks. "Those aren't standard-sized racks. They're at least half a meter too long. And aren't standard troop carrier racks four-tiered instead of three?"

"Yes," Thrawn said. "These quarters are clearly de-signed for large passengers."

"Doesn't look temporary, either," Vanto said. "The racks are permanently bonded to the walls, deck, and ceiling. So what kind of passengers was the *Sempre* de-signed to . . ." *His words stop. His eyes focus on the connection rings set into the walls beside two sets of racks. His fingers squeeze together with sudden ten-sion.* "They weren't passengers," he said quietly. "They were prisoners."

"Not just prisoners," Thrawn said. "Slaves."

· · ·

Faro was waiting when Thrawn and Eli returned to the bridge. "Report, Commander," Thrawn ordered.

"I have the analysis of the attack, Commodore," Faro said, pulling up a schematic on the sensor display. "Looks like the most damaging fire came from the V-19s—they took out the shield generators, hyperdrive, and sublights—with the frigate mostly serving as a distraction."

"Not unexpected," Thrawn said. "Established military doctrine—" He looked at Eli. *"Nikhi."*

Mentally, Eli shook his head. All these years speaking Basic, and there were still occasional words that escaped him. "Notwithstanding," he supplied.

Thrawn nodded his thanks. "Established doctrine notwithstanding, if a well-trained starfighter squadron can penetrate point defenses, it is often more effective in striking power than capital ships. Note that the deliberate destruction of the hyperdrive indicates that their goal was never to capture the ship for their own use."

"They were here to free the slaves," Eli murmured.

"Exactly," Thrawn said. "Was there anything to indicate the attackers' species of origin or training methods?"

"Ah, nothing we spotted, sir," Faro said, frowning. "I'm not even sure how we'd go about determining that."

"There are ways," Thrawn said. "We will discuss them later." He turned to Lomar. "Senior Lieutenant?"

"We've finished scrubbing the *Sempre*'s audio," Lomar said. "There are half a dozen species that could have made the sounds we pulled up, but only Wookiees match up to the size you described for the slaves."

"Good." Thrawn pulled out his datapad. "In that case, this blood mark can be interpreted as an emblem instead of writing. Very well. Commander Vanto, to the computer."

"Yes, sir." Eli sat down at the nearest terminal. "Ready."

"The slaves will have come from Kashyyyk," Thrawn said, his eyes narrowed as he scrolled through pages on his datapad. "But there will have been an offworld processing center to test for health and other qualifications before they were sent on to their final destination. Using Kashyyyk and our current position as end points, search for that center's likely location."

"Unless they were in a hurry, there's no reason they had to come direct," Faro pointed out. "They could have been processed anywhere from here to Alderaan."

"Haste is not so much an issue as efficiency, Commander," Thrawn said. "If there has been a steady stream of such transports . . ." He paused, then continued scrolling. "At any rate, the *Sempre* was permanently altered to carry Wookiees or creatures of their same size. It seems reasonable that the processing center is equally permanent. Commander Vanto?"

"I've pulled up everything within a ninety-degree double cone, sir," Eli reported. "There are a *lot* of systems in there."

"It will be a military base," Thrawn said. "Owned and operated solely by the Empire. It will be relatively isolated, closed to outside traffic, and with a higher level of imported material than the listed crew complement would suggest."

"Why don't you just look for shipments of Wookiee food?" Faro suggested.

"I don't think there's anything special about Wookiee food, ma'am," Eli said as he continued keying in the parameters. "Even if there were, the shipments would be disguised as machinery or other items. Not much use having a secret slave center if you're announcing to the galaxy that you're feeding a lot of extra mouths."

"Precisely," Thrawn said. He was still gazing at his datapad, Eli noted, but the rapid-fire scrolling had ended. He must have found what he was looking for. "There will also most likely be another Imperial base nearby, less secretive but larger and close enough to provide a rapid response if necessary."

"Yes, sir." Eli keyed in the final parameters. "And that gives us . . . Lansend Twenty-Six. It's an old customs clearing station the Separatists took over during the war and converted into a staging area. The Empire took it back but hasn't done much with it."

"Until now," Faro murmured. "Do you think we should warn them that one of their transports got whacked, sir?"

"We will do more than that," Thrawn said. "Signal the helm, Commander Vanto, to take us to Lansend Twenty-Six at all possible speed."

"Yes, sir," Eli said. He keyed the intercom and delivered the orders.

"Why would the attackers head there, sir?" Faro asked. "Wouldn't they be more likely to bypass the station and take the Wookiees to some refugee planet?"

"You assume they already have all the Wookiees that they want," Thrawn said.

"You mean you think they're going to raid the station for more prisoners?" Faro asked, frowning.

"Consider, Commander," Thrawn said.

Eli hid a smile. He knew this tone.

"Bringing the *Sempre* out of hyperspace at the precise point where the attackers were waiting would have been nearly impossible without assistance," Thrawn continued. "That assistance would have had to come from either Lansend or the *Sempre* itself. Either way, the implication is that the attackers had an ally and saboteur aboard the station."

"And if he's still there," Faro said, nodding understanding, "why not sabotage the station's defenses while he's at it?"

Thrawn inclined his head to her. "Very good, Commander."

"If they've got a saboteur aboard, shouldn't we warn them?" Lomar put in. "Either them or—Commander Vanto, was the commodore right about there being another station nearby?"

"Yes," Eli said. "Baklek Base, a twenty-minute flight away."

"We must maintain comm silence," Thrawn said. "We do not wish to alert the raiders that we are in pursuit."

"With all due respect, sir, this still sounds like a bit of a stretch," Faro said. "If someone sabotaged the *Sempre,* there's a fair chance Lansend picked up the same distress call we did and has already figured out they have a problem. Hitting an unsuspecting transport is one thing; hitting a station that's primed and ready is something clse."

"Agreed," Thrawn said. "Nevertheless, I believe they will make the attempt."

"Because they're crazy idealistic meddlers and that makes them suicidal?"

"No," Thrawn said. "Because they told us they were."

Faro shot a startled look at Eli. "They *what?*"

"The drawing left behind amid the bodies," Thrawn said. "We know now that the slaves were Wookiees. The mark we found was a clan symbol, underscored by a mark indicating warning or defiance."

Eli winced as he saw where Thrawn was going. "And defiance results in vengeance?"

"With tribal cultures like that of the Wookiees, very often," Thrawn confirmed. "Even if there are no more Wookiees aboard the station to rescue, they will seek vengeance upon those who participated in the slaving. Since there is still the possibility that the station is unaware of their actions, they must attack as soon as possible."

"Only Lansend *might* be ready for them," Eli pointed out.

"We shall hope," Thrawn said. "Regardless, I fully expect us to arrive in time to catch the attackers in the act."

. . .

"Still no signals from the station," Vanto reported. *His voice is brisk with the anticipation of battle, his tone hinting of the swirl of possibilities and patterns within his mind.* "Breakout in fifteen seconds."

"Weapons systems and crews standing ready," Faro said. "TIE squadrons ready to launch."

"Signal to Baklek Base standing by," Lomar said. "Pre-recorded message loaded and ready."

A flicker of starlines, and the *Chimaera* arrived.

To find the battle had begun.

"Base is under attack," Vanto snapped. "Reading one frigate—twenty-two V-19 starfighters. Base's starboard laser cannons slagged and silenced; portside weapons still firing."

"Launch TIEs," Thrawn ordered. "Their first priority is to disable the frigate without destroying it. Signal Baklek Base, adding Commander Vanto's details to the alert. Signal Lansend and request status."

In many cases an opponent's attack strategy betrayed his origin. Here, the battle had already devolved into chaos, with each attacking starfighter effectively its own strategist and tactician.

But even in large-scale disorder could be found local patterns and connections. Thrawn studied the V-19s' movements, watching for repetition and predictability.

"*Chimaera*, this is Colonel Zenoc." *The voice from the bridge speaker is tense but not panicked.* "Welcome. Your timing is excellent."

"Colonel, this is Commodore Thrawn," Thrawn said. "You have a saboteur on your station."

"Found her, disarmed her, and locked her up," Zenoc said. "Unfortunately, not before she disabled the long-range comm and shut off the starboard-side defense systems. Baklek Base is supposed to be on call—can you whistle them up for us?"

"I have already done so," Thrawn said. "I need the schematics of your base."

"Right," Zenoc said. "On their way. I'm including a real-time internal sensor feed."

"Very good," Thrawn said. "Commander Vanto?"

"Schematics and sensor feed coming up now," Vanto said.

The schematics appeared, with moving dots indicating the positions of the attackers and defenders.

"We've been breached from the starboard docking hatch," Zenoc continued. "So far we're holding, but we're being pushed back. It looks like they're trying to take down our portside defenses so that they can send in another boarding party from that end and catch us in a pincer."

"My starfighters are engaging those attackers," Thrawn said. "Commander Vanto?"

"Portside V-19 force has split," Vanto reported. "Half turning to engage TIEs, half continuing attack on station defenses. Starboard V-19s turning to defend frigate."

"Too late," Faro called. *Her voice holds grim satisfaction.* "We've taken out the frigate's hyperdrive. Our visitors aren't going anywhere."

"Order the TIEs to shift focus to the V-19s," Thrawn said. The movements of the station personnel had now revealed a pattern. "Colonel Zenoc, are any of your personnel in sections A-four, A-five, or B-five?"

"No, sir."

"Are any slaves in that area?"

There was a short pause. "I'm not at liberty to discuss such matters, Commodore."

"If you wish to save your station, Colonel, you will answer my question."

Another pause. "There are some . . . nonmilitary personnel in section B-five," Zenoc said.

"Thank you," Thrawn said. "Pull all your personnel back to B-eight and hold there."

"To B-*eight*?" *Zenoc's voice holds confusion.*

"Yes," Thrawn said. "Commander Faro: I have marked seven target points on the starboard part of the station.

I require pinpoint accuracy from the turbolasers. Can you do it?"

"Absolutely, Commodore," Faro confirmed. "Sending targets to gunners . . . gunners await your command."

"Colonel Zenoc?"

"We've pulled back," Zenoc said. *His voice still holds confusion, and now also wariness and distrust.* "But this isn't a tenable position, sir. If we get pushed back any more, we're going to be in trouble."

"You will not be pushed back," Thrawn assured him. "Your battle is over. Turbolasers: *Fire.*"

On the schematic, the seven marked points flashed as hull plates disintegrated. Behind them, the sensors painted four of the internal sections bright red as the air within them boiled into space.

"What the *hell*?" Zenoc barked. "*Chimaera,* did you just *fire* on us?"

"Yes," Thrawn confirmed. "I believe you will now find your intruders trapped in their current positions."

Another pause. "I'll be roasted," Zenoc said. *The earlier wariness and confusion are gone. His voice now holds surprised understanding.* "And B-five?"

"Is intact, though it is now also isolated from the rest of the station," Thrawn said. "We will continue the battle against the frigate and V-19s. I suggest you call on the intruders to surrender before you begin emergency access operations."

"Yes, of course." *Zenoc's voice holds relief and even a small degree of humor.* "Thank you, Commodore. Excellent work."

"You are welcome, Colonel," Thrawn said. "We will continue operations until the Baklek reinforcements arrive. After that, we will leave you to deal with the prisoners while we retrieve the *Sempre* and return it here. I presume you have orders that cover such contingencies?"

"We do," Zenoc said. *His voice sobers as the imme-*

diacy of the battle fades and he remembers the loss of the transport's crew. "We'll be ready when you return. And again, Commodore, thank you."

"Commander Faro?" Thrawn said.

"Enemy forces are down to the crippled frigate and three functioning V-19s," Faro reported. "I assume you'd like us to corral and capture the remaining fighters intact if possible?"

"If possible," Thrawn said. "If not, the Empire will have sufficient prisoners for interrogation among the rest of the survivors."

"Yes, sir."

Vanto came up beside him. "Commodore?" he asked, his voice quiet and disturbed. "What are we going to do about the Wookiees?"

"We will leave them here."

Vanto is silent a moment. "I'm not completely comfortable with the idea that the Empire is using slaves, sir."

"Terms are not always as they seem, Commander," Thrawn said. "They are called *slaves,* but they may in fact be indentured servants. They may be prisoners working off their sentence. They may have sold themselves into slavery as a means of repaying debts to others on their world. I have seen all those situations at times."

"You really think any of those are likely?"

"No," Thrawn said, his tone hardening. "But it does not matter. However these beings were pressed into service, they are now Imperial assets. They will be treated as such."

"Understood, Commodore."

CHAPTER 21

Each culture is different. Each species is unique. That presents challenges to the warrior, who often must ascertain from limited clues the strategy, goals, and tactics of an opponent.

But the danger of misreading an opponent is sometimes even greater in politics. There, one seldom has the clearness of weapons activation or troop movement to warn of impending danger. Often, the only indication of conflict is when the battle has already begun.

The shuttle hatch opened, letting in the warm afternoon air.

After all these years, Arihnda had come home.

She paused at the top of the ramp, taking a moment to let her gaze drift across the buildings of Capital City before turning to the more rustic Lothal landscape surrounding it. After the massive cityscape of Coruscant, the sight of wild vegetation was almost a shock.

"Welcome home, Governor," a voice called from the bottom of the ramp.

Arihnda looked down. Maketh Tua stood there, dressed in the blue and gray of an Imperial minister, a hint of her blond hair glinting from beneath her close-fitting conical helmet. Her hand held a datapad; her smile held a hint of nervousness.

"Thank you," Arihnda said, walking down the ramp and stopping in front of her. "It's been a while, hasn't it?"

"Yes, Governor," the woman confirmed. "Over a year since you succeeded to the governorship, in fact."

Arihnda felt her lip twitch. And in that year she'd spent less than a week here, usually only a few hours at a time, ruling by proxy the world she'd worked so hard to get. Most of her time had been spent on Coruscant, making friends, bolstering Lothal's standing among the Empire's thousands of worlds, and chasing down incriminating bits of information for Grand Moff Tarkin.

But finally, *finally*, she was here to stay.

After the glittering lights of Coruscant, she still wasn't entirely sure how she felt about that.

"Which also makes it over a year since you were appointed overseer of industrial production," she said. "So tell me: How is Lothal's industrial production getting along?"

"Quite well, Your Excellency, quite well," Tua said. "I have all the relevant data whenever you're settled in and ready to examine it."

Silently, Arihnda held out her hand. Tua's cheerful expression slipped, just a bit, and she hastily handed Arihnda the datapad. "It's the file on top, Your Excellency."

"Thank you." Arihnda keyed to the file, watching Tua out of the corner of her eye. The woman had been an assistant minister during the last couple of months of Governor Azadi's administration. Azadi's sudden removal and arrest on charges of treason had been a traumatic event for the entire governmental staff, and even after all this time it was clear that Tua wasn't completely over it.

Hopefully the others were feeling likewise. Nervous subordinates worked extra hard, and kept their noses *very* clean. Until they had a better feel for their newly returned boss, they would be polite, energetic, and easy to control or intimidate.

Which was just as well, because the intimidation was about to start in earnest. "What's this decline in refinery output?" she asked, turning the datapad around. "Twenty percent in the past four months?"

"It's the mines, Your Excellency," Tua said. "They've been worked so hard over the past few years that they're running out of quality ore."

"Really," Arihnda said, letting her voice cool a bit.

Tua's throat tightened. "They've been worked very hard," she repeated. "It's also more and more difficult to find qualified miners. A lot of young people go into the Academy—Commandant Aresko has set up a whole string of incentives for them. They just don't want to work the mines anymore like they used to. With the Empire running them instead of the old mining families—"

"Then you bring in miners from offworld," Arihnda cut in. She'd already noted that the Imperial-run mines had logged the quickest decline in workers. "My parents—" She broke off as a number on the list caught her attention. "That doonium vein is tapped out *already*? That's impossible."

"I'm sorry, Your Excellency, but it's true," Tua said. "I've been down the mine myself. All the doonium has been extracted."

"I see," Arihnda said, pulling up the full data spread on Pryce Mining. The fact that Renking had blatantly kept the name was just one additional irritation. "In that case, Pryce Mining isn't worth the effort being put into it. Shut it down."

Tua's eyes widened in shock. "Excuse me, Your Excellency?"

"Was the order unclear?"

"No, Your Excellency," Tua said hastily. "Do you want it . . . is it to be closed right now?"

"Right now," Arihnda confirmed. "At the end of the current shift. See to it personally, Minister."

"Yes, Your Excellency." She turned and started to go—
"Minister?"

Tua turned back. "Yes, Your Excellency?"

Arihnda held out the woman's datapad. "I understand Senator Renking is on Lothal at the moment," she said as Tua hastily retrieved the device. "Have someone inform him that I want to see him in my office at his earliest convenience."

Her office in the government building was just as she'd left it: neat, but only sparsely decorated. Azadi's supporters had looted the room of all his personal effects after his arrest, and Arihnda hadn't bothered to replace any of them.

Nor did she intend to. She was here to work, not relax among trinkets and sentiment.

She spent the rest of the afternoon and early evening reading through the data that had accumulated since Azadi's last report to Coruscant. Lothal's industrialization was proceeding at a gratifying pace, but there were still some serious deficiencies that needed to be addressed.

It was almost sundown when the droid in the outer office announced that Renking had arrived.

To Arihnda's complete lack of surprise, the senator barged through the door without waiting for permission to enter. "Welcome back, Your Excellency," he said, without a shred of actual welcome in his voice. "How long are you here for this time?"

"Hopefully, I'm going to be here permanently," Arihnda said.

"Wonderful." He stopped at the edge of the desk, his face darkening. "Now what the hell is this about closing my mine?"

"*Your* mine," Arihnda countered calmly. "Forgive me, but I didn't realize you *had* a mine. I thought all mines on Lothal were owned or overseen by the Empire."

"You know what I'm talking about," Renking ground

out. "Your old mine—Pryce Mining. My agreement with the Empire was for ten percent of the profits."

"That would have been reason enough right there to shut it down," Arihnda said. "But don't flatter yourself. Closing it was a strictly business decision. The doonium vein has tapped out, and there aren't enough experienced miners left to waste them on underperforming rock. Hence, Pryce Mining will be shut down and its employees transferred elsewhere."

"And I suppose you'll decide which people go where?" Renking asked suspiciously.

"I'll leave that up to Minister Tua," Arihnda said. "But it seems only fair that the employees with the highest seniority be offered the best positions."

"Those being the ones left over from when *you* ran the mine, I suppose?"

"That *is* how seniority works."

Renking hissed between his teeth. "I don't have to just sit here and take this, you know," he said. "I can bring in my own experts and show you that the mine's production is at least on a par with every other mine on Lothal."

"You could," Arihnda agreed. "But you won't. Would you like to know why?"

"I'm dying to find out," he bit out sarcastically.

"One: Because Pryce Mining is too small to be worth a fight," she said, counting off fingers. "You have other interests that pay much better, especially now that the doonium is gone. Two: Because every favor you burn on a worthless mine is a favor you can't call in for something else. I know how you work. You can't afford to waste favors on pride."

She let her expression harden. "And three: The only way I could have obtained this governorship so young is if I have powerful friends and patrons. *Very* powerful friends . . . *and after all your digging I dare say you* still *have no idea who they are*. Until you do, you don't dare raise a finger against me."

For a long moment they stared at each other across the desk. Then, with another soft hiss, Renking inclined his head. "In that case, Governor, I believe our conversation is over."

"I believe it is, Senator," Arihnda agreed. "Good evening."

She waited until he was gone from her office, and the doorwatch droids reported that he'd left the building. Then, keying the holo on her desk, she punched in a familiar number.

The display lit up with the triangular face, bright eyes, and lumpy headcrest of a female Anx. "Hello, Eccos," Arihnda said. "This is Arihnda Pryce. How have you been?"

For a moment the eyes goggled. Then, abruptly, the Anx mining boss let loose a stream of Shusugaunt.

"Easy, Eccos, easy," Arihnda said. "Basic, if you please—my Shusugaunt is quite rusty. Yes, I'm back; and yes, I'm still governor. But that doesn't mean we can't still work together. *If* you're still in the business of making money, that is."

"Of course," Eccos said, the words barely understandable through her thick accent.

"Good," Arihnda said. "You're aware, of course, that Pryce Mining had a vein of doonium they were working. I presume you're also aware that the vein has played out."

"Yes, to both," Eccos said, her voice heavy with regret. "It is very sad."

"Not really, since we both know it isn't true," Arihnda said calmly. "I saw the report, and I know that the granite block that supposedly marked the end of the vein is nothing more than an intrusion. The doonium continues on the other side."

"Really?" Eccos said, sounding surprised. "Are you sure?"

"Of course I'm sure," Arihnda said. "Because you've been mining it."

The wrinkled cheeks puckered with dismay. "Governor Pryce—"

"Don't bother denying it," Arihnda interrupted. "Because I've seen *your* numbers, too. The reason I called was to tell you that I've just shut down Pryce Mining. That means that starting tomorrow morning you can go full-bore on that vein without worrying that one of Renking's stooges will hear your machines behind the granite."

The cheeks puckered again, this time in the opposite direction. "I . . . do not know what to say."

"Then don't say anything," Arihnda said. "Just get that doonium out and into processing." She looked briefly at the map she'd pulled up on her datapad. "Depending on where the vein goes, we might need to relocate another farmer or two to get it out. Let me know if you need me to do that."

"Yes, Governor Pryce," Eccos said. "May you rest tonight in the warmth of your dreams."

"And may you," Arihnda said.

She keyed off, the sheer low-mind commonness of the traditional farewell grating across her ears and mind. She'd always thought Lothal painfully rustic, but life on Coruscant had seriously sharpened the contrast. She turned back to her computer.

And paused. Through the west-facing window, the sun was beginning to set.

For a moment she watched, thinking back to the evening when her mother was arrested and their lives had changed forever. At the time she'd thought how the people in big cities probably never saw the horizon or the sunset, and had wondered if they ever thought about such things. Or whether they even cared.

Arihnda had lived on Coruscant, in the galaxy's ultimate big city.

And as she gazed out the window, she realized that she really *didn't* care.

Keying the blinds closed, she turned her back on the distant horizon and got back to work.

The next few months were an unpleasant mix of frantic work, irritating dealings with the locals, and unrelenting tedium. Lothal was exactly as Arihnda remembered it: filled with backwoods humans, even more backwoods nonhumans, patterns of cronyism that often undercut the Imperial interests on the planet, and a social structure that provided no quality entertainment whatsoever.

The cronyism was the worst part. During her years away in the capital the Empire had steadily built up Lothal's industries, expanded the mines, and gradually brought in more troops to oversee it all.

But not everyone was happy with the planet's new direction. The old leaders and families resented the slow erosion of their power, and they weren't quiet about lining up their friends, associates, and everyone else within their web of influence to denounce the New Order. The Imperial response had been predictable: repression of speech and curtailment of freedoms, followed by business as usual.

Part of that business involved moving farmers off their land, sometimes to establish a new factory or military facility, more often to enhance mining operations. Naturally, the farmers complained about the forced relocation and drew their friends into the quarrel, occasionally to the point of violence.

It was a pointless argument. Lothal had more than enough cropland for its purposes, and in fact was still a net exporter of foodstuffs. The relative handful of lost farms was negligible. But the displaced farmers seldom saw it that way, and the offer of jobs in factories or mines was usually rejected out of hand.

Still, despite the complaints of a small minority, the work continued to progress. Those who had claimed that the new development would create jobs and prosperity were vindicated. Those who had decried the heightened Imperial presence and preached doom were reduced to quiet muttering.

But not all the threats were internal. Arihnda had been on Lothal three months when an unexpected danger quietly reared its head.

"Yes, Your Excellency, I noticed this report a few days ago," Minister Tua said, frowning in confusion at the page Arihnda had pulled up on her computer. "I don't see why it's a problem."

"Don't you," Arihnda said darkly. For all Tua's expertise at managing Lothal's industrial infrastructure, the woman was utterly blind in certain matters. "The governor of Kintoni is offering to expand her military-grade landing and maintenance facilities, and you don't see why that's a problem?"

"No, Your Excellency," Tua said, looking more confused than ever. "I would think the more naval presence we have in the area, the better. With all the pirates and smugglers—"

"We don't want an enhanced naval presence in this area," Arihnda ground out. Did the woman understand *nothing*? "We want an enhanced naval presence *on Lothal*. Do you understand? *Only* on Lothal."

Tua shrank back into her chair, her eyes wide with surprise and fear. Good. "Your Excellency—"

"We want Lothal to be the center of this part of the Outer Rim," Arihnda said quietly. Somehow, the softer tone seemed to frighten Tua more than the outburst had. "That means industry, mining, commerce, expanded youth and military academies . . . *and* a powerful navy presence to maintain it all. If Kintoni starts drawing away our ships, everything else will follow."

She raised her eyebrows. "Do *you* want to live on Lothal the way it was, Minister Tua? Or do you even remember that far back?"

With a visible effort, Tua found her voice. "I understand, Your Excellency. But . . ."

"But you don't see what we can do about it," Arihnda said, suddenly disgusted. All of Tua's offworld schooling, and yet here she was drifting back to thinking like a native. That is, barely at all. "I'm leaving immediately for Coruscant," she said, blanking the display and standing up. So much for settling in permanently. "You'll be in charge until I return."

"Yes, Your Excellency," Tua said, belatedly getting to her feet. "Ah . . . may I ask how long you'll be gone?"

"Until I finish this," Arihnda said. "One way or another."

"I'm sorry, but Grand Moff Tarkin isn't on Coruscant at the moment," the receptionist at Tarkin's office said, her voice polite but vacant. "If you wish, I can send him a message."

"No need," Arihnda said. She hadn't really expected Tarkin to be here, but it had been worth a try. "Just add a note to whatever you next send him that Governor Arihnda Pryce of Lothal sends her greetings."

"Yes, Governor."

So she didn't recognize Arihnda, either by face or by name. Not surprising, really. There were thousands of governors in the Empire, and no one could be expected to memorize even a tenth of them.

Still, Arihnda had hoped.

The airspeeder's holocomm was blinking a waiting call when she returned. She glanced at the ID, smiled to herself, and keyed it. "This is Governor Arihnda Pryce," she identified herself to the uniformed man who answered. "I'm returning a call from Commodore Thrawn."

"One moment, Governor." The display blanked. A minute later, Thrawn's familiar blue face and red eyes appeared. "Ms. Pryce," Thrawn said, inclining his head toward her in greeting. "Rather, I should say, Governor Pryce."

"Thank you for returning my call, Commodore," Arihnda said, deciding not to make an issue of the slip. She was familiar enough with Thrawn's lack of grace in social and political matters to know it hadn't been a deliberate insult. Besides, it was never a good idea to berate someone who was—hopefully—about to be useful. "Have you had a chance to look over the proposals I sent you?"

"I have," Thrawn said, lowering his eyes to something off-screen. "If I understand correctly, you want my opinion as to whether Lothal or Kintoni would be the better location for an expansion of the navy's presence in that part of the Outer Rim."

"That's correct," Arihnda said, mentally crossing her fingers. Against her natural instincts she'd discarded her original plan to subtly weigh the data and proposals in Lothal's favor. Thrawn might detect such manipulation, and that would be the end of any chance to get him on her side. "Obviously, I have an interest in this matter, but I tried to present the choice in as fair a manner as possible."

"And so you did, Governor," Thrawn acknowledged, his eyes still focused off-screen. "I took the liberty of confirming your notes and maps through the navy archives. Your presentation was remarkably evenhanded."

"Thank you," Arihnda said, feeling a shiver run up her back. Just as well she hadn't tried to slant it. "Your conclusion?"

"Both systems offer advantages," Thrawn said, finally looking back up at her. "But if I had to choose one, I would choose Lothal."

Arihnda exhaled silently. "Thank you, Commodore," she said. "May I quote you when I make my presentation to the High Command?"

"No need, Governor," Thrawn said. "I have worked

up a full analysis that includes my conclusions. I can send it to you now, if you like."

"I would indeed," Arihnda said. "Thank you."

"No thanks needed," he assured her. "I always stand ready to assist the Imperial navy in any way I can. Is there anything more?"

"Not at this time, Commodore," she said. "Hopefully, we'll cross paths again soon. Goodbye."

"Goodbye, Governor."

It took a few moments for the report to load, first to her airspeeder and then to a data card. Arihnda watched the progress, running it all through her mind. With Thrawn's blessing in hand, there was only one person yet she needed to see before she would be ready to take her case to the High Command.

And there was a reason she'd put this contact last on her list. Securing the data card in her pocket, she took a moment to mentally prepare herself. Then, joining the traffic flow, she headed across the center of the Federal District toward a familiar—a far too familiar—place.

The office of Senator Domus Renking.

"I hardly expected to see you here today," Renking commented stiffly as he ushered Arihnda to a chair. Still seething over his loss of Pryce Mining, Arihnda guessed, but still not ready to try a countermove against her. "I heard you were on Coruscant, but assumed you'd be spending your time with all those powerful friends and patrons you once threatened me with."

"Social calls can wait," Arihnda said, pulling out a data card. "I presume you've heard about Kintoni's request for a larger navy presence in their system?"

"Of course," Renking said, frowning as he sat down behind his desk. "So?"

"So even the navy hasn't got infinite resources," Arihnda said as patiently as she could. She should have guessed Renking would be so focused on his petty political intrigues that he would miss the full significance of Sanz's power play. "So every credit they spend on Kintoni is a credit they *don't* spend on Lothal. So we have to put a stop to it."

"All right, fine," he said. "Points well taken. I presume you have some ideas?"

"Of course," Arihnda said. "The plan is threefold. First, I have a proposal showing what Lothal could do in the way of landing and maintenance facilities. Here are the details." She handed him a data card. "Second, I have an analysis and recommendation for Lothal from Commodore Thrawn. Third—"

"Thrawn?" Renking cut in, frowning again. "That blue-skinned lieutenant we met at that Ascension Week party?"

"Yes, only he's a commodore now," Arihnda said. "*And* is highly respected by the High Command. His opinion ought to carry significant weight. And third—" She raised her eyebrows. "—I want you to work on Governor Sanz."

"Work on her how?"

"I don't know," Arihnda said impatiently. "Talk to her, argue with her, persuade her—however you want to do it is up to you. Just get her to withdraw her proposal."

"I can try," Renking said. "How long do I have?"

"The presentations will be heard six days from now," she said. "I'm going to spend that time fine-tuning my proposal and looking for allies in the Senate. I suggest you spend that time working on Sanz."

"Got it," Renking said. "However I want to do it?"

Arihnda lifted a hand. "Just do what you do best, Senator. Do what you do best."

"All rise," the warrant officer standing beside the short table intoned.

Seated among the crowd in the petitioners' gallery,

Arihnda stood up, Renking beside her, as an officer and two civilians filed into the room. Across the narrow aisle, she spotted Governor Sanz as she rose with the rest of the people on her side of the gallery. Sanz's back, it seemed to her, looked unnaturally stiff.

The board took their seats, and as the petitioners sat down the civilian in the middle picked up the datapad lying on the table in front of her. "The select committee of the Imperial High Command has studied the various proposals that have been brought before it," she said. "We are here to make their decisions known." She tapped the datapad. "First: in the matter of Lothal versus Kintoni regarding a contract for the expansion of navy facilities. The contract is awarded to Lothal."

Arihnda felt a flood of relief wash over her. She glanced across the aisle, and it seemed to her that some of Sanz's stiffness drained away.

Odd, given that her bid had just been turned down. Perhaps she hadn't wanted the contract as much as she'd let on.

"We can go now," Renking prompted quietly, tapping her sleeve.

"Go ahead," Arihnda murmured back, studying her datapad. "The next few petitions are also Outer Rim matters. I'd like to see how those go down."

Renking grunted. "Fine," he said, and lapsed into sullen silence.

Arihnda had been keeping an eye on the various petitions, and none of the board's decisions came as a surprise. Finally, after twenty minutes, she nodded and gestured Renking to the aisle. He stood up and slipped past the rest of the people in their row, Arihnda right behind him.

"That worked out well," Renking commented as they left the audience room and headed toward the building's exit. "I suppose congratulations are in order."

"Thank you," Arihnda said. Out of the corner of her eye she saw a woman in a white ISB tunic angling across the entryway toward them. "But we couldn't have done it without you."

"I'm glad I could do my part—"

"Senator Domus Renking?" the woman said.

Renking turned to her, giving a small twitch as he spotted the uniform. "Yes," he said cautiously.

"Major Hartell, ISB," the woman identified herself. "I need you to come with me, sir."

"What for?" Renking asked, his face starting to darken. "What's this about?"

Passersby were beginning to pause and slow down, Arihnda noted peripherally, and heads were starting to turn. "Do you really want to have that discussion here, Senator?" Hartell asked.

"I'll tell you what I *don't* want," Renking countered, his voice starting to rise. "I don't want some ISB flunky throwing my name on a list just so some other ISB flunky can play power games with the Imperial Senate. I demand to know the charge, if there even is one, and who the claimant is."

"As you wish, Senator," Hartell said. "The claimant in this case is the Imperial Security Bureau itself. The charge is bribery."

Renking caught his breath. "What?" he asked, the words coming out from between stiff lips.

"Don't act so surprised," Hartell said. "Four days ago, you approached Governor Sanz of Kintoni, offering a substantial bribe if she would withdraw her planet's petition before the High Command. Governor Sanz declined on the grounds that a withdrawal at this late date would look suspicious, but then agreed to your counter-proposal that she deliberately sabotage her presentation, with double the original bribe to be paid if Lothal won the bid."

Renking had taken on the look of a hunted animal. "That's a lie," he insisted. "All of it." But to Arihnda his tone sounded more worried than defiant. "Whatever Sanz told you—"

"Governor Sanz hasn't told us anything," Hartell said evenly. "But she will. She's already in custody for her part in this conspiracy."

Renking caught his breath, twisting his head to look at Arihnda. *"Pryce?"*

"You really shouldn't discuss criminal acts with someone else's data card in your card pouch," Arihnda said calmly.

"But—" Renking shot a look at Hartell, looked back at Arihnda. "You *told* me to do it."

"I told you to talk, argue, or persuade her," Arihnda corrected. "I never suggested or even hinted you try to bribe her." She gestured at Hartell. "All of which is also on the recording."

"Indeed," Hartell said. "Thank you for your assistance, Governor Pryce. You may go. Senator Renking, follow me, please."

Renking gave Arihnda one final look, his expression a mix of disbelief and hatred. Then, without a word, he turned and followed Hartell out.

All around them, with the drama now over, the people of Coruscant resumed their activities.

"I'll be leaving for Lothal in the morning," Arihnda told the receptionist at her Coruscant office as she gathered the data cards she'd forgotten to pick up earlier that day. "I shouldn't be gone long, though. There are a few meetings and conferences next month I'll want to attend, Grand Moff Tarkin has invited me to visit Eriadu, and I'll certainly want to be back for Ascension Week. So you might as well keep everything open and running."

"Yes, Governor," the receptionist said. "Oh, and you got another message about two hours ago from a Juahir Madras."

Arihnda froze. "Juahir Madras?"

"Yes, Governor, from the Oovo Four detention center. She's written, oh, about twenty of these messages over the past year or so. I send them on, but your Lothal office always turns them back. Do you want to take them with you now?"

Arihnda took a deep breath. Juahir Madras. Her old friend. Her old, traitorous friend. "No, keep them here," she said. "I'll let you know when I'm ready to read them."

CHAPTER 22

The soldier in the field and the crew member aboard a warship inevitably see a war from a limited perspective. Their goal is to carry out their mission or their appointed task, and trust that their commanders are aware of the larger situation and the vast matrix of facts, positions, options, and dangers. Leadership is a role and a task that should never be aspired to lightly. Neither should loyalty be given without reason. Even if the primary reason is nothing more than the soldier's oath and duty, a true leader will work to prove worthy of a deeper trust.

But leadership and loyalty are both two-bladed weapons. Each can be twisted from its intended purpose. The consequences are never pleasant.

"Persuade them if you can," Fleet Admiral Jok Donassius said, his face on the holo grim and angry. "Devastate them if you have to. But stop them, one way or another. And stop them *fast*."

"Understood, Fleet Admiral," Thrawn said, his voice steady and cool. A lot steadier, Eli thought, and a lot cooler than he himself was feeling right now.

And from the expressions he could see on the rest of

the *Chimaera*'s bridge crew, he wasn't alone in his misgivings.

Small wonder. It hadn't been all that long since the Separatist crisis sparked the bloody devastation of the Clone Wars. Billions had died in that conflict, with hundreds of planets all but destroyed and thousands more still clawing their way up from the brink. The last thing the galaxy could afford was a repeat of that horror.

But Governor Quesl and the people of Botajef were apparently ready to give it a try.

Thrawn and Donassius finished their conversation, and the holo blanked. For a moment Thrawn continued to gaze at the empty projector, as if pondering the orders he'd just received. Then, lifting his head a few centimeters, he turned to face his senior officers. "Commander Faro, instruct the helm to lay in a course for Botajef," he ordered.

"Yes, sir." Faro looked over at the helmsman—who was, Eli noted, already watching her closely—and lifted a finger. The helmsman nodded back and turned to his board. "On course for Botajef, Commodore," Faro confirmed.

"Thank you." Thrawn looked around the group. "Comments? Senior Lieutenant Pyrondi?"

"With all due respect, sir, I think they're crazy," Weapons Officer Pyrondi said, a bit hesitantly. As the newest addition to the *Chimaera*'s bridge officer corps, she was still getting used to Thrawn's unique style of open tactical consultation. "Do they really think they can secede from the Empire all by themselves?"

"Who says they *are* all by themselves?" Faro countered soberly. "There's a lot of unrest out there in the galaxy, and it's growing."

"Though it's mostly just grumbling," Eli said.

"So far," Faro said pointedly. "But who's to say Quesl hasn't got a hundred other systems quietly backing him, all of them just waiting to see how far he gets before making independence proclamations of their own?"

"*Not far* is exactly where he's going to get," Pyrondi said. "I mean, seriously, ma'am? We've got enough firepower here to carve our initials into Botajef's bedrock."

"A fact Governor Quesl is undoubtedly aware of," Thrawn said. "What then does he hope to gain by his words of defiance?"

"That's the question, sir," Faro agreed. "If he's the representative for a lot of other systems, just slapping him down won't necessarily solve the problem. It might even exacerbate it. If he's alone"—she gestured to Pyrondi—"then Lieutenant Pyrondi is very likely right. The man is crazy."

"Though if he is, he's picked a great place to show it off," Pyrondi said. "I've met a few Jefies in my life. They're the best followers in the world. You persuade them you're their leader, and they'll follow you anywhere. And even with all the immigration over the past century they're still a solid eighty-five percent of the planetary population."

"Yet they didn't complain about Coruscant appointing a human governor over them?" Eli asked.

"Like I said, sir, they're followers," Pyrondi said. "Prove you're a leader, and they're there. Quesl must have proved it, and then some."

"That is my reading of the Jefies, as well," Thrawn agreed. "Which suggests that the best strategy may be to create a new leader for them."

"Assuming they're just blindly following Quesl, sir, and haven't bought into this secession thing themselves," Pyrondi warned. "You get a group of Jefi true believers, and they may not need a leader to tell them what to do. There's a lot we don't know about them."

"Then we should learn," Thrawn said. "Commander Faro, how long until we reach Botajef?"

Faro checked her datapad. "Approximately fifteen hours, sir."

"I'll be in my quarters," Thrawn said. "You have the

bridge, Commander Faro. I want the *Chimaera* fully ready for combat fourteen hours from now."

"It will be, Commodore," Faro said grimly, and in her eyes Eli could see the flickering, burning memories of her own Clone Wars experiences. "Count on it."

The history of Botajef was one of long periods of passive allegiance, followed by brief episodes of often fiery conflict, followed by new leadership and another era of passive allegiance.

Jefi art followed that same pattern: curves interrupted by stark lines or sharp angles, with a color palette mirroring the group emotional and ethical spectrum. Sculpts were low-contrast, perhaps indicating that the Jefies themselves recognized the shortcomings in their cultural matrix. In contrast, the hanging tressiles, with their quick-dampening balances, indicated they also recognized the basic stability of their political system.

"Commodore?" Vanto's voice came.

"Enter."

Vanto crossed the floor, passing through the holograms. "Jefi art?"

"Yes."

"Nice," Vanto said, his gaze moving between the pieces. "A bit jagged for my taste, but nice. I came to inform you, Commodore, that we're two hours from Botajef and the *Chimaera* is ready for battle."

"Thank you, Commander," Thrawn said. "You seem troubled. Are you concerned about the upcoming confrontation?"

"I am," Vanto said. "But probably not in the way everyone else is. I'm concerned that we were given this assignment because certain people are trying to set you up."

"Have you any evidence for this?"

"No evidence, but plenty of logic," Vanto said. "We know there are government officials who don't like you, many of whom also dislike nonhumans in general. So now we have a largely nonhuman world proclaiming independence, with a hefty system defense fleet to back it up. The two most likely outcomes are, first, that you'll stomp the Jefies into the dirt; or, second, that the Botajef Defense Force will overwhelm us and chase us out of the system."

"Fortunately, there are more than just those options."

"I hope so," Vanto said. "Because in my first scenario Coruscant can paint you as the mad alien run amok who stomped a world of innocent Jefies and humans who were just obeying their appointed leader. In the second scenario, you get painted as incompetent and they kick you down to commanding an ore carrier."

"Interesting that you should choose that example," Thrawn said. The Jefi art holos vanished, replaced by a map of the Empire. "Do you recall the position Captain Filia Rossi held before commanding the *Blood Crow*?"

"First officer on an ore freighter escort, wasn't it?"

"Yes," Thrawn said. "I'm aware that you and some of the others had reservations at the time about her capability and seniority. But consider what we now know about how doonium and other metals are being taken from the general market. It may be that the ore freighters she was escorting were more important than anyone knew at the time."

"Interesting," Vanto said thoughtfully. "Not just that, but I seem to recall now that her previous posting was to Socorro. Lots of doonium in the asteroid belts there. I wonder . . . as you say, no one knew what those freighters meant. I wonder if that could have led to someone being a little less careful with security than they are now."

"Indeed," Thrawn said. "In which case, it should be possible to track the shipments and discover where this operation is occurring."

"I can try." Vanto frowned as the word caught his

attention. "Operation, singular? You think this is a single project?"

"I do," Thrawn said. "Consider. Hyperdrive components are being taken from supply depots, but no assembled hyperdrives are disappearing. Sublight engine components are likewise being taken, but no completed engines."

"Interesting," Vanto said slowly. "Though that could just mean they don't want to lug around things that are that bulky."

"Perhaps," Thrawn said. "Though there are certainly transports large enough to carry such items. My conclusion is that they may be creating hyperdrives and sublight engines of a size never before seen."

Vanto's eyes widened in shock. "You're saying something bigger even than a Star Destroyer?"

"From my reading of the data, considerably larger," Thrawn said. "I confess I feel a certain foreboding at that conclusion. I've seen this same . . . *omseki*."

"Syndrome."

"I've seen this syndrome before," Thrawn continued. "Star Destroyer-sized capital ships and large numbers of supporting starfighters are the most efficient and flexible naval array for both deterrent and combat. Yet there are many who consider *larger* to be the equivalent of *better*. Even the Empire has limited resources, and I fear that those resources are not always allocated wisely."

"The realities of a large bureaucracy," Vanto said ruefully. "Two bureaucracies, in this case, if you count both the government and the navy. There are always boondoggles—sometimes really big ones—that slip through the cracks of the review process."

"That is unfortunately true," Thrawn said. "Perhaps I will yet have an opportunity to express my thoughts on the strategies of such large-scale weapons systems."

"Well, you get invited to Coruscant often enough," Vanto pointed out. "Maybe . . ." He trailed off, suddenly understanding. "You know where it is, don't you?

You've figured out where they're building this monstrosity."

"I have an idea."

"I should have guessed you would," Vanto said. "I take it you've tracked Rossi's ore freighters?"

"I was unable to discover their final destination," Thrawn said. "However, I did find the most likely vector for the shipments."

"Which only gives you . . ." Vanto smiled with fresh understanding. "But we also have the likely vector for that Wookiee slave ship. So assuming they were all headed to the same place, you crossed the vectors . . . ?"

"And found a location," Thrawn said. "It may not be the correct location, of course. Perhaps an opportunity to visit will present itself at some point. In the meantime, we have Botajef to deal with."

"Yes," Vanto said. "I presume you have a plan?"

"I do." The galactic map disappeared, replaced by the image of a human standing behind a podium. "This is the recording of Governor Quesl's declaration of independence thirty hours ago."

"Yes, I've seen it," Vanto said. "Speechwise, the man really lights up a room."

"Did you notice the artwork hanging on the display wall behind him?"

"All fifty-seven pieces of it." Vanto smiled wryly. "Yes, I counted them. I also made holos of every piece visible on that recording, in case you wanted to see what you could pull out about the man."

"Thank you," Thrawn said. "However, it won't tell us anything about the governor. The artwork has been collected over the centuries by the Jefi people, and neither the pieces nor the placement have been altered by Governor Quesl."

"Which you know because you've already checked the older archives," Vanto said, a bit crestfallen. "Well, it seemed like a good idea at the time."

"It was an excellent idea," Thrawn said. "In other

circumstances it might well have been highly useful. But I draw your attention to the governor's words and speaking manner. What do you hear?"

"Well, he's not shy about his goals or feelings," Vanto said. "Makes it very clear he has no intention of keeping Botajef in the Empire."

"Yet should he not also show some recognition of the power that will surely be brought to bear against him?"

"One would certainly think so," Vanto said, rubbing his chin in concentration. "Now that you mention it, he's almost daring Coruscant to come in and stop him."

"I make a prediction," Thrawn said. "I believe that upon our arrival we will find heavy weaponry situated around the main governmental building. I also predict that Governor Quesl will repeat his challenge directly to the *Chimaera*."

"Really," Vanto said. "And the planetary defense forces?"

"He will initially deploy them to keep the *Chimaera* at a distance. At some later point, they will be sent to the attack."

"Interesting tactics," Vanto said. "We'll find out soon enough."

"Indeed," Thrawn said. "You may return to the bridge now. When you arrive, have Starfighter Commander Yve and Stormtrooper Commander Ayer report to me here. I have some final orders for them."

The *Chimaera* reached Botajef exactly on schedule.

And damned if Thrawn hadn't been right.

"Two CR90 corvettes rising from orbit," Eli reported, running a quick eye over the tactical readout. "Coming in from starboard and port, possibly trying to flank us, but keeping out of effective firing range. Five squadrons of V-19 Torrent interceptors rising from the north-polar base; two more squadrons coming from south-polar."

"Both corvettes' weapons systems are running cold," Faro added. "We may have taken them by surprise."

"Reading three ground-based turbolaser clusters," Eli said, smiling to himself. "Coordinates on tactical. Note that one of them is in the capital, five turbolasers grouped around the governor's palace."

"Around the *palace*?" Faro echoed disbelievingly. "He's *really* counting on Imperial self-restraint, isn't he?"

Eli thought back to the battle over Umbara, and the pinpoint fire the *Thunder Wasp* had later delivered to the pre-spice vein on Cyphar. "More likely he doesn't understand Imperial gunner accuracy, ma'am."

"Perhaps we will have the opportunity to instruct him," Thrawn said. "Senior Lieutenant Yve, launch TIEs."

"TIEs launching, Commodore," Yve acknowledged. "Targets?"

"Send four each to the corvettes," Thrawn ordered. "They are not to fire, but are to perform close-line fly-bys, two each starboard and portside. The other TIEs will move to form a screen between us and the V-19s."

"Including the special unit, sir?"

"Yes," Thrawn said. "They are not to fire until and unless I so order."

"Yes, sir." Yve turned to her board.

Eli frowned. He hadn't heard anything about a special TIE unit. Something Thrawn and Yve had cooked up after he left Thrawn's quarters for the bridge?

"You're not letting the TIEs defend themselves, sir?" Faro asked.

"I am offering the Jefies one free shot, Commander," Thrawn replied calmly. "That said, I do not believe they will make the first attack."

"Commodore, we're getting a signal from Governor Quesl," Lomar called.

"Put it through."

The comm display lit up with the same wizened, scowly face Eli had seen on the previous recording. Quesl was standing closer to the cam this time, and up close he looked even more unpleasant and shifty. "This is Governor Quesl of the free system of Botajef," he intoned. "You have intruded into Jefi space. If you do not leave, you will be fired upon."

"This is Commodore Thrawn, commander of the Imperial Star Destroyer *Chimaera*," Thrawn said. "I'm afraid you are acting under a misapprehension, Governor. According to the treaty signed by the Jefies after the Clone War, any change in status must follow the formal rules called for in Section Eighteen, Paragraph Four."

The wizened face drew back from the cam, and Eli caught a glimpse of the artwork hanging on the wall behind him. "What are you talking about?" he demanded. "There is no such treaty."

On the tactical, the four TIE fighters swept past the starboard corvette as Thrawn had ordered. Eli held his breath, wondering if the corvette would see it as an attack and open fire.

Fortunately, it didn't. Aside from a brief twitch of its bow, in fact, it made no response at all. The portside corvette was even more sanguine in the case of its starfighter flyby, without even that small reflexive twitch.

"Your lack of knowledge regarding your assigned post is puzzling," Thrawn said. "Under the circumstances I must draw your attention to Paragraph Seven. That proviso states that before any talks may be opened, the governor or other leader must fully disarm." He gestured toward the tactical. "I must therefore insist that those turbolaser emplacements around your palace be removed."

"Oh, you insist, do you?" Quesl retorted in a condescending tone. "So. Commodore or not, Imperial Star Destroyer or not, you still dare not face a free people and their weapons? Afraid our bite is as bad as our bark?" He folded his arms across his chest, a mocking smile on his face. "You want those turbolasers gone, Commodore Thrawn? Fine. Do it yourself."

"Very well," Thrawn said. He gestured to Yve. "Senior Lieutenant?"

"Yes, sir," Yve said. "Special Unit One: *Go.*" On the tactical, six of the TIE fighters that had been moving to intercept the V-19s abruptly broke formation. Weaving easily through the defenders' formation, they headed straight in toward the capital and the palace.

"What? *No!*" Quesl shouted. "Defenders—*defend!*"

The turbolasers opened fire, their brilliant blasts sizzling through the air toward the incoming fighters.

It was an exercise in futility. Yve had trained her TIE pilots superbly, and the starfighters themselves were fast and nimble. They evaded the blasts with ease, approaching the palace even as the defenders' fire increased. "It is not too late to surrender, Governor," Thrawn said.

"Never," Quesl spat. His face was taut with expectation, his eyes focused somewhere off cam. "I will die with dignity and grace, and with the full strength and defiance of the Jefi people at my side."

"Your spirit is admirable," Thrawn said. "But your dramatics are quite unnecessary. Observe the power and the skill of the Imperial Navy."

The TIEs had reached the palace, and their laser cannons opened fire.

But they weren't targeting the palace. Even as they twisted and turned and jinked to avoid the frantic turbolaser blasts, they instead poured salvo after salvo into the weapons themselves. One of the turbolasers disintegrated in a brilliant blast of shattered metal and ceramic. The second went . . . then the third . . .

"Commander Faro?" Thrawn called.

Eli blinked. So engrossed had he become in the deadly dance at the planet's surface that he'd forgotten to keep track of the situation in the *Chimaera*'s immediate vicinity. He looked at the tactical—

To discover that, while he'd been distracted, the *Chimaera* had somehow drifted a significant distance to starboard toward the corvette still holding position there. A blue line appeared on the tactical, marking the activation of one of the Star Destroyer's tractor beams—

And on the comm display, Quesl gasped as his image gave a violent jerk.

Eli looked back at the tactical as it belatedly hit him. "He's on the *corvette*?"

"Indeed," Thrawn said, the faintest hint of satisfaction in his voice. "Along with the extremely valuable art collection that you see behind him. My apologies, Governor, for failing to cooperate in your hoped-for destruction of the palace. It would have rather effectively covered up your theft, as well as enraging the Jefies into launching a full attack on the *Chimaera*. I expect you hoped to slip away to freedom during the resulting chaos."

On the display, Quesl was breathing heavily, his face a mask of hatred and despair. "They'll never believe you," he bit out. "The Jefies are loyal to me."

"They are loyal to a respected leader," Thrawn countered, his voice going cold. "I do not believe they will see you as such beyond this day."

For a moment Quesl glared. Then he seemed to wilt. Offering Thrawn another mocking smile, he half turned to look at the wall behind him. "They're worth hundreds of millions, Commodore. Maybe even billions. And all they do is sit collecting dust in a third-rate building on a fifth-rate world. *Billions*."

He turned back, some of the melancholy replaced by puzzlement. "But there are two identical corvettes. How did you know I was on this one?"

"The starfighter flyby," Thrawn said. "Your pilot twitched with reaction to what he feared would be an impending collision. Human crew. The other corvette trusted their leader implicitly, and thus showed no such fear. Jefi crew. You, of course, could not rely on Jefies to assist you in their betrayal."

Quesl sighed. "So that's it?"

"Hardly," Thrawn assured him. "You and your crew must still be brought aboard the *Chimaera*, the artwork must be returned, the Jefies need to be enlightened, and a new leader must be chosen until Coruscant can send a new governor." His eyes glittered. "Later, of course, there will be your trial."

He let the last word hang in the air for a moment, perhaps inviting Quesl the chance to respond. But the governor remained silent.

Thrawn gestured for the comm display to be blanked. "So I gather there *is* no Clone Wars–era treaty?" Faro asked.

"No," Thrawn said. "I merely wished to keep him in view until his movement under the tractor beam's pull gave final confirmation of his presence."

He took a deep breath. "Senior Lieutenant Lomar, contact the chief of the Botajef Defense Force and explain the situation. I'm sure he'll want proof; you may invite him aboard at his convenience. Commander Faro, bring the governor's corvette into the hangar bay. Major Ayer, your stormtroopers will board as soon as the vessel is secure. Take care with the prisoners; take even better care with the artwork. Senior Lieutenant Yve, bring Special Unit One back to screen position with the other TIEs. Inform all pilots they are to remain alert, but that no further combat is anticipated."

He looked at Eli, and Eli thought he could detect a small smile on the Chiss's lips. "Commander Vanto, you will contact the High Command on Coruscant. Inform them that the situation on Botajef has been resolved."

CHAPTER 23

It is believed by many that the military life is one of adventure and excitement. In truth, that life more often consists of long periods of routine, even boredom, with only brief intervals of challenge and danger.

Enemies seldom seek out their opponents. The warrior must become a hunter, searching and stalking with craft and patience. Successes are often achieved by a confluence of small things: stray facts, unwary or overheard conversations, logistical vectors. If the hunter is persistent, the pattern will become visible, and the enemy will be found. Only then will the routine be broken by combat.

It's not surprising, therefore, that those seeking excitement sometimes weary of long and arduous pursuits. They are relieved when the enemy appears of his own accord, standing firm and issuing a challenge.

But the wise warrior is especially wary at those times. He knows there are few things more dangerous than a skilled enemy on his own carefully chosen ground.

"Code cylinders, please," the door warden said. *Her voice is brisk and formal, but her face shows suspicion.*

"Here," Vanto said, handing over both his cylinder and Thrawn's.

The warden takes the first and slips it into the ID reader. The confirmation procedure takes longer than usual. Perhaps she doesn't believe that the IDs are genuine.

Vanto notices the delay, as well. "Is there a problem, Warrant Officer?"

"No problem, Commander." *Her face still holds suspicion as she returns the cylinders. But she does not hold enough doubt to summon assistance.* "You're cleared to enter, Commander Vanto." *Another brief but noticeable hesitation.* "As are you, Admiral Thrawn."

They passed through the doorway into the High Command headquarters. "I wonder what it is this time," Vanto murmured as they made their way among the other navy personnel hurrying about their appointed tasks.

"The pattern of communications during the past four days indicates that the One Oh Third and One Twenty-Fifth task forces have also been summoned," Thrawn said. "I conclude a major mission is being planned."

"Interesting," Vanto said. "How much sifting through the chatter did it take to dig out those bits of information?"

"Not much," Thrawn assured him. "There are patterns in Imperial communications, as there are in everything else. Once the pattern is known, knowledge is easier to obtain."

"That's quite a skill," Vanto said. "It would take me hours with a computer and matrix sheet to get anywhere."

The rest of the group was waiting, seated in a half circle in front of a holoprojector with their backs to the newcomers as Thrawn and Vanto arrived. Four of those in attendance were navy officers and four were civilians, the latter dressed in upper-class governmental style.

There were two empty seats between the officers and the civilians.

Standing at one side of the projector was Fleet Admiral Donassius. *His expression is controlled, but his body stance holds tension.* Standing at the opposite side was Colonel Yularen. *His face and stance also hold tension, though he conceals it better than Donassius.*

"Admiral Thrawn," Donassius said, nodding gravely in greeting as Thrawn and Vanto approached the ring of seats. "May I introduce Admiral Durril of the ISD *Judicator* and the One Oh Third Task Force; Admiral Kinshara of the ISD *Stalwart* and the One Twenty-Fifth. Admiral Thrawn of the ISD *Chimaera*, recently assigned the Ninety-Sixth."

"Honored," Thrawn said, nodding greetings as he and Vanto passed the end of the row. *Kinshara returns the greeting politely, his expression holding no rancor or ill will. Durril's expression and body stance hold displeasure at the presence of a nonhuman. The other two officers, one a captain, the other a commander, hold the normal courtesy and wariness of aides meeting an unknown flag officer for the first time.*

"And these are the governors of the relevant systems," Donassius continued. "Governor Restos of Batonn; Governor Wistran of Denash; Governor Estorn of Sammun—"

The fourth governor in the line is unexpected.

"—and Governor Pryce of Lothal."

"Honored," Thrawn repeated. "It is good to see you again, Governor Pryce."

"Likewise," Pryce said. *Her expression is cool, her voice professional. But her body stance holds a hidden tension.* "I wish it could have been under more pleasant circumstances."

"Circumstances you've been called upon to deal with," Donassius said. *His voice holds grim concern.* "Sit down, please, and we'll get right to it. Colonel Yularen?"

"Thank you, Admiral," Yularen said. He tapped a key on his remote, and a holo of a section of the Outer Rim appeared. "Batonn sector," he identified. "We've been noting a rise in criminal and insurgent activities here for the past several months. Up until now it was assumed to be the usual random flailings by malcontents. However, we now have indications that some of these groups may be starting to work together, or at least to share information and coordinate plans. None of them is much above nuisance level, but we feel this is a trend we need to stamp out before it spreads."

"How deep is this cooperation?" Thrawn asked.

"Not very at the moment," Yularen said. "Insurgent groups are paranoid, practically by definition, and they typically don't trust one another any more than they trust their own governments. But as I say, they're starting to talk."

"So we need to shut them up," Pryce said.

"A question, Colonel," Governor Restos put in. "There are four governors here, representing four affected systems. Yet I see the commanders of only *three* task forces. May I ask which of our systems you're planning to ignore?"

"The insurgents of Lothal are already being dealt with by Admiral Konstantine," Donassius said. "Governor Pryce requested to be here as an observer, since her system is close to the area of concern and is experiencing much of the same trouble."

"I see," Restos said, eyeing Pryce with a look of suspicion. "As long as Batonn will be getting sufficient attention."

"Absolutely, Governor," Yularen said. "In fact, we're going to start with your world, since it seems to be the focal point for activity in the sector. If we can push back the insurgents there, the other groups should wither away."

"What do you mean, *push back*?" Wistran asked. "Where are you pushing back from?"

"At the moment, from a place called Scrim Island, three hundred kilometers west of Batonn's main continent," Yularen said. "Five days ago, a group of insurgents overran and took command of the Imperial garrison there. They're holding at least a hundred hostages, mostly navy troopers and techs, but also some civilian workers. They have full control of the island's energy shield, its shoreline defenses, and three of its ion cannons. Admiral Thrawn, this one will be yours."

"Have you a schematic of the facility?" Thrawn asked.

"Certainly." The holo changed to an aerial view of Scrim Island.

"You said there were three ion cannons," Thrawn said. "Yet I see eight fortified emplacements along the shoreline."

"The last status report, about six weeks ago, stated that five of the cannons were awaiting replacement cathtron tubes," Yularen said.

"Which five?"

"Irrelevant, I'm afraid," Yularen said. "The insurgents have had enough time to switch out the three functioning tubes, so we don't know which three cannons are operational."

"Shouldn't matter," Admiral Durril said. *He waves a hand in casual dismissal.* "You're not going to breach from above anyway. Best approach is by low-altitude incursion."

"The shoreline defenses are more than adequate to repel even a sizable attack," Thrawn pointed out.

"You haven't been with the navy long, have you?" Durril asked. *His tone holds condescension. His gaze drops to the new admiral's insignia plaque, his expression holding disapproval and resentment.* "If you had, you'd know that if more than half the island's ion cannons are down, then at least half the shore defenses are, too. A few assault boats' worth of stormtroopers, and it'll be over."

"Perhaps," Thrawn said. "I will need more time to study the situation."

"There *is* no time," Donassius said. "Every hour the garrison is held, the reputation of the Empire is tarnished a little more. Your orders are to proceed at once to Batonn and release the insurgents' hold on Scrim." *His lip twists.* "Destroy the island if you have to, but remove the rebels."

"Destroying the island would also kill the hostages," Thrawn said. "There are better ways. But they require more reconnaissance and planning."

The room is silent. The others' body stances hold disapproval and discomfort. "Very well," Donassius said. *His voice is stiff.* "If you don't think you can handle it, the Ninety-Sixth can go to Sammun instead. Will that assignment be more to your liking?"

"I will go wherever the navy wishes," Thrawn said.

"You've had enough time with the Ninety-Sixth to operate smoothly together?"

"I have, Admiral."

"Very well. Admiral Durril, you seem confident that the rebels on Scrim can be easily neutralized. Your One Oh Third will deal with them."

"With pleasure," Durril said. *His voice holds eagerness and gloating.*

"Good." *Donassius gestures to Yularen, his expression holding disappointment.* "Colonel Yularen, you may continue your briefing."

"You disapprove of my decision," Thrawn said as he and Eli walked down the outer steps toward the landing pad where their transport waited.

"I think *everyone* disapproved of your decision, sir," Eli said sourly. "Whatever capital you might have had with the High Command, I think you've just burned it."

"For the moment," Thrawn said calmly, pulling out his datapad and keying it on. "That will change."

"I don't see how," Eli said, trying to see what Thrawn was doing. Images were flashing across the datapad's display, but from Eli's angle he couldn't get any details. "Admiral Durril seemed awfully certain he could take back the island."

"Admiral Durril is always certain of himself," Thrawn said. "But he has a tendency to value speed over precision. Sometimes that serves him well. More often, it leads to miscalculation."

"You think this is one of those miscalculations?"

"I am certain of it," Thrawn said. "And that failure will be costly, both to his task force and to him personally."

"Wonderful," Eli muttered. More men and women hurt or killed because of the arrogance of their superiors. "Should we say something?"

"I *did* say something," Thrawn reminded him. "I said the situation required more study."

"So we just let him and the One Oh Third walk into the wall?"

"Admiral Durril has taken a stand," Thrawn said. "We have offered advice. He has not taken it. We must now stand aside and allow him to test his confidence."

"I suppose," Eli said, craning his neck. The images were still flowing across Thrawn's datapad. "May I ask what you're doing, sir?"

"Studying Sammuni art," Thrawn told him. "I need a better sense of the culture."

They were in sight of the landing platform by the time Thrawn finally put the datapad away. They walked toward their shuttle, and Eli winced with fresh embarrassment at how pathetic their nondescript light freighter looked tucked in among the more impressive Lambda shuttles of the other admirals. He still didn't know why Thrawn had chosen that particular craft, one they'd taken from their most recently defeated smuggler gang, instead of bringing his own Lambda. Eli's best guess had been that he'd hoped to show it off as a trophy to the other admirals. Somehow, he'd never gotten around to that.

"You disapprove of my choice of transport, as well."

Eli glared sideways at him. "Do you *have* to do that?"

"I find it tends to bypass unnecessary conversation," Thrawn said, pulling out his comlink. "Admiral Thrawn for Commander Faro."

"Yes, Admiral," the *Chimaera*'s new captain said briskly. "Have we orders, sir?"

"We do, Commander," Thrawn said. "You are to take the task force to Sammun. There is insurgent activity there that we are tasked with eliminating."

"Yes, sir," Faro said, a hint of uncharacteristic uncertainty in her voice. "You say *I'm* to take the force? You won't be with us?"

"That is correct," Thrawn confirmed. "Commander Vanto and I have an errand elsewhere."

"I see," Faro said. She was still getting used to being the *Chimaera*'s captain, Eli knew, and he could tell she wasn't entirely happy about being thrown into a mission this soon without her admiral there to watch over her shoulder. But her usual self-confidence was already starting to reassert itself. "Very well, Admiral. Any specific instructions?"

"Of course," Thrawn said. "You will enter the system at a distance and disperse the rest of the task force. You will then bring the *Chimaera* in close to Sammun and demand surrender of the insurgents. Our intelligence indicates that they are protected from ground or air assault, but their shields and bunkers are unlikely to withstand Star Destroyer turbolasers for long."

"So I'm to threaten an attack, but the real goal is to drive them out of their positions?"

"Exactly," Thrawn said. "You may need to fire a few times to persuade them to abandon their stronghold, but you should not have to utterly destroy it. The task force may also need to destroy some of the fleeing ships, but you should be able to capture the majority undamaged."

"What if they head instead to other locales on the planet itself?"

"I think that unlikely," Thrawn said. "Their first instinct will be to seek the safety and darkness of space."

"Understood, sir," Faro said. She was with the plan now, and Eli had no doubt she would carry it to completion. For all her casual attitude toward proper decorum, she was smart enough and generally knew what she was doing. "If there's one thing they won't get out there, it's safety."

"Very good, Commander," Thrawn said. "Before you depart for Sammun, detach the *Shyrack* for my use. Inform Captain Brento that I'll speak with her privately once I've decided on her course of action."

"Yes, sir," Faro said. "Shall I report when I've completed my mission, or shall I wait for you to initiate contact?"

"The latter would be best," Thrawn said. "Good hunting to you."

"And to you, Admiral."

Thrawn returned the comlink to his belt. "And now to our errand," he said.

"Yes, sir," Eli said. "Ah . . . are we treading on dangerous ice here, sir? Donassius ordered us to go to Sammun."

"Not precisely," Thrawn assured him. "Fleet Admiral Donassius said the Ninety-Sixth was to deal with the insurgency there. No specific mention was made of you or me."

Eli grimaced. A fine distinction, and one he doubted anyone involved would appreciate. But Thrawn was an admiral, and Eli was a commander, and he'd been given his orders. "Yes, sir," he said. "May I ask where we're going?"

"To Batonn, of course," Thrawn said. "Admiral Durril is convinced he'll have no difficulty capturing Scrim Island. I am interested in seeing if he is correct."

"Standard siege array," Vanto murmured. His tone held interest and alertness, but so far he was withholding judgment on Admiral Durril's tactics. "No obvious response yet from the island."

"They may be negotiating," Thrawn pointed out. *The ships are indeed set out in a siege array, but it is not precisely standard. Two of the light cruisers are farther out from the* Judicator *than normal, and Durril has launched no starfighter screen.* "We wouldn't pick up a tight comm signal from here."

"True," Vanto agreed. "I keep expecting someone to notice us and order us away."

"Our transponder identifies us as a properly licensed freighter," Thrawn reminded him. *There is a ping from one of Durril's screening corvettes. The freighter's transponder pings back. A moment of hesitation, one final ping, and then the corvette ceases further inquiry.* "They no doubt assume we're waiting to assess the extent of the battle before committing ourselves to resume travel toward the surface."

"Yes," Vanto said wryly. "Lucky for us you had the foresight to pick this as our transport." He raised his eyebrows. "Or *was* it luck? Did you pull something out of the comm traffic that made you suspect we might need something lower-key than a military Lambda?"

"I had some suspicions," Thrawn said. Vanto's insight and perception had grown remarkably over the years. He saw many of the patterns now, quickly grasping the underlying reasons and motivations.

The deeper reasons still sometimes eluded him. But there was time. The young commander's tactical abilities continued to grow, though Vanto himself was not fully aware of his progress. The focus now would be on improving his observation and training his mind to assemble data and reach conclusions more quickly. In battle, such reflexive decisions often meant the difference between victory and defeat.

There is a series of flashes from the distant task force. "First salvo away," Vanto announced. "Full turbolasers from the *Judicator*. Island's energy shield . . . looks like it's holding."

"Any reduction in strength?"

"Not that these sensors can detect from here," Vanto said, his forehead furrowed in concentration. "Second salvo away. Third salvo away. Looks like Durril's got all his ships firing now. Still no response from the insurgents."

"That will soon change," Thrawn said. *The screening corvettes are now being brought closer to the Star Destroyer as Durril responds to his initial failure to destroy the island's shield.* "By ordering fire from all of his ships, Durril has now demonstrated their full capabilities."

"And has also close-marked all their positions," Vanto pointed out. "If the island's commander is smart, he'll counterattack before those positions change . . . and there they go. Shield seems to be contracting—I can see bits of the western and southern shorelines. Durril's still pounding at the center—"

On the main display two streams of red-tinged green bursts shoot up from the edges of the island. "Ion fire!" Vanto snapped. "Direct hits on the *Judicator*."

"Incapacitated?" Thrawn asked. *The light cruisers and frigates have opened fire again as Durril orders their turbolasers to target the ion cannons on the northern and western shorelines.*

But the action was too late. The shield edge had expanded again following the ion cannons' salvos, and the turbolaser bolts spattered harmlessly away. The escort ships continued firing, some at the now protected ion cannons, others at the center of the shield in an attempt to overload the generator.

"Now Durril's just flailing," Vanto muttered, his earlier withholding of judgment turning rapidly to scorn. "Probably ordered everyone to keep firing while he tries to get his systems running again. Okay, shield's contracting again. This time it's the northern shoreline opening up—"

Again, Durril fails to notice or react. The escort ships continue to fire uselessly toward the western and southern emplacements as an ion cannon on the northern shoreline opens fire.

"Damn," Vanto breathed. "Perfect timing. Whoever's in charge down there is good."

"Damage?" Thrawn asked. The latest ion blast had targeted the frigate and two cruisers on the *Judicator*'s portside flank, sending sputtering sheets of energy across their hulls, damaging sensors and turbolaser targeting and control systems.

"Hits on the portside escorts," Vanto reported. "They'll be down to secondary weapons and auxiliary drives now. Probably can still get out of there if Durril releases them, but another blast or two in the right places and they'll be drifting."

Again, Durril continues his ineffective attack instead of adjusting to his opponent's tactics. The escorts are still holding position as another ion salvo shoots upward from the island.

But this time, as the bursts raked across the same group of escorts, a stream of eight small space freighters appeared from beneath the eastern edge of the shield and headed toward the continent three hundred kilometers away.

"*Judicator*'s definitely lost its turbolasers," Vanto said grimly. "Might still have auxiliary drive, maybe enough to get clear. Durril's not trying, though. The two light cruisers and frigate that took that last attack seem to have been immobilized."

"An attack focused on the *Judicator* and the escorts on Durril's portside flank," Thrawn said. *The freighters con-*

tinue to fly low over the water. Their commander continually veers the group back and forth, taking advantage of both the minimal cloud cover and the reflected sunlight glare to achieve minimal observability from above. "The flank opposite to the direction he sent his freighters."

"Freighters?" Vanto asked, frowning. "Where?"

"Flying eastward from the island," Thrawn said. "Running low and on minimal power, which renders them largely invisible to ships already under ion attack."

"*And* to ships that aren't under attack but are concentrating all their attention on the ships that are," Vanto said. "Okay, I've got them now. I fell for the trick, too." He looked at Thrawn. "I gather you were expecting it?"

"It was one possible reason the starboard escorts were being ignored at the expense of the portside ships," Thrawn said. "Interesting, though. Standard procedure would have been the exact opposite: to target the escorts on the *Judicator*'s starboard side in order to minimize response to the freighters' departure."

"It's a long way to the continent," Vanto pointed out. "No point in getting clear if everyone knows you're on the way and where you're going."

"Yes." *Seven of the freighters are still traveling eastward at wave-top altitude. The eighth, now effectively clear of the battle zone, is rising toward space. An interesting moment for the commander to split his convoy.* "Which raises the question of where they *are* going. In particular, the one that's broken off and is heading into space. Your analysis?"

Vanto pondered a moment. "I can't tell from here whether those are freighters or personnel carriers," he said slowly. "But there's no reason for them to ship people off the island in the middle of a battle, either their own forces *or* their hostages. So, freighters. One obvious reason for taking Scrim is all the military ordnance stored there, so those ships probably represent everything that wasn't fused to the ground. Seven to insurgent cells on the mainland; one to Denash or Sammun?"

"Or to elsewhere," Thrawn said.

"Yes." Vanto leaned closer to the sensor display. "Shield's shifting again. Looks like they're going to give the *Judicator* another blast."

But this time it wasn't an ion cannon burst that shot upward from the island's western shoreline. Instead, it was the intense green fire of a turbolaser salvo from an emplacement to the north of the western ion cannon. The barrage struck the *Judicator*'s starboard superstructure, burning into and through the hull metal.

Vanto caught his breath. "Damn. A *turbolaser*? Donassius never said the island had functional turbolasers."

"He may not have known." *A second burst of fire shimmers through the atmosphere, again delivering its energy against Durril's flagship. Again, Durril makes no move to counter or evade.* "The freighter angling away from the planet is likely to make the jump to light-speed soon. Hail it."

Vanto shot him a startled look. "You want me to *hail* it?"

"Yes," Thrawn said. "A tight comm signal, of course, to keep the conversation private. We're the *Slipknot,* and you're a weapons smuggler named Horatio Figg."

Vanto's momentary confusion cleared into understanding. "So that's the *real* reason you put us in a captured smuggling ship. Am I buying or selling?"

"Whichever will gain us an invitation to visit his base."

"An invitation to his base." Vanto took a deep breath. "Okay. Here we go." He keyed the comm and adjusted for tight beam. "Unidentified freighter, this is the freighter *Slipknot,*" he called. "Looks like you're scorching out of here. Need any assistance?"

There was no response. "Again," Thrawn said quietly.

Vanto nodded. "Let me try it another way, freighter.

I'm guessing you have some fresh merchandise. I'm also guessing you want to keep it. You want to be civil, or you want me to call you out to the Imps?"

"Don't even *think* about it, *Slipknot*." *The voice is dark and angry, holding both suspicion and threat.*

"Not thinking it," Vanto assured him. "Just trying to start a friendly conversation. If I'm right about your current cargo, there might be something there I could take off your hands."

"Forget it. Already spoken for."

"Fine," Vanto said. "In that case, maybe you'd like to add a little frosting to your new cake."

There was a long pause. "You deal?" *The voice still holds suspicion, but also now holds cautious interest.*

"A little of everything," Vanto told him. "Since you hit a military base and not a spice dealer, I'm guessing you're mostly interested in weapons. So, arms dealer it is. You in the market, or aren't you?"

There was another silence from the other end. "We might be," he said. "The boss says he's willing to talk." A light flickered on the board. "I've sent you the coordinates. Jump whenever you're ready."

"Got it," Vanto said. "Be right there."

Vanto cut off the comm channel. "Well, we either fooled him or we didn't," he said. "What now?"

"We prepare to follow," Thrawn said.

"You mean, right *now*?" Vanto asked. "What about the *Judicator*?"

A third turbolaser salvo rakes the Star Destroyer. The four undamaged escort ships fire toward the weapon, but once again are too late as the island's shield closes over it. There is a pattern to the attacks, but Durril fails to recognize or exploit it.

"There's no aid we can render," Thrawn said. "I've already transmitted an emergency distress signal on Admiral Durril's behalf. Our efforts are best directed elsewhere."

"Understood," Vanto said, frustrated but recognizing the reality of the situation.

The shield shrinks again, this time opening the eastern shoreline. The escort ships alter their aim, directing a fresh attack against the ion cannon emplacements now exposed. It is much the same response Durril has already attempted several times.

But as anticipated, the island commander now changes tactics. No ion cannon blasts come. Instead, as the Imperial ships continue to fire, the shield shrinks again from the western shoreline, unnoticed by the preoccupied and battered Imperial ships. The escorts are still firing at the eastern emplacements when a new barrage of ion fire from the western emplacement silences their weapons.

"Odd," Vanto said.

"Explain."

"Our friend in the freighter," Vanto said. "He's far enough out to jump, but he hasn't. I wonder if he's having trouble with his hyperdrive."

"Perhaps," Thrawn said. "What other possibilities are there?"

"He could be waiting to see how the battle goes," Vanto suggested. "Grabbing as much data as he can before jumping. Or he could be sending—or receiving—some last-minute instructions."

The freighter abruptly flickered with pseudomotion and was gone. "I guess he got all he wanted," Vanto said. "So now we follow?"

On the island, the shield once again shrinks to expose the insurgents' turbolaser. But the Imperial ships are no longer in a position to respond in a sufficiently timely manner. As before, the Judicator *is the target of the attack.*

Neutralize, attack, feint, attack. It was an efficient pattern, carried out with expert timing. "You're having doubts?"

"I don't know," Vanto said slowly. "He gave up those coordinates awfully easily. This could be a trap."

"True," Thrawn said. "On the other hand, I doubt he would be foolish enough to offer his base's true location. More likely we have a rendezvous point where we can be studied more closely."

"Not sure that sounds any better."

"There are risks," Thrawn said. "The outcome will depend on how eagerly they want new weapons. Allow me to suggest one other possible reason for him to have delayed his departure. Tell me, what are the other seven freighters doing?"

"The other—? Oh, right—the rest of the group." Vanto readjusted the sensors. "Still heading for the continent. Only—interesting. Their vectors are diverging. They're not headed for the same place anymore, but seem to be going to seven different spots."

"If there were an Imperial observer watching, he would now be offered a choice," Thrawn said. "He could attempt to follow the eighth freighter into space, or remain here and track the seven to the insurgents' other strongpoints."

"After the eighth drew all the attention to himself," Vanto said. "Good chance he's out there somewhere waiting to see how quickly we follow him."

"Or if we follow him at all," Thrawn said. "If you were in command, which would you choose: the one, or the seven?"

The island's turbolaser blasts continue to batter the Judicator, *tearing at its hull and weapons. The ion cannons have again opened fire, sending fresh barrages at the escort ships, preventing them from moving to assist.*

"I'd probably go with—wait a minute," Vanto said with sudden understanding. "I don't *have* to choose, do I? You already guessed we'd need backup, which is why you detached the *Shyrack* from the Ninety-Sixth. I assume it's lurking around here somewhere?"

"It is indeed," Thrawn said. Excellent. "Captain Brento is observing the planet, including those seven freighters. We may therefore turn our attention to the eighth freighter."

"Yes." Vanto gave the sensor display one final look, clearly reluctant to leave the 103rd locked in desperate battle. "All right. Let's do it."

CHAPTER 24

There are times in every commander's life when he must yield the stick of authority to a subordinate.

Sometimes the reason is one of expertise, when the subordinate has skills the commander lacks. Sometimes it is positional, when the subordinate is in the right place at the right time and the commander is not. Often it is anticipated there will be loss of direct communication, which means the subordinate may be given general instructions but must then carry them out on his own initiative as the situation flows around him.

No commander enjoys those moments. Most subordinates fear them, as well. Those who do not fear already betray the overconfidence that nearly always leads to disaster.

But the moments must be faced. And all will learn from them, whether to satisfaction or to sorrow.

They reached the coordinates to find the freighter waiting for them.

"Took your sweet time about it," the other growled. "Trouble?"

Eli took a deep breath. If there was one group he'd really gotten to know during his time in the navy it was smugglers, arms merchants, thieves, and general assorted scoundrels.

He knew how they behaved, talked, and thought. The trick was to make himself think and talk the same way.

He keyed the comm. "Weren't planning on using the hyperdrive at all until you showed up. Didn't think you'd get bored so easy."

"Yeah. Ha-ha. Who are you?"

"Name's Horatio Figg."

"What were you doing at Batonn?"

"Trolling for bargains and customers," Eli said. "I heard about your Scrim Island thing and thought I'd come see if you were interested in doing some business. Buying *or* selling—like I said, I do both."

"Well, personally, I'd just as soon blow you into dust and be done with it," the other said. "But the boss wants to see you, so I guess you get to live a little longer. Follow me."

"Thanks," Eli said, turning onto the freighter's vector. "You won't regret this."

"I already do. And don't try to run—I'm not the only one out here."

The comm clicked off. "Now what?" he asked.

"Now we prepare," Thrawn said, unstrapping and climbing out of his seat. "Stay with him and keep watch. I'll be back in a moment."

Ten minutes later, with their destination visible on the displays, he returned. "I see we've arrived."

"Just about," Eli said, frowning. Thrawn had his tunic draped over his arm with a small hold-out blaster in his other hand. "It looks like an old Clone Wars–era Nomad."

"I'm not familiar with those."

"They were a sort of traveling ship–repair shop that came into systems after the battles were over and the fleets left," Eli explained. "Repair facilities were usually hit pretty hard, and these ships came in to pick up some of the slack for the locals. You realize taking off your tunic isn't going to fool anyone, right?"

"It isn't intended to," Thrawn said. "Take off your tunic and put on this one."

"Okay, but it won't fit—whoa," Eli interrupted himself as he spotted the fresh blaster burn in the tunic. "What's *that*?"

"You took this tunic from an officer you killed," Thrawn said. "That's why it doesn't fit. You wear it because it intimidates people."

"Okay," Eli said, frowning at the tunic as he quickly stripped off his own. Thrawn's admiral insignia plaque, he saw, had been replaced by a lieutenant's plaque.

A *lieutenant's* plaque?

He sent Thrawn a sharp look. "Yes," the admiral confirmed. "My old remote, modified for the current need. When the time comes, press the tile closest to the center of your chest."

"That time being?"

"You'll know. Here." He offered Eli the hold-out blaster. "Hide it somewhere. They'll take it from you, but it would look suspicious if you weren't carrying a backup weapon."

"So I keep this one, too?" Eli asked, nodding toward his blaster as he smoothed the sealing strip on Thrawn's tunic. The garment was definitely two sizes too big for him.

"Yes," Thrawn said. "It will be a sample of the merchandise you have for sale."

"Okay," Eli said, fresh doubts nagging at him. Playing this insane role on a comm was one thing. Playing it in person was something else.

He forced the thought away. The whole essence of being a scoundrel was self-confidence. If he couldn't fake that, he was dead. "Where will you be?"

"Engineering our escape," Thrawn said. "In the meantime, learn as much about them as you can."

"Right." The Nomad was coming into view ahead,

and Eli could see that there were six small ships already lined up in its long, full-flank repair bay. Tucked in among the parked vessels were three empty slots, with flashing approach lights marking the one in the center.

"Just remember that I can't keep this role up forever."

"I'll be as quick as I can," Thrawn said. He left the cockpit, taking Eli's tunic with him.

"Figg, there's a landing slot marked for you," the freighter pilot said, veering out of Eli's path. "Land and come outside. Someone will be waiting."

Eli keyed the transmitter. "Understood," he said. "I hope there's something to eat. I'm starving."

"Just be ready to talk," the other said sourly. "Because you'll be doing a lot of that."

Three armed men were waiting for Eli when he walked down the freighter's ramp. "Well, well," one of them sneered. "An Imperial. What a surprise."

"And you're exactly the kind of idiot I wear this for," Eli said, putting tired contempt into his voice. "Did you even notice that it doesn't fit?"

"Or see the blaster burn?" one of the others added, pointing his blaster toward Eli's stomach.

"Which you can't see if I angle the comm cam just right," Eli said. "Guaranteed to get people's attention and cooperation."

"Not here it doesn't," the first man said. "That blaster. Pull it out—slowly—and kick it over."

"Be careful with it," Eli said, drawing his blaster from its holster and setting it on the deck in front of him. A gentle nudge with his toe sent it spinning across to the guards. "That's part of my stock. Genuine Imperial Navy sidearm. Can't get those just anywhere."

"You'd be surprised," the first man said. "Arms out and stand still."

Eli complied. The man gestured, and his two companions laid their own blasters on the deck and walked over to Eli, purposeful expressions on their faces.

He'd hoped they wouldn't find the hold-out blaster hidden under his arm. They did.

"More stock?" the first man asked, taking the weapon and frowning at it as the others retrieved their own weapons.

"Part stock, part insurance," Eli said. "You'd be surprised how many customers try to walk off without paying for their purchases."

"I'll bet. Come on."

The docking bay had three hatches leading into the rest of the massive ship. The three men took Eli through the center one, the hatch nearest his freighter. A short walk down a rust-edged corridor, a turn into another corridor, and they arrived at a compartment with a faded plaque that said SHIPMASTER beside it.

The first man stepped forward and tapped the release. The hatch opened, and he gestured Eli forward.

Eli took a careful breath. *Self-confidence,* he reminded himself. *Arrogant self-confidence.* With a casual nod at his captor, he walked through the hatchway.

And froze. Seated behind an old desk, a small smile on his face—

"*Cygni?*"

"So you remember me," the man said, his smile widening a bit. "It's good to see you again, Commander Vanto.

"And please—call me *Nightswan.*"

For a long moment, Eli couldn't breathe. Ever since that first run-in aboard the *Dromedar,* Nightswan had always kept to the shadows and background. Always. He was the last person Eli had expected to see in charge of the Scrim Island operation.

Was this something new? Or had they never really known the man at all?

He started as someone poked him hard in the back. Forcing his muscles to unfreeze, he stepped into the room. "Have a seat," Nightswan said, gesturing to a chair at the corner of his desk. "What was he carrying?"

"Standard blaster," the first guard said, brushing past Eli and laying the navy sidearm on the desk. "Plus this," he added, setting the hold-out blaster beside it. "Never seen one like it before."

"An antique of some sort," Nightswan said, peering closely at it. "Clone Wars era?" he asked, looking up at Eli.

Eli shook his head. "No idea."

"Doesn't really matter," Nightswan said, turning both weapons a few degrees so that they were pointed away from him and directly at Eli. "I'm glad that Admiral Thrawn sent you to seek me out, by the way. I always thought you'd been handed a bad set of cards, and your presence here means you'll be spared what the rebels on Scrim Island are doing to him right now." He frowned, his gaze dropping to the tunic's insignia plaque. "You *are* a commander, aren't you? I saw the announcement. You haven't been demoted, have you?"

"No, I'm still a commander," Eli confirmed, some of his mental haze burning away in a sudden surge of cautious excitement. Nightswan thought it was *Thrawn* directing that botched attack on the island? "This is just part of the camouflage."

"Ah," Nightswan said. "Not much of a disguise. You really weren't expecting to be challenged?"

"Oh, I was expecting to be challenged," Eli said, his mind racing. Nightswan clearly thought Eli was here alone. His best chance now was to stall. "I just wasn't expecting there to be someone aboard who'd ever seen me before, let alone you. So, what, you've thrown in with a bunch of crazies?"

"They're hardly crazies," Nightswan said. "Your Empire is corrupt, Commander. Corrupt, dangerous, and ultimately self-defeating. It's going to fall anyway. I'm just helping it along."

"I'd go easy on the overconfidence if I were you," Eli offered. "As long as there are commanders like Admiral Thrawn, you're going to have an uphill job of it."

"Ah, but there *are* no commanders like Admiral Thrawn," Nightswan said with a tight smile. "Not anymore."

The smile faded. "Please understand that Scrim Island was my last resort. I'd tried destroying him politically. I'd tried persuading the High Command that he was more trouble than he was worth. But he skated clear every time. Killing him was the only way I could think of to neutralize him."

"I'm sure he appreciated your earlier restraint," Eli said, frowning as the patterns of Nightswan's earlier challenges suddenly became clear. "Still, Star Destroyers are pretty tough ships. The island also has only one turbolaser, and it's firing through atmosphere. He may wiggle out yet."

Nightswan shrugged. "Perhaps. At this point, though, it doesn't really matter. Losing his command ship—and the ship *is* lost, whether he personally survives or not—is a blunder even he can't withstand. Whoever his friends are, however highly they're placed, they'll have no choice now but to turn their backs on him."

Eli had to smile at that one. "Maybe," he said. "You seem to have taken an interest in his career."

"I have," Nightswan said, frowning at Eli's smile. "Ever since he turned the tables on my little tibanna gas theft. What's so funny?"

"Oh, nothing," Eli said. "Speaking of the tibanna, that was a nice trick of your own. How did you get the gas out without leaving any damage to the cylinders?"

"Sorry. Professional secret."

"So what?" Eli countered. "You're going to kill me anyway."

"Actually, I'm not," Nightswan said. "Not unless you make trouble. My target was Thrawn, not you."

"Thanks," Eli said drily. "Not sure whether to be flattered or insulted. Though even Scrim Island may not be enough. I gather you don't know how Thrawn happened to be admitted into the navy in the first place."

"I assume the appointment was pushed through by one of his friends." Nightswan's eyes narrowed as he studied Eli's face. "No," he said slowly. "Not just a friend. A nonhuman from the Unknown Regions . . . it would have to be someone *very* highly placed. No—wait." His eyes widened. "Hell and brimstone," he breathed, leaning forward over the desk. "That was *him*?"

"That was who?" Eli asked, reflexively shrinking back a little. Nightswan's sudden intensity was more than a little intimidating.

"Hell and brimstone," Nightswan murmured again, his eyes fixed on Eli. "You really don't know?"

"Apparently not."

"So *that* was Thrawn," Nightswan said, his gaze drifting to somewhere over Eli's shoulder. "I heard about it a couple of years ago, from someone working the Thrugii asteroids. There was this unknown nonhuman—blue skin, glowing red eyes—who'd somehow teamed up with one of the Jedi generals fighting in the Clone Wars."

Eli felt his throat tighten. "Anakin Skywalker," he murmured.

In a flash Nightswan's eyes came back, an invisible hatch seeming to slam shut over the memories. "Yes, General Skywalker," he said, his voice wary. "So you *do* know the story."

"All I know is that Thrawn once met the man," Eli said. "He wouldn't tell me anything else."

The desk intercom beeped. For a moment Nightswan continued to lock gazes with Eli. Then, leaning back in his chair again, he touched a switch. "Yes?"

"We searched the freighter, sir," a faint voice came.

"No one else aboard. But listen—the engine compartment's showing a radiation leak."

"A radiation leak, you say," Nightswan repeated, raising his eyebrows at Eli.

"Yes, sir, and it looks bad. You think we should tractor the whole thing out of the bay before the reactor goes critical?"

"Oh, I doubt we need to go to such extremes," Nightswan said. "How many troops do you have with you?"

"All six. You said to be careful."

"So I did," Nightswan said. "Get everyone together by that hatch and figure out how to get in. There should be an override control near the main release."

"Wait a minute," the man protested. "You want us to go *in*? Without radiation suits?"

"You won't need them," Nightswan assured him. "It's just another Imperial or two hiding among the baffles. They'll be armed, of course, so continue being careful."

"Got it," the man said.

Nightswan touched the intercom switch again. "Really?" he asked Eli with a wry smile. "A radiation leak?"

Eli shrugged, stifling a curse. Of all the ploys for Thrawn to pull out of his hat, it had to be one Nightswan already knew. "It *is* a classic."

"So it is," Nightswan agreed. "Though like you, I don't know whether to be flattered or insulted. You're probably wishing you'd tried something else."

"I didn't know I'd be playing to an audience who'd already put on the same show."

"True," Nightswan said. "I hope that whoever's in there doesn't put up a fight. Simmco's people aren't too bright, but they're very good shots."

"I'm sure they are," Eli said with a sigh. However this worked out, Nightswan was in for a surprise. He'd either have Thrawn himself, or he'd have his body.

"But you were telling me about Thrawn and Skywalker," Nightswan continued.

"No, I already told you about Thrawn and Skywalker," Eli corrected. "Everything I know. That Thrugii story sounds interesting, though."

"I'd rather talk about you," Nightswan said. "With Thrawn about to leave the stage, your career will finally be out of his shadow." He raised his eyebrows. "It *has* been rather in his shadow, hasn't it?"

Eli smiled. Once, he'd indeed felt that way.

But not anymore. Not for a long time.

"I'm not worried about it," he assured Nightswan. "The future is what you make of it, as my father used to say. I'm a commander, I have a fairly decent list of victories on my ledger, and I'd like to think I've picked up one or two friends along the way."

"Really?" Nightswan said. "Because Thrawn doesn't seem to have. Not politically astute at all, from what I hear." He snorted. "As for you, my young idealist commander, do you really think you have any friends on Coruscant? A Wild Space nobody who's spent his entire career as a house pet to a nonhuman?"

"It's not like that," Eli insisted. "You saw how they came around with Thrawn."

"Probably because favors were bought or sold," Nightswan said. "You really need to learn more about Coruscant." The intercom pinged again, and he tapped the key. "Yes?"

"Sir, it's Simmco," the man's voice came. "We've searched the engine compartment, and there's—"

He was cut off by an explosive concussion erupting from the intercom speaker. An instant later Eli felt a quieter echo of the blast through the bulkhead behind him.

And suddenly the room erupted with the thunderous cadence of the universal *abandon ship* alarm.

Nightswan snatched up Eli's blaster from the desk with one hand, jabbing at the intercom with the other.

"Captain?" he called over the cacophony. "Captain, what's going on?"

Eli braced himself. *You'll know,* Thrawn had promised. Reaching casually to his insignia plaque, Eli pressed the innermost tile. Nightswan caught the movement, turned the blaster warningly toward his prisoner—

As the hold-out blaster in front of him exploded into a blinding cloud of smoke.

Eli was out of his chair in an instant, wincing as Nightswan's blaster bolt sizzled through the space he'd just been occupying and shattered the back of the chair. For a fraction of a second he thought about trying to counterattack, realized it would be suicidal, and instead sprinted for the hatch. If he could get it open before Nightswan's vision cleared he might make it.

He was nearly there, his hand stretched out toward the release, when the hatch slid open of its own accord and a looming figure charged inside, a blaster gripped in his hand. Eli slammed into him at full speed, sending the man toppling backward onto the deck and squeezing out an agonized *whoof* as the impact knocked the air out of his lungs. Eli grabbed his blaster, twisted it out of his grip, slammed it across the side of his head to make sure he stayed down, then scrambled to his feet and made for the docking bay.

Even over the noise he could hear multiple shouts and running footsteps as the rest of the crew reacted to the alarm. Fortunately, he didn't have far to go. He burst through the hatchway into the repair bay—

Into a churning honeyhive of activity. Everyone who hadn't yet made it out of the main ship seemed to be there, some of them climbing into damage-control equipment, most of them sprinting toward the various ships with the clear intent of getting out.

And more men and women were streaming into the bay every second. Sooner or later, Eli knew, one of them would spot him. Clenching his teeth, he turned toward his freighter, hoping that blast had been Thrawn getting rid of Simmco's boarding party.

A blaster bolt sputtered past him, jerking him back and nearly throwing him off his feet. He grabbed for balance, lost the fight, and came down awkwardly on one hand. Spinning around, he brought up his borrowed weapon, wondering if he would even have time to get off a shot before his attacker nailed him—

And spotted Thrawn a quarter of the way down the bay, a blaster in his hand, beckoning to Eli from the entryway of one of the other freighters. Bounding back to his feet, Eli sprinted for the ship.

Thirty seconds later he was there, racing up the ramp and through the hatch. Thrawn had already disappeared, presumably to the cockpit. Eli locked down the hatch, double-checked that the seal was holding, then headed forward.

Thrawn was seated in the pilot's chair, the displays and indicators already up and running. "Welcome aboard, Commander," he said as Eli maneuvered his way through the cramped space to the copilot's seat. "We should be clear before they realize we're not part of their group."

"So that's why we're taking this one instead of ours?" Eli asked as he began strapping in.

"An unexpected bonus," Thrawn said. "My primary goal was data that might have carelessly been left uncleared on this ship's computer. Navigational records in particular that might point us to bases and supply lines." He sent a quick sideways look at Eli. "You were taken to their leader, I assume. Was it Nightswan?"

"Yes," Eli said, frowning in sudden understanding. "You *knew* it would be him?"

"I didn't know for certain. But I suspected."

"Why didn't you tell me?" Eli demanded. Thrawn always played his cards close to his plaque, but this was pushing it too far. "Knowing who I was up against could have been extremely useful."

"On the contrary," Thrawn said. "You would hardly

have been able to produce a convincing performance had you not been genuinely surprised."

"So you just walked us into his trap?"

"He needed to believe we'd been caught unawares," Thrawn said. "Otherwise, he would have been on his guard."

"He *and* his crew," Eli said, the anger fading. As usual, once Thrawn explained things, he could see the tactical logic. "I presume you were never in the engine compartment?"

"Correct," Thrawn said. "I hid in the escape pod cowling until the boarders had moved aft, then left and found the abandon-ship control."

"After setting up a bomb," Eli said. "Let me guess. The same gimmicked blaster power pack trick you used to get off your exile planet?"

"Yes," Thrawn said. The status board went green. "Time to return to Batonn."

He keyed the drive, and they shot out of the bay. Eli tensed, but no one opened fire on them. "And see how much of Admiral Durril's task force survived?"

"Hopefully, more than you fear," Thrawn said. "But we shall see."

"I told Nightswan that Star Destroyers were tough ships," Vanto said, shaking his head in amazement as he gazed out the viewport at the regrouped 103rd. "But this is borderline unbelievable."

"They weren't under bombardment for long," Thrawn said. "Captain Brento had instructions to move in as soon as we were gone, coordinate the remaining functional ships as best she could, and use their combined tractor beams on the *Judicator*."

"You had a handful of light cruisers tractor a *Star Destroyer*? And it *worked*?"

"They didn't need to move it very far," Thrawn said. "Just far enough downward to reach an orbit that would take it out of the ion cannons' range. Once the attack was halted, the *Judicator*'s power systems came up quickly enough for it to move away from Batonn and out of danger."

"Ah," Vanto said. "I wonder if Durril will acknowledge the *Shyrack*'s assistance."

"It would be difficult for him to ignore it."

"True. But I'll bet he'll try."

". . . and after that we were able to make running repairs on the engines and get out of range," Durril concluded his report. *His flickering holographic image is difficult to read, but his voice holds anger and embarrassment.* "I apologize for my failure, Fleet Admiral Donassius. But now that I know what we're up against, my next assault will succeed."

"Perhaps," Donassius said. *His holographic image turns to the third hologram floating over the* Chimaera's *projector.* "Admiral Kinshara. Your report?"

"The insurgents at Denash have been dealt with, Fleet Admiral," Kinshara said. *His voice holds satisfaction at his success, and a more subtle satisfaction at Durril's failure.* "There was little there, as it turned out. However, our preliminary prisoner interrogation suggests that a large portion of their ships and matériel may have already been transferred to Batonn."

"Excellent," Durril said. *His voice holds brisk confidence.* "All the barks in a single hound. That much easier to roll up the lot of them."

"Admiral Thrawn?" Donassius invited.

"Sammun is likewise pacified," Thrawn said. "Two enemy ships were destroyed, four ships captured. A considerable array of small-arms ordnance was also captured."

"Without your actual presence, I'm told?"

Commander Faro shifts her feet. Her usual confidence is muted; her body stance holds discomfort.

"The action was carried out under my direction, Admiral."

"I see." *For a moment, Donassius continues to gaze at Thrawn.* "Admiral Durril, when will the One Oh Third be able to travel?"

"We can reengage in thirty hours, sir," Durril said. *His embarrassment is gone, his voice now holding anticipation.*

"I didn't ask when you could fight, Admiral," Donassius said. "I asked when you could travel."

"Ah . . . five hours, perhaps," Durril said. *His voice holds sudden caution.* "Sir, with all due respect—"

"In five hours you are to bring your task force to the Marleyvane shipyards for repair," Donassius said. "Admiral Thrawn?"

"Yes, Fleet Admiral?"

"You said you needed to gather intelligence on the Scrim Island insurgents. How much time will you need?"

"Sir, I must protest," Durril said. *His stunned disbelief transforms into outrage and wounded pride.* "This operation was given to *me*. I'm perfectly capable of seeing it through."

"Admiral Thrawn?" Donassius repeated.

"Actually, Fleet Admiral, the gathering is complete," Thrawn said. "I can take back the island whenever you wish."

"Good." *Donassius's image looks at Durril, then back to Thrawn. His voice holds satisfaction.* "At your convenience, Admiral."

CHAPTER 25

At one time or another, every warrior wishes to have an unconquerable fortress. Such a fortress is perceived as a refuge, a place of defiance, or a rock upon which enemies can be goaded into smashing themselves to their own destruction.

Politicians, too, yearn for such fortresses, though they envision them in terms of power and authority instead of stone and weapons and shields. Industrialists wish to be similarly protected against competitors and marauders, while pirates hope for defense against system authorities. In one way or another, all people wish for ultimate safety.

But ultimate safety does not exist. Those who trust in such will find that hope dashed upon the very rock behind which they seek to hide.

The captains had their orders. The ships of the 96th Task Force were in position.

It was time.

"All ships, report in," Thrawn called from the center of the command walkway. Making a final check, as he always did.

Eli smiled to himself. For all of Thrawn's interest in

observing and establishing his opponents' patterns, the admiral had plenty of his own.

"Interesting plan," Faro murmured from Eli's side. "At the very least it holds the prospect of taking them by surprise."

"Admiral Thrawn's plans usually do that," Eli murmured back.

"So I've noticed," Faro said. "You've been with him a long time, haven't you?"

Eli shrugged. "All my career."

"Must have been nice," Faro mused. "Minds like his are few and far between. Too often the men and women in senior command positions are there because of *who* they know rather than *what* they know."

"Yes, I've served under my share of those."

"As did Thrawn, I assume," Faro said. "It must have driven him crazy at times. Good thing you were there to keep him sane."

"There's nothing special about me, ma'am," Eli said. "In fact, I was on track to be a supply officer before he showed up."

Faro shook her head. "That would have been a waste. You belong on the bridge, not the conveyer."

"Not sure I agree, ma'am," Eli said, feeling a twinge of embarrassment. "I certainly don't have the admiral's genius for tactics."

"Maybe not," Faro said. "But once the plans are explained, you understand them."

Eli had to smile. "Once they're explained, ma'am, *anyone* can understand them."

"You think so?" Faro countered. "You really think all the captains and their senior officers out there in the Ninety-Sixth understand how this is going to work?"

"Of course," Eli said, frowning. "It's obvious."

"To you and to me, Commander," Faro said. "Not to everyone."

Eli stared at Thrawn's back, his brain automatically

counting down the ships' acknowledgments as they came from the comm station. Was Faro right?

And if so, was that why Thrawn had manipulated Eli's career to keep him as his aide? Not as a punishment, or even on a whim, but to train him in the art of command?

The last ship reported in, and Eli saw Thrawn's back straighten a bit. It was time. "Very good," the admiral said. "*Shyrack, Flensor, Tumnor:* Move in."

"Hold position," Faro added quietly to the *Chimaera*'s helmsman.

Eli took a breath, let it out slowly and silently. Sending all three of the task force's light cruisers into harm's way was a terrible risk, one that most commanders would be hesitant to make. But it was the only way this plan would work.

He frowned. Was Faro right? *Was* Eli one of a relative few who could genuinely understand Thrawn's tactics?

The cruisers were moving inward toward the planet, their turbolasers firing at Scrim Island. At the moment it was a waste of effort; even without the island's shield, the shots would have been mostly ineffective. But as the warships dropped lower and penetrated deeper into the stratosphere, the level of energy delivered would become progressively higher. Eventually, if the cruisers continued, the blasts would begin to stress the shield and possibly overload the generator. Before that happened, the insurgents would have to make their move.

They didn't wait until the situation became that critical, of course. The cruisers were still in the upper atmosphere when the shield contracted simultaneously from the entire shoreline, opening firing vectors for all three ion cannons. "Ion cannons clear," Thrawn called. "Cruisers: Fire at will."

The three warships shifted their targeting vectors from the center of the shield toward the new targets. It was, Eli thought, like a replay of Admiral Durril's first attempt.

But this time something new had been added to the mix. Even as the cruisers' turbolasers hammered at the ion cannon emplacements, a fourth ion cannon opened fire from a position on the southeast shore.

The *Shyrack* spotted it and tried to shift its aim. But the ship's response time was too slow for that large an angular shift, and the hazy ion blasts shooting up from the surface were too fast. Before the cruiser's fire could track to its new target the ion clusters splattered across its hull, knocking out sensors and silencing weapons. Before the *Flensor* and *Tumnor* could shift their own aim, the fourth cannon had sent a salvo at each of them, as well, and their attacks also went silent.

"So the admiral was right," Faro commented. "They *did* have a fourth active cannon. Must have had a spare cathtron tube when they first took the island."

"We've tangled with Nightswan before," Eli reminded her. "You learn not to take anything at face value."

"Cruisers: Report," Thrawn called.

Eli listened closely as the reports came in. Nightswan was smart, all right. But he didn't know everything.

Including how tough even Imperial light cruisers were. All three ships had lost primary weapons and main drives, but their communications and some of their secondary weapons were still intact.

Most important of all, so were their auxiliary drives.

"Final maneuvering," Thrawn ordered. "*Flensor:* Now."

The *Flensor* began drifting to starboard. Thrawn watched it a moment, then gestured. "*Shyrack:* Now."

In turn, the *Shyrack* and the *Tumnor* moved casually to their assigned positions. "What about that fourth ion cannon, Admiral?" Faro asked.

"It will not be a problem," Thrawn assured her. "Captain Yelfis? The *Tumnor* took the last salvo. What were your observations?"

"The cannon was already sputtering, Admiral," Yelfis's voice came from the speaker. "My engineering officer says that's the sign of a cathron tube emitter in the process of burning out. Whatever black-market dealer they got it from, they were robbed."

"Given that its primary goal was to force us to withdraw and reevaluate, I would say its brief functionality was probably worth the cost," Thrawn said. "Fortunately, we are not so easily dissuaded. Commander Faro, take us in."

Ahead, the planetary horizon rose a little higher as the *Chimaera* shifted position. It moved in behind the three partially disabled cruisers, entering the stratosphere and moving ever closer to the surface . . .

"Northern ion cannon clear to fire," *Flensor*'s captain warned.

"Compensate, Commander," Thrawn ordered.

"Compensated," Faro confirmed calmly.

Eli smiled tightly. The insurgents had seen the *Chimaera* moving in and had hoped to take it out as they had the *Judicator*. But a small shift in the Imperial ships' positions had put the Star Destroyer directly behind the damaged cruiser.

"Commander?" Thrawn asked.

"Still moving inward, Admiral," Faro reported.

"Western ion cannon clear to fire," Brento reported from the *Shyrack*. "Adjusting . . . you're covered, *Chimaera*."

"Thank you, Captain," Thrawn said. "All ships, continue as planned."

Faro took a step closer to Eli. "I wonder if they're getting worried yet," she murmured.

"I doubt it," Eli said. "Whoever they've got running things down there, he's clever enough to know that shadows work in both directions. If his ion cannons can't hit the *Chimaera*, the *Chimaera*'s turbolasers can't hit his ion cannons."

"What about the island's turbolaser?"

"He'll wait until we're closer," Eli said. "With only that one target still available to us, he'll assume we've already locked in on it. He won't want to open the shield until he's got his best chance at a kill shot."

"As you said, a clever man," Faro said. "I almost feel sorry for him."

The island's three ion cannons continued with sporadic fire, clearly trying to get a shot past the cruisers to the *Chimaera*. But Thrawn had positioned his ships well, and the four captains had followed their orders precisely. Each time the cannons fired, their bursts merely expended themselves against the cruisers.

The standoff couldn't last forever, of course. If the cannons continued to fire, the cruisers' systems would eventually become so frozen that the ships would have no power or mobility of any sort and be unable to restart. At that point, they would begin the slow inward spiral that would ultimately send them crashing to the surface.

Fortunately, that wasn't going to happen. The *Chimaera* eased its way inward . . .

"Optimal firing distance, Admiral," Faro reported. "Turbolasers standing ready."

"Thank you, Commander," Thrawn said. "Target One. Turbolasers: *Fire.*"

Through the viewport, Eli watched the sky light up as the brilliant green bolts hammered their way toward the planet below.

But not to the island itself. As Admiral Durril and the *Judicator* had so painfully demonstrated, the insurgents' defenses were more than adequate to fend off any orbital attack.

But Scrim was an island . . . and the ocean immediately off its shore was not under the protection of that shield.

"Direct hit on Target One coordinates," a voice came from one of the 96th's two frigates, flying high observation over the battle zone. "Water crater—implosion—waves heading outward—"

"Impact!" a voice shouted from the second frigate. "Tsunami-scale wave has slammed into the western shoreline."

"Target Two: *Fire*," Thrawn ordered. "Damage at Target One?"

"Unclear, Admiral," the second frigate's observer said. The man was trying to stay calm and professional, but Eli could hear the awe creeping into his voice. "But the tsunami made a direct hit on the western ion cannon emplacement."

"Report on Target Two," the first frigate's observer cut in. "Turbolaser emplacement also hit. Looks even more swamped than Target One—the ground must be level or even bowl-shaped there."

"Alternate fire," Thrawn said. "Targets One and Two."

"Shield retracting," the *Flensor* reported. "Turbolaser clear to fire—"

"Second tsunami has hit Target Two," the first observer called.

"Second tsunami on Target One," the second added. "Western ion cannon is awash. Turbolaser—" He broke off. "Explosion at turbolaser emplacement, Admiral. Looks like the water shorted the capacitors. I'd say the weapon is out of action."

"Comm, open transmission," Thrawn ordered. "Scrim Island, this is Admiral Thrawn aboard the ISD *Chimaera*. Lower your shield and surrender, or we will continue to inundate your heavy weapons and shore defenses until they have been destroyed and those operating them killed. Repeat: Lower your shield and surrender or be destroyed."

There was no response. "Do we continue firing, Admiral?" Faro asked.

"Alternate fire between Targets One and Three,"

Thrawn said. "Alert the assault boats for imminent action."

Another burst of turbolaser fire sizzled from the *Chimaera* into the now seething ocean. "Tsunamis on Targets One and Three," the first observer reported. "Looks like a fire has started in the area around Target Two."

"Sir, the shield is down!" the sensor officer called excitedly. "Looks like they're surrendering."

"Confirm that, Admiral," the comm officer added. "The insurgent leader is formally asking for terms."

"Tell him he and his men are to leave their weapons in the buildings and wait outside for the assault boats," Thrawn said. "Any attempts at further resistance will be met with deadly force."

He half turned to the crew pit, and Eli could see an especially harsh glitter in his glowing red eyes. "And tell him," he added quietly, "that the cost will be severe if any of his hostages are harmed."

He waited for an acknowledgment, then turned and walked back along the command walkway to where Eli and Faro were standing. "You may signal Coruscant with news of our victory, Commander Vanto," he said. "Once the island has been fully retaken, Commander Faro, you will oversee the task of tractoring the three cruisers safely out of Batonn's gravity well so that they may initiate repairs."

Eli nodded. "Yes, sir."

"Yes, Admiral," Faro said. "And may I add my congratulations. A brilliant plan, perfectly executed. An outstanding victory."

"Victory, Commander?" Thrawn shook his head. "This battle is over. But the war for Batonn has not yet been won."

He turned and looked back along the walkway. "Should I be needed, I will be in my cabin. Inform me when the island has been secured."

· · ·

"Have you ever been aboard an Imperial Star Destroyer, Governor?" Yularen asked as his corvette rode the docking tractor beam into the *Chimaera*'s hangar bay.

"No, I haven't had the privilege, Colonel," Arihnda said. In point of fact, she'd never even seen one of the massive ships this close, let alone been invited aboard one.

But ships were ships, men were men, and admirals— even ones who'd risen as rapidly through the ranks as Thrawn—were still just admirals. She'd handled her share, and she would handle this one.

Thrawn was waiting when Arihnda and Yularen emerged from the docking tunnel. "Governor Pryce," the admiral greeted her. "Colonel Yularen. Welcome aboard."

"Thank you, Admiral," Arihnda said. Commander Vanto was standing a few steps behind him, along with a woman wearing a commander's insignia plaque. "We appreciate you seeing us on such short notice."

"Especially considering how busy you obviously are," Yularen added. "But I think this meeting may prove worthwhile."

"We shall see," Thrawn said. "The conference room is this way."

The conference room, when they finally reached it, turned out to be little more than a pilots' briefing compartment. The refreshments that had been laid out were plain and perfunctory, probably from the same pilots' mess.

Thrawn hadn't introduced his subordinates, either. Fortunately, both Arihnda and Yularen already knew Vanto, and the other woman by default and rank had to be *Chimaera*'s captain, Commander Faro.

Mentally, Arihnda shook her head. After all this time, Thrawn still didn't have a solid handle on the political requirements of his position.

"We understand you've pinpointed the insurgents' main Batonn stronghold," Yularen said as they sat down around the table. "The Creekpath Mining and Refining complex outside Paeragosto City."

"Yes." Thrawn's eyes flicked to Vanto. "While the freighters that fled from Scrim Island landed in different locations on the continent, Commander Vanto was able to sort out shipping vectors that indicated their cargoes ultimately ended up in Creekpath."

Arihnda felt her stomach tighten. "And of course, you're planning to go in there in force."

"I don't see that we have a choice, Governor," Commander Faro said. "The complex's shield blocks orbital assault."

"Even if it did not, there are approximately thirty thousand civilians within the complex's boundaries," Thrawn added.

"Yes, I know," Arihnda said. "Two of those civilians are my parents."

Those disturbing red eyes narrowed. "I see."

"Which is not necessarily all bad," Yularen said. "Governor Pryce has for obvious reasons been following events on Batonn very closely. Two days ago she came to me with a proposal." He gestured. "Governor?"

"It's very simple, Admiral," Arihnda said, slipping her voice, expression, and body language into what she liked to call Persuasion Mode. "I visited my parents several times when I worked for Senator Renking. I know some of the people down there, and my parents probably know most of them. I want to go down there, reacquaint myself with my parents and their friends, and get a close-up look at the insurgents' defenses and weapons setup. That way, when you send in your forces, they won't go in blind."

"Depending on the setup, they might even get a crack at the shield generator," Yularen pointed out. "Taking that down would make this operation considerably easier."

"Yes," Thrawn said, eyeing Arihnda closely. "A question. When you last visited Batonn you were a senator's aide. Now you're an Imperial governor. Your position and reputation may precede you."

"They won't," Arihnda said. "I can wear a disguise, but the simple fact is that for most people expectations override observations. They won't be expecting to see Governor Pryce of Lothal, so they won't see her."

"Your parents will know."

For a second Arihnda flashed back to that terrible day on Lothal, the day she'd had to tell her parents that they would have to leave their home, maybe for years, maybe forever. She'd talked long and hard during those three hours: cajoling and arguing, extolling the opportunity they were being given while warning of the dangers if they refused Renking's offer, promising she would help in the future while conceding she was helpless in the present. In the end she'd persuaded them, and they'd moved to Batonn, eventually settling into their new life with reasonable comfort and contentment.

But it was Arihnda who'd persuaded them. Not Renking and his threats, but Arihnda.

"Don't worry about them," she assured Thrawn. "I'll make sure they keep quiet."

"I assume you're not going alone," Vanto put in.

"Of course not," Arihnda said. Though that was, in fact, exactly what she'd been hoping to do. She'd argued long and hard with Yularen before ultimately being forced to concede the point. "One of Colonel Yularen's men will go with me."

"The story will be that they're hunting down a friend who's gotten mixed up in the mine situation," Yularen said. "That gives them a reasonable excuse to come into a potential combat zone, and to persuade her parents to get her past the insurgent checkpoints."

"It also does not require her to take either side in the dispute," Thrawn said. "All to the best, since we do not know which side her parents support."

Arihnda felt her lip twitch. She hadn't thought about that point. "I'm sure they're loyal to the Empire."

"Perhaps," Thrawn said. "Nightswan is quite persuasive. I must also point out that even with an ISB escort this will be a dangerous undertaking."

"I'll be fine," Arihnda insisted. "More important, you need the information."

"The collecting of which you're hardly an expert on," Faro pointed out. "It seems to me that limits your value."

Arihnda had to smile at that. If Faro only knew how good she was at collecting information. "One: Agent Gudry *is* trained in those things," she said. "He knows how to pull up the raw data. Two: *I* know mines, mining, and refining. I'll know what equipment is supposed to be in those facilities and what isn't, and what's worth tagging for orbital destruction and what isn't. Between his gathering and my sifting, we'll be a very effective team." She looked at Thrawn. "The most effective, I daresay, that you can get on such short notice."

Thrawn eyed her a moment, then shifted his gaze to Yularen. "Do you vouch for this Agent Gudry, Colonel?"

"Absolutely," Yularen said. "He's highly competent, both as an investigator and as a protector. He'll keep her safe. Count on it."

Thrawn was silent another moment. Then he gave a microscopic nod. "Very well. How do you intend to get her to the mine?"

"I'll take her to Dennogra and put her and Gudry aboard the regional planet-hopper," Yularen said. "They'll come in to Paeragosto City like any other visitors."

"I see," Thrawn said. He still had his doubts, Arihnda could tell. But he also knew he had limited power over what an Imperial governor did, especially when that governor already had ISB's blessing. "Time frame?"

"We can have her to Dennogra and back to Batonn in twelve hours." Yularen glanced at his chrono. "That should get her to Creekpath about two hours before sunset, local time." He nodded behind him. "From the looks of your light cruisers, I doubt you'd be ready to take any action before then anyway."

Arihnda pursed her lips. Yularen was right on that score, certainly. Their corvette had passed close to one of the cruisers on their way in, and the damaged ship's entire flank was a solid mass of maintenance tugs and huge repair barges. From what they'd seen of the other two cruisers, positioned far from the *Chimaera* where they'd be out of the way of any firefights, those weren't in any better shape.

"The cruisers were more heavily damaged in the ion cannon attack than was first thought," Thrawn conceded. "Still, their state of repair is largely irrelevant, as they would be of little use in a ground assault."

"Unless Nightswan also has a space component to his plan," Yularen warned. "Remember that Admiral Kinshara reported most of the insurgents' ships had already left Denash when the Hundred Twenty-Fifth arrived."

"That report merely repeated the statements of his prisoners," Thrawn reminded him. "The presence or number of insurgent ships that were in the system has yet to be independently confirmed."

"Maybe," Yularen said. "You'll still want to keep a close watch on the sky."

"I always do, Colonel," Thrawn assured him with a small smile. "For the record, I disapprove of Governor Pryce's plan, on both safety and effectiveness issues. However, as I am sure she is prepared to remind me, Batonn and Paeragosto City are not yet considered full military zones, which limits my authority over her movements there."

"And yet, disapproving or not, I know I can count on your instant assistance if there's trouble," Arihnda said. Her long years of political combat had taught her that being gracious in victory never hurt. "For that, Admiral, I thank you."

Thrawn inclined his head to her. "Governor." He looked at Yularen. "Will you be returning to the *Chi-*

maera after you take Governor Pryce and Agent Gudry to Dennogra?"

"Sadly, I have urgent business elsewhere," Yularen said. "But I trust we'll meet again soon."

"I will look forward to it," Thrawn said. "You will provide the comms and data collectors that Governor Pryce and Agent Gudry will need?"

"Yes, and I'll coordinate with Commander Vanto on frequencies and passcodes," Yularen said.

"Very well." Thrawn again inclined his head to Arihnda. "Success with your mission, Governor. Be cautious, and be safe."

"And bring back useful data," Yularen added. "Better yet, see if you can take down the shield. Make things a lot simpler."

"Don't worry," Arihnda assured both of them. "We'll do our best."

". . . and the passcodes will decrypt anything they send back," Yularen said, handing Eli a data card as they walked toward the hangar bay.

"Thank you," Eli said, slipping the card into his datapad and giving it a quick check. Everything seemed to be in order. "I presume you want this kept isolated from the rest of the ship's computer system?"

"If possible," Yularen said. "It's one of ISB's best encryptions, and we really don't want it wandering around the galaxy by itself."

"Understood," Eli said, pulling the card from his datapad. The docking tunnel entrance was just ahead, and Governor Pryce had already drawn away from the others, picking up her pace as she headed toward it. She really *was* anxious to get this mission started. "Admiral Thrawn's already been in contact with the Imperial forces on the ground. They'll be ready to move if and when Governor Pryce and her escort find them a soft way in."

"Yes," Yularen said, his voice going subtly odd. "Governor, go on in and get settled. I need a quick word with Commander Vanto."

Pryce sent a slightly puzzled look over her shoulder but disappeared into the tunnel without comment.

"A problem, Colonel?" Eli asked quietly.

"I don't know," Yularen said. "Can you tell me who set up the positioning of the *Chimaera* and the rest of the task force?"

"I believe the admiral did that himself. Why?"

"Because it's decidedly nonstandard," Yularen said. "In fact, it's borderline insane." He gestured. "Your three light cruisers are at the corners of an equilateral triangle nearly a hundred kilometers on a side. That means they're not only too far from your flagship, but too far from one another. None of them can support the others, and none of them are within covering range of the *Chimaera*."

"They're not exactly fit for battle at the moment," Eli said. Still, he'd wondered about the placement himself. Thrawn's explanation had been that he wanted plenty of space around each of the cruisers so that the huge and bulky repair barges he'd brought into the system from somewhere wouldn't get in one another's way.

But was that an explanation? Or was it simply an excuse?

"Their lack of combat capability is precisely my point," Yularen said. "As I said: They can't support the *Chimaera*, and the *Chimaera* can't support them. They're basically belly-up turtles surrounded and hemmed in by other belly-up turtles. A few armed ships popping out of hyperspace, and you'll be down by one cruiser and a whole lot of support ships. Three forces attacking in unison, and all three ships and support clusters would be gone."

"Not in unison," Eli murmured. "They'd come in sequence. *Shyrack,* then *Flensor,* then *Tumnor.* They'd want to give the *Chimaera* just enough time to turn its turbolasers toward one cruiser before the second was attacked."

"I see you're learning to think tactically," Yularen said. "The question is, why isn't Thrawn doing the same?"

"I'm sure he is," Eli said.

But Yularen was right on all counts. Which left only one reason Eli could think of why the cruisers had been set that far away.

They were Thrawn's equivalent of traffic zags. Something to slow down a sneak attack by encouraging the raiders to deal with a tempting trio of outlying ships while the *Chimaera* came to full combat readiness.

Only the bait was helpless . . . which meant that any attack would instantly degenerate into a slaughter.

Eli felt his throat tighten. Thrawn wouldn't do something that coldhearted. Surely he wouldn't.

"Well, I for one can't see the logic in this one," Yularen said darkly. "But I suppose that's his business, not mine. All I'm saying is that you should keep an eye on things. Nightswan . . . I've had the feeling ever since that first tibanna gas encounter that the man's gotten under Thrawn's skin. Deeper, probably, than the admiral would ever admit. With him orchestrating this whole thing, I'm not at all sure how clearly Thrawn's thinking."

"He's thinking just fine," Eli said firmly. "And whatever he does, it'll be for the good of the Empire."

"I hope so," Yularen said. "Keep an eye on him anyway." With a final, lingering look behind them, Yularen headed into the tunnel.

Leaving Eli alone in the passageway. With new and disturbing thoughts.

He waited until the corvette was safely on its way. Then, fingering Yularen's data card, he headed for the bridge.

He would watch Thrawn, all right. He would watch everyone.

Because Nightswan was somewhere in the area, with some plan of action already in place.

And as Thrawn himself had pointed out, the man was quite persuasive.

CHAPTER 26

Each person has goals. Some of those goals are open, visible to all who care to observe. Others are more private, shared only with one's closest friends or associates.

Some are dark secrets that one hopes will never see the light of day.

But eventually, inevitably, those deepest goals must be made manifest if they are to be reached. They must be opened for someone to hear, or see, or offer assistance.

Everyone who brings those goals into the light must be prepared for either acceptance or rejection. And he must be ready to bear the consequences.

All of them.

Back aboard the *Chimaera,* Thrawn had said that Paeragosto City wasn't yet a full military zone.

If it wasn't, Arihnda had no interest in tackling the real thing.

The first gauntlet was at the spaceport, where everyone leaving the transport had to show ID and answer some questions on their purpose for visiting Batonn in general and Paeragosto City in particular. After that was the Batonn Defense Force soldiers and navy troopers who'd set up a roadblock on the main road leading from the city to the Creekpath mining complex. It didn't look like they'd set up a full cordon yet, but Arihnda guessed it was just a matter of time and numbers. And finally there was a checkpoint just under the edge of Creekpath's shield, this one guarded by what appeared to be a mixed group of insurgents, malcontents, excitement seekers, and flat-out paid-for mercenaries and would-be mercenaries.

But the IDs that Yularen had given them—partial real name and fake planetary address for Arihnda, fake everything for Gudry—did the trick, bolstered by some amazingly good patter from Agent Gudry. Arihnda had expected to have to carry that load. Clearly, Yularen hadn't been overstating Gudry's abilities.

"You did very well, Governor," Gudry murmured as they headed for a line of four-seater personal transports just inside the last checkpoint. "Better than I expected."

"I'm glad I met with your approval," Arihnda murmured back. "We'll start with my parents' house, then head into the mine area for a look around."

"We only needed your parents to get in," Gudry said. "We're in."

"We're only in past the barricade," Arihnda pointed out. "Not into the mine complex itself."

"Not a problem," Gudry said. "Anyway, I want to see what's going on before it gets dark."

Arihnda closed her fingers around his upper arm. "One: Don't be an idiot," she said, lowering her voice. "My father's a foreman, and my mother's an administrator. Having a familiar face along will get us past checkpoints or security patrols a lot easier than ISB bluster talk. Two: A mining facility is as bright at night as it is in the daytime. It's just the shadows that move to different places. And three: Since by-the-book Imperials like to attack enemy positions in the dark, sundown will draw the insurgents' attention outward. Night is *exactly* what we want."

Gudry was silent another couple of steps. "Fine," he growled. "We'll do it your way. For now."

"We'll do it my way," Arihnda agreed. "For always."

Her first fear was that her parents might have been shifted to a different work schedule. That would have entailed hunting them down or risking a comm call. To her relief, her mother answered the door on the second ring. "Yes?" she said cautiously. She looked back and forth between them, her eyes settling on Gudry. "What can I do for you?"

"You could start with a hug," Arihnda suggested.

Elainye jerked, her gaze snapping back to Arihnda. There was a split second of confusion, and then her eyes widened. "Arihnda!" she gasped, stepping forward and wrapping her arms around her daughter. "I had no idea you were coming. What have you done to your hair?"

"It was a spur-of-the-moment thing, Mother," Arihnda said, giving Gudry a triumphant smirk over her mother's shoulder. Gudry had argued that the long blond wig over Arihnda's short black hair and the darkening lenses over her blue eyes wouldn't fool anyone. Obviously, Arihnda had been right. "I heard about the trouble here and wanted to make sure you and Father were all right."

"We're fine," Elainye said into Arihnda's shoulder. "Though that could change at any moment." She pulled back and held out a hand to Gudry. "I'm Elainye Pryce."

"Mattai Daw, ma'am," he said. "Arihnda's told me so much about you that I feel I already know you."

Arihnda felt her lip curl. In fact, everything Gudry knew about her parents had been relayed in brief snatches of conversation aboard the transport, dialogue that had consumed maybe fifteen minutes of their time together. The rest of the voyage from Dennogra had been spent in silence as Gudry buried himself in schematics, maps, and the latest ISB dispatches. "We need to talk, Mother," she said. "Is Father in?"

"Yes, of course. Come in, come in."

A minute and another round of hugs later, the four of

them were seated together in the living room. "So what's going on out there?" Talmoor asked. "Did you come here to talk to the governor about fixing this mess?"

"Unfortunately, Governor Restos doesn't listen much to anyone," Arihnda said, running a critical eye over her father. He'd aged considerably in the weeks since their last holocall, with his face more lined, his eyes more careworn, and his posture slumping. "In fact, I'm here *very* unofficially, which is why the hair and the eye lenses. Aside from making sure you two were safe, we need your help. A friend of Mattai's may be inside the mine area, and we need your help to find him and get him out."

"Oh, he's in there, all right," Gudry said with just the right mix of concern and embarrassment. "He's just the type to jump into something like this without thinking. I need to find him and get him out before the whole thing goes up."

"Let's hold on just a minute here," Talmoor said. "First of all, there's no one in the mine who isn't there of his or her own free will. They're fighting for people's rights against a repressive and dangerous government."

Arihnda felt a knot form in her stomach. Thrawn had wondered which side her parents would be on in the standoff. At the time, Arihnda had reflexively defended their loyalty. To hear her father talking like this—"I think you may be painting with too wide a brush," she put in. "The Empire is quite multifaceted."

"Maybe on Coruscant it is," Elainye said. "Maybe on Lothal. Not on Batonn. Here, the governor and his friends are—well, I'll just say it. They're corrupt, Arihnda. Utterly corrupt. And the galaxy needs to hear about it."

Arihnda began to breathe again. So it was just the local politics that were the problem? She could handle that. "I'll look into it when I get back to Lothal," she promised. "I can petition the Senate, possibly even the Emperor. There are procedures for that kind of thing."

"Yes, there are," Talmoor said grimly. "They're called revolution. I understand your concerns about your friend, Mattai, but there's really nothing you can do."

"And I'm perfectly willing to accept that," Gudry said. "But I need to hear that from him. I've heard too many stories about people being press-ganged by pirates and insurgent groups—and yes, I know most of them are probably apocryphal. But I need—" He swallowed hard. "I just need to hear it from him."

"So we're going in," Arihnda said. "You don't have to take us if you don't want to, but it would help if you could call ahead to someone you know."

Talmoor sighed. "You'll never get through the cordon without me. Fine, I'll take you. What's your friend's name?"

"Who knows?" Gudry said. "I mean, he hasn't always been on the right side of the law, if you get my meaning. I knew him as Blayze Jonoo, but I don't know what he's using here."

"That's helpful," Talmoor said with a touch of sarcasm. "Will you at least recognize him if you see him?"

"Absolutely," Gudry assured him. "And he's a weapons electronics guy, so that should give us a clue as to where they might have him working."

"Okay," Talmoor said, snagging his jacket from a coat tree by the door. "We'll go in and take a quick look around. But if and when they tell us to leave, we leave. Clear?"

"Clear," Arihnda said. "Before we go, I need to use the restroom."

"Okay," Talmoor said. "You remember where it is?"

"Unless you and Mother have moved it," Arihnda said with a tight smile. "I'll be right back."

She was, too. But on the way to the restroom was the kitchen, and her mother's handbag hanging by its strap as usual on a peg behind the door. Out of sight of the others, Arihnda opened the side pouch, hoping fervently that her mother hadn't changed her comm make and model since the last time she'd visited.

But her mother was a creature of habit, and to Arihnda's relief the comm was the same one she'd had before. Quickly, Arihnda swapped it out for the identical one she'd brought from Coruscant, then continued on to the restroom.

It would have been nice to simply borrow the comm without bothering with the switch. But she didn't dare risk it. If her mother noticed it was missing, she'd use a finder ping to locate it, and that could bring up awkward questions at the wrong time and place. This way, unless Elainye decided to make a call, her comm's disappearance shouldn't be noticed.

Gudry was still going on about his missing friend when Arihnda rejoined them. "Ready?" Talmoor asked.

"Ready," Arihnda confirmed. "Thanks, Father."

"You're always welcome," Talmoor said. "All right. Let's do this."

The terminator line had passed Paeragosto City. The sky over the enemy stronghold at Creekpath was darkening with the approach of night.

It was time.

Thrawn's office was quiet, filled with the same twilight the insurgents below were experiencing. Surrounding him were holograms of Batonnese art, hovering like messengers from the past, each piece speaking to the ethos, attitudes, and modes of thinking of the people and culture that had created it. Shape and flow, color and texture, style and medium—it all spoke to him. Even such factors as the type of art and the reputed value of the pieces offered clues as to how the people would act and react in warfare.

Unfortunately, with this kind of insurgency the patterns weren't as clear as a simple planetary uprising would be. Most of those under Nightswan's leadership were Batonnese, but there would be others who had journeyed here to join their cause. Those outside elements would distort and dilute the patterns laid out by the art.

Ideally, he would have had time for a more leisurely, more focused study of the enemy. But there was no more time. Scrim Island had been a diversion, something loud and obvious with which Nightswan had hoped to hold Imperial attention while he gathered his forces and weaponry under Creekpath's protective shield. Most likely he had expected the island's recapture to persuade the Empire that Batonn was no longer a threat, leaving him time for further preparation after they withdrew.

But for once he'd miscalculated. His time was coming to an end, along with the Batonn insurgency.

It was Thrawn's responsibility to do everything in his power to ensure it ended in the best possible way.

His desk comm was already set to the proper frequency. "Yes?" a woman answered.

"This is Admiral Thrawn aboard the ISD *Chimaera*," he said. "I wish to speak to Nightswan."

There was a pause. "Excuse me?" the woman said. *Her voice holds disbelief and astonishment.*

"This is Admiral Thrawn," Thrawn repeated. "Please inform Nightswan that I wish to speak with him."

This time, the pause was longer. "One moment."

It was forty seconds before the comm came active again. "This is Nightswan," the familiar voice said. *His tone holds caution but little surprise.* "How did you get this frequency?"

"It was one of many contained in the records of the freighter Commander Vanto and I took from your Nomad."

"Ah," Nightswan said. *His voice now holds dark humor within the caution.* "Careless of whoever flew that ship last. Well. With anyone else I'd expect an ultimatum or at least some gloating. But neither strikes me as your style. Why did you call?"

"I wish to speak with you."

"We are."

"Together, face-to-face, with no barriers between us."

There is a quiet snort. "Certainly. Do you want to come to my heavily armed camp, or shall I come to yours?"

"There is a field two kilometers northeast of the Creekpath facility," Thrawn said. "It includes a ridge of low hills that block it from casual observation, but is easily accessible from your camp."

Another pause. "You're serious, aren't you?" Nightswan said. *His voice holds confusion.* "You really want me to come there, out from under the shield?"

"If it would make you feel more comfortable, I will arrive first," Thrawn offered. "As you know, I have a civilian freighter, one that would not draw undue attention."

"You'll have guards, of course."

"I will order them to stay with the freighter and out of firing distance. Be assured that I do not seek your death."

"Just my capture?"

"You misunderstand," Thrawn said. "Your value to me cannot be realized by your capture. It certainly cannot be realized by your death."

"You've piqued my curiosity," Nightswan said. *Caution, but also a rising interest.* "What *is* my value to you?"

"I will only speak of it face-to-face," Thrawn said. "I will not discuss it in a comm conversation."

"I see." Another pause. "You say you don't want to kill me. I like that part. What makes you think I won't kill *you*?"

"Because you value life," Thrawn said. "Because I am the only guarantee that the civilians crowded within your stronghold will not be slaughtered. Should others lead the attack, they will almost certainly kill everyone and destroy everything in their path. You do not want that."

"I didn't ask the civilians to come here," Nightswan said. *There is fresh pain, and anger, and resentment.* "Some I couldn't help, the ones whose homes are under the shield. But the others . . . I asked them not to come. But we couldn't keep them out."

"I understand," Thrawn said. "I also understand that you see that burden the way I would see it. I pledge to do all in my power to prevent unnecessary deaths. That is why I know you will allow me to return to the *Chimaera* in peace."

The pause this time was longer, nearly eleven seconds. A reading of expression and body stance would be useful. But the connection was only audio.

If Nightswan accepted his invitation, a more complete reading would be possible.

"As I say, curiosity," Nightswan said. "All right, why not? The northeast field. When?"

"I will be there in one hour," Thrawn said. "You may arrive at your convenience."

"One hour," Nightswan said. "I'll be there."

It took some fancy talking on Talmoor's part, but eventually he, Arihnda, and Gudry were allowed through the mine's outer perimeter. There were no personal transports in sight, but Talmoor assured them the central part of the complex was only another kilometer inward, and they set off on foot.

And as they did, as Arihnda had expected him to, her father launched into a monologue of Creekpath's recent history.

". . . the irony is that the governor has himself to blame for the fact we've got a shield at all," he said as they stepped out of the way of a speeder truck heading inward, its cargo bay loaded with boxes. Arihnda squinted as the vehicle went past, caught the words MAKRID STRING on the sides. "When the trouble started on Denash, Creekpath's owner pleaded with him for some protection. All he really wanted was a couple hundred troops to beef up his checkpoints, but the governor wanted to save all the soldiers for his own protection. So instead he found a used DSS-02 regional shield and had it set up."

"Nice," Arihnda said, glancing behind him at Gudry walking on her father's other side. The sun was long since gone, but as she'd predicted the complex's lights more than made up for it, and in their glow she could see a small smile playing around the agent's lips.

Small wonder. DSS shields were used all across the Empire, and somewhere in Gudry's ISB training he'd undoubtedly learned how to take them down.

Yularen had suggested they eliminate the shield, but in the kind of offhanded way that had implied he was mostly joking. Before the evening was over, he might find himself surprised.

"I'd have thought the operators would have tried to sabotage it before you kicked them out," Gudry commented.

"Before the *insurgents* kicked them out," Talmoor corrected, a bit stiffly. "I might agree with some of their grievances, but I'm not one of them. Anyway, from what I understand they were rounded up and escorted off the premises before they even knew what was happening."

"And then Nightswan came in?" Arihnda asked.

Talmoor frowned at her. "Who's Nightswan?"

"The group's leader," Arihnda said. "Didn't you know?"

"I told you, I'm not with these people," he said shortly. "You said your friend was a tech, Mattai?"

"Mostly a tech, but he dabbled in a lot of things," Gudry said. "He might even have been brought in to keep the shield running. You know where the generator is?"

"Over there somewhere," Talmoor said, pointing. "I

guess we might as well head in that direction as any other."

Arihnda let them get a couple of steps ahead. Then, picking her moment, she slipped behind a parked speeder truck and angled off. She passed that truck, slipped around another one, and dropped to one knee where she'd be out of sight if Gudry or her father looked in her direction. She pulled out her mother's comm and punched her father's frequency.

He answered on the second signal. "Elainye? Is something wrong?"

"I don't feel well," Arihnda said, wheezing as if she were having some sort of reaction. "I think it was—I think it's something in the air."

"Hang on, I'll call the hospital," Talmoor said, his voice anxious.

"No, it's not that bad," Arihnda said, wheezing a little more. She had no idea how good her impression was, but the strain and wheezing would hopefully cover up any deficiencies. "Can you come home? I need you and Arihnda to come home."

"Yes, of course," Talmoor said. "Arihnda—"

He broke off, undoubtedly wondering where she'd disappeared to. "Please hurry," Arihnda said. She turned off the comm, slipped it into her shoulder bag, and stood up.

Just in time. Even as she turned back, her father and Gudry appeared around the end of the speeder truck. "Arihnda!" Talmoor called.

"Here," Arihnda called back, hurrying to them. "Sorry—I saw a group of men and wanted to check them out."

"What did they look like?" Gudry asked.

"Nothing like the description you gave me, I'm afraid," Arihnda said. "Is something wrong?"

"Your mother's been taken ill," Talmoor said, taking her arm. "We have to go home right away."

"Is it serious?"

"She says no," Talmoor said. "But we're going anyway. Come on, Mattai."

"Wait a minute—I need to find my friend," Gudry objected. "Can't I stay? I promise I won't get in anyone's way."

"I don't think—" Talmoor began.

"That's a good idea," Arihnda interrupted him. "You can find your way back to the house, right?"

"Sure," Gudry said. "You two go on. I'll be fine."

"I can't let you stay without me," Talmoor said. But the words were mechanical. His thoughts were clearly with his wife. "I promised—"

"Let me talk to him," Arihnda offered. Without waiting for a response, she took Gudry's arm and pulled him a few steps away.

"Well, this is damn awkward," Gudry whispered. "The old cow gets sick *now*?"

"You can do this alone, right?" Arihnda asked, trying hard to ignore the fact he'd just insulted her mother.

"Of course," he growled. "Trouble is, your old man won't let me."

"I'll change his mind," Arihnda said. "That last speeder truck, the one with the Makrid String crates? You'll want to find out where it went. Makrid String is a—"

"Is a wire explosive," he interrupted. "Thanks, I know. I'm more worried about Nightswan's collection of police gunships and skim fighters."

Arihnda felt her jaw drop. "You saw *gunships*? How many?"

"I didn't see *them*," Gudry said patiently. "I saw a spare parts dump, with enough material to patch up a couple dozen of them."

Arihnda winced. Air combat vehicles. Just what they needed. "You need to find and tag them," she said. "And—"

"Yeah, thanks, I know my job," he said. "You just get your old man off my back and out of here, okay?"

"Okay." Still holding his arm, she turned back to her father. "Okay, we've made a deal," she told him. "You and I will go home and see to Mother. He'll stay for one hour—*one* hour—and look for his friend. If he hasn't found him by then, he'll come out. Okay?"

Talmoor hesitated, his face screwed up with indecision. "Arihnda—"

"It'll be all right, Father," Arihnda said, letting go of Gudry's arm and taking her father's. "He'll be fine, and Mother needs us. Come on. Come *on*."

"All right," Talmoor said reluctantly as he allowed her to pull him back toward the perimeter. "Just be careful, Mattai. And don't mess with anything."

With her father distracted by worry, it was easy to guide him back out through a different checkpoint, one where the guards didn't know that three had gone in but only two were coming out. Fortunately, the men and women at this point, too, knew Foreman Talmoor Pryce, and didn't search or even question him.

How many of them, Arihnda wondered, would still be alive when morning came?

But that wasn't her problem. These people were in the center of a combat zone, they'd willingly placed themselves here, and what happened next was on their own heads. That went for Gudry, too.

As for Arihnda, she had a more important task before her. The job she'd planned from the very beginning of this standoff. The one only she could pull off.

Time to get started.

CHAPTER 27

An enemy will almost never be anything except an enemy. All one can do with an enemy is defeat him.

But an adversary can sometimes become an ally.

There is a cost, of course. In all things in life there is a cost. In dealing with an adversary, sometimes the cost is paid in power or position. Sometimes it is paid in pride or prestige.

Sometimes the cost is greater. Sometimes the risk is one's future, or even one's life.

But in all such situations, the calculation is straightforward: whether or not the potential gain is worth the potential loss.

And the warrior must never forget that he and his adversary are not the only ones in that equation. Sometimes, all the universe may hang in the balance.

Nightswan was waiting at the appointed place when Thrawn arrived. "I understood you would wait until my arrival," Thrawn said.

"I got bored," Nightswan said. *His voice holds a casual dark humor. His body stance holds tension but also weariness. His facial heat is heightened with a low level of caution.* "Besides, I was curious to see if you'd told me the truth." He gestured toward the stars above them. "Even now you could kill me and there would be nothing I could do to stop you."

"You are no use to me dead or captured."

"So you said," Nightswan said. "I assume you're calling on me to surrender, and to persuade my followers to surrender as well?"

"Interesting that you should call them followers," Thrawn said. "When we first met, you were merely a consultant. You hired out your tactical skill to those who would pay, without thought of consequences."

"You make me sound quite the amoral mercenary," Nightswan said. *His voice holds acceptance and agreement. His body stance holds tension, but also a subtle admission that the assessment is accurate.* "But you're mostly correct. Though I'd like to point out that I *did* save your life during the *Dromedar* hijacking."

"How so?"

"I persuaded Angel to take that buzz droid back aboard his ship with you and the other prisoners," Nightswan said. "I was pretty sure you had something in mind for it, and I wanted it to be available to you."

"Why?"

Nightswan shrugged. "I'd told him to deliver all of you to the drop point. But I suspected he was going to kill at least you and the other Imperials. I couldn't stop him on my own, so I had to hope you were clever enough to survive if you had the tools. Hence, the droid."

"Thank you," Thrawn said. "Allow me to point out in turn that, had you not, I had a second droid already moored to the hull."

"Ah. Of course you did." *Nightswan's smile holds irony.* "So much for playing the card of appealing to your sense of obligation."

"I find obligations are not a stable basis for a relationship," Thrawn said. "Perhaps it is different in the Mining Guild."

Nightswan's eyes widen. "Not really," he said. *His tone holds disbelief and rising fear. His arm muscles tense as his body stance shifts to an escape posture.* "How did you know?"

"You knew mining and metals," Thrawn said. "You noticed the disappearance of doonium more quickly than was likely for one not familiar with metals and the metal marketplace. You also spoke of the Thrugii asteroid belt to Commander Vanto, which supports many Mining Guild operations."

"I knew that was a mistake the minute I said it," Nightswan said. *He shakes his head, his body stance relaxing from escape mode to acceptance of defeat.* "So how much do you know?"

"I know that a group observed the rising confusion in the Empire's metal markets and broke from the guild in an attempt to manipulate that confusion for their own gain. I know that several members subsequently left and went their separate ways. I presume you were one of those."

"Yes." *Nightswan's expression now holds a cautious calmness.* "The chaos in metal prices was hurting a lot of small businesses, shipbuilders in particular. I joined the group hoping we could siphon off enough from the navy's demands to help them out." *His lips compress, his expression holding frustration and a brief flash of anger. His facial heat rises briefly, then subsides.* "When I discovered they were simply selling our stolen metals back to the Empire through the black market, I left."

"And joined instead with insurgents?"

"Not then," Nightswan said. "Not until much later. Most of the people I worked with at first were just ordinary citizens who'd been hurt by the Empire and couldn't get any redress. Justice costs money, and stealing and smuggling metals like doonium was the most efficient way to generate that money."

"Doonium *and* tibanna gas?"

Nightswan smiled. "I wish I could have seen your expression when you found out I'd pulled that one off.

Part of that one, anyway." *His expression and body stance hold memory and thoughtfulness.* "Come to think of it, that was probably the first time I worked directly with an insurgent group. The first time I knew I was working with one, anyway. Ground-based, though, with no ships, or I wouldn't have had to hire Angel and his Culoss crazies."

"They will not bother the galaxy ever again."

"Yes, I heard," Nightswan said. "After that . . . I don't know. For a while I straddled the line, still mostly just helping out innocents but also working with occasional insurgents when they popped up. I thought about going back to the Mining Guild, but by then they'd gotten wise to the group I'd left with and turned the Empire loose on them. You can guess the result." He smiled. "Or don't have to guess because you already know."

"I do," Thrawn confirmed. "So you no longer had anyone to turn to but insurgents?"

"Oh, I could have made a comfortable life for myself without them." *Nightswan purses his lips, his expression holding sudden dread.* "But then I started hearing rumors. Stories about something nasty the Empire was up to out in the middle of nowhere. The project that was sucking up all the doonium, iridium, and other metals that they were yanking out of the markets. I heard about whole planets being strip-mined. The old Thrugii facilities I used to work are still officially under Kanauer Corporation control but are now effectively an Imperial operation. I started getting curious." *His lips compress. His expression holds regret.* "Sometimes it's a very bad thing to be curious."

"It is never wrong to be curious. But it can sometimes be dangerous. This project you seek. Do you wish to stop it?"

Nightswan frowns, his expression and body stance holding suspicion. His facial heat again rises. "Why? Are you in charge of protecting it?"

"No."

"You probably should be." *His suspicion is fading.* "If they *really* want to protect it, that is. Would I stop it? I don't know. I suppose I'd first need to know what it is, so I could judge whether or not it's worth all the chaos it's causing. Why do you ask?"

"Because I, too, am interested in the project. I would like to hear what you have learned."

"Sure." *Nightswan waves a hand toward Creekpath. His expression holds sardonic humor.* "Take off that uniform, come join us, and I'll tell you everything I know."

"You know I cannot do that."

"And I can't give up information that someday might be vital to these people," Nightswan said. "Obligations, you know."

"Yet you also have a higher obligation to greater ideals," Thrawn said. "Tell me about Cyphar."

"Cyphar?" *Nightswan's frown holds surprise.* "What about it?"

"You claim obligation to the people of Creekpath," Thrawn said. "The money you would have obtained from the Cyphar pre-spice smuggling operation would have purchased weapons and supplies for them. Yet you deliberately used the same seashell technique I had seen before in the hope that I would notice and destroy the operation."

Nightswan shakes his head. His expression holds both resignation and admiration. His arm muscles relax, indicating he no longer expects combat on any level. "Sometimes I forget how good you are," he said. "Other times, I'm glad of it. You're right, I set that one up hoping you'd bring it to a crashing halt. I've seen what spice does to people, and I wanted no part of it."

"Yet you worked with them."

"Under false pretenses." *His voice holds bitterness.* "They told me they were being squeezed between the Afes and the Cyphar government and couldn't get the Empire to pay attention to them. By the time I found out what they were *really* smuggling I was already on the ground and couldn't bow out without risking a blaster shot to the head."

"You could have alerted the authorities."

"Who might or might not have done anything." *Nightswan's smile holds dark humor.* "Besides, I had a reputation to maintain. No, my best hope was that you would notice it and deal with it. And you did."

"As I also dealt with Higher Skies on Coruscant," Thrawn said.

Nightswan holds up his hands, palms outward. His body stance holds caution and protest. His face holds a mix of anger and contempt. "Whatever you think you know about Higher Skies, believe me when I say that assassinations or attempted assassinations were *never* part of the plan. The sole reason they were suborning bodyguards was to gain access to high-level files for data on the Empire's secret project."

"Did you learn anything?"

"We learned plenty," Nightswan said. *His expression holds determination.* "We learned that Grand Moff Tarkin's involved at the top, for one thing. We learned the work is being done at a single location, as opposed to being spread out all across the galaxy."

"Not entirely correct," Thrawn said. "There is a main work site, but there is also a subsidiary one."

"Really?" Nightswan frowned. "Interesting. I don't usually miss things like that."

"An excusable error," Thrawn said. "Most of the materials for the subsidiary location were delivered some time ago, with only small additions since then. As I say, the main work site is absorbing the bulk of the current shipments."

"Thanks, that makes me feel a little better." *Nightswan's voice holds dry humor.* "Still, it sounds like we're talking a single main structure or interwoven structure, rather than a group of large ships or battle stations.

Otherwise, it would be safer to split off the ships to different locations."

"I agree."

"And I'm getting close. Another few weeks . . ." *He stops, the determination fading again into weariness.* "But I don't *have* a few weeks, do I?"

"That decision is still yours."

"Is it?" *Nightswan shakes his head. The weariness spreads from his face to his full body stance.* "These people have attached themselves to me, Admiral. I can't turn my back on them."

"I see," Thrawn said. "I have always known that you were a master tactician. I see now that you are also a leader."

"Am I?" *His expression holds bitterness.* "Let me tell you a secret. At one point I had a grand plan for bringing all these insurgent and rebel groups together under one roof."

"What stopped you?"

"Paranoia," he said. "Distrust. Squabbling. Pride." *Again, he shakes his head.* "I don't know if anyone will ever bring them all together. I just know I couldn't. So much for my leadership skills." *He gestures to Thrawn, his expression holding an edge of confusion.* "What I don't understand is why *you* still serve the Empire. Can't you see the evil you're helping to perpetuate?"

The lights of the mining complex behind Nightswan shone faintly against the low scattered clouds. Thousands of people waited there, preparing for the inevitable Imperial attack. "I'll give you a scenario," Thrawn said. "You and I face a dangerous predator intent on slaughter. Running is impossible; tools and weapons are limited. What are your options?"

"The obvious one is for us to join forces," Nightswan said. *His voice holds hesitation and thoughtfulness.* "But you're clearly going for something else."

"Not necessarily," Thrawn said. "Unity against the common foe is one choice. But there is another."

"Which is?"

"You already know," Thrawn said. "You strike me down so as to make me the easier prey. While the predator devours me, you hope to find or build a weapon you can use to assure your own survival."

"Logical," Nightswan said. *His tone holds quiet revulsion. His body stance indicates a desire to back away from such a thought.* "Cold-blooded, but logical. Your point?"

"My point," Thrawn said, "is that it was that choice that lay before me when I decided to visit the Empire."

Nightswan frowned. "The story I heard was that you were rescued from exile."

"I was unaware that knowledge had been released to the general public."

"It wasn't." *Nightswan's smile holds wry humor.* "I had to do some serious digging to find it. As I had to dig to find the records of your time at Royal Imperial Academy, as well as all the other details of your career."

"I am honored you found me worth such dedication."

Nightswan shrugs. "To defeat an enemy, you must know them. Not that I've defeated you very often, but you've always been a fascinating study. Now you tell me you *weren't* exiled?"

"It was intended to so appear. But that was not the reality."

Nightswan smiles faintly. His expression holds anticipation. "Tell me this reality."

"I was exploring the edges of the new Empire shortly after the Clone War. I had witnessed a small part of that conflict, and had seen the chaos the collapse of the Republic had created throughout the region."

"There are theories that both the conflict and collapse were engineered by outside agents."

"The causes do not alter the fact that the Republic was unstable," Thrawn said. "There were too many different points of view. Too many different styles of political thought and action. The system was by its nature sluggish and inefficient."

"And you found the Empire to be the opposite?"

"At the time I knew little about the Empire," Thrawn said. "But during one of my surveys I discovered a colony of refugee Neimoidians. Once they learned who I represented, they pleaded with me to bring the Chiss to battle against Coruscant. They promised their people would rise up in response, and that together we would bring down Emperor Palpatine and restore the Republic."

"I hope you didn't accept their offer." *Nightswan's tone and expression hold contempt.* "The Neimoidians have a severely overblown opinion of themselves and their capabilities."

"I certainly did not trust their unsupported word. Nor did I make any promises. But my superiors were nevertheless concerned by my report."

"Because of the Empire? Or because of the Neimoidians?"

"Because of reality," Thrawn said. "There are evil things in this galaxy, Nightswan. Far more evil than the Empire, and far more dangerous to all living beings. We know of some, while of others we have heard only rumors. We needed to know whether the Empire that was rising from the ashes of the Clone War could be an ally against them."

"Or whether it should instead be collapsed into an easy prey," Nightswan said. *His voice holds dread.*

"You understand now my scenario," Thrawn said. "I had met a Jedi general during my Clone War investigations. That gave me credentials to offer the new Empire's leaders. I was thus the best choice to send."

"And so they dropped you somewhere and made it look like you'd been exiled?"

"Yes," Thrawn said. "The encampment was designed to appear as if I had been abandoned for years. In truth, I was only there a few months. We tried several lures to bring an Imperial ship to the planet. On the third attempt we succeeded. I used my tactical skills to slip aboard the ship, hoping to impress its captain. I succeeded, and was taken to Coruscant."

"Where you were made an officer in the Imperial Navy."

"A totally unexpected occurrence," Thrawn said. "I had hoped merely to persuade the Emperor to allow me to study the Empire's political and military structure under the pretext of sharing information about distant threats. But his offer gave me the opportunity to learn much more."

"And your study convinced you that it was better to hope the Empire would someday be your ally than to bring it down?" *Nightswan shakes his head. His expression holds disappointment.* "I'm afraid that uniform has blinded you to reality."

"Not at all," Thrawn said. "Certainly the Empire is corrupt. No government totally escapes that plague. Certainly it is tyrannical. But quick and utter ruthlessness is necessary when the galaxy is continually threatened by chaos."

"And what happens when the ruthlessness breeds more chaos?" Nightswan asked. *His tone holds challenge, his body stance briefly throwing off the weariness to hold fresh energy.* "For that *is* what happens. Repression and revolt feed and devour each other."

"Then the revolt must die," Thrawn said. "The danger is too great. The stakes are too high. If the Empire falls, what can replace it?"

"Justice. Mercy." *Nightswan's smile holds sadness.* "Freedom."

"Chaos," Thrawn said. "Lawlessness. The Clone War."

Nightswan shakes his head. "Perhaps I have a more optimistic view of my fellow beings than you do. So you consider tyranny to be a bulwark against evil. For how long?"

"Explain."

"How long will you accept tyranny as a necessary part of Imperial rule?" Nightswan asked. "Until all resistance is silenced? Until all evils are vanquished?"

"Perhaps your optimism is not as strong as you claim," Thrawn said. "The tone of a government is set by its leader. But Emperor Palpatine will not live forever. When it comes time for his authority to be handed to another, my position as a senior officer will allow me to influence the choice of that leader."

"And do you expect that new leader to spread light into the darkness?"

"There is hope that he will," Thrawn said. "But if evil is victorious, that hope will be extinguished. Forever."

"Hope." *Nightswan shakes his head. His body stance holds no such hope.* "I fear, Admiral, that you're still dangerously naïve on political matters." *He lifts a hand. His body stance holds defeat.* "I hope you're right. But I fear you're wrong."

"We shall see."

"Some of us shall," Nightswan said. "Others of us will be long gone. What about the Neimoidians? What happened with them?"

"To my knowledge, they are still where I left them, nursing their resentments and dreaming of a long-delayed victory," Thrawn said. "As I said, I made them no promises. Still, that initial contact was the reason I first created and then nurtured an acquaintanceship with the young Cadet Vanto. When I overheard him speak the name *Chiss,* I thought he might have been planted aboard the *Strikefast* by them to secretly observe me."

"I assume that wasn't the case?"

"It was not," Thrawn said. "By the time I was convinced, I had seen other qualities in him, qualities I have spent the past few years helping him develop. Like you, he has the rare combination of tactical aptitude and leadership."

"Ah," Nightswan said. *His voice holds sadness.* "And now we come to the part where you ask me to abandon my people and my cause and join you in your fight for a better Empire."

"Not at all," Thrawn said. "After your activities here, you would never be accepted by the navy."

"Nor would I accept such an offer."

"But you are correct in that I wish to offer you a position," Thrawn said. "Not with the Empire, but with the Chiss Ascendency."

Nightswan's eyes widen. His expression holds complete surprise. His arm and torso muscles tighten, his body stance straightening. "You want—? Admiral, that's crazy."

"Is a human among the Chiss more implausible than a Chiss among humans?" Thrawn asked. "It would offer you the chance to stand against forces far more evil than you face now. Moreover, your work there might someday save the lives of all those who currently stand with you at Creekpath."

"And what of those people right now? What would happen to them?"

"I offer them a promise," Thrawn said. "If they disperse, leaving their weapons behind, this will be the end."

"What, no retribution?" *Nightswan's expression and tone hold sarcasm.* "No tyrannical hammer to beat back the chaos?"

"The people of Batonn are Imperial resources," Thrawn said. "A wise commander never wastes resources without need."

Nightswan shakes his head. His expression holds disbelief and sorrow. "I should have guessed that was how you see people."

"I see reality," Thrawn said. "Your followers may return to their homes and jobs. There will be no reprisals or other action taken against them."

"Until you leave." *Nightswan's expression holds*

bitterness. "Even if Governor Restos honored your deal—which he wouldn't—it still wouldn't last. The injustices against the people are too great, the arrogance of those in power too deep. Sooner or later, they would rise up again. Only this time, they would have no one to lead them. They would be cut down like grain in a field, their voices silenced before they were ever heard."

"So you will stay?"

"I have no choice," Nightswan said. "We have the same sense of duty, Admiral Thrawn. Perhaps we ultimately seek the same end, at least for the distant future. But we see vastly different roads to that end."

He straightens again, his body stance holding a sense of imminent departure. "May I count on your promise to protect the civilians—excuse me; the Imperial resources—of Creekpath as best you can?"

"You may," Thrawn said. "I will seek to preserve all the lives under your leadership, combatant or otherwise, to the best of my ability. And my offer of clemency in surrender also stands."

"I appreciate that. Good evening, Admiral, and thank you for your time. We've been distant adversaries for a long time. My curiosity is now satisfied."

"Is it?" Thrawn asked. "There is still the matter of the Empire's new project. If I were to aid you in your search for answers, would it persuade you to join me?"

Nightswan stares across the gap between them. His expression is tight, his eyes narrowed. His body stance once again holds surprise. "What exactly do you know?"

"I have no direct knowledge," Thrawn said. "But I, too, have gathered some of the pieces of the puzzle to myself. I may also know where the main work site is located."

"But you haven't gone there to see?"

"I have not found an opportunity."

"Haven't found one? Or have refused to make one? And if you did find it, what then? What would you do?

You serve the Empire, and this project, whatever it is, represents a great deal of Imperial resources."

"I do indeed serve the Empire," Thrawn said. "But I also serve the causes of the Chiss Ascendancy. If I deem this project to be a threat against them, I might find it necessary to reconsider my path."

Nightswan's expression holds interest and temptation. His fingers rub restlessly against his leg, the movement holding uncertainty. "And if I surrender and accept your terms? What are you offering?"

"We will journey to the site together."

"And the people of Creekpath and Batonn?"

"I have given you my terms."

"And what of their grievances against Governor Restos?"

"I will do what I can."

Nightswan shakes his head, his body stance holding resignation. "And therein lies the problem. This is a political situation, and you have no political power. On one hand, we have a puzzle, and a fear of what the Empire is planning. On the other hand, I have real flesh-and-blood people to protect. I'm sorry."

"As am I."

Nightswan turns and begins walking toward the mining complex. "I have read about the nightswan," Thrawn called after him. "Have you?"

Nightswan turns partially back. His face is obscured by shadow. His body stance again holds weariness, along with a quiet dread. "You refer to the fact that it sings only as night is falling?"

"Yes," Thrawn said. "You do not expect your stand to succeed, do you?"

"I know that it won't succeed," Nightswan said.

"That does not necessarily mean the end. I can give orders for you to be taken unharmed."

"They'll be ignored. Half the troops here are Batonn Defense, and Restos is determined to get rid of me."

"Then come with me now."

"A man must do what he must, Admiral Thrawn. Even if his stand is against the fall of eternal night."

He began walking again. A minute later he was out of sight behind the hills. A minute after that, the sound of an airspeeder whispered across the stillness of the night.

"Thank you for not killing him," Thrawn said.

"Don't thank me yet." *Colonel Yularen's voice comes from behind. It holds anger and suspicion.* "Tell me why I shouldn't shoot *you* as a traitor to the Empire."

Elainye was surprised to see her husband and daughter home so soon. But she wasn't nearly as surprised as Talmoor.

"Are you all right?" he asked, enveloping her in a quick hug. "You sounded terrible. Has whatever it is passed?"

"Has whatever *what* is passed?" Elainye asked, frowning at him in confusion. "I have no idea what you're talking about."

"That was me, I'm afraid," Arihnda spoke up, pulling out her mother's comm and holding it out to her. "I needed to get back here, and I needed to get away from Mattai. This was the simplest way to do it."

"To get—*what*?" Elainye asked, her eyes on Arihnda as she mechanically took back the comm.

"There's going to be a battle soon," Arihnda said. "A big one. I need to get you out of here before it starts. So you need to start packing—"

"Arihnda, Arihnda," Talmoor soothed. "It's okay. They're not going to attack the mine—really. The governor wouldn't dare take any of his precious troops from their bodyguard duty to use against us."

"He won't have a choice," Arihnda gritted out. "There's an Imperial task force overhead, and their admiral has orders to neutralize the insurgents on Batonn. That means Creekpath, and he *is* going to take it. So you need to gather up everything you can't live without—"

"Arihnda, please—"

"There's no *please*, Mother," Arihnda snarled at her. "There's no please, and there's no time. You need to go pack, and you need to pack *now*."

She hadn't intended to shout that final word. But she did, and she felt a flicker of guilt as her mother jumped at the unexpected vehemence.

But if that was what it took to get them moving, Arihnda could live with it.

"Come on, Elainye," Talmoor said, squeezing his wife's hand. "Do as she says."

He started toward the stairs. Elainye didn't move. "What about our friends?" she asked, pulling back against her husband's grip, her voice under rigid control. "What about the men and women we work with in the mine?"

"I'm not here for them," Arihnda said. "I'm here for you."

There was another long silence. "I see," Talmoor said. "All right. Come on, Elainye."

"And make it fast," Arihnda warned, glancing out the window at the lights of the mining complex in the distance.

Because Gudry didn't know anything about this part. And if Gudry found out, she was damn sure he wouldn't like it.

"I thought you said you had urgent business elsewhere," Thrawn said as Colonel Yularen came down the hill, a blaster carbine in his hands. *Like his voice, his body stance holds caution and suspicion.*

"You asked if I'd be returning to the *Chimaera*," Yularen reminded him. "I said I wouldn't. And I didn't."

"You did not want Governor Pryce and Agent Gudry to know you were coming here to watch them from afar."

"Correct," Yularen said. "Both would have been insulted, though for different reasons. You can imagine my surprise when Commander Vanto informed me that you'd left the *Chimaera* in that freighter you took from Nightswan's Nomad."

"I see you asked Commander Vanto to be extra vigilant, as well."

"And now you're stalling," Yularen said. *He continues forward until he is four meters away. His blaster is pointed a few degrees to the side, not directly threatening but ready to be brought onto target.* "I want to know what you're doing here, and what your business was with Nightswan."

"I am an admiral," Thrawn said. "You are a colonel. I could order you to withdraw."

"Theoretically, yes," Yularen agreed. "As a practical matter, the ISB carries more weight with Coruscant than our respective ranks might suggest." *He hesitates a second, then lowers the carbine to point at the ground.* "I don't believe you're a traitor, Admiral. But this meeting has the appearance of treason, and that's all your enemies would need to bring you down. Bottom line: You talk to me now, or someday you face them. Which is it going to be?"

"I invited Nightswan here to offer him a position with my people," Thrawn said. "Not only would that have benefited them, but the loss of the insurgents' leader would have collapsed opposition on Batonn."

"I see," Yularen said. *His voice holds uncertainty.* "He turned you down, did he?"

"You saw him leave."

"Maybe he just went for a change of clothes," Yularen countered. "You sure he's not coming back?"

"He is not."

"Fine," Yularen said. "Now tell me about your light cruisers. Specifically, why you've positioned them so far away from the *Chimaera* with those dog-ugly barge things you dragged in from somewhere wrapped around them."

"The cruisers are under repairs and unable to fight," Thrawn said. "I positioned them at a distance so they would be out of range of any attack from the surface."

"Uh-huh," Yularen said. "Sounds reasonable . . . except that where they are right now completely opens them up to an attack from space. You remember those ships that got away from Kinshara at Denash?"

"The existence of such ships has not been proven."

"Proof is for jurists and politicians. I'm talking about tactics and strategies, subjects you suddenly seem to know nothing about. Those cruisers are far enough outside Batonn's gravity well that someone could just swoop in, board them, and take them to hell and gone." *He raises his eyebrows, his expression holding a question.* "Their hyperdrives *are* working, correct? That's what Vanto deduced from the repair logs."

"Commander Vanto is quite capable in the area of supplies and repairs," Thrawn said. "If he states the hyperdrives are functional, you may rely on it."

"Glad to hear that," Yularen said. "You haven't answered my question."

"You are correct that a determined and quick attacker might be able to spirit the cruisers away," Thrawn said. "But did you fail to notice the turn of that scenario?"

Yularen frowns. The frown vanishes into understanding. "That the cruisers can also jump if an attack is imminent?"

"Exactly," Thrawn said. "That is why I placed them where I did. The repair barges are attached loosely enough that they will not be a hindrance."

"And you separated them widely because . . . ?" *His expression holds anticipation.*

Thrawn remained silent. *Yularen's expression changes to cautious understanding.* "Because you don't want any potential thieves to have all three of them lined up in a nice neat row ready for plucking."

"Precisely," Thrawn said. "You possess the same tactical abilities as Commander Vanto, Colonel. I do not know if you also possess his quality of leadership."

"You really *don't* have much political sense, do you? Never mind. I got a transmission from Gudry as Nightswan was leaving. He's made it deep into the Creekpath base and has mined both the shield generator and an explosives cache he found. He's keyed both of the triggers onto his comm's remote." *His expression holds sudden frustration.* "He also said that once he retrieves Pryce he'll be ready to get out, and that he can trigger either or both of the mines at your command."

"When he *retrieves* Governor Pryce?"

"That's the part that has me worried, too," Yularen said. *Frustration and anger.* "Apparently, she wandered off somewhere, possibly with her parents in tow, and he can't raise her or locate her comm. He said he'll try their house first. If she's not there—" *He shakes his head.*

"We will find her," Thrawn said. "I need to return to the *Chimaera*."

"Go," Yularen said. "Let's just hope we don't have to tell Grand Moff Tarkin that he needs to find Lothal yet another governor."

CHAPTER 28

———————————

All strive for victory. But not all understand what it truly is.

To a soldier or pilot on the line, victory is surviving the current battle. To a politician, victory is an advantage one can bring to a bargaining table. To a warrior, victory is driving an enemy from the field of battle, or bringing him to surrender.

Sometimes the victory is greater than the warrior could ever hope for.

Sometimes it is more than he is able to bear.

"You're kidding," Arihnda said, eyeing the stack of twenty data cards her mother had handed her. "*All* of them?"

"*All* of them," Elainye said firmly. "And if I find that other box before you drag us out of here, there'll be ten more."

"It's the record of your life, Arihnda," Talmoor reminded her. "Your dance recitals, your school debates, your first day working the mine. Everything up until you left for Coruscant."

"Fine," Arihnda said, managing to check her chrono without spilling the data cards all over the floor. "You've got fifteen minutes. And don't forget to grab some of your own mementos."

"You're the most important part of our life together, Arihnda," Talmoor said quietly.

"Well, get some of your own things anyway. You must have *some* memories from before I was born. The carrybags are where?"

"Downstairs, in the closet off the kitchen," Elainye said. "There's one big one and three smaller ones."

"Okay," Arihnda said. "I'll load these in one of the small ones and bring the big one up. Remember: fifteen minutes."

She headed downstairs, holding the data cards in a vertical stack pressed between her palms. Fifteen minutes should be enough time to get out of here before Gudry came back.

She was wrong. By exactly fifteen minutes.

"*There* you are," Gudry's voice came from behind her as she reached the bottom of the stairs.

Arihnda jerked, nearly spilling the cards as she spun around. Gudry had emerged from the dining alcove, a suspicious scowl on his face, a line of dried blood tracing out a path from the corner of his chin.

A small blaster gripped in his hand.

"Of course I am," Arihnda said as calmly as she could. *Damn.* "Where else would I be?"

"Oh, I don't know," Gudry said sarcastically. "Maybe at the hospital? Your mother being deathly ill and all."

"False alarm," Arihnda said. "We made her some tea, had her put her feet up, and she started feeling better."

"Yeah, I can tell," Gudry said. "I can hear the party they've got going on upstairs. A packing party, sounds like. Where's the teacup?"

Arihnda felt her stomach tighten. *Stupid,* she berated herself. She knew better than to tell unnecessary lies, especially ones that could be easily checked. "What exactly are you implying?"

"I'm *saying* that you deliberately gave me the slip," he said, taking a step toward her. "I'm *saying* that you were never going to help me find what we needed in there."

"You're the professional. I didn't think you needed any help."

"Whereas your parents *do* need your help to get out before this place goes to hell?" Gudry shook his head. "Sorry, sweetheart. This isn't a rescue mission. It's search and destroy." He held up his comm. "Luckily for the Empire, I *didn't* need you. I did the search, and now we're ready for the destroy."

Arihnda took a deep breath. *Damn* him, anyway. How could he have been so fast?

Or maybe how could she have been so slow? "Excellent," she said. "What have we got?"

"We have an explosives cache and the shield generator." He grinned slyly. "Oh yeah, I got all the way to the shield generator."

Arihnda looked at his new blaster. "I assume that's where you got the weapon?"

"Let's just say the previous owner won't need it anymore," Gudry said. "I tied the triggers into my comm. Signal One is the shield, Signal Two is all the explosives."

"*All* the explosives?"

"All of them," he said. "Hell of a cache—it took four of my caps to cover all the piles. Never mind that. We're ready, the navy task force and troops are ready, and it's time to get the hell out of here. So put down those cards and let's go."

"We can still take my parents with us," Arihnda said. "They won't slow us down."

"I don't care if they can turn into Arkanian dragons and fly us out," Gudry retorted. "A party draws attention we can't afford. I'm in charge, and they're not going."

"I'm a governor," Arihnda bit out, taking a step toward him.

"I've got the blaster."

There was a sudden gasp from the stairs. Arihnda's mother had frozen halfway down the steps, gripping a shimmering multicolored crystal, her eyes bulging at the sight of Gudry's blaster. Arihnda took another quick step toward Gudry as he reflexively spun to face the unexpected noise—

And as he spun back toward Arihnda, she hurled her stack of data cards into his face.

He was quick. But he was also half turned, his balance was off, and his blaster was pointed the wrong way. He ducked his head away from the flying data cards, flinging up his free hand to fend them off, then spun back toward Arihnda.

Too late. She caught his wrist with her right hand, and as he tried to break it free she swung the arm upward, ducked under it, grabbed the blaster with her other hand, and pulled his elbow down sharply across her shoulder. There was a faint sound as the joint snapped, a barely louder grunt as Gudry reacted to the pain. Arihnda twisted the blaster free of his grip and started to dive out of his reach—

And gasped in pain as he slammed the heel of his other hand against the back of her head.

She fell forward and away from him, her head spinning, her knees wobbling. She threw out her free hand blindly, managed to catch the arm of a chair as she fell past it. She pivoted around the arm and slammed onto her back on the floor.

"Cute," Gudry growled as he strode toward her, clutching his broken elbow with his other hand. "We'll try that again in the dojo after they put my arm back together. Get up—it's time to go."

"With my parents," Arihnda managed between gasps of air.

"No," Gudry bit out. "Let 'em die here with all the rest of these Outer Rim freaks."

Lifting the blaster, Arihnda shot him three times in the chest.

He collapsed in a heap, dead before he even had time to change expression. Holding the back of her head, wincing at the knives of pain shooting through her skull, Arihnda climbed back to her feet.

Her mother was still standing on the stairs, her eyes even wider than before. "See?" Arihnda managed, pointing her blaster at the crystal clutched in Elainye's hands. "You *do* have memories of your own."

"Arihnda," Elainye breathed. "Oh, Arihnda—"

"I had no choice, Mother," Arihnda interrupted. "He was going to leave you and Father behind. And he was probably going to kill me once I'd gotten him out of the area." Which wasn't true, of course. But if it made her mother feel better, she was more than happy to tell the tale. "Let me get the suitcase—"

"*I'll* get the suitcase," Elainye said, finally coming unglued from the stairs and hurrying toward her daughter. "You just sit down. No—wait—let me get the medpac first."

"Just get the suitcase," Arihnda said. "I'll get the medpac. We haven't got much time."

Elainye looked at Gudry, turned quickly away. "We'll be ready," she murmured.

With a last look at her daughter, and no look at all at the dead man lying on her floor, she headed toward the closet and the carrybags.

For a long moment Arihnda stared at Gudry, wondering if she should feel something at what she'd done. But there was nothing. No guilt, no sorrow, not even any queasiness. Gudry had threatened her parents. He'd gotten in her way.

He'd paid the cost.

Carefully, mindful of her shaky balance, she walked over to him. He still had all their special gear, after all, including the blasting caps, the comm trigger mechanism he'd set up, and whatever else he'd decided to bring along.

Arihnda might not need anything except the trigger. But then again, she might.

Easing down onto her knees, she began to search the body.

"Still no response from Pryce or Gudry." Yularen's voice came from the *Chimaera*'s bridge speaker. "Have you received anything?"

"Not since Agent Gudry's transmission confirming the shield had been sabotaged," Faro said. "I assume you also have the necessary triggering code?"

"Yes, but I'd rather not use it until and unless we give them up as captured. Or dead."

Eli looked forward along the command walkway. Thrawn was standing by the forward viewport, his hands clasped behind his back, unmoving as he gazed at the planet below.

The admiral hadn't had much to say since his return from that clandestine visit to the Creekpath area. Eli had received a private communication from Yularen as Thrawn was returning to the ship, but the message hadn't said much except that questions about the admiral's motives or strategies had been satisfactorily answered.

Satisfactorily for the colonel and ISB, maybe. Not so much for Eli. The fact that Thrawn had returned safely from Batonn had relieved a lot of his concerns and stress. But the matter of the vulnerable cruisers still hung over the situation like a dark nebula.

Especially since Eli had now proved, at least to his own satisfaction, that Admiral Kinshara had been right about the insurgents sneaking ships off Denash.

It hadn't been just a few ships, either. His estimates, gleaned from the lists of spare parts and equipment shipments that Kinshara had retrieved from the captured base, indicated there were no less than thirty midsized ships lurking somewhere nearby. All of them armed, all of them ready to pounce.

Even for an Imperial Star Destroyer, a force of thirty armed ships wasn't to be taken lightly. In a situation like that, the *Chimaera* needed its screening vessels close at hand.

Only it didn't have them. The three cruisers were still sitting in their private little circles of isolation, far distant from the *Chimaera,* each half cocooned with supply ships and repair barges. The two frigates were useless, having been sent by Thrawn to high observation duty in case Nightswan attempted to bring new weapons or personnel to his ground forces.

Eli had reported his findings to Faro, who had responded by emptying the *Chimaera*'s hangars and doubling the TIE fighter sentry screen around the planet. But the TIEs couldn't begin to cover everything, and the nearest warships that could respond to a call were over thirty hours away. By the time any aid could arrive, the battle would be over.

Eli looked at the tactical, feeling his stomach knot up. Every ship of the 96th was vulnerable. But there was only one that truly mattered. If Nightswan's thirty lurking ships took out the *Chimaera,* the whole system was open to them. If they didn't, they'd already lost.

The *Chimaera* wasn't just a target. It was *the* target.

"Colonel Yularen, what is your troop status?" Thrawn called.

"We don't have enough for an encirclement, Admiral, but we can probably mount a solid punch-through," Yularen said. "I should also mention that Gudry's report of an unknown number of gunships and skim fighters has the ground commanders a bit worried."

"Once the shield is down, those fliers should not be a problem," Thrawn assured him. "The *Chimaera* can descend to effective firing distance within three minutes, more than enough time to deal with combat aircraft of that size."

"We'll probably need that support, sir."

"You shall have it," Thrawn said. "Before all the troops are committed to battle, I want you to separate out a special-duty squad for me."

"Yes, sir. Their mission?"

"Once the battle begins, I want them to make their way to the house of Governor Pryce's parents," Thrawn said. "If she and Agent Gudry were compromised, they might have taken refuge there."

"Understood, sir," Yularen said. "Actually, we may not need to wait for the battle to get under way. If I'm reading the maps and images correctly, the house is far enough out from the center that we should be able to slip a squad in whenever we want."

"That was also my conclusion," Thrawn said. "But the situation on the ground is often more complex than it appears from orbit. How long will it take the squad to reach the house?"

"Give me fifteen minutes to cut out a squad and prep them," Yularen said. "Probably thirty more to slip them through the outer picket line and make their way inward. Forty-five minutes, an hour at the most."

"Good. Proceed."

"Yes, sir."

"And inform the commanders that they are to ready their troops," Thrawn added. "If Governor Pryce and Agent Gudry are not at the Pryce home, and if we have not otherwise heard from them by then, we will assume their mission has failed and proceed accordingly."

"Yes, sir," Yularen said.

"Captain Faro?"

"Admiral?" Faro replied, taking a step down the walkway.

"Prepare the *Chimaera* for combat," Thrawn said. "I expect enemy forces to appear at any moment."

"Yes, sir." Faro gestured to the crew pits. "Turbo-lasers stand ready. Shields at standby power."

"Shields at standby, sir," a voice acknowledged.

"Turbolasers at—" a second voice began.

"Incoming!" the sensor officer snapped. "Midsized ships—ten—incoming on vector one-ten by eighty. Range, one hundred thirty kilometers."

Eli turned to the tactical, his throat tightening. The ten ships had jumped out of hyperspace thirty kilometers behind the *Shyrack* and were heading straight toward it, accelerating to attack speed as they came. Exactly as he'd feared. "Admiral—the *Shyrack*—"

"Incoming!" the sensor officer cut him off. "Eleven more midsized on vector—"

"Two more groups incoming," the secondary sensor officer corrected, her voice tight. "This one also eleven vessels. Admiral, they're targeting the cruisers."

"I see them," Thrawn said, his voice like glacial ice.

Then do *something!* The words screamed in Eli's brain. The three attack squadrons hadn't yet opened fire, but the respite would only last another few seconds. Another twenty kilometers, and their blaster cannons would cut through the defenseless cruisers like a fruit knife through a demi-husk.

And once they'd destroyed the cruisers, there was nothing between them and the *Chimaera*.

Eli gazed at the display, his mind beating furiously at the situation, trying to find a way out. But there wasn't one. The *Chimaera* was too deep in Batonn's gravity well to jump to lightspeed. With the main drive still on standby, it would take nearly ten minutes to climb to the necessary distance. There were no ground-based weapons that could assist, and Batonn had no orbiting weapons platforms. All that remained was for the Star Destroyer to sit here and slug it out with the enemy ships.

Was that Thrawn's plan? To make the attackers waste

energy on the cruisers, possibly burning out some of their weapons in the process, then hope that the *Chimaera*'s armor and weapons would be enough to hold them off? Certainly the admiral couldn't want the newcomers joining Nightswan and his insurgents on the ground— was this his way of making sure they stayed in space and out of Nightswan's reach until the Creekpath battle was over?

A motion caught Eli's eye, and he turned to see Thrawn walking back along the command walkway. Not hurrying, as if he were concerned about being too close to the viewport when the attack began, but with the measured tread of a man secure in his plan and his command.

He paused beside the comm section of the crew pit, almost as if it were an afterthought. "Signal the ground commanders," he ordered. "The units on the west and north may open fire on the Creekpath insurgents. But they are to remain on the edges of the complex— harassment fire only—until the shield is down or until I give further orders."

"Yes, sir."

Thrawn continued down the walkway, stopping before Eli and Faro. "Colonel Yularen's retrieval squad will benefit from diversionary fire elsewhere on the perimeter," he said.

"Yes, sir," Eli said, a small part of his mind feeling a twinge of chagrin that he'd been so preoccupied with the attacking ships that he hadn't put those pieces together. "Sir . . . the ships?"

"Yes, Commander: the ships," Thrawn agreed, turning again to gaze out the viewport. "Let us now discover how well I have read our opponent."

"And whether we're about to die," Eli muttered.

"Yes," Thrawn said. "And whether we are about to die."

. . .

Arihnda and her parents were nearly to the insurgents' outer picket line when the complex to the north and west lit up with blasterfire.

"Talmoor?" Elainye murmured tensely, clutching at her husband's arm.

"I hear it," Talmoor said, his voice grim. "So it's happened. I hoped it wouldn't."

Arihnda peered across the semi-lit area in front of them, trying to spot the Imperial troops out there. But they were still hunkered down and quiet, just as they'd been when she and Gudry headed inward earlier across their line. Had those squads missed the order to attack?

Hardly. If they were still in place, it was because they'd been ordered to stay that way.

In which case the attacks in the distance were either a single-vector penetration or a diversion.

She smiled tightly in the darkness. Of course. She'd been ignoring the increasingly frequent calls on her comm and the comm she'd taken from Gudry, not wanting to speak to Thrawn until she knew exactly what she was going to say. If that blasterfire was a diversion, it was so that a team could head in from some other direction to look for her.

Her smile faded. The logical place to start a search would be her parents' house. If the team made it there and found Gudry's body . . .

She might be able to talk her way out of it. But she might not. The fact that Gudry was dead without Arihnda and her parents sporting so much as a blaster scorch would require a very tricky lie to explain.

"We need to go," Elainye said, her eyes still on the flickering lights in the distance. "Arihnda?"

"In a minute," Arihnda said, looking around. A few meters to her right was a bulldozer-type machine, probably set there by the insurgents so that this part of their picket line would have somewhere to fall back to when the shooting started. "Stay here. I'll be right back."

Gudry's bag of tricks had included six comm-triggered blasting caps. She had a single one of them left.

Affixing it beneath the bulldozer was the easy part. Keying Gudry's comm to detonate it was the trick. He'd run through the procedure with her on the transport, but it had been a perfunctory explanation from a man who'd clearly never expected her to have to use that knowledge.

But after a few false starts, she got it keyed to the Signal Three setting. Tucking the comm invisibly in her hand, she returned to her parents.

They were still staring into the distance, as if by sheer willpower they would be able to see what was happening over there. "Time to go," she murmured to them. "Let me do the talking."

She'd hoped the guards on the insurgent line would have all their attention directed outward, and that she and her parents would be able to slip through without being spotted. Once again, luck was against them. "Halt," a quiet voice ordered from just ahead. "Where do you think you're going?"

"I need to get my parents out of here," Arihnda said. He was an older man, and he held his blaster like he knew what he was doing. A Clone Wars vet, maybe. "Mother's not well," she added as she started toward him, gripping Gudry's comm tighter in anticipation. "I need to get her to—"

"Let's see some IDs," the guard cut in. "All of you."

This was it. So far everyone they'd met had known her father, by name if not by face, and the odds were good that this man would, too. If he did, and if he started asking questions—or worse, if he called over a suspicious superior—

"That won't be necessary," Talmoor said, stepping forward. "I'm Talmoor—"

Clenching her teeth, Arihnda triggered the comm.

The blasting caps had only limited power, and the explosion wasn't a huge one. But it was big enough, and

loud enough, to draw everyone's attention to the bulldozer as it shuddered and rocked up briefly onto one
side.

As the guard gaped, Arihnda stepped close to him,
pressed the muzzle of her blaster against his chest, and
fired.

With the sound of the shot muffled by his body and
further covered by the echoes from the explosion, she
doubted anyone heard it. The guard certainly made no
noise as he crumpled to the ground, his blaster clattering
softly against the pavement. Arihnda glanced around as
she slid the blaster back inside her tunic, but saw no
other pickets.

"Arihnda, what was—*Arihnda!*" her mother gasped.
"What happened?"

"Probably caught a piece of shrapnel," Arihnda said,
taking her arm and pulling her along. "Father? Come
on."

"But we have to help him," Elainye said.

"It's too late," Arihnda said, tugging harder. "Father,
come on."

"In a moment," her father said, his voice strange.

Arihnda looked back over her shoulder, the movement sending another needle of pain through the back
of her head. Talmoor was standing over the freshly dead
body, gazing down at it. "Father!" she said in a loud
whisper. "Come *on*."

He looked at the body for another moment. Then he
stirred and followed.

And even in the faint light Arihnda could see the pain
and revulsion in his eyes.

She'd expected to be challenged at least once more
before they reached the Imperial line. But the explosion
had apparently sent the rest of the insurgents scrambling
for cover while they figured out whether or not the attack was starting. Ahead, she could see a line of armored
personnel carriers, their bulks dark against the lights of
Paeragosto City in the distance—

"Halt!" a brisk professional voice came from behind them.

Arihnda looked back. Two men in black navy trooper uniforms were striding toward them, blaster carbines held ready. She had no idea where they'd been hiding. "It's all right," she said quickly. "I'm Arihnda Pryce. I'm here on special assignment from Colonel Yularen."

"*Governor* Arihnda Pryce?" one of the troopers said, picking up his pace. "About time, Governor. The colonel's been worried about you. You'd better give him a call—the team's already gone in."

"What team?" Arihnda asked.

"The rescue team heading to your parents' house," the trooper said. "These them?"

"Yes, these are my parents," Arihnda confirmed, her heart beating faster. She'd hoped the team would wait until the battle started before going in.

Maybe there was still time to stop them. "When did they leave?"

"I don't know," he said, giving her pass a quick look. "Probably twenty minutes ago. You'll have to ask Colonel Yularen. Wasn't there supposed to be someone else with you?"

"We got separated," Arihnda said, clenching her teeth. Twenty minutes. Depending on how stealthy they'd had to be on the inward trip, they could be within sight of the house by now.

For that matter, they could already be inside.

"I'll call him right away," she said, glancing up. The stars, what could be seen of them through the hazy glow from the complex, showed the extra flicker that came from their light being sifted through an energy field. They were still under the edge of the Creekpath shield. "Where's your HQ?" she asked the troopers. "I need to get my parents to the city and some proper care."

"HQ's over there," the man said, pointing to a larger version of the armored carrier. "Major Talmege. He'll arrange for transport."

"Thank you." Arihnda beckoned to her parents. "Come on, let's find a place where you can sit this out."

They headed off, Arihnda herding her parents in front of her. *Another few steps,* she told herself. *Just another few steps.*

The attacking ships, all three clusters, were within firing distance of the cruisers now. Eli clenched his teeth, wondering when they would begin the slaughter. The attackers continued on, reached point-blank range—

And in smooth unison their formations split apart, the ships swinging wide around the cruisers and support vessels. They cleared the obstacles, re-formed their clusters, and continued inward toward the *Chimaera.*

Without firing a single shot.

"What in the *world*?" Faro muttered.

"Nightswan learned from our attack on Scrim Island," Thrawn said calmly. "You see how he brought his ships in along the precise vectors where our fire would be blocked by the cruisers for the first leg of their attack."

"Yes, sir," Faro said. "Speaking of our fire . . . ?"

"Patience, Commander," Thrawn said. "Senior Lieutenant Lomar, inform the cruisers to break free of the barges immediately."

"You're sending them away *now,* sir?" Eli asked. "I thought you put them out there so they could jump *before* an enemy force could open fire."

"An incorrect assumption, Commander," Thrawn said calmly. "The attackers were never going to fire on them. Remember, we face Nightswan, who insisted that the *Dromedar*'s crew be held captive by pirates who wanted to kill them. He would never order his forces to fire on ships that could not fire back." He gestured out the viewport toward the *Shyrack.* "From a purely tactical point of view, having our undamaged ships and their crews behind his attackers and directly in our line of fire should also make us hesitate to open defensive fire."

"And that's why you're sending them away?" Faro asked. "So we can finally fight back?"

"I am not sending them away." Thrawn gave her a small smile. "Patience, Commander. Commander Vanto, report on the repair barges."

"They've pulled away from the *Shyrack,*" Eli said, studying the display. "Same for those around the *Flensor* and *Tumnor . . .*" He paused, peering at the group of repair structures. Was something emerging from behind them? "Admiral? Are those—?"

"They are indeed, Commander," Thrawn said quietly. "TIE fighters, a full squadron from each location. Brought into the Batonn system concealed inside the repair barges."

Eli exhaled a quiet breath, the knot in his stomach suddenly loosening as he finally understood. "Waiting for the attacking ships to pass by."

"Yes," Thrawn said. "And now, thanks to Nightswan's strategy, they are perfectly positioned behind their targets."

Even as Eli watched, the TIEs curved smoothly around the barges and accelerated to attack speed, bearing down on the incoming insurgent vessels. "Our TIEs are still on sentry screen," he said. "Where did these come from?"

"The *Judicator,*" Thrawn said. "Admiral Durril was kind enough to loan them to us. Commander Faro?"

"Sir?"

"Instruct our turbolasers to stand by to fire," Thrawn said. "Remind them not to overshoot against the TIEs."

"Yes, sir," Faro said, a tight smile on her face. "Fire control, you heard the admiral. Enemy incoming. Get ready to take them down."

It was time.

Arihnda's parents were safely inside Major Talmege's

HQ. Arihnda was standing behind the vehicle. The steady light of the stars overhead showed they were finally out from under the Creekpath shield.

And no one was watching.

She couldn't stop Yularen's special squad. She couldn't prevent them from finding Gudry's body. All she could do was make sure they never reported it.

Raising Gudry's comm, she keyed the remote.

Not the Signal One remote, the one that would destroy the shield. The Signal Two remote, the one that would set off Nightswan's cache of explosives.

And suddenly, the world shattered into a blaze of fire.

Whatever Eli might think of Durril's abilities as a tactician, the *Judicator*'s starfighter pilots were among the best he'd ever seen. By the time the attackers reached the *Chimaera*'s close-firing range, their numbers had been decreased by nearly two-thirds.

It was the *Chimaera*'s turn now.

The sky was filled with speeding ships and the green flashes of turbolaser blasts when, out of the corner of his eye, Eli saw the display centered on the Creekpath strongpoint light up with a brilliant burst of light.

He spun to the display, his breath catching in his throat. For another fraction of a second the smoke-swirled fire remained a near-perfect circle—

And then, with a second flicker of light from the very center, the circle vanished and the roiling mass of smoke and debris became a tangle-edged cloud as it blew farther outward.

Someone in one of the crew pits swore . . . and abruptly Eli understood.

The explosives Gudry had rigged had detonated. But with the shield still in place the massive blast had been contained and deflected inward and downward, demolishing not only the insurgents' stronghold but also the multitude of civilian homes clustered around the mine complex.

What the *hell* had the insurgents just done?

The *Chimaera*'s bridge had gone quiet. Thrawn was the first to break the silence. "Commander Faro, signal Colonel Yularen and the ground commanders," he said, his voice calm but with an edge to it. "The troopers are to enter the insurgent complex immediately.

"But not for combat. For search and rescue."

"Understood, sir," Faro said, her voice under rigid control. "And those?" she added, pointing at the enemy ships swarming through the blaster cannon and turbolaser fire.

"If any break off and run, let them go," Thrawn said. "Their tales of what happened here today will hasten the demoralization of any other such groups."

"And those that stay to fight?"

Thrawn didn't hesitate. "Destroy them."

"Did you see that?" Elainye asked yet again, her voice still shaking. "Did you *see* that?"

"I saw it, Mother," Arihnda confirmed as she half led, half dragged her parents to the waiting shuttle. Behind them, the whole Imperial line had come alive as men and vehicles moved into the blazing buildings and scattered debris that had been the Creekpath mining complex. "And no, I have no idea what happened."

"Such a terrible thing," Elainye murmured. "How could the Empire have done something like that?"

"You want to blame someone, blame the insurgents," Arihnda countered, more harshly than she'd intended. "They're the ones who forced this confrontation."

Her mother fell silent. Her father hadn't spoken at all since they'd left Talmege's vehicle.

Arihnda had to admit to a certain queasiness of her own. The shield-contained blast had been far more devastating than she'd expected.

But it had served its purpose. The explosion or the resulting firestorm had surely obliterated her parents' home, and with it the evidence of Gudry's murder.

In the end, that was all that mattered.

"Here's what you're going to do," she said, shaking both her parents a little to make sure she had their attention. "The pilot has instructions to take you to the Paeragosto City landing field and a transport called the *Duggenhei*. Your passage to Lothal has already been paid. Once there, go to the governor's mansion—I'll call ahead and instruct them to put you in one of the guest suites. I'll join you as soon as I can, and we'll figure out then what you want to do. Clear?"

"But—" Elainye began.

"No *buts,* Mother," Arihnda said. "Just go, and wait. Okay?"

Elainye sighed. "All right."

"Father? Okay?"

Talmoor merely nodded.

"Okay," Arihnda said, stopping at the foot of the shuttle's ramp and releasing their arms. "Get going. I'll be there as soon as I can."

She watched as they made their silent way aboard, both still moving like dreamers trapped in a horrible nightmare. The hatch closed, and the shuttle took off, heading for the distant lights of the city.

"Your parents?"

Arihnda turned. Colonel Yularen was standing a few meters back, his eyes hard on her. "Yes," she said. "I'm sending them back home. There's nothing here for them now."

"Nothing much here for anyone, really," he said. "I came to tell you that Admiral Thrawn requests our presence aboard the *Chimaera.*"

Which the colonel could have told her via comm, Arihnda knew. But if he'd done that, he wouldn't have been able to follow her and see what she was up to.

Fine. Let him watch. Let him watch, and wonder, and

suspect. She was Governor Pryce now, ruler of a vast array of mines, factories, and industries vital to the economic and military well-being of the Empire. As long as she continued to deliver what Coruscant wanted, she was untouchable. "Thank you, Colonel," she said. "Do you have a shuttle ready?"

"I do, Your Excellency," he said. "Shall we go?"

CHAPTER 29

All people have regrets. Warriors are no exceptions.

One would hope it was possible to distinguish between events caused by one's carelessness or lack of ability and those caused by circumstances or forces beyond one's control. But in practice, there is no difference. All forms of regret sear equally deeply into the mind and soul. All forms leave scars of equal bitterness.

And always, beneath the scar, lurks the thought and fear that there was something else that could have been done. Some action, or inaction, that would have changed things for the better. Such questions can sometimes be learned from. All too often, they merely add to the scar tissue.

A warrior must learn to set those regrets aside as best he can. Knowing full well that they will never be very far away.

"It was, by anyone's standards, a slaughter," Yularen said. *His voice is under control but holds deep regret and the echo of dark memories.* "I saw some horrendous things during the Clone Wars. This ranks right up there with the worst of them."

"You have the numbers?" Thrawn asked.

"Yes, sir," Yularen said, keying his datapad. "As you can see, the number of civilian deaths far exceeded the number of insurgents killed."

"How do we know which were which?" Governor Pryce asked. *Her voice holds scorn and caution but no sympathy. The muscles of her arms and shoulders are tight beneath her tunic.* "This *was* a citizen uprising, after all."

"We can assume the people inside the central cordon and the ones holding weapons on the sentry lines were insurgents," Yularen said. *His tone is polite but holds barely concealed contempt.* "The people in their houses when the firestorm blew them apart probably weren't."

"There's no need for vehemence, Colonel," Pryce said. *Her voice holds calmness now, with the scorn fading. Her hands, resting on the conference table, show rigid self-control.*

"You do not know how the explosives came to be detonated before the shield generator?" Thrawn asked.

"I'll tell you what I told Colonel Yularen," Pryce said. "I went to my parents' house to get them ready to leave. We waited there for Agent Gudry. He didn't return by the time we'd agreed on, so we left. I can only assume he was trapped or disabled by the insurgents, and rather than allow them to take him alive triggered the caps."

"Those on the explosives cache first?" Yularen asked. *His voice holds suspicion. His eyes are fixed unblinkingly on Pryce.*

"Or he triggered both at once," Pryce said. *Her voice holds impatience and challenge. Her hands begin to move, then become motionless again as she regains control.* "Or he tried the generator first and it failed. We won't know the details until a full investigation is made."

Commander Vanto stirred in his chair, also frustrated and suspicious. But he said nothing.

"The Senate has already ordered an inquiry," Yularen said. "But I doubt they'll find anything useful. The inner section of the complex, where the explosions took place, was reduced pretty much to dust."

"Again, I don't have much sympathy for the insurgents," Pryce said. "But I do mourn the loss of Agent Gudry. He was a good agent, and a loyal protector."

"I trust you also mourn the troopers who died in the blast," Yularen said. "Including those who had been sent to rescue you."

"A mission I was unaware of," Pryce said. *Her voice holds coolness. The tightness is fading from her muscles.* "As I told you earlier, I didn't want to use my comm more than absolutely necessary."

"Have we information as to the insurgents' ability to tap into such communications?" Thrawn asked.

"We don't know that they could, sir," Vanto said. "But it *is* theoretically possible. And someone like Nightswan would certainly have wanted to keep tabs on who was communicating from inside his stronghold if he'd had the capability."

"Yes," Thrawn said. "Your report, Colonel, said his death was confirmed?"

"Yes, sir," Yularen said. "His body was found and identified in one of the outer areas, where the damage was less severe. He was probably checking on the perimeter." He hesitated. "Possibly preparing to stand alongside the defenders there."

"Yes," Thrawn said.

And so it was over. The path had ended. The pattern was broken.

The song of the Nightswan was silenced. The galaxy would be the worse for its loss.

"Still, the Emperor is pleased with the outcome," Pryce said. *Her voice holds pride and satisfaction as she looks at Thrawn. Her head is held high.* "Very pleased indeed."

"Is he?" Thrawn said.

Pryce's eyes slip away from his gaze. Her throat muscles tighten, her expression holding caution and discom-

fort. "He is," she said. "I expect he'll find a tangible way to show his thanks."

There was a signal from the conference room intercom. "Yes?" Thrawn asked.

"A message from Coruscant, Admiral," Faro reported. *Her voice holds controlled excitement.* "The Emperor requests your presence at the Imperial Palace at your earliest convenience."

"Thank you, Commander," Thrawn said. "Transmit my acknowledgment, and inform Coruscant that we will travel there as soon as the Batonn matter has been finalized."

"Yes, sir." The intercom clicked off.

"You don't want to keep the Emperor waiting, Admiral," Pryce warned.

"Agreed," Yularen said. "With respect, sir, we can handle things from groundside."

"And the cruisers can follow on as soon as their repairs are complete, sir," Vanto added. "They shouldn't be more than a couple of days behind us. If you'd like, we can leave the frigates here with them so that they can all convoy together."

"An excellent thought," Thrawn said. "Very well. Inform Commander Faro to make ready. The *Chimaera* will leave Batonn in three hours, with the rest of the task force following as able. Colonel Yularen, if during the next three hours you find my attention here is further needed, please inform me so that I may delay our departure."

"Yes, sir." *Yularen, Vanto, and Pryce stand up from the table.*

"Governor Pryce, a word with you in private, if I may," Thrawn said.

Vanto and Yularen exchanged glances. But they collected their data cards and left the conference room without further comment.

"A question, Admiral?" Pryce asked when the others were gone. *She remains standing by her chair, her body stance holding no indication that she is preparing to sit down again.*

"A statement, Governor," Thrawn corrected.

Pryce shakes her head. Her cheek and throat muscles show fresh tension, but her back is stiff and straight and her head is held high with defiant confidence. "No."

"Excuse me?"

"That's not how you bring an accusation against a powerful member of the Imperial government," she said. "For all your tactical skill, Admiral, you still don't know the first thing about dealing with politicians."

"Do I not?"

"You do not," Pryce said. *Her voice holds confidence.* "Your entire career has been one of military triumphs and political bumps, and every one of those bumps has required someone with political skill to get you out of it."

She leans forward and sets her hands, palms down, on the table in front of her. "Let's lay out our cards. Or rather, I'll lay out *my* cards, since you're not the cardplaying sort. You clearly suspect me of knowing more than I've said about what happened on Batonn. Fine. Suspect me all you want. But don't lose track of the fact that you need me."

"In what way?"

"To smooth out your future political bumps," she said. "And trust me: There *will* be more bumps. You're a successful admiral. That makes you a target for people who want to siphon off some of your power for themselves."

"People such as you?"

She smiled again. *Her expression holds irony. Her body stance holds a slightly grudging respect.* "At least you've learned *some* political lessons. But no, I don't want to take your power away. I merely want to direct it along a line that will do us both the most good."

"Such as?"

"The fact is that I have something of an insurgent

situation on Lothal," she said. *Her voice holds reluctance. Her facial heat increases. Her body stance holds resentment and anger, but directed elsewhere.* "I wanted to make my world the Outer Rim's best and finest source of high-grade metals, as well as the premier manufacturing and military center for the sector. In the process, I may have pushed the locals a bit too hard. Regardless of the cause, we have a problem, and Admiral Konstantine has been less than effective in dealing with it."

"You've spoken to the High Command?"

"The High Command has a lot of hot spots to deal with right now." *Her voice holds impatience and scorn.* "With more popping up every day, I've had some discussions with Grand Moff Tarkin, and he isn't any happier about the situation than I am. He's especially not happy that our local rebels are starting to take their brand of annoyance to other places in the region. He's made it clear that I need to find a solution."

"Have you?"

"Yes," she said. "You."

"And what would my benefit be?"

"I already detailed one of those benefits," Pryce said. "If you don't think my political guidance of enough value, then consider the gain to your prestige from another victory or two. That's all Coruscant values, you know: results." *She cocks her head to the side.* "My sources tell me that Fleet Admiral Sartan of the Seventh Fleet is going to be replaced soon. Batonn is just the kind of victory that could put you in line for that command."

"I am content with the Ninety-Sixth Task Force."

"You'd be more content with the Seventh Fleet," Pryce retorted. *She pauses, her expression and body stance showing her effort to regain control.* "One last card, a card I know you care about. The Seventh Fleet carries a lot of firepower. It's sent to major conflicts, where there are powerful and desperate enemies. If you don't command it, someone else will. Do you think there's anyone else in the Imperial Navy who cares as much as you do about limiting casualties?"

"You make interesting points," Thrawn said. "I will consider your proposal."

"Do that." *Her body stance holds complete confidence. Her expression holds quiet triumph.* "In the meantime, go have your meeting with the Emperor. Smile and thank him for whatever accolades or trinkets he heaps on you." *She smiles, her expression holding cynicism.* "Who knows? He might even make you a grand admiral. The point is, get through it, and we'll see each other again soon."

"We may indeed," Thrawn said. "Farewell, Governor. Safe journey."

She had been gone for eighteen minutes when Vanto returned to the conference room. "Governor Pryce just left," he reported, eyeing Thrawn closely. "What did she say?"

"She offered herself as my adviser on political matters."

"You could definitely use someone like that," Vanto said doubtfully. "Not sure she's the right one for the job, though. What did she say about Creekpath?"

"She didn't admit to playing any part in the destruction," Thrawn said. "But I believe she bears at least some of the blame."

"But you have no proof?"

"None."

"Figured as much," Vanto said, his voice grim. "And from what Yularen said, we're not likely to get any. So she gets away with it."

"Perhaps," Thrawn said. "Perhaps not. I've noted there is often a symmetry to such things."

"We can hope," Vanto said. "So. To Coruscant?"

"To Coruscant," Thrawn said.

"I know you're not going to like accepting the credit for the action down there," Vanto said. "But try to smile and act grateful anyway." He frowned. "What are you smiling about?"

"Governor Pryce had much the same advice."

"Oh." Vanto shrugged. "Well, it's still a good idea. With your permission, I'd like to go see if there's any final data from groundside before we leave."

"Please do," Thrawn said. "Remember, too, that others have served the Empire well. I trust the Emperor will have enough honors to award to all."

"I wouldn't hold my breath," Vanto said. "Doesn't matter. I'm quite content to be your aide, Admiral. It's where I'm supposed to be."

"Perhaps," Thrawn said. "Perhaps not."

The throne room was as Thrawn remembered it, though he saw it now with different eyes. The new uniform he'd been given was white, with gold shoulder bars and silver collar insignia, completely unlike anything else in the Imperial Navy. The rank insignia plaque the Emperor held in his gnarled hand was equally impressive: twelve tiles in blue, red, and gold.

The Emperor's face was as Thrawn had never seen it. *His expression holds satisfaction, with hints of both amusement and malice.* "Congratulations, Grand Admiral," he said as he held out the insignia plaque. "An excellent day for you. An excellent day for my Empire." *The amusement grows.* "Though I fear many will not see it that way."

"I will endeavor to set their hearts and minds at ease," Thrawn said. "But I must first calm my own heart and mind."

The smile leaves the Emperor's face. Some of the satisfaction fades, replaced by displeasure. "Must you, now," he said. "Very well. Speak your mind, Grand Admiral."

"Tell me about the Death Star."

The amusement vanishes. The malice grows. "When and how did you hear of that project?"

"I learned the name from unguarded dispatches," Thrawn said. "I deduced the size and power from resource allocations. I now wish to learn from you its purpose."

The amusement reappears, mixed now with understanding and triumph. "Ah," he said, lowering his hand to his side. "Your thoughts are laid bare, Mitth'raw'nuruodo. You fear that, once I have dealt with the rebels within my borders, I will turn my unstoppable weapon against your Chiss. Is that your concern?"

"That is part of it," Thrawn said. "I would certainly not wish to see my aid to you and your Empire subverted into conquest or destruction. But I would also warn against diverting too many of the Empire's resources from a flexible navy of capital ships and starfighters to massive projects that can bring the Imperial presence to only one system at a time."

"Allow me to allay your fears," the Emperor said. "I have no designs against your people. Indeed, I have noted that despite your assistance in mapping the Unknown Region hyperspace routes you have kept the location of Chiss worlds and bases secret. That is acceptable. I don't begrudge you the defense of your people. As to Imperial resources—"

He smiles again, the triumph growing and turning strangely brittle.

"—there will soon be no need to spread the Imperial presence across the galaxy. Once the Death Star is fully operational, its very existence will suppress all opposition. And so . . . ?"

He raises his arm, again holding out the rank plaque. This time, Thrawn took it.

"Good," the Emperor said. *His smile again holds satisfaction. The malice fades, but never entirely disappears.*

At the side of the throne room a door slid open and a tall, black-clad figure appeared, a long black cloak swirling behind him. "Ah—Lord Vader," the Emperor called a greeting. *He beckons to the figure. His body stance holds a sense of mastery and domination.* "Come; join us. I don't believe you have met Darth Vader, Grand Admiral Thrawn."

Vader approaches, his pace measured but confident. His face is hidden, his muscle movements muted and unreadable beneath his armored clothing. But his stance holds power and authority.

It also holds confidence. More than anything else, it holds confidence.

"You are correct, Your Excellency," Thrawn said. "I greet you, Lord Vader."

"Grand Admiral," Vader said, inclining his helmeted head. *His voice is deep and partially mechanical. It, too, holds power and confidence.*

"I have heard a great deal about you," Thrawn said. "I am pleased we have finally met."

"Yes," Vader said. "As am I."

EPILOGUE

---

*It is said that one should keep one's allies within view,
and one's enemies within reach.*

*A valid statement. One must be able to read an ally's
strengths, so as to determine how best to use him. One
must similarly be able to read an enemy's weaknesses,
so as to determine how best to defeat him.*

But what of friends?

*There is no accepted answer, perhaps because true
friendship is so exceedingly rare. But I have formulated
my own.*

*A friend need not be kept either within sight or
within reach. A friend must be allowed the freedom to
find and follow his own path.*

*If one is fortunate, those paths will for a time join.
But if the paths separate, it is comforting to know that
a friend still graces the universe with his skills, and his
viewpoint, and his presence.*

*For if one is remembered by a friend, one is never
truly gone.*

Eli read the entry a second time. Then, with a sigh, he
shut down his datapad.

He still didn't know why Thrawn had left him his
journal. Perhaps he'd seen it simply as history. Perhaps

he'd seen it as one final opportunity for training and instruction.

Or perhaps the reason was encompassed somehow in that final entry.

Distantly, Eli wondered if there had been any more to the journal. And, if so, if he would ever find the other entries.

He doubted it. But it didn't really matter. The galaxy had Thrawn's legacy and his accomplishments. Those who could learn from that legacy had presumably already done so. Those who couldn't never would.

Eli hoped he was part of the first group.

Setting aside the datapad, he gazed again at the pattern of numbers flowing across his display. For most people, he knew, numbers were next to meaningless. For Eli, by life and by training a supply specialist, they were like music. Whether they formed themselves into inventory lists, targeting calculations, or hyperspace course and position data, numbers were at the heart of everything that made the universe function. They spoke to a grand symphony of people, humans and nonhumans alike; of worlds and trade routes; of the lifeblood of good and evil alike.

Perhaps that was why he and Thrawn had worked so well together. Eli had his numbers, Thrawn had his art, and neither skill could be fully understood by anyone else.

He smiled at the thought, and at his own conceit. No, he had never fully understood Thrawn. He doubted anyone ever had.

But that was Eli's past. This was Eli's present. His present, and hopefully his future.

The flowing course numbers reached their end, and Eli threw the hyperdrive levers. The view through the cockpit canopy changed from mottled sky to starlines to the cold beauty of unfamiliar stars.

And in the center of the grandeur, a single ship. A *large* ship, shimmering with muted running lights, bristling with weaponry, crewed by men and women whom Eli had never met.

He had arrived.

The comm screen lit up with a face: regal and blue-skinned, with glowing red eyes. Her blue-black hair was tied in a tight knot at the back of her head; her collar insignia those of an admiral. "I am Admiral Ar'alani of the Chiss Defense Fleet," she said in a clear voice, her Sy Bisti heavily accented. "Are you he?"

"I am he." Eli took a deep breath. "I am Eli Vanto. I bring greetings to you from Mitth'raw'nuruodo. He believes I can be of some use to the Chiss Ascendancy."

"Welcome, Eli Vanto," Ar'alani said, inclining her head in greeting. "Let us learn together if he was correct."

Read on for an excerpt from

Star Wars: Battlefront II: Inferno Squad

by Christie Golden
Published by Del Rey Books

CHAPTER 1

The firm control of one's emotions was an unspoken criterion for those who would serve the Empire. One did not gloat, or cheer, or weep, or rage, although cold fury was, upon occasion, deemed an appropriate reaction to particular circumstances.

Senior Lieutenant Iden Versio had been familiar with this stipulation since she was old enough to understand the concept. Even so, now, at this hour of the Empire's unequivocal and absolute triumph, the young woman raced across the gleaming black surface of the Death Star's corridors with her helmet cradled in one arm, trying and failing to smother a grin.

Today, of all days, why shouldn't she smile, at least when no one was watching?

When her orders had come to serve on the space station—which a scant few hours ago had reduced an entire planet into rocky chunks of glorious rebel *rubble*—Iden had endured resentful, sidelong glances followed by murmurs pitched exactly too softly for her to catch. But Iden didn't need to hear the words. She knew what the others were saying about her. It was nothing more than a variant on what had always been said about her.

She's too young for this position. She couldn't have earned it on her own.

She got it because of her father.

The self-righteous mutterers would have been startled to discover the degree to which their assumptions were wrong.

Inspector General Garrick Versio might well be one of the highest-ranking members of the powerful and secretive Imperial Security Bureau, but Iden had gotten nothing out of the joyless task of being his daughter. Every honor, every grade, every opportunity she had, she'd fought for and obtained *despite* him.

She'd been primed for the military academy while barely more than a child, studying at the Future Imperial Leaders Military Preparatory School on her homeworld of Vardos, located in the Jinata system, where she had, literally, been bloodied. There, and afterward at the Imperial Academy on Coruscant, Iden had graduated top of her class, with honors.

All that felt like a mere prelude to this moment. For the last several months, Iden had been part of a small, elite TIE fighter unit aboard what was arguably the pinnacle of Imperial design—the massive space station known as the Death Star. And she was rather unprofessionally excited.

Even as she tried to rein in her enthusiasm, she could sense that others hastening to their own TIE fighters shared it. They betrayed themselves with the surging tattoo of booted footfalls, their upright positions, even the brightness in their eyes.

It wasn't new, this happy tension. Iden had seen it bubbling under the surface after the first test of the station's capabilities, when the Death Star's superlaser had targeted and obliterated Jedha City. The Empire had landed a one–two punch in a handful of seconds. It had destroyed not only the rebel terrorist Saw Gerrera and his group of extremists known as the partisans, but also the ancient Temple of the Kyber, held sacred by those who secretly hoped for the return of the disgraced and defeated Jedi. Jedha City represented the first real demonstration of the station's power, but that fact was known only those who served on the Death Star.

For now. To the rest of the galaxy, what had happened at Jedha was a tragic mining accident.

Things had happened with shocking speed after that, as if some galactic balance had suddenly, drastically, been tipped. The superlaser was again employed at the Battle of Scarif, this time wiping out an entire region and several rebel ships trapped under Scarif's shield along with it. Emperor Palpatine had dissolved the Imperial Senate. His right hand, the mysterious caped and helmeted Darth Vader, had intercepted and imprisoned secret rebel and now former senator Princess Leia Organa. The Death Star's director, Grand Moff Wilhuff Tarkin, had used the princess's home planet of Alderaan to demonstrate the true breadth of the power of the now fully operational battle station.

As nearly all on the Death Star had been ordered to do, with their own eyes or on a screen, Iden had stood and watched. By their treasonous actions, the rebels on Alderaan had brought destruction not only on themselves, but on the innocents they always seemed so keen to protect. She couldn't get the image out of her head: a planet, a world, gone in the span of a few seconds. As, soon, would be virtually all the Empire's enemies. In a very, very short time, the galaxy would receive an implacable and thorough understanding of just how useless resistance would be. And then—

Then, there would be order, and this ill-thought-out, chaotic "Rebellion" would subside. All the extensive hours of labor, all the credits and brainpower spent on controlling and dominating various unruly worlds could, at last, be turned to helping them.

There would, finally, be peace.

The event would be shocking, yes. But it had to be, and it was all for the greater good. Once everyone was under the auspices of the Empire, they would understand.

And that glorious moment was almost here. Tarkin had located the rebel base on one of Yavin's moons. The base—and the moon—were but a few moments from oblivion.

Some of the rebels, though, were not going to go quietly.

These few had taken to space and were presently mounting a humorously feeble attack on the gigantic space station. The thirty Y- and X-wing fighters the rebels had mustered were small enough to dodge the station's defensive turbolaser turrets, zipping about like flies. And, like flies, this nominal, futile defense would be casually swatted down by Iden and the other pilots in ship-to-ship combat, as per orders from Lord Vader.

Within the span of seven minutes, Yavin's moon and all the rebels it had succored would be nothing more than floating debris. On this day, the Rebellion would be no more.

Iden's heartbeat thudded in her ears as she all but jumped down the ladder into her fighter, sealing her flight suit and pulling on her helmet. Slender but strong gloved fingers flew over the consoles, her gaze flitting over the stats as she went through the preflight checklist. The hatch lowered, hummed shut, and she was encased in its black metal belly. A few seconds later she was swirling in cold, airless darkness, where the distinctive scream of her vessel was silent.

Here they came, now, mostly the X-wings—the Rebellion's answer to TIE fighters. They were impressive little single-occupant vessels, and they skimmed along close to the surface of the station, a few of them misjudging the distance and slamming into the walls around the trenches that crisscrossed the Death Star's surface.

Suicide, Iden thought, even as she knew the term was just as often applied to those who flew TIE fighters. You either loved the small starfighters or you hated them. A TIE fighter was fast and distinctive, with its laser cannons quite deadly, but it was more vulnerable to attack than other vessels as it wasn't equipped with deflector shields. The trick was to kill the enemy first—something Iden was better at than anyone else in her squadron. Iden liked that everything was compact and immediately to hand—flight controls, viewscreen, targeting systems, equipment for tracking and being tracked.

Iden listened to the familiar beeps of the tracking equipment as it targeted and locked onto one of the X-wings. She swung her vessel back and forth with easy familiarity as the enemy ship frantically jigged and jagged in a commendable, but ultimately useless, effort to evade her.

She pressed her thumbs down. Green lasers sliced through the X-wing, and then only pieces and a flaring sheet of flame remained.

A quick count on her screen told Iden that her fellow pilots were also efficiently culling the herd of rebels. She frowned slightly at the tiny, ship-shaped blips on her screen. Some of them were veering off from the group, going deeper in toward the Death Star, while others seemed to be trying to draw the TIE fighters away from the station. Iden's gaze flickered to another ship, a Y-wing—one of those enemy vessels that always looked to her like a skeletal bird of prey—and she went in pursuit, rolling smoothly and coming up on its side. More streaks of green in the star-spattered blackness, and then it, too, was gone.

Her gaze now lingered on the more suicidal of the enemy fighters, watching as they dropped into the trenches. As far as Iden knew, no one in her six-pilot squadron had been told *why* the rebels had adopted this peculiar tactic of flying through the trenches. Iden had grown up with nearly everything—from what it was her father actually *did* for the Empire to what her mother was designing that day, even what was for dinner that night—being on a need-to-know basis. She had grown accustomed to the situation, but she would never like it.

"Attention, pilots," came the voice of her commander, Kela Neerik, in Iden's ear, and for a brief, beautiful instant Iden thought her squad commander was going to explain what was going on. But all Neerik said was, "Death Star is now six minutes out from target."

Iden bit her lip, wondering if she should speak up. *Don't. Don't,* she told herself, but the words had a life of their own. Before she realized it, out they had come.

"Respectfully, Commander, with only six minutes until the entire moon's destruction, why are we out here? Surely thirty one-person ships won't be able to do anything resembling damage to the Death Star in that amount of time."

"Lieutenant Versio"—Neerik's voice was as cold as space—"don't assume your father's position gives you special privileges. We are here because Lord Vader *ordered* us to be here. Perhaps you'd like to put your question to him personally when we return to the station? I'm sure he'd be delighted to explain his military strategy to you."

Iden felt a cold knot in her stomach at the thought of a "personal" conversation with Lord Vader. She'd never met him, thankfully, but she had heard too many chilling rumors.

"No, Commander, that won't be necessary."

"I thought not. Do your duty, Lieutenant Versio."

Iden frowned, then let it go. She did not need to understand the rebels; she needed only to destroy them.

As if they sensed her renewed resolve, the rebel pilots suddenly upped their game. There was a brief flash at the corner of Iden's vision, and when she turned to look, she realized with sick surprise that the debris hurtling off in all directions was black.

Iden didn't know who had just died. TIE fighters were so uniform as to be practically indistinguishable from one another. Their pilots weren't supposed to think of their ships in the warm, fuzzy way the rebels were reported to do. A ship was a ship was a ship. And Iden understood that, as far as most in the Empire were concerned, a pilot was a pilot was a pilot: as expendable and interchangeable as the ships they flew.

We all serve at the pleasure of the Emperor, her father had drilled into her since she was old enough to comprehend what an emperor was. *None of us is indispensable.* Iden had certainly seen Imperial ships shot down before. This was war, and she was a soldier. But *indispensable* be damned.

The half smile she'd been wearing during most of the combat vanished, and Iden pressed her lips together angrily. She veered, perhaps a touch too violently, to the right and targeted another X-wing. In mere seconds it exploded into a yellow-orange fireball.

"Gotcha, you—" she muttered.

"No commentary, Versio," warned Neerik, her voice rising a little; more hot than cold, now. "We will be having the honor of Lord Vader joining us momentarily. He and his pilots will be focusing on the hostiles navigating the meridian trench. All remaining units are ordered to redirect their attacks to the rebel ships on the magnetic perimeter."

Iden almost shouted a protest, but stopped herself just in time. For some reason *still unknown to the squadron,* this perplexing tactic by the rebel pilots was clearly of great concern. Lord Vader wouldn't trouble himself with appearing personally to take care of it otherwise.

Almost everything Iden knew about Darth Vader was pure speculation. The exception was a single revelation on the part of her father, in one of those rare moments when he was feeling less taciturn than usual with his only child.

"Lord Vader has great power," Versio had said. "His instincts and his reflexes are uncanny. And . . . there are certain abilities he possesses that our Emperor finds to be of tremendous value."

So yes. Vader was head and shoulders above the rest of them—literally and figuratively. But it wasn't Vader's friends who were dying in this battle, and Iden burned to be the one to make the rebels pay.

With a huffing sigh that she was certain was audible, she swerved from tailing the X-wing, frowning as red laserfire came perilously close to her fighter's fragile wings. That was on her; she hadn't been focusing.

She corrected that oversight immediately, zooming away from the station toward a pair of Y-wings that was, successfully, attempting to get her attention. Any other time, Iden would have enjoyed toying with them—they were decent pilots, although the ones in the X-wings were superior—but right now she was too irritated to do so.

She targeted the closest Y-wing, locked onto it, and blew it to pieces. Watching the fragments of the starfighter hurtling wildly was some small compensation for the deaths of her fellow pilots.

"Death Star is two minutes to target. Be aware of your distance from the planet."

Ah, so that was why Neerik was giving the countdown. Iden had to give the pilot of the Y-wing credit for courage, albeit of the foolish kind; the ship was now racing *away* from the Death Star at top speed. Were they heading back to Yavin's moon, nobly choosing to die with their base, or were they just trying to evade her?

Not happening, Iden thought, and continued her pursuit. She got the vessel in her sights and fired. She didn't slow as the ship exploded, but simply pulled back and looped up and over the fireball and debris, snug in her crash webbing, and smoothly dipped the TIE fighter in front of the second Y-wing for the perfect shot.

The pale moon-shape of the Death Star loomed behind the vessel, its gargantuan size making the rebel ship look like the toys she'd been allowed to play with as a child. The Y-wing was making for Yavin as fast as it could, swerving erratically enough that Iden frowned as she tried to get a lock on it.

A sudden scalding brightness filled her vision.

Temporarily blinded, Iden hurtled wildly, her TIE fighter tumbling out of control. As her vision returned, she realized debris was coming at her as intensely as if she had suddenly materialized inside an asteroid field. Her focus, always powerful, narrowed to laserlike precision as she frantically dodged and swerved, maneuvering around the biggest pieces and wishing with all her being that TIE fighters had shields.

Iden pivoted and tumbled, breathing the mercifully still-flowing oxygen deeply and rhythmically. But she knew in her heart this was just a matter of time. There was too much debris, some of it the size of a standard escape pod, some of it as small as her clenched fist, and she was right in the thick of it. The smaller pieces were pelting her TIE fighter already. Sooner or later, one of the big chunks would hit her, and both Senior Lieutenant Iden Versio and her ship would be nothing more than smears on what was left of Yavin's moon.

Somehow, she'd wandered too close to the Death Star's target and had gotten swept up in the chaotic sweep of its destruction—exactly what her commander had been warning her against.

But how was that possible?

"Mayday, mayday," Iden shouted, unable to keep her voice calm as she desperately dipped and dived to avoid disaster. "This is TIE Sigma Three requesting assistance. Repeat, this is TIE Sigma Three requesting assistance, do you copy, over?"

Silence. Absolute, cold, terrifying silence.

The inevitable occurred at last.

Something struck the TIE fighter, hard. The ship shuddered, tumbled off in a different direction, but did not explode. A piece of one of the sleek, fragile wings flashed across Iden's field of vision and she realized that control of the vessel was out of her hands.

Others would panic, or weep, or rail. But Iden had been raised to never, *ever* quit, and now, at this moment, she was grateful for her father's implacability. The ship was careening and, as she could do nothing to stop it, she took a few seconds to observe.

The prospect of her own violent and, possibly, painful and prolonged death was something that held little fear for her. But what she saw in those seconds struck terror down to her bones.

It was the blue-green moon of Yavin. And it was completely intact.

Not. Possible!

She thought of the dreadful silence on the comm. And now that she knew, now that she had wrapped her brain around something that was not supposed to happen, that no one had ever imagined *could* happen, she recognized some of the pieces that she was trying so desperately to evade.

They were of Imperial construction.

Imperial.

Pieces of the greatest battle station that—

A single short, harsh, disbelieving gasp racked her slender frame. Then Iden Versio clenched her teeth against a second outburst. Pressed her lips together to seal it inside her.

She was a Versio, and Versios did not panic.

The destruction of the Death Star was brutal and irrevocable truth that the impossible was now possible. Which meant she could survive this.

And she was going to.

Iden clawed her way back to control and assessed the situation with a bright, sharp, almost violent clarity.

The impact of the debris strike had, fortunately, served not only to damage the wing but also to push her toward the moon, and without the pull of the Death Star to counter it, the gravity of Yavin's small satellite was greedy. She couldn't direct her trajectory, but she could manage it. Iden went on the offensive—a preferred tactic—but this time not against a rebel vessel. This time, her enemy was the debris that hurtled toward her.

She spun toward the moon's surface, targeting anything in her path and blasting it into rubble. This sort of thing was second nature, so she let part of her mind deal with how to manage the process of reentry, a controlled crash, and ejection.

There would then be avoiding capture, stealing a vessel, and absconding with it, presuming she landed on Yavin's moon in one piece.

There it was again, that frisson of bestial, primitive panic, closing her throat. Iden swallowed hard even as cold sweat dewed her body—

—beneath the uniform of an Imperial officer—

—beneath the helm of a TIE fighter pilot—

—and again took a deep, calming breath. The oxygen was finite, but it was better to use it now to help her focus than later as she panicked.

Iden was, as far as she knew, the sole survivor out of over a million victims of this act of rebel terrorism. She *had* to survive, if only to honor those who hadn't. Who hadn't chased the foe in an impulsive act that ought to have been a mistake, but instead had gifted her with a chance to live.

She would find a way back to Imperial space ready to continue the fight against the Rebel Alliance for as long as it took to eliminate every last one of the bastards.

Her jaw set and her eyes narrowed with determination, Iden Versio braced herself for a bumpy landing.